The circle began to move and Janis moved with it. Round and round they accelerated until they were whirling freely, their scanty costumes blowing in the draught. Janis felt more and more exhilarated: her body burned with desire and her mind was floating in a sea of erotic imagery.

As the circle broke up the first chords of the opening number were sounded by the musicians on the dais at the back of the stage and, like clockwork, everyone moved into their positions or retreated to the wings. Janis watched the stage being lowered over Blade and saw the four girls take up their stances around the bars. While she waited her hands roamed over the smooth material of her costume, stroking the skin beneath, teasing her nipples into prominence, pressing into the niche between her thighs . . .

The sight of Pam caressing Lucille's full, black breasts in their spangly bra while Diane and Suzanne kissed and fondled each other was a real turn-on. Then Virgo appeared at the top of her steps, cracking her whip, and the whole audience erupted in glee. She looked magnificent in her ringmistress's costume of black top hat, red tailcoat opened to show her black and red bra, pants and suspender belt with long, high-heeled boots of black leather . . .

Also in New English Library paperback

Arousal

House of Lust

The Uninhibited

Submission!

Haunting Lust

Depravicus

The Splits

In the Pink 1: Stripped for Action

In the Pink 2: Sin City

In the Pink 3: Getting It

Lustathon

Vampire Desire

Midnight Blue

Rock Hard

Nadine Wilder

NEW ENGLISH LIBRARY
Hodder and Stoughton

First published in 1996
by Hodder and Stoughton
A division of Hodder Headline PLC

The right of Nadine Wilder to be identified as the Author of
the Work has been asserted by her in accordance with the
Copyright, Designs and Patents Act 1988.

10 9 8 7 6 5 4 3 2 1

British Library Cataloguing in Publication Data
A CIP catalogue record for this title is available from the British Library

ISBN 0 340 66056 2

Typeset by Avon Dataset Ltd, Bidford-on-Avon, Warks

Printed and bound in Great Britain by
Cox & Wyman, Reading, Berks

Hodder and Stoughton
A division of Hodder Headline PLC
338 Euston Road
London NW1 3BH

CHAPTER ONE

Janis had been to many rock gigs before, but never one like this. She recognized the tension between the excited audience and the bustle of the crew on stage. She relished the sweaty press of bodies all around her, and the thrill of being amongst a number of individuals who would soon merge into one heart and mind, fused by the music.

But this was no ordinary rock band, and the crowd's lust for entertainment was spiced with something dirty, something wicked. Whatever was happening in the way of preparation on stage was hidden from view behind a giant screen bearing an image of a man with arms and legs outstretched, like the Leonardo drawing. Except that he was standing against a huge depiction of a devil's head in the shape of a five-pointed star, and from his groin sprang an erection the size of a baby's arm.

Already Janis could smell the musky odour of sexual arousal seeping from her neighbours. To her right was a girl in black leather trousers and a red stretch bra that clearly showed the prominence of her nipples. On the other side a heavily tattooed man with cropped hair was wearing a 'Grass Blade' T-shirt, with the rock star's head silhouetted against a marijuana leaf. Janis had the same one at home, but for her first live Shaft gig she'd chosen her favourite: a black T-shirt with 'Blade of the Shaft' written in white Celtic-style script beneath a portrait of Blade's head with his hair streaming out like the rays of the sun. It was an exclusive design, number thirty-one of a limited edition, and she was very proud of it.

Janis heard the scornful voice of Adam, her boyfriend, saying, 'What did you waste your hard-earned money on that for?' The memory still had the power to hurt her. Adam had been jealous of the rock star ever since they'd swapped sexual fantasies and she'd told him about what she imagined doing with Blade. Earlier that evening, when she'd surprised him by saying she had two tickets for the Shaft gig at the Pyramid, an ugly scene had erupted and she had stormed off. Janis had hoped to involve him in her enthusiasm for the band and end his ridiculous jealousy. But it had backfired on her so badly that she had given up all hope of, or even desire for, reconciliation and was already thinking of Adam as her 'ex'.

Now, standing there alone in the midst of an increasingly turned-on crowd, she felt both vulnerable and immensely elated. Maybe Adam hadn't been so good for her after all. She was only twenty-three, too young to think about settling down. It would be good to play the field awhile, find out more about herself and what she wanted from others. In any case, sex with Adam had become boringly routine. Stuck in the comfortable rut they'd created for themselves Janis hadn't wanted to admit that to herself, but now it was staring her in the face.

The warm-up video by a minor rock band ceased abruptly and the electric buzz of voices dropped to an expectant murmur. As soon as the Shaft logo appeared on the screen a roar of approval erupted and people near the front began jumping up and down with impatience. A slow handclap began, shouts of 'We want Blade!' together with stamping feet and loud whistling. Janis gazed up at the familiar symbol, remembering how it had taken her some time to realize how it was constructed. The devil's face behind Blade's aggressive stance made up an inverted pentacle, with the five points being a pair of horns, Spock-shaped ears and a goatee beard.

Yet Shaft was not just another heavy metal band flirting with black magic. Its charismatic leader was the originator and undisputed king of Porn Rock, a steamy blend of hard rock and hard porn that was attracting the over-eighteens in their thousands. The tabloids were screaming with hypocritical outrage, the politicians promised to do something about it, but a European court had decided that, provided identification was checked at the door, there was nothing illegal about adults watching what was, as far as they were concerned, just a live porn show.

Slowly the giant screen at the front of the stage began to lift, accompanied by crashing guitar chords, thudding percussion and bursts of real fire. The audience cheered as the scene was revealed, instantly recognizable as some kind of harem, with a fountain centre stage round which six semi-clad women were reclining on gaudy satin couches. The spouting water changed colour as the music swelled into the familiar melody of 'Ready for You', and the ecstatic screams reached new heights. Janis swayed to the driving rhythm, utterly transfixed, and let the bass vibrations from the speakers set her heart and groin throbbing.

'Ready for you, I'm ready for you!' sang the women, rising from their couches and starting to strip off their flimsy garments. The audience first started clapping then took up the song, dragging slightly behind the beat.

'I'm ready, are you coming? I want to come too!
I want to feel the power, the power in you!'

Janis sang along with the rest, familiar with the song from the CD Rom *Shafted!* She preferred the harem setting to the computer images of Blade riding Virgo dressed as a highwayman, which she'd thought was a bit daft.

Now the troupe of gorgeous females were coming to the

front of the stage, showing off their charms amidst roars of
approval. They'd been carefully chosen to cater to everybody's
taste. A redhead with small, pert breasts and boyish hips
cavorted next to a tall, buxom brunette. A willowy blonde with
hair to her waist and a perfectly proportioned figure held
hands with an earthy black woman who was wiggling her large
hips and showing off her ample but firm buttocks. The third
pair consisted of a petite Asian girl and a brown-haired woman
with enormous breasts that swayed like tethered balloons in a
high wind.

One by one the girls were singled out by a man's voice
calling from the wings. Everyone in the hall recognized it as
Blade's, and the screams multiplied. He sang, '*Hey Pam, are
you ready? Ready for me?*' and the redhead stepped forward
to tumultuous applause singing, '*Oh yes, Blade, I am ready,
Ready for you!*'

While she sang Pam began to caress herself all over. She
squeezed her dainty breasts with both hands and wiggled in
ecstasy, then she smoothed her palms down her sides and
stroked her thighs. When she put one hand between her legs
the response was deafening. Although she continued singing
while she stroked her own body the words were punctuated by
moans and sighs.

> '*Oh yes, Blade – uh! – I am ready – ah!
> Ready for – ooh! – you!*'

After she had apparently reached a climax – it was impossible
to tell whether it was real or simulated – she stepped back in
line to applause and whistles. Then it was the turn of Carol, the
brunette, to show just how ready she was. More exhibitionist
than Pam, she pulled at her dark pink nipples until they stood
out against the creamy skin of her breasts, then dangled them
over the front of the stage for the men to grab at, like bobbing

apples. Laughing and winking, she informed the crowd that she was 'very, very ready' for Blade.

Diane, the blonde, spent a while stroking her tanned buttocks with her long mane before turning to give the audience full view of her firm breasts and lithe hips. She slid her finger down through her bush and into her quim, then licked it, to the delight of everyone. Lucille, the black girl, was bolder still and made the men in the front row reach up and feel her moist crevice. '*Am I ready?*' she sang at them, with a giggle.

'*Yes, you're good and ready! Ready for Blade!!*' came the delighted reply.

The little Chinese girl, Suzanne, pretended to be shy and used a fan as a prop, peering coyly at the audience and giggling whenever she touched herself intimately. Finally the well-endowed Tina produced a fluorescent green dildo and was rewarded with a cheer. Some of the audience had brought similar devices along, some green and some pink, which they waved triumphantly in the air above their heads. Tina proceeded to rub hers between her giant breasts, much to everyone's amusement. When she put it between her thighs there was uproar, and suddenly all the other girls on stage began fighting her for it.

The show was turning into a female wrestling match, and the audience loved it. Tina had the advantage of bulk and managed to toss Suzanne and Diane right into the fountain before there was a sudden crashing chord and Blade appeared on the balcony at the back of the stage, silhouetted in black against a simulated night sky. Everyone went crazy, and Janis felt her legs turn to jelly. It was all she could do to remain upright. The build-up to Blade's appearance had been cleverly designed to get the onlookers worked up and as 'ready' for him as the women on stage were. So when he finally appeared it was quite a shock.

A voice behind her ear whispered, 'Don't worry, darlin', I'll
make sure you're all right!'

Janis felt strong arms squeezing her waist, smelt the
unmistakable scent of beery sweat and musk, and knew that
she was no longer alone in the hall. Tempted as she was to turn
round, she decided it would be more exciting not to face her
anonymous partner, just feel his masculine presence right
behind her. He was holding her tight against him, with the
bulge in his jeans pressing against her backside, and a surge
of pure lust went through her. But she was distracted only for
a moment. With a blinding flash the lights went up on stage,
flooding the carved wooden balcony with glowing colour and
illuminating the Prince of Porn.

The crowd went wild as Blade began descending in golden
light from the balcony, followed by his musicians dressed as
eunuchs. He was wearing a simple white gown, his head tied
with an Arab-style turban, and his blue eyes glittered with
fierce intensity against the dark tan of his face.

'Are you ready?' he sang out, this time addressing the
question not just to the swooning women on stage but to the
entire audience.

'YES!' came the tumultuous reply.

Janis watched in fascination, dividing her attention between
the charismatic figure on the stage and the close-up of him on
the video. She saw his handsome features distort into a snarl
as he strode up to Carol, who now had the dildo, and snatched
the thing off her, throwing it into the audience. He took half a
dozen running strides back up onto the balcony where he stood
on the podium with his back to the crowd, legs apart and arms
spread above his head in the manner of the Shaft logo, The
pure white drapery fell dramatically from his wrists to his
ankles, making him look like an angel in flight.

The music had dropped in volume now, a repetitive riff
emphasizing the suspense as Carol slowly climbed the steps

behind him. Tall as she was, she had to stand on tiptoe to reach up to his shoulders. As she did so the music built towards a crescendo. The garment must have been held by something like Velcro because when she gave it a slight tug it fell off him in two halves, front and back slipping down to make two white pools at his feet.

At the sight of his naked back and buttocks, Janis felt her cunt contract with sudden desire and the man behind her began to rub her breasts through the T-shirt, arousing her even more. She wriggled her bottom against his groin and he gave a low chuckle, but all Janis's attention was concentrated in her eyes. Milking the effect to its maximum, Blade began swaying as the beat quickened, flexing his taut brown buttocks but maintaining his posture. The music flowed into the introduction to one of the band's best-known songs and the place erupted, screams and yells threatening to raise the roof. Then, with slow deliberation, Blade began to turn around, the first line of the lyric pounding out at full volume:

'Hard man, I'm a hard man,
I can rock hard, all night long . . .'

The lighting was carefully designed to make him look like a bronzed Greek god as he displayed his naked body in all its splendour. Janis found it suddenly moving, and felt tears prick her eyes. How long had she dreamed of seeing her hero live, just like this, and now he was even more wonderful than she had imagined. Below the muscled chest and flat stomach, between his sinewed thighs, was the focal point of everyone's image of Blade, the giant phallus that had made the man a legend and inspired thousands of love-sick fans to worship him.

Slowly, arrogantly, Blade descended to the level of the women who were bunched in awe around the fountain. The huge erection seemed to move before him, like the mast on the prow of a ship. The music changed into another of Blade's big hits. His voice filled the auditorium with its rocking up-beat and insistent message:

'*Gonna fuck you, pretty baby, from your head down to*
  your heels,
Fuck you, little darlin', till you know how good it
  feels . . .'

Everyone in the audience was moving their hips now and Janis was no exception. She could feel the tight embrace around her waist as she rocked from side to side and her anonymous partner fell into the rhythm with her. After the dramatic impact of Blade's first appearance the mood had lightened. The girls on stage were on their feet too, prancing around the fountain, showing off their wares and vying with each other to be the first to win Blade's favour. He took the hand of each as they twirled past him, and on the video Janis could see the exaggerated expressions he was making as he sang, pretending to look as if he were giving the choice some serious consideration.

At last the music slowed and quietened, the lights dimmed, and Blade took Diane and Lucille by the hand. The rest of the girls skipped off stage making disappointed noises while the part of the stage containing the fountain was pushed to the back and, in its place, a large round bed descended slowly, to tumultuous applause. Janis held her breath as Blade led his two concubines towards the silken nest that was covered in cushions. After all the drama, fun and games, the mood was now one of sultry sensuality, helped along by the slow tempo of the next song, 'Sweet Pussy', and the subtle scent of jasmine and roses that was wafting through the air ducts to every corner of the concert hall.

The rich, sexy tones of Blade's voice now filled the place

as effectively as the perfume, making Janis sigh with longing.
How she envied those two chosen beauties as they lay on either
side of Blade's magnificent body, ready to take part in the love
ritual.

'Come here, sweet pussy, let me stroke your fur,
Come here, sweet pussy, let me hear you purr . . .'

The luxurious bed began to revolve slowly, letting everyone
have a good view of what was taking place upon it. Blade lay
there passively, letting the two women worship his body with
their hands and lips. On the video screen was a close-up of his
monumental prick which two feminine hands, one black and
one white, were alternately caressing. At the top of the great
shaft was the shiny dome of his glans, swollen and pinkish-
purple. Janis wondered how any woman could possible accommodate such a monster: she gave an involuntary shudder. She
could feel hands creeping up beneath her T-shirt now, lightly
crossing the bare skin of her midriff, and she tensed with
expectation. She was not wearing a bra.

When the stranger's fingers reached both of her stiff nipples
at once and began to pinch them gently, Janis let out a gasp of
relief that was either ignored or unheard by all those around
her. She leaned back against him and felt again the urgency of
his erection, pressing between the back pockets of her jeans.
On screen she could see blonde Diane positioning herself on
top of Blade, preparing to lower herself down onto that
gargantuan spike of flesh. Like everyone else in the audience
her gaze was riveted to the action as the intrepid woman
manoeuvred herself slowly, slowly, into docking position.

'Sweet pussy lips, with your little red mouth,
I could kiss and lick you, from the north down to the
*   south . . .'*

The words of the song were now directed towards Lucille, who was kneeling over his face with her dark labia drawn back and her pink quim exposed. The all-seeing camera caught the moment when the tip of Blade's long tongue probed into that wet, warm interior and the crowd gave out a collective gasp of envious lust. Looking around for a second, Janis could see that furtive movements were going on almost everywhere, with people groping each other beneath their garments, kissing and caressing as far as they could while keeping their eyes fixed on stage or screen.

Diane was now rising and falling with easy grace, looking perfectly at home in the saddle as she slid up and down on Blade's hefty pommel. Her buttocks were spread out over his thighs and her breasts pressed against Lucille's back as the other girl wriggled her mound in Blade's face, all three of them now rocking to the rhythm of the song. While he munched at the black girl's hairy delta Blade was rubbing her large breasts, making the dark nipples strain for his touch.

The pace of the action quickened with the music, and Janis felt a hand drop from her breast to the buckle of her jeans. She offered no resistance as first her belt was undone, then her zipper. The hand insinuated itself beneath the band of her panties and went on down, finding her damp bush. Janis slackened her thighs to allow him further access and was gratified when his finger found the swollen button of her clitoris, already bursting out of its sheath and hungry for stimulation. Clumsy at first, he let her guide his hand to the best spot and then applied just the kind of firm pressure she liked. Relieved that her own lust was soon to find an outlet, Janis turned her attention back to the performance on stage.

Now the two women were nearing their climax and so, it seemed, was half the audience. Blade's voice was singing about a 'hot, pulsating pussy' as Diane gasped her way through

the final stages of her arousal and Lucille was proclaiming her
delight in moans and groans. The whole place was filled with
sex. It oozed from screen and stage, from the bodies below that
swayed and screamed and stroked and gasped until it seemed
as if they were all going to come at once in one huge, orgiastic
release. Relentlessly the musicians played on, half hidden in
the shadows at the back of the stage, moving towards their own
peak of sound while they subtly orchestrated the responses of
the two women and, through them, those of the whole
audience.

Then came a sudden trilling fall of notes, accompanying the
shrill cries of Lucille as Blade's tonguing of her finally
achieved its goal. Her huge breasts shuddered in tune with her
vagina as the racking spasms passed through her body and
Janis, watching through dim eyes, felt her own orgasm begin.
She heard, but scarcely saw, the last voluptuous paroxysms of
Diane as Blade pumped his prick into her with forceful pride,
and then her eyes closed as the bliss swept her up, out of the
heaving morass of sweaty bodies and into a private space
where she could wallow in the delicious sensations flowing
through her. Only the music remained, thumping out its heavy
erotic pulse while she wallowed in the ecstatic flutterings
within.

Afterwards she wanted to lie down, but there was only the
body of the stranger who had pleasured her to lean against. He
held her firmly round the waist, kissing the back of her neck
as she came down from her orgasmic high. Eventually she was
able to look towards the stage again where she could see Blade
escorting the two women towards the wings amidst much
cheering and whistling. The smell of sweat and love-juice was
overpowering, making Janis feel slightly sick now that her first
appetite was sated. There was a hiatus when the screen came
down, blotting off the stage from view, and the video showed
the Shaft logo again.

Janis felt the whole audience relax when Blade moved off the stage and she gave a long, satisfied sigh. There was only so much sexual tension you could bear. She knew more or less what to expect in the second half of the show where the band's female star came into her own. While the other six women were very much Blade's sex slaves Virgo was his equal, and the encounter between them promised to be most exciting. There was a photo of the beautiful star on Janis's bedroom wall, next to Blade's. Sometimes Janis tried to look like her, giving her hair a dark rinse and putting on the heavy, Egyptian-style eye make-up that Virgo used to make her green eyes look an even more startling shade of emerald.

When the band struck up with what had become Virgo's signature tune, the place was in uproar once again. It was not just the female vocalist they wanted. It was to see her and Blade together, in sexual combat, playing out the age-old antagonism between man and woman which could only have one outcome.

Slowly the screen was raised and a new set appeared, to an enthusiastic reception. The band was strumming the introduction to 'Hard to Get' as the crypt of a church was revealed, with pillars supporting a low ceiling, a coffin and some tombs in the corner. The four women who'd not had the pleasure of Blade's company in the previous set now came on dressed as vampire maidens in white gauzy dresses with wildly flowing locks, their pointed teeth tinged with red.

As the girls danced in a ring around one of the pillars, a coffin lid began to move and soon the black-caped figure of Blade appeared. The girls squealed excitedly when they saw him and hurried towards him, their excitement echoed by the crowd. He threw off his cloak and stood naked before them, letting each of the four fondle his erect penis. Then the girls knelt in turn to suck his cock, before they tripped off and concealed themselves within a stage tomb. Suddenly there was a bright glare of simulated sunlight through the window and Blade hid his eyes with a grimace, creeping back into his coffin as well.

The music swelled and the light brightened, spotlighting the fabulous figure of Virgo as she stood at the top of the stone steps leading down into the crypt. She waited for the applause to die down and then descended slowly, letting everyone see her costume. On the video screen Janis could take in every detail. Beneath the mask-like beauty of her features, Virgo's magnificent body was clad in a skin-tight strapless dress of peacock blue that accentuated both the turquoise in her eyes and the tantalizing depth of her cleavage. A side-slit up to her waist showed off her long, slender legs in black, high-heeled shoes. She wore long black gloves, and her blonde hair was piled on top of her head in a cascade of curls. As she walked her lithe hips swayed lazily from side to side, giving her an air of voluptuous indolence.

Once Virgo reached centre stage she began to sing:

> *'Hard to get, I play hard to get,*
> *I've not met the man who can catch me yet . . .'*

A male voice directly behind Janis murmured, 'God, what a babe! I could fuck her to kingdom come!' and she knew it must be her faceless lover, but she wasn't going to turn round and find out. She preferred to imagine Blade's hands and lips on her body, pleasuring her.

There was a different atmosphere in the crowd now, less raucous, almost respectful. Janis was intrigued, wondering if people were simply worn out by their various activities during the first set. Somehow she didn't think so. The presence of such a beautiful sex object seemed to demand more reverence than Blade's raunchy act had done.

While Virgo stood there singing, the lids of the tombs were

raised one by one and out crept the vampire virgins, apparently lured by her siren-song. They put out tentative hands to touch her, but she slapped them away angrily as if they were merely annoying insects. The sight of her appeared to send them into a frenzy of desire, and they began to fondle each other, stripping off the gauzy garments until they were all nude. Whenever they came too close Virgo would dodge behind a pillar, all the time insisting that she 'played hard to get', but the girls grew increasingly lascivious and were soon engaged in a sexual free-for-all, licking and stroking and kissing and fingering each other quite indiscriminately.

Then the lid of the coffin began to move again and the Dracula-figure of Blade emerged, hissing at the promiscuous girls who squealed and fled back into their tombs. Slowly emerging from the shadows, Blade began to harmonize with Virgo, singing his own version of the words:

> 'Hard to get, don't play hard to get,
> You've just met the man who can get you wet . . .'

A titter went round the audience as Blade's parody on Virgo's lyrics sank in. He was mimicking her actions too, standing right behind her and posing like a drag queen. The crowd loved it and burst into applause, but then abruptly ceased as they realized they might miss the words if they clapped too loud.

> 'Hard to find, men are hard to find,
> They just fuck your body and ignore your mind,' trilled
>   Virgo.

With wicked glee, Blade's alternative version ran:

> 'Hard to find, I'm not hard to find,
> If you suck my body it'll blow your mind!'

Suddenly Virgo turned to confront Blade, and everyone cheered. She pushed her hand right in his face and he reeled backwards, staggering histrionically to the delight of the crowd. The pace hotted up. Virgo came right onto the apron and, with a contemptuous glance over her shoulder at the punch-drunk Blade, began to peel off her long, black gloves. She began singing very quietly, seducing the audience with her incredible eyes all the while. Blade kept his distance, lying on the floor and gazing up at her with lust emanating from every pore. She dangled each glove over the upturned faces of the crowd before tossing them casually into the air where they drifted down like black bats to be snatched at by hands eager for a trophy.

Slowly the rock diva turned round until she was facing the prone Blade once more. Her hand crept to the long zipper down her back and, to the frenzied approval of the crowd, she began to pull it slowly down. The creamy whiteness of her back was revealed, smooth as silk, then the top of the crevice between her bum cheeks was visible and the audience stamped and cheered wildly, wanting more, more! The band slid into another of Virgo's songs, 'Are you man enough for me?' and Blade jumped to his feet. He began to brandish his fully erect organ, strutting around with his hand at the base of his shaft, waving the purplish glans at Virgo in mocking assertion that he was, indeed, man enough for her.

The turquoise sheath slid to the ground showing Virgo naked from the back. Her exquisitely formed buttocks curved with pert assurance above slim thighs, shapely calves and trim ankles. Now everyone in the audience was envying Blade, with his full frontal view, but the video cameras remained resolutely on her back. The suspense was almost tangible. Virgo went through two choruses of the song, wiggling her behind at the audience while Blade continued his absurd parade. Everyone wanted to see the two of them together, in action, and the teasing tension was mounting to fever pitch.

Then, at long last, Blade began to approach Virgo with wary strides, his features contorted by a grossly lascivious smile. She pretended to be alarmed and, in dodging away from him, revealed herself more fully. There was a brief side view of one large, shapely breast, the nipple disappointingly concealed beneath a stick-on red heart, then she fled behind one of the columns.

Now the real teasing began, as Virgo displayed fleeting glimpses of her almost-naked body. She clutched the column and wrapped her long legs around it, pretending to make love to it as she moved her body up and down. It was an obvious jibe at the size of Blade's dick and he came forward angrily, trying to snatch at her, but she dodged behind another column, offering another fleeting glimpse of herself as she went. By now everyone could see that she was wearing three strategically placed red hearts.

Next time Blade did manage to seize her momentarily by the hair, which promptly came tumbling down about her shoulders altering her image dramatically. Now she had the look of a tousled seductress. Suddenly Blade put his arms around the column where she was sheltering and the pair of them were embracing the giant phallic symbol, drawing roars of enthusiasm. Someone near the front of the crowd started chanting, 'Shaft! Shaft! Shaft! Shaft!' and everyone took it up until the noise was deafening.

Slyly, Virgo crept from behind the column and Blade grabbed her around the waist, trying to sink his teeth into the skin of her neck. She chopped at his thigh, just missing his prong, and he jumped back howling. Virgo preened herself, showing off her magnificent figure to the audience who by now were going crazy, stamping and whistling and screaming. She offered her large, firm breasts for inspection, holding them underneath but being careful not to dislodge the protective hearts. She smoothed her hands down her slim hips and, with a smug grin, patted the heart that covered her pubic area.

Her complacency was ill-timed, however. Blade was on his feet behind her and moved quickly to imprison her in his arms. His mouth came down at once on the side of her neck and she screamed, but then her screams dwindled to moans of sensual delight as he sucked away. Now that he had her in his power his hands moved to her breasts, removing the flimsy hearts – which he threw into the audience – and revealing her incredibly large and red nipples. He tweaked them in turn, making her writhe with sensual glee, and removed his mouth from her neck where he had given her a great purple love-bite.

Sensing that the great moment was approaching, everyone watching was well aroused and Janis felt her own libido rising too. Again the hands of her invisible lover crept under her T-shirt to caress her breasts and she had to fight the urge to close her eyes and give herself up to her own pleasure instead of watching the show. Her belt was still undone, and this time he pushed her jeans down her thighs until her pants were exposed. Janis didn't care. No one else was looking, and most of them were already engaged in similar activity with their partners. Some were already joined at the crotch, pumping away excitedly to the music.

As she felt warm hands slip down her pants and caress her buttocks, Janis turned her gaze to the video screen. Blade had his fingers on Virgo's strawberry nipples now, pinching them and making her squeal with pleasure, as his lips continued to graze her neck. Only one red heart remained on her body, concealing her mound. Slowly Blade's hand slipped down over her flat, creamy stomach. Then his fingers reached the stuck-on motif. With a sudden growl he pulled it off, tossing it disdainfully into the crowd who roared in frenzy as Virgo's smoothly shaven pubis was revealed. Janis gazed in fascination at the star's pouting pussy lips and the dark slit between.

With a slow and sensual movement, as if falling under a spell, Virgo parted her legs and stood astride at the front of the stage. Blade thrust between her thighs from behind and his huge dick reared up in front of his partner's naked mound, making her look like some kind of weird hermaphrodite. She grasped the jerking tool, throwing her head back with a sigh, and began to rub it between her labia to loud encouragement from the crowd. The music changed again, this time moving up tempo into the vigorous beat of 'I want it now and I want it hot!' The audience joined in with the second line, '*So give it everything you've got!*' and the couple on stage got into a fucking rhythm, moving their hips in unison until Virgo was sliding back and forth along Blade's organ. He was squeezing her breasts and she was gasping, pulling open her love-lips to allow the video camera to catch every detail of her arousal, including the erect red tip of her clitoris.

The driving rhythm of the music was moving rapidly towards a climax. When the song reached the lines that ran, '*Please don't make me wait, just make me! Any way you want to take me* . . .' Virgo dropped to her knees and then went down on all fours, her breasts hanging down like firm globes made of smooth, lightly tanned leather. Everyone cheered as Blade finally thrust into her from behind, riding her like a cowboy on a bucking bronco. She seemed to be trying to unseat him, rotating her pelvis at high speed and jerking her bum up and down, but still he held on and continued to prod away, his well-defined chest and stomach muscles straining hard to maintain control.

The sight was obviously too much for the guy behind Janis. With a groan he pulled her pants right down and pushed his cock in between her thighs. She clenched them together tightly, making a meat sandwich of the long, thin prick. Janis began to squeeze her thighs together rhythmically, feeling him thrust, and the action had a stimulating effect on her labia. She put her hand down and touched the slippery glans that was already seeping juice, then she applied some friction to her own love-button that was clamouring to join in the fun. Soon she was on the verge of coming, but she wanted to delay the moment. When she felt herself about to tip over the brink she withdrew and let her excitement fade a little. With her eyes fixed glassily on stage she knew that she would only let herself come when Virgo did.

It couldn't be long now. The sweat was running down the porn star's brow, highlighted by the fierce stage lighting that was revealing every detail. Her full-lipped mouth was open and her emerald eyes were staring out blindly into the crowd. Janis saw little beads of moisture dripping down from the tips of her huge nipples and somehow that was the biggest turn-on of all. The video camera homed in on them as they fell from the perfect orbs of her breasts to the floor, and Janis felt the first shock waves of her orgasm approach. Unable to help herself, she seized the stiff cock that was between her legs and rubbed it hard against her throbbing clitoris. At the same time a great roar went round the hall and, despite the fact that her eyes were closed and she was swiftly entering a world of her own, she knew that Virgo must be climaxing too.

The realization intensified her pleasure, giving her deep and satisfying spasms that went on increasing in strength over and over, until she thought she would collapse with rapture. Eventually they faded to a warm, tremulous glow. It was only then that she became aware of an emptiness between her thighs and two slow streams of wet gloop that were making their way steadily down her legs. She groped in her bag for a tissue and wiped herself, then pulled up her pants and jeans. The man behind seemed to have retreated, for the time being at least.

The show proceeded to a virtuoso display of fellatio from a

conquered and satiated Virgo, leading to a silly episode of phallus worship, but for Janis the best was already over. When the couple finally left the stage, with Virgo in Blade's arms followed in procession by the vampire maidens, Janis was still in a star-struck daze. The cheers rang in her ears as the crowd began to disperse, turning towards the various exits. Janis didn't want to turn round, didn't want to meet the eyes of the man who had shared her body in that clandestine fashion. Now that the glamour and excitement had faded the whole business seemed sordid and embarrassing.

So instead of making for the nearest exit she headed towards one on the far side, waiting until the crowd had thinned enough to let her through. She still felt keyed up inside, thrilled to have seen her idols in the flesh, listening to the tunes replaying over and over inside her head. At last she got to the door, which turned out to be a fire exit, and pushed the bar to open it. Cool night air streamed over her, blissfully refreshing, and she came out into a car park.

Disorientated, she'd thought she was heading for the front of the building but in fact she was going round the back. Her car must be parked at the far end. Stumbling through the dark she suddenly found herself near a door with a light over it and two burly men standing on guard. The door opened and a face looked out. With a shock, Janis recognized Virgo, still in her stage make-up and with a blanket around her shoulders. 'Where's that fucking taxi?' she asked one of the men.

He shrugged. 'We phoned for it, like you said. It's supposed to be here by now.'

A small crowd of fans were rushing around the corner of the building. 'There she is!' one called. The others screamed and accelerated their pace. For a moment Janis found herself meeting the annoyed gaze of her heroine. She moved forward, dazzled by those fantastic eyes, and heard herself saying with surprising audacity, 'If you're in a hurry I could give you a lift.'

The star hesitated only for a second. Then, just as the crowd of fans were bearing down on her, she made a dash towards Janis, hauling her after her. 'Come on, run!' Virgo urged, taking Janis's hand. 'Where's your car? Hope it's nearby.'

'Just over here!'

With trembling fingers Janis thrust the key in the lock and flung open both front doors. She switched on the ignition, praying that the trouble she'd had starting that morning would not repeat itself. Her luck was in. The engine caught first time and soon they were moving through the car park and across the forecourt. It was only when they got stuck in the stream of traffic trying to get out that the adrenalin high that had been propelling Janis through the last few minutes began to abate, and she realized exactly what she was doing.

Fucking hell! she thought, glancing down to where Virgo was crouched on the floor with a blanket over her head. *I've just had an orgasm simultaneously with the sexiest woman in the world, and now she's in my car!*

CHAPTER TWO

Janis was so excited she could hardly keep her hands on the wheel but somehow she made it through the traffic, waved out onto the street by a young policeman whose eyes would probably have popped out if he knew who was in her car. Once they were away from the Pyramid, London's newest and smartest rock venue, Virgo tossed the blanket into the back seat and relaxed. She was wearing black stretch jeans and a grey mohair sweater.

'Whew! I thought I'd never get out of there alive! Mind if I smoke?'

'No, that's OK.' As the nostalgic smell of Gitanes filled the car, Janis stared nervously at the road ahead. It took her a few minutes to realize that she didn't have a clue where she was going. 'Er . . . where do you live, Virgo?'

The star leaned back in her seat and puffed out a long smoky breath, reeking of the Paris Métro. 'Docklands. Just follow the signs and I'll direct you when we get nearer. It should only take about half an hour this time of night. What's your name, by the way?'

'Janis. With an s.'

'Like Joplin?'

'That's right. My Mum was a rock fan.'

'Good for her! And now it's in your genes, eh?' Virgo patted her denim-clad knee, making a pun of it. 'Well, it's good of you to give me a lift, Jan. I hope this isn't out of your way.'

'Oh, not at all!' Janis lied. *If this woman lived in Edinburgh I'd have driven her home*, she thought. The brief contact between Virgo's hand and her knee was still sending tingles up her spine. To think that scarcely half an hour ago she had been watching that same hand caressing Blade's penis on stage!

'I don't usually rush away from a gig so fast, but tonight I'd had it up to here!' Virgo went on. 'Sometimes it's like that. You just don't want to meet the fucking fans. I know I'll get a bollocking from Sam – Sam Woods, our manager – because he says it's bad for my image. But I tell him I've already got a bad image, so what the hell?'

She gave a coarse laugh, taking another loud drag at her fag. Janis was nonplussed. Virgo was turning out to be nothing like she'd imagined.

'So what did you think of the show?'

The question caught Janis off balance. She heard herself gush, 'Oh, it was just marvellous!'

'You got off on it, then?'

Virgo's throaty drawl was tinged with amusement. Janis gave her a sidelong look and found she was being smiled at, the translucent green eyes scanning her face.

She grinned back. 'Yes, I did, actually.'

'All by yourself?' Her tone was mocking, but at the same time self-mocking.

'I was there on my own because I'd had a row with my boyfriend. But there was this guy standing behind me . . .'

'Naughty!'

'But nice!'

Janis was pleased with herself when Virgo gave another belly laugh. It seemed they were getting on famously. Or was the other woman high on something? A cloud descended over her spirits when she thought that Virgo might forget all about this by tomorrow morning, that she was just a convenient vehicle, nothing more. She quashed the thought firmly, telling herself not to spoil things, but to enjoy it while it lasted.

'Take a left here, or we'll get caught up in the one-way system,' Virgo said. She sounded very lucid, not out of it at all. They fell into silence for around five minutes but all the time Janis was wondering frantically what she could say that wouldn't make her sound like a complete twat of the 'I'm your number one fan' variety.

She wanted to tell Virgo that she thought her stage act with Blade was incredible, that her singing was amazing, that her face and figure were an ideal to which every woman should aspire. She also wanted to ask her about Blade. What was he like off stage? How did he maintain an erection throughout the show? And, above all, what was he like as a lover?

But just then Virgo stubbed out her cigarette on the dashboard, letting the dog-end fall to the floor.

'God, Jan, it's so nice to be able to chat to you instead of having some prick of a cab driver chatting me up. You've no idea! Shall I hire you as my chauffeur, darling? Would you like that?' She giggled, and Janis joined in until she added sourly, 'But don't give up the day job!'

'I wouldn't mind. Tell me about how you got started, Virgo. I'd love to know.'

'Would you really? What do you want, the official version or the true one?'

'The true one, of course.'

'You'll get both. The official story is that Blade and I were discovered in some sleazy pub talent contest.'

'But that's not true?'

'Only if you believe in fairy stories. No, the truth is that Blade and I had separate bands. We were both signed up by this poxy record company that had us sitting around on our arses and living on promises before they got taken over by a major outfit.'

'You mean you and Blade didn't play together?'

'We didn't even know each other! Poxy Records didn't like its artists talking to each other in case they found out that they were getting an even bummer deal than the bum deal some other sucker was getting.'

'Um . . . sorry to interrupt, but I think we're in Docklands now, aren't we?'

'Christ, we've missed the turning! Take first left, then first right. Now where was I?'

'About to get taken over by the big boys.'

'Oh, yeah. Well, once that happened there was a big rationalization programme. Lots of unprofitable bands got the chop. Blade and I were lucky. No one knew whether we were a golden goose or a cold turkey, so they teamed us up to see what hatched.'

'And you certainly succeeded!'

'Not straight away we didn't! Our first band was called Interface, would you believe? Known locally – and back then we were *only* known locally – as "In yer face". It was utter crap! But then some senior A & R guy said we should be more sexy on stage. We travelled to Hamburg, saw some live sex shows, and reckoned we could combine that with music. Then we came back to England, hired new backing musicians and Shaft was born.'

Janis sighed. 'You make it sound so easy.'

'Well, it wasn't. And it still isn't. Porn is a hard business and Rock is a harder one. Combine the two and you've got one hell of a tough time ahead. Second left, then we're there.'

They drew up in front of a towering apartment block that looked like an ocean liner with wings. 'A touch post-modernist for my taste, but the address looks good on my letterhead,' Virgo said in response to Janis's awe-struck reaction.

Janis was bewildered. One minute the woman was swearing like a trooper, the next second she sounded like someone on the South Bank Show. She waited as Virgo undid her seatbelt, steeling herself for some quick thanks and then the abrupt ending of this fantastic dream. Who would believe her, if she told them her story? Not Adam, that was for sure. But then she wasn't sure she wanted to see him, ever again. Tonight had just confirmed . . .

'Well, are you coming up or not?'

Suddenly it dawned on Janis that, absorbed in her reverie, she'd missed an invitation. She smiled broadly, unable to believe her luck. 'You mean, up to your flat?'

'No, darling, up into the stratosphere! I've got my own personal space rocket standing by!'

Hastily Janis undid her seatbelt and switched off the engine. Afraid that she was going to miss this incredible opportunity she scrambled from her seat, got her leg tangled in the belt and gave herself a thud on the shin with the side of the door. 'Ow!'

'Hey, take it easy! You'll put a nasty dent in the body work if you're not careful!'

Giggling through her pain, Janis hobbled to the pavement. Virgo put her arm around her waist. 'Come on, lean on me. I've got some miracle cream in my bathroom cabinet. Arnica. If you put it on straight away it stops a bruise forming.'

If it hadn't been for the searing pain in her leg, Janis reflected as they made for the door, she would have been overwhelmed by being that close to her heroine. Beneath the enveloping aroma of French cigarettes she could detect other smells, sweat overlaid with deodorant and another faint odour that was very sexy. Could it possibly be the scent of Blade, she wondered, and a shiver went through her. Virgo's arm was giving her real support and she could sense that there was a good deal of strength there. It was obvious that she worked out. No one could maintain a figure like hers without spending at least some time in the gym.

As they waited for the voice-activated security system to let

them in, a vision of Virgo's exquisite body flashed into Janis's
mind and she felt weak at the knees. A hot flush of pure desire
caught her unawares, shocked her with its frontal attack upon
her senses, and she felt herself begin to crumple. She groaned
and reached for the wall to support herself. Virgo turned round
with a look of genuine concern. 'Are you OK? Is it your leg?'

Janis knew it was the thought that Virgo might want to
make love to her that had fazed her, but she just nodded.

'You poor thing. Come on, I'll carry you into the lift.'

'No, it's all right . . .'

Janis's protests were over-ridden and she was picked up
bodily. She clung to Virgo like a baby, letting her head fall
against the firm twin pillows of her breasts. *This is amazing*,
she kept telling herself, but by now the whole thing had taken
on a kind of dream logic, with one part of the adventure
seeming no more extraordinary than the rest.

'Light as a fucking feather!' Virgo declared as she strode
into the waiting lift. 'What do you weigh? Must be less than
eight stone.'

'Nearer nine, last time I weighed myself.'

'Hm.' Gently Janis was restored to an upright position. She
leaned against the back of the lift for support as it rose almost
soundlessly through five floors with Virgo smiling at her all
the way. She felt absurdly shy, but aroused at the same time. It
was a familiar feeling from long ago. Then she remembered it
was like finding herself suddenly alone in the cloakroom with
a sixth-former that she'd had a crush on.

'Here we are. Can you stagger a few yards, or must I carry
you across the threshold?'

Janis gripped the hand that was held out to her. She limped
across the blue monogrammed carpet of the hallway and
waited for Virgo to unlock the door of her apartment. Following
her in, Janis gasped as subdued lights came on and the vast
room was displayed in all its glory. The curtains were still open

to the night sky and out towards the horizon the lights of London made a dazzling display, golden constellations mirroring the silver ones above.

'Oh, how wonderful!' Janis breathed, forgetting her pain momentarily.

'You just sit there, put your feet up and admire the view while I get the arnica.'

Janis sank into the plump lap of a vast armchair with a foot rest and let her head fall back. She closed her eyes and listened to the silence. She was aware of being in a place of quiet luxury, a place where only the best was good enough and where anything – and anyone – could be taken care of. Janis had never been in a five-star hotel but she imagined it must be like this.

'Here we are! Take off your jeans and put your foot on this stool.'

Virgo's manner was brisk, like a friendly nurse, and Janis obeyed automatically. It no longer seemed strange to her that she was with a famous – infamous – rock star. Success, money, notoriety hadn't spoilt Virgo. On the contrary, it seemed to have made her more ordinary, perhaps to compensate for her extraordinary stage persona. Janis undid her belt and pulled down her jeans, blushingly recalling her behaviour at the concert. Virgo helped to remove them, then unscrewed the top of the tube and squeezed a splodge of white cream onto her fingers. 'Now then, where does it hurt?'

'On my shin, about halfway down.'

The touch of Virgo's fingertips was soft and gentle, stilling Janis's fears that she would be caused further pain. She rubbed the cream in delicately until it had all disappeared. 'There you are, you'll be as right as rain in the morning.'

Somehow, from the way she said it, Janis knew that Virgo expected her to stay the night. Another of those strange shivers went through her and this time it was noticed.

'Are you cold? I could turn the heating up.'

'Oh no! It's just a reaction, I suppose.'

Virgo smiled knowingly, and rose to her feet. 'I'll get you some hot choc, laced with brandy. It'll settle your nerves.'

Before Janis could reply she'd gone into the adjacent kitchen and was humming to herself as she put milk on to heat. It was strange having someone look after her like this, stranger still when she thought about who it was. When she'd been ill, say with 'flu, Adam hadn't fussed over her at all. On the contrary, he'd been sulky and irritated, as if he suspected her of malingering. The more she thought about it, the better off she felt without him.

'So, you had a row with your boyfriend,' she heard Virgo say as she appeared bearing two white mugs.

'That's weird, I was just thinking about him.'

'Hardly surprising, is it?' Virgo handed Janis one steaming, fragrant mug with the pale brown liquid still whirling round. 'Want to talk about it? You can tell Aunty Virgo everything, you know. Not only am I completely unshockable, but I also used to be an agony aunt on a teenage magazine. Now you didn't expect that, did you?'

Janis laughed. 'Certainly not! But I bet you had loads of street cred!'

'Oh, I wasn't Virgo then. No one had heard of me. I got the job through a friend. But for God's sake stop me talking about myself, will you? Tell me your troubles, for a change.'

Janis sipped the hot, sweet liquid and felt instantly cheered. 'Nothing much to tell, really. I've been living with Adam for two years. It was OK at first, a kind of novelty, playing at being a housewife. I used to love shopping with him on a Saturday afternoon . . .'

She paused, afraid that she must be sounding really pathetic to someone who led the exciting life of a rock star. But Virgo grinned encouragingly at her. She took off her sock and started to massage her right foot. Janis found her firm, sure touch very relaxing.

'If I'm honest, I have to admit that it only felt good for about a year. It's been going downhill ever since. Well, ever since I told him how much I fancied Blade.'

Virgo laughed, disconcertingly, 'Why did you tell him?'

'We were swapping fantasies. It wasn't fair because he made me go first so I told him the truth. I said I fancied being on stage with Blade and having him tie me up and stuff.'

'You did?' Virgo was leaning forward now, eyes glowing with interest. Janis felt herself blush. She didn't want to go into detail. In fact, she wished she hadn't mentioned it at all.

'Mm. Anyway, I said he had to tell me his favourite fantasy too, because that was the deal. He came out with this story about taking me boating in summer with me in a frilly dress. When we were moored in the centre of the lake he'd perform cunnilingus on me under my skirt.'

'Far out!'

'It was, actually, for him. He didn't like going down on me, said I smelt funny. That's what made it all the more annoying when he started to get jealous of Blade. I mean, my fantasy was obviously something that was never going to happen. But his fantasy was something that could happen, except that he didn't want it to. It all seemed . . . perverse.'

'Yes, I see that. So his fantasy was one you wanted to act out, was it?'

'Not particularly. But I'd have liked him to . . . you know, in bed sometimes.'

Janis felt Virgo's hands caressing her legs, almost absent-mindedly, as she sat on the carpet at her feet. It seemed the wrong way round: Janis should be sitting at *her* feet. She looked down at the star's tangled mane of honey-blonde hair, caught in a loose knot at the nape of her neck, and thought for the hundredth time how lovely she was. Beneath the greasy remains of her stage make-up it was obvious that she had a stunning natural beauty, and even below the shapeless sweater she was wearing her breasts jutted proudly, firmly. Again Janis felt sudden, gut-wrenching desire. Her legs were warm and relaxed now, not trembling at all, and the hurt had disappeared. She smiled down at Virgo, who suddenly rose and went over to the expensive-looking sound system that took up part of the opposite wall.

'Some music, I think. What do you like?'

She reeled off a list of names. They had similar taste in music, it seemed. They finally agreed on Billie Holiday, and the rich dark tones of the jazz singer soon filled the apartment with mellow harmonies. Janis leaned back into the embrace of the armchair and closed her eyes. Suddenly she felt very tired. She sensed that Janis had come to sit on the floor beside her again but she kept her eyes closed. Then she heard Virgo say, quietly, 'Sleepy?'

Janis responded with a nod and a smile, keeping her eyes closed. She felt the light touch of the other woman's hand, on her thigh this time, and a distinctly sexual thrill flashed through her groin. *Something's going to happen*, she thought, her pulse racing excitedly. Didn't she remember reading about Virgo being bisexual? Janis had never made love with another woman before, never really fancied it. Now she was surprised to find it didn't seem so strange. After all, she had adored both the stars of Shaft for some time. To be close to Virgo was to be close to Blade, and that was what she wanted more than anything in the world right then.

Virgo was still stroking her thighs with firm, massaging fingers. What if it was just that, a therapeutic massage, and she was reading too much into it? The sweet, sultry voice of the singer was casting its spell over them both and all conversation had ceased, touch being their only communication now. Janis sighed, all her awareness concentrated in her thighs and the flowing warmth that was smoothing away the pain and replacing it with pleasure.

The tactile experience changed and, still without opening her eyes, Janis recognized the soft, hot wetness of lips against the sensitive skin of her inner thigh. The kisses were like the gentle mouthings of a baby, provoking warm flurries deep within her and an involuntary groan. Virgo's hands crept upward to stroke Janis's bare midriff beneath her T-shirt. Now her intentions were beyond doubt. The arousal she'd felt at the concert returned in full force, making her writhe and moan with urgent longing. Her breasts were tingling, lusting after the touch of those teasing fingers as they moved with delicate precision around the tickly node of her navel.

'You're such a little peach, Janis.'

Hot breath fanned her pubis and Janis opened her eyes to see Virgo staring lustfully at the mini-triangle of her panties. A swooping gust of raw passion caught her unawares, and she gasped. Virgo grinned. 'Not used to having a woman make love to you, eh?'

Janis nodded, speechless. She still couldn't believe this was happening to her. Virgo perched on the arm of the chair, forcing her to look into those mesmerizing eyes. 'Is this your very first time?' Again, Janis nodded. Virgo gave that sexy, throaty laugh again and bent her lips to Janis's mouth.

The kiss was exquisitely sensual, not thrusting and forceful like kisses with Adam were but lazily exploring the outer and inner surfaces of lips, tongue-tips meeting and retreating, tasting and softly sucking, in a dance of endless delight. Janis imagined how that same expert mouth might play with the even more intimate parts of her body, and the thought set up eager expectations in those very erogenous zones. She could feel herself growing limp from head to toe, her body Virgo's for the taking as she lay there in languid ease.

After the long bliss of their mouth-to-mouth encounter,

Virgo's lips left a moist trail of kisses across her cheek and
Janis felt a shuddering wave pass down her spine as she felt her
T-shirt being lifted up and her breasts exposed. Virgo made a
little guttural noise of appreciation and swiftly bent to take one
rearing nipple between her lips. Janis groaned. She could feel
her nipple thrusting in between the other woman's lips,
growing huge and stiff and ravenous as if it, not the sucking
mouth, were the hungry party. Titillating little sparks were
firing down her nerves from her breast to her clitoris, making
her press her thighs together in a vain attempt to ease the
growing itch between them.

Her clothes were becoming a nuisance now. 'Wait . . .' Janis
whispered, when she could bear the encumbrance no longer.
She lifted her arms above her head and pulled off her top,
exposing the pale golden hemispheres of her bosom. Virgo's
eyes smouldered with emerald fire as she gazed at them, lifted
them gently with her hands and squeezed until the tawny-pink
nipples stood out like fruits ripe for the picking.

Flick, went that agile tongue, flick, flick, back and forth
over first one nipple then the other until the hungry vortex in
the pit of Janis's stomach grew almost unbearable. Now that
tormenting mouth was sucking her with lips and tongue going
at full tilt, drawing in the throbbing nub of her passion and
nibbling at it unmercifully. Hips and thighs writhing with
naked desire, Janis dug her fingers into the thick silken knot
at the nape of her lover's neck and felt the tangle loosen,
falling about her shoulders. The freed tresses brushed against
her own breasts and stomach, rousing her further. Down below
Virgo was still stroking her thighs in a rhythmic way, sneakily
reaching almost up to her heaving pussy, but not quite.

If this goes on much longer I shall burst, Janis thought. She
wanted to scream out her desire, to tell Virgo exactly what she
wanted her to do, but a residual shyness prevented her. This
was, after all, her female idol and she was, after all, only a fan.

An incredibly privileged fan to be sure, favoured beyond her wildest dreams, but she didn't want to spoil things by being too demanding, too hasty.

Then – Oh, incredible joy! – those sneaky fingers began to creep beneath the close-fitting leg of her panties. The pouting lips of her quim slid open to let the naughty intruder feel how deliciously wet she was, how achingly ready for some direct contact at last. Virgo was nipping quite hard at her nipples now, grazing them with her sharp little teeth, notching her desire up to the next level where it was earthy and strong and unscrupulous in the pursuit of its own satisfaction. She pushed down the waistband of her panties, revealing the dark curls of her bush, and Virgo's hand retreated for as long as it took to get the last garment sliding down her thighs. Impatiently Janis kicked the panties off into the air and lay back again, thighs outspread in a blatant invitation to explore the hidden depths between them.

The star sang softly, self-mockingly, 'Hey Janis, are you ready? Ready for me?'

Quick as a flash, she replied, 'Yes, Virgo, I am ready, Ready for you!'

Testing fingers probed between Janis's sleek labia and found her swimming in love-juice. 'Oh yes, you're ready all right!' Virgo murmured, her voice faltering as she found the entrance to the other girl's vagina wide open. Without delay she slid her fingers right in, making Janis gasp with surprise and delight as her cunt was suddenly filled. Virgo pushed her hand in and out, making squelching noises as the secretions overflowed in response to the stimulation. At the same time she nibbled at Janis's taut nipples more fiercely, sucking and biting excitedly like a tiger cub that hardly knows its own strength.

Janis was overwhelmed by the rapid onset of her orgasm at it swept her on through peak after peak of shuddering pleasure.

Dimly she sensed that Virgo had swapped the positions of her
hands and mouth, that she was now pinching her nipples,
digging into them with her sharp nails, while she sucked thirstily
at every new gush from Janis's weeping cunt and licked out
every crevice. The combined effect was to prolong her climax
longer than she would have thought possible. Moaning and
thrashing, Janis gave herself up again and again to the
onslaught of ecstasy until she was utterly shattered and
completely sated.

For a long while afterwards she lay flopped back in the
chair, unable to think or speak, letting the tide that had ripped
through her like a hurricane wash her up gently onto the shore
of her consciousness again. When she finally came to she was
aware of Virgo cradling her head in her lap. She looked up and
the exquisite eyes gazed down at her fondly, the full lips
curving into a smile of recognition. 'Are you OK?' she
whispered, needlessly.

Janis laughed in delight, 'Oh my, oh my! If that's what
lesbian love is all about . . .'

Virgo's smile faded a little, her eyes dimming like stage
lights before a sad song.

'Sex, Janis dear. Let's get it straight from the start, shall we?
I do sex, not love.'

A chill gripped at Janis's heart. She hated being reminded
that this was probably going to be her one and only close
encounter with the rock goddess. The golden glow that had
bathed her, body and soul, only a moment ago faded abruptly
and a sour realism took its place, 'Of course,' she said, flatly.
'Look, would you like me to leave now?'

A soft hand caressed her cheek. 'Not unless you want to.
You're welcome to stay. You can share my bed, or there's a
spare.'

A little of the glow returned. Janis sat up. 'Are you sure?
Then I would like to stay with you. May I use your bathroom?'

'We'll have a bath together, shall we?'

Wallowing in fluffy clouds of scented bubbles, the giggling pair groped and smothered each other like a couple of kids at bath time. Every time Janis caught hold of a piece of Virgo's gorgeous, slippery body she marvelled at its sleek perfection. Her questing fingers touched now a thick, rubbery nipple, now a smooth toe. Her hands groped until they found one large, impossibly firm breast but then Virgo's body flipped over and it was an equally taut buttock she was feeling. Once or twice she found herself making contact with her shaven mound smooth as a cowry shell, but she fought shy of it, unwilling to invade that forbidden territory unbidden. Although she was happy to offer up every secret corner of her own body to Virgo's expert caresses, she was less relaxed about reciprocating. It was all so new too her, and there was only so much that she could take in one go.

Afterwards they patted each other dry with fluffy warm towels and then Janis lay on the vast bed while Virgo massaged perfumed cream into her skin. It was so late, and she was so tired, that once she had completely relaxed Janis fell asleep where she lay.

She came to in the early morning and when she remembered where she was a slow excitement filled her veins. The duvet had been pulled up and there beside her lay Virgo, her profile unfamiliar in the faint light with black sweeping lashes resting on her pale cheeks like the sinister petals of a Venus flytrap, and her mouth half open in a seductive pout. The glorious mane tumbled about her shoulders, one lock falling between her gently heaving breasts.

Gazing at her, Janis tried to imagine how Blade must feel making love to such a magnificent creature and she felt a jealous stab. But then Virgo opened her eyes and gave her such a sweet smile that all such negative thoughts were instantly banished. 'Hi! Nice to wake up beside such a pretty face,' she said.

'I beg your pardon? Are we talking about me first thing in the morning here?'

Virgo reached up and kissed her firmly on the mouth. 'Oh yes, sugar lips. Now you just lie there while I get us some nosh. Don't know about you, but I'm starving!'

Soon they were sitting side by side munching cinnamon doughnuts and drinking coffee. The chummy vibe of the night before returned as they swapped memories of the bands they used to like.

'I always wanted to be in a band myself,' Janis confessed at last. 'I wrote a couple of songs, learned a few chords on a guitar and went along to audition for a local band. But they were all blokes and they completely sapped my confidence. It was awful. I never tried again.'

'Bastards! Men are such bastards!' Virgo spoke so vehemently that she spat sugar all over the duvet. 'You know why? They're scared that a woman will turn out to be better than them. They can't stand the competition.'

'You don't have problems like that with Blade, then, or the rest of the Shaft band?'

Virgo's green eyes took on a wary slant. 'Look, don't fish, OK? What goes on inside Shaft is no one's business but our own. We're fed up with people making things up about us.'

'I'm sorry. I didn't mean . . .'

'Of course you didn't.' Virgo gave her a long, serious look. 'You're very sweet, Janis. You don't want to get mixed up with the rock world. It's not very nice. It changes you.'

'But it's the only time I feel alive! Last night, at the gig, being there on my own and really getting into the music, the sex, was utterly fantastic. It's what I live for, that . . . buzz.'

Virgo smiled, wistfully. 'I know what you mean. I still get that feeling sometimes, although mostly I'm just going through the motions. But you don't want to hear about that.'

'Oh, I do! I want to know about anything and everything!

Blade has been my hero for three years, you too. I just think
you're fantastic!'

She bit her lip, afraid of sounding too much like the gushing
fan. Virgo slipped from the bed, her lithe figure moving
towards the door where a black kimono covered with pink,
green and white flowers hung. She pulled it around herself,
tying the sash. 'Blade is not what he seems, Jan. Don't get too
hung up on him, will you?'

Janis felt disappointed. She'd hoped there was a chance of
being introduced to him. Her feelings must have shown on her
face because the star went on, 'If you wanted his autograph I
could get you that. Why don't you come to the show tonight?
I'll put you on the guest list.'

'Really? Would you?'

'Of course, no trouble. And I'll make sure you get a
backstage pass so you can get to my dressing-room.' Again her
expression darkened, mysteriously. 'But Blade and I have
separate dressing-rooms, so don't expect to meet him.'

'OK.' Not wishing to seem ungrateful, Janis tried to inject
a brighter note into her tone. 'It's really good of you, Virgo. I
can't believe I'm going to see the show again, so soon.'

'Just returning a favour.'

Janis quailed. Was this supposed to be some kind of
payment for last night? But then Virgo added, 'I really needed
that lift. You helped me more than you realize.'

Virgo opened the bedroom door and disappeared. She
returned in a few seconds with Janis's clothes that had been left
strewn on the living-room floor.

'Look, I'm not trying to throw you out or anything but I
have to get to the gym in half an hour or I'll miss my session.'

'Oh yes, of course!' Janis scrambled out of bed and into her
clothes. Before she left, Virgo took her in a long embrace. It
was a sisterly hug, and Janis felt reassured. She was told to
report to the box office at seven that night, then shown out of

the apartment and into the lift, departing as smoothly as she had arrived and in the same star-struck, dreamlike state.

While she drove back through the unfamiliar streets Janis lived her night with Virgo over and over again, impressing every small detail on her memory. Then she thought about going back to the Pyramid that night, going backstage, being one of the privileged few to get really close to the stars. Was there really no chance of meeting Blade, of bumping into him by accident in some corridor? It had seemed odd the way that Virgo had tried to warn her off him. Was it possible that she was jealous? The idea was so ludicrous that Janis laughed aloud, but the more she thought about it the harder it was to come to any other conclusion.

CHAPTER THREE

The second Shaft gig was even more fantastic than the first. Janis was standing nearer the front because she'd been able to get in earlier, thanks to being on the guest list. All around people were eyeing her 'Access All Areas' sticker with an envy you could almost smell.

Yet, strangely enough, they kept their distance. This time no arms sought to embrace her from behind, no lips whispered in her ear, no crotch rubbed against her bum. It was almost as if by virtue of her pass, she were rendered exclusive, untouchable.

Not that Janis minded that in the least. It left her free to concentrate on what was happening on stage, and she was already high as a kite. She'd been feeling exhilarated all day, but when she finally walked out on Adam and slammed the door behind her she believed she'd done the right thing.

It had been inevitable, of course, the final showdown, but she hadn't been prepared for the sheer idiocy of the scene that had developed between her and her ex. Coming back around noon she had almost been inclined to forgive him, but when he asked sullenly where she'd been she had made the mistake of telling him the truth.

'Liar!' he'd sneered, his face contorted into a sullen mask.

'Why should I lie to you?' she'd replied, stunned. 'I'm telling you the truth, damn it! I gave Virgo a lift home after the gig, then spent the night at her place.'

She hadn't wanted to tell him that they'd made love. It was too private, too special. And the way he'd ridiculed her made her glad she hadn't mentioned it. But things had degenerated into a slanging match after that until Janis had asked herself why she should put up with it any more and simply walked out on him in mid-tirade.

The sense of freedom, of a new life opening before her, buoyed Janis up all the way to the Pyramid. She watched the first half of the show in a daze, but when the second half moved through its preliminaries and reached the point where Blade began to shaft Virgo with his enormous prick, Janis knew that she needed no help from anyone else to get her aroused to the point of climax. The memory of last night's steamy sex with Virgo was turning her on a treat, making her hard where she should be hard and meltingly soft where she should be soft.

The animal cries of a well-fucked Virgo were enough to trigger Janis and soon she was reeling under the impact of a cataclysmic orgasm, achieved almost without the benefit of human contact, unless you counted the tight squeezing of her own thighs as she swayed ecstatically to the music. The crescendo of the drums and guitar faded along with the roars of the crowd as she surrendered to the insistent beat of her own pulsating body.

Later, as the screen with its devilish image of Blade came down and the crowd began to stream towards the various exits, she made her way towards one of the stewards. Seeing her pass he grabbed her hand and led her through a door manned by a couple of heavies and into a corridor that led to the dressing-rooms. She asked him where she could find Blade's.

He leered at her. 'Straight down to the end, turn left and it's the third door on the right.'

With her heart thudding like a steam hammer, Janis followed his directions and came to a door that stood ajar. The black guy hovering outside gave her a nod and called in through the doorway, 'Blade? Here's your sacrificial virgin, mate!'

A face looked out, not Blade's but that of a shaven-headed man, the lines on his forehead deeply etched and with a black beard on his chin that looked as if it had been stuck on as an afterthought. His cold grey eyes surveyed her impassively, sending a chill through her. For a moment she feared she would be refused access, but he asked how she had got her pass.

'I'm . . . er . . . a friend of Virgo's.'

His grin was not encouraging. 'You'll find her dressing-room back there.'

But then came a voice from inside the room, a voice that Janis recognized as Blade's. It sent her already racing pulse into overdrive when he said, 'Let the chick in, Gore.'

The door opened wide to reveal a muddle of discarded clothes, instrument cases, beer cans, wine bottles and paper plates strewn with the remains of food. In the middle of it all, in a dark green leather armchair near a huge mirror, sat Blade. He wore a black silk dressing gown tied loosely at the waist and showing his tanned, heavily muscled chest with its mesh of dark hair. The hair on his head was held back by a coloured bandanna so that he could clean the make-up off his face. The black eyes glittered at her from beneath heavy lids that still bore traces of purple shadow.

'What d'you want? Did Virgo send you?'

'No, I just wanted to see you. I . . .'

Now that her great opportunity had arrived, Janis felt nervous and gauche. She desperately wanted to deliver her message to the star, but was afraid of sounding presumptuous. Hovering in the doorway she was ready to flee, but at the same time felt rooted to the spot.

Blade turned back to the mirror and picked up a wad of

cotton wool which he proceeded to dip in a pot of cold cream. 'Well, now you've seen me you can fuck off, can't you?'

The words were spoken in a strangely polite tone. Janis felt more encouraged than put off. She walked towards him, mentally rehearsing her speech. 'I wanted to talk to you about the show, Blade. I've seen it twice, and I thought it was great. But I had this idea . . .'

He swivelled round briskly in his chair. 'Idea, huh? Look, if Virgo sent you . . .'

Already Janis was beginning to realize that her association with Virgo cut no ice with Blade. She also knew she had to talk fast to get him interested. 'No, she doesn't know I'm in here. I just had this fantasy about what I'd like to see in the show. It starts with you being in a cage on stage with the girls outside, teasing you with whips as if they were lion-tamers.'

His eyes showed a glint of interest. 'Go on.'

'Then you break out, like a wild animal. You round up the girls and tie them to the bars of the cage so you can prowl round and do what you like to them. Getting your own back, sort of.' Janis thought she saw her vision failing to impress and lost confidence. 'Anyway, it was just an idea I had. I don't know what I'm talking about, really.'

She turned to go, but Blade said, 'Wait, what's your name?'

'Janis.'

'OK, Janis, I think you might be onto something. It'll need working on, of course.'

The man called Gore stepped in. 'Are you gonna let some fuckin' punter tell you what to do? Sign the bitch up, why don't you?'

Blade's dark eyes flared. 'You come up with something better then, arsehole! We got to do some new material for the new tour. Maybe it's time we listened to the fans for a change, gave them what they wanted. There's no guaranteed shelf life in this biz, you know.'

Gore retreated, scowling, and Blade turned back to Janis, eyeing her thoughtfully up and down. She'd put on her sexiest outfit for the occasion: black leather mini-skirt and skimpy silver top that made her tits look big and her waist look small.

Blade grinned. 'How would you like to be in the show, Janis?'

Gore made an explosive noise of disgust and left the dressing-room. Blade looked pleased that he'd scored a point or two. He held out his hand and she moved near enough for him to put his strong arm around her waist, provoking wild shivers down her spine. The combined scents of sweat, musk, alcohol, tobacco and greasepaint that emanated from his body made an intoxicatingly aphrodisiac perfume.

'Do you really mean that?' she whispered.

He drew back, pretending to be affronted. 'Do I look like the kind of guy who doesn't mean what he says?' She shook her head. 'Well, then. You're a friend of Virgo's, you say. How good a friend?'

'We only met last night. I gave her a lift home.'

'And you're still friends? Must be some kind of record! OK, Janis, if you want the gig it's yours. Come along to rehearsal next Monday morning and we'll put your idea into practice. If it works, you're in the show. Tell Virgo you'll be replacing Carol.'

Sensing that she'd been dismissed, Janis walked towards the door hardly able to take it all in. The thought that she was fated to become intimately involved with both Virgo and Blade was thrilling her to the core. It had all happened so swiftly, so naturally, that she was sure it was meant to be. The black guy pointed the way down the corridor to Virgo's dressing-room, but before she'd gone more than a few yards another door opened and Gore appeared.

'So you've got what you wanted, bitch!' he snarled, abruptly bursting Janis's bubble. Somehow she'd managed to make an enemy of this man without in the least meaning to.

'But I didn't expect . . .' she faltered.

'Neither did I. This is supposed to be a professional outfit. You had experience?'

'Not really.'

'Thought so. Well, Blade ain't got the only say-so around here, you know. You better be fuckin' good or you're out on your arse, girl. Tell Virgo that, from me!'

By now it was obvious to Janis that she'd somehow got herself mixed up in the internal politics of the band. But it seemed unfair to make her a scapegoat and, by the time she got to Virgo's dressing-room, she was full of righteous anger.

'Jan!' Virgo's smile of greeting was like balm to her troubled soul, defusing her annoyance. 'I was hoping you'd make it. What did you think of the show tonight? I sang like a frog on heat, don't you think?'

Janis laughed. 'You were great, honestly! I enjoyed it even more than last night.' Virgo was wearing a sludgy green velour track suit but she still looked beautiful, with her blonde hair tied back in a pony tail and her face pink and shiny, devoid of make-up. She opened her arms to Janis and gave her a loving kiss on the lips. 'I've been thinking about you.'

Janis blushed. 'Have you?'

'What have you been up to since this morning?'

'Well, I've split up with Adam.'

'That's a good start!'

'Only I don't have anywhere to live.'

'You can stay with me.' Virgo sounded so decisive that Janis didn't see the point in arguing. What had she done to deserve such an incredibly lucky break? Even so, mixed feelings surfaced when she thought of Adam's sceptical response. He'd better believe her now!

'That would be great. Especially if I'm going to be in the show.'

'You what?'

'I just saw Blade and told him my idea for a new act. He liked it, and said I might be able to replace Carol. I'm coming to rehearse with you next week.'

To her dismay, Virgo's face darkened. 'Shit! Oh, shit!'

'What's the matter?'

'How did you get to see him? Did you go sneaking off to his dressing-room?'

Janis shrank from the fury in her voice. She nodded, wondering what can of worms she had inadvertently opened. It was horrible to see Virgo looking so incensed, her lovely face distorted with ugly emotions.

Then Virgo seemed to get a grip on herself. Her expression relaxed and she held out her hand, drawing Janis close again. 'I'm sorry, it's not your fault. You weren't to know.'

'Know what?'

'Never mind. It's true, we do need a replacement for Carol. Silly cow got herself knocked up. I just didn't want it to be you, that's all.'

Again Janis had the feeling that Virgo was jealous of her, afraid that Blade might bed her. And it was probably justified. If Janis had to choose between the pair of them she would go for the charismatic Prince of Porn every time, despite the wonderful night she'd spent with Virgo.

'I didn't mean to upset you,' she said, feeling hypocritical now. 'Anyway, he's only trying me out. I'll probably be no good anyway.'

'Don't be so frigging modest, girl! I can teach you a thing or two, don't forget that. And we've got a week to practise.'

Virgo had apparently decided to make the best of a *fait accompli*. Janis admired her for that. The idea of being trained by the sex-rock goddess to make love with Blade was sending her imagination reeling off into space, creating visions of one long, mind-blowing orgy.

'Have some wine,' Virgo offered, pointing to the opened bottle nearby. 'Soon as I'm dressed we'll go home, pick up a pizza on the way. I'm starving!'

'Home'. Was that luxurious dwelling really going to be her home for the next however long? Tomorrow, when Adam was at work, she'd go back to the flat and collect all her things. A twinge of regret caught her unawares as she knocked back a mouthful of the sweet white wine and she wondered if she'd really done the right thing in ending their relationship. Her doubts didn't last long, though. After months of stagnating her life was moving into the fast lane and there were bound to be casualties along the way.

By the time the first rehearsal for the new tour came round, Janis already felt part of the show. It had been an amazing week. Her first experience of lesbian love-making had been almost entirely passive, but now she had to learn to take a more active rôle. As Virgo said, there was no room for passengers in the Shaft road show. She had to both do and be done to, whether her partners were male or female, single or multiple, The whole act would be choreographed like a ballet and she must do whatever she was told.

'Making love on stage isn't like doing it in private,' Virgo explained. 'You have to let people know what you're doing, for one thing. We have the cameras to catch the detail, but it still has to look good from the back of the hall.'

One day Janis was taken into the West End for a makeover. Virgo had gone through her wardrobe ruthlessly, throwing out two-thirds of it, so there were new clothes to buy from the leather and fetish-wear shops of Soho. They also visited an exclusive underwear shop and stocked up on delicious corsets and bodices, bras and girdles in a range of coloured silks and satins. Her hair was cut short at a fashionable salon, since she would have to wear a variety of wigs, and she was inducted into the mysteries of the gym where Virgo worked out three times a week. The day ended with a relaxing swim and sauna followed by a massage and pampering beauty treatment.

'You really think I'm going to make it into the show, don't you?' she asked Virgo, as they took a taxi back to Docklands.

Virgo grinned. 'Of course you are. Blade may look as if he wears the trousers but I can assure you he doesn't. In the band, what I say, goes.'

But Janis couldn't help wondering where the balance of power really lay.

That night Janis had her first taste of pussy. Virgo had been leading her up to it slowly, knowing that she wasn't a naturally active lesbian and that cunnilingus was still a bit of a taboo for her, even though she'd been on the receiving end several times. Janis had found it strange when she was presented with one of her lover's huge, rampant nipples but she had licked and sucked at it conscientiously and eventually came to like it very much. She never tired of stroking and squeezing those wonderfully pneumatic breasts. There was a strong element of wish-fulfilment in her fondling of them since she had always longed for larger tits for herself, and she was fascinated by the different ways they behaved: firm and jutting in the shower, soft and malleable in a hot bath, or taut and thrusting in bed.

But to explore that shaven crevice, to become closely acquainted with those musky secrets that were also her own, was a whole 'nother ball game. That night, after bath time frolics and a long session of having her own vulva well serviced, Janis was invited to take a good peep at what lay between Virgo's outstretched thighs.

Shyly Janis parted the puffy pink labia and began to examine her. The dusky inner flaps opened as Virgo flexed her muscles and her dark hole was revealed, sticky with juice. Up above Janis could easily see the swollen clitoris with its eager red tip protruding from its fleshy cowl. She stroked the wet folds with a cautious finger and Virgo gave a moan.

'Poke me, rub me, do what you like to me. I'll tell you what's good and what's not so good,' she told her.

So Janis grew bolder, probing into the slick entrance first with one finger, then two, then three. She could feel the thick fleshy walls gripping her as she penetrated further in, with the hard external nub pressing against her thumb. Virgo began to move against her, pleasuring herself with practised motions of her pelvis until she suddenly came, and Janis gasped as the fierce undulations rippled again and again over her knuckles.

'There, now you know what an orgasm feels like from the outside,' Virgo smiled. 'Now you have to discover what it tastes like.'

At first Virgo's quim tasted really strange, both sweet and sour, but Janis found she liked the soft feel of the other woman's vulva against her lips and tongue. She soon learned where and how to lick and suck to maximum effect, how to speed up the onset of a climax and how to slow it down. That, Virgo informed her, was essential in making love for real but not so important on stage where an orgasm could, in any case, be faked.

'I don't like it when I have to do that, though,' she smiled, as Janis came up for air after a lengthy tonguing session. 'It gets boring if you don't come. You have to remember to make all the right moves. It's much easier if it's happening naturally.'

'It certainly looks convincing,' Janis assured her.

Virgo made a face. 'I find I have to fake it more and more with Blade. He's such a bloody poser. It was OK at the beginning, but I know him too well now. You know what they say about familiarity breeding contempt.'

Janis found it hard to imagine getting bored with a rampant sex machine like Blade. 'But don't you find getting screwed by that incredible penis exciting?'

Virgo gave a giggle that soon turned into a belly laugh. 'Oh, my dear! If only you knew!'

'Knew what?'

Virgo shook her thick mane, her laughter subsiding. 'You'll find out soon enough. I don't want to spoil the joke for you. Come here, darling, put your sweet little labia near my lips and your sweet little lips near my labia and we'll see if we can come at the same time.'

It was an invitation that soon put all thoughts of Blade out of Janis's mind.

Despite the intensive training that Janis had been put through, she was still feeling very nervous when Virgo drove her across town to the rehearsal studio. For one thing, she would have to perform with the other girls. What if they didn't accept her? Virgo had promised to do all she could to smooth her path but in a way that only made things worse. She was so afraid of letting her friend down by doing something stupid.

The large warehouse which they used for rehearsal space had been only minimally transformed. The walls were still bare brick, the windows still small and the heating inadequate. Seeing the others standing around in thick jumpers and woolly leggings Janis was glad she'd taken Virgo's advice and worn a track suit instead of her leotard and tights.

Blade was looking hung over in a leather jacket and jeans. Stripped of his stage persona he was still desirable, still capable of making Janis's heart take a flying leap when those sultry black eyes looked in her direction. He took her by the hand and led her into the centre of the informal circle of girls.

'I want you all to meet Janis, Carol's replacement,' he began. 'She's new to this game but I'm sure she'll catch on quick. Otherwise she'll be out on her arse. And the same goes for the rest of you!'

A tired laugh travelled round the circle dwindling to a weak smile by the time it reached Janis. She had just seen Gore enter, becoming a darkly brooding presence in the corner. Something about that man gave her the willies.

'OK, here's the new scenario,' Blade went on briskly, handing out sheets headed 'Caged Beast'. 'There's a lyric to go with it over the page. I've got a recording to play to you in a moment.'

Janis took her handout in amazement. He was a hell of a fast worker! From the germ of an idea that she had given him Blade had worked out a whole sequence and written a song to go with it. Her admiration for his professionalism grew as she read through the script of the act.

But if she was hoping for any acknowledgement of her input she was to be disappointed. The whole thing was being put forward as Blade's idea. Inwardly fuming, she sat tight-lipped as he proceeded to describe the set, but she realized there was no point in making a scene. As the newcomer to the troupe she had to tread warily. Even so, it went against the grain that her idea was being passed off as Blade's. Perhaps she would tell Virgo about it later.

Certainly he had developed the theme far beyond her initial concept. It was now a circus act, with the girls performing tricks while Blade roared in frustration behind fake iron bars.

'We need to cast the various parts,' Blade announced. 'Diane, you do yoga. Fancy being our lady contortionist? I think your tongue can reach the parts other tongues can't reach, if you catch my drift.'

Diane grinned, as if she knew exactly what Blade had in mind. The other rôles were quickly allotted. Pam was to be the 'pork-sword swallower', Suzanne would put saddle and bridle on Lucille and ride her up and down, while Tina juggled with her enormous breasts.

'That leaves you, Janis,' Blade said. 'Any ideas how you could contribute?'

Virgo said, 'I think she would be perfect as a clown. She has a very expressive face.'

Gore gave a snort of derision which they all ignored. Janis wasn't sure whether she liked the idea or not, but Virgo winked at her so she had to have something in mind.

'I want you to come on as Ringmistress, Virgo, cracking a huge whip,' Blade grinned. 'Top hat and tails, black leather boots, the lot. So, ladies, let's start thinking about how we're going to turn this into the greatest show on earth, shall we?'

It was far harder work than Janis had imagined. There was so much to remember. Blade played the song over and over again until they all became familiar with their cues.

'You can lock me up, but you can't put me down,
You can fence me in and make me look a clown,
But I'm still wild,
Wild about you!'

At this first rehearsal they just worked on the overall sequence of events. Blade said each girl must work out her own individual act by the next rehearsal. Janis was dismayed.

'Don't worry,' Virgo whispered, 'I'll help you with yours.'

By the end of the day everyone was knackered. The raw energy of 'Caged Beast' was still thudding in Janis's ears and her head ached horribly. But Blade hadn't said she was hopeless. Despite the sneering face of Gore that had haunted her throughout her attempts to do what was required of her, she sensed that she had passed the first test.

One thing had disappointed her, however. She'd imagined that the day would be excitingly erotic whereas it had merely been hard work. As they drove back to the flat Virgo sensed that it had not been quite what Janis had expected.

'Now you know what bloody hard grind it is,' she said. 'But don't be put off. It can be fun, especially in the later stages of rehearsal when everyone knows what they're doing and the band is there to create some atmosphere. By the time we get to the dress rehearsal you'll be entering into the spirit of it like a seasoned porn star, you wait and see!'

Her words hit home. Janis Young, the Porn Rock Queen! What would Adam say if he could see her now? He wouldn't understand, she thought sadly. There was another Janis inside of her, one that had been longing to get out all these years but somehow had lacked the guts. Well, they'd managed to lock that other Janis up but they hadn't put her down, and now she was going to break free with a vengeance!

CHAPTER FOUR

When Janis had walked out on Adam she had expected to have nothing more to do with him. But after a few weeks had gone by she realized that she'd have to give him a forwarding address. For one thing, she was expecting her P45 to be sent back, and possibly a tax rebate. The office job she'd had before that fateful meeting with Virgo had now been jettisoned so that she could start the tour with Shaft at the beginning of May.

By the time she got around to contacting Adam again she was also feeling rather sorry for him. Maybe it had been unfair to blame him for being jealous. After all, she could recall numerous occasions when she'd given him a hard time for chatting up girls at parties. His job as a rock journo meant that he was constantly in the company of glamorous singers and groupies but, as far as she knew, he hadn't taken advantage of any of his opportunities while they were together.

So she sent him a postcard with a fat Persian cat on it, a bit like his old moggy 'Darius', whose surly presence she missed almost more than Adam's. On the back, along with Virgo's address, she told him she was now in the show and invited him to come to one of the gigs, enclosing a list of tour dates. She didn't think he would turn up unless he was asked to cover the event for the music press. And even if he did come she didn't know how he would react to the sight of her cavorting naked on stage. Probably it would just confirm all his worst fears about her. At least he would know she hadn't been lying.

On the day of the dress rehearsal Janis felt really sick, but Virgo said it was just nerves.

'You'll get used to it, love,' she told her. 'And once you're in your costume with make-up and a wig on you'll get into the part and forget who you are. Trust me, I'm a trouper!'

They were doing the first show at the Pyramid again, before touring the country. As she stood on the huge stage, posing with the others for the lighting crew to practise their craft, Janis couldn't help remembering that she had been down there in the stalls only eight weeks ago, just another fan, and now look at her! Sometimes the realization hit her with such force that she felt like bursting into tears.

Fortunately, there was no time for histrionics. Once the lighting men had finished with the girls, Blade called them all into a circle behind the front curtain and gave them their pep talk. He was the only one out of costume, dressed in a black polo-necked sweater and black jeans.

'OK, I know it's going to be difficult for you to do this cold, but we have to get the timings right,' he began. 'If any of you want a little help go and see Gore, but I don't want any of you completely out of it, OK?'

Janis gave Virgo a questioning look, but she seemed to be purposely avoiding her eye. Blade continued, 'We'll be working to recordings because Virgo and I want to save our voices. I hope that won't be a problem. Also, the musicians won't be on stage so you'll have to imagine they're there. And my costume is still being made, so you'll have to imagine me as a tiger. Otherwise, it's going to be more or less exactly as per performance, apart from the obvious.'

Janis felt even more confused. She sensed that he was referring to some other element, some missing ingredient, but had no idea what it might be. She would ask Virgo later.

Once the familiar music started pounding out Janis felt

more confident. She wore a flouncy clown costume, at least for the first few minutes, and her rôle required her to run around the cage making obscene gestures, 'peeing' on the imprisoned Blade with water from a bladder concealed in her pocket, divesting the other girls of their costumes and generally creating mayhem. She relished the part, since it was so over the top that her fear of making a fool of herself was irrelevant, that was the whole idea!

Her only worry was that she would forget to do something and put someone else off their cue. The sex part she was secretly rather disappointed with. She'd imagined that Blade would want to screw her since she was the new girl, but Virgo had explained that he only had direct sexual contact with the more experienced girls. They had to work up to it, so to speak. Instead, Janis would be involved in some lesbian play with two other girls, and that was all.

They'd rehearsed it dozens of times, but when it came to performing cunnilingus on Diane in front of the roadies, lighting and sound crews, Janis still felt self-conscious. She needn't have worried. The men were more concerned with how the whole thing looked and sounded and paid little attention to other details. While she sucked away mechanically at Diane's fuzzy blonde bush she could see the video cameraman in the wings getting an angle on the action, his face screwed up in concentration, and she knew it was all in a day's work to him.

Likewise, when Tina thrust a dildo into her cunt from behind and she began the mechanical bump and grind routine it didn't seem in the least stimulating. She was more concerned with timing her movements to the beat. It was strange how unsexy the whole procedure seemed, but at least Janis was relieved that her part in the action went like clockwork.

In fact, all the hitches at rehearsal occurred between Blade and Virgo, much to Janis's surprise. She'd presumed that they knew each other so well there would be a rapport between them, but they seemed niggly with each other. Perhaps it was a case of two perfectionists – or two prima donnas. At any rate it was tedious to have to stand for ages in the wings while they sorted things out to their mutual satisfaction.

Sometimes Janis almost wished she'd never become involved with them this closely. The glamour and excitement that had surrounded them when she was merely a fan had faded somewhat now she saw them with feet of clay, swearing and carping at each other. It was clear that there was no love lost between them.

Things had cooled off between her and Virgo, too. Although they were still friendly, Janis sensed that she'd lost her novelty value and there had been several nights when Virgo had not come home, presumably spending the night with another lover. Not that Janis was jealous. Her feelings for the star had been ambiguous from the start, and she had always seen her more as a chance to get near to Blade than as a desirable partner in her own right. Their lesbian love-making had been sensual and fulfilling, but it had lacked that extra dimension that she got from making love with a man.

On the other hand, despite witnessing all Blade's moods and petty foibles she still found him devastatingly attractive. His arrogance, his moodiness, his occasional bursts of bad temper hadn't put her off him – quite the reverse. She'd often tried to analyse why women like her were turned on by bad boys like him, but it was unfathomable.

At the end of a long day Janis and Virgo returned to Docklands exhausted. In the car Janis asked her, 'What did Blade mean about doing it "cold"?'

Virgo's expression took on the sly cast that was now familiar. 'Oh, he just meant without an audience, I expect,' she said, airily. But Janis had the distinct impression she was lying.

Janis woke next morning feeling terrified. No matter how often Virgo assured her that doing a live show was far easier than rehearsing, the thought of being observed by several thousand people while she performed sexual acts on stage was horrifying. None of them would know who she was, of course. Unless Adam came. Suddenly she wished she'd never sent him that invitation. She felt guilty about ending their affair so abruptly and this would just be rubbing salt into any wounds he might still have.

There was nothing she could do about it now, though. As the time for them to go approached, Janis began to think about Blade. He had been her inspiration all along, and if she did well perhaps he would take more interest in her. There was nothing she wanted more than to be his lover, preferably off-stage as well as on, but his personal life was still a mystery. It was obvious that Virgo and he had nothing to do with each other outside the show, and when she'd made a few tentative enquiries Virgo had refused to be drawn. Perhaps, she thought wistfully, he was just waiting for the right woman to come along.

By nine o'clock Janis was waiting in the dressing-room with the other girls, listening to the continuous roar of the crowd as they yelled impatiently for the show to begin. The excitement was reaching fever pitch out in the hall and it was impossible not to feel it backstage too. In her silky clown costume, with the heavy paint on her face, Janis began to feel randy. She pressed her hands between her thighs, feeling the buzz of her already aroused clitoris, and knew that she was going to lose all her inhibitions once she was on stage.

The call came to gather behind the curtain. They made a circle as they had at rehearsal, but this time Blade was in his tiger costume and looked magnificent. Even his giant penis was striped black and yellow. Janis couldn't take her eyes off it – him!

Blade told them all to close their eyes and from somewhere a single humming note began, louder than the music from the warm-up video. The note reached a crescendo, ringing in their ears. Then Janis was aware of someone chanting something in a weird voice. Meaningless syllables were being uttered in a stage whisper, and when she half opened her eyes she saw that Blade was doing it, his head thrown back and his eyes rolling in his head in a crazy way.

A chill shudder passed down her spine as Janis saw that everyone had their mouth open as well as their eyes closed. She watched Gore pass around the ring placing something on each tongue, like a parody of a priest. What was it, some kind of drug? No one had told her about this. A wave of panic almost made her break ranks and run, but she felt rooted to the spot. There was thick smoke in the air, scented with heady perfume and sapping her will to move.

By now she was convinced that the whole show was to be performed under the influence of some mind-altering chemical. Gore was near her now, his hooded eyes blank and cold. She stared at him openly and he stared back, his full lips curving into a faint smile. The strange sounds continued to come from Blade and the disorientating smoke was filling her nostrils, sapping any remaining will to resist. That one, piercing note was maddening in its unwavering intensity, confusing her further.

At last Gore stood before her, his expression cynical. She had the impression that he knew how much she wanted to opt out, yet he also knew it to be impossible. Meekly she opened her mouth to receive the fake sacrament that tasted bitter but began to dissolve in her saliva as soon as it touched her tongue. She was almost the last in the circle. All around she could see the others swaying with a spaced-out look on their faces and soon she was joining them, swaying from side to side and feeling light-headed. A sudden ecstasy filled her veins and she began to feel incredibly randy.

The circle began to move and Janis moved with it. Round and round they accelerated until they were whirling freely, their scanty costumes blowing in the draught. Janis felt more and more exhilarated: her body burned with desire and her mind was floating in a sea of erotic imagery. Breasts and buttocks, cocks and cunts swam before her eyes as objects of devotion and when the whirling finally slowed she felt the urgency of her longing become lulled until she was in a state of calm voluptuousness, robbed of all will to resist.

As the circle broke up the first chords of the opening number were sounded by the musicians on the dais at the back of the stage and, like clockwork, everyone moved into their positions or retreated to the wings. Janis stood at the side of the stage awaiting her cue. She watched the huge cage being lowered over Blade and saw the four girls take up their stances around the bars. Everyone looked perfectly ready and focused on the job in hand.

Despite her initial bewilderment, Janis too was ready to play her part. There was an urgency within her, an eagerness to touch and be touched that she knew would put fire into her performance and relieve her of all inhibition. While she waited her hands roamed over the smooth material of her costume, stroking the skin beneath, teasing her nipples into prominence, pressing into the niche between her thighs and rubbing against the hard bulge of her clitoris.

The sight of Pam caressing Lucille's full, black breasts in their spangly bra while Diane and Suzanne kissed and fondled each other was a real turn-on. Blade was striding up and down his cage in a rage, the huge striped penis waving around in frustration as he was forced to witness the girls' lascivious play. Then Virgo appeared at the top of her steps, cracking her whip, and the whole audience erupted in glee. She did look magnificent in her ringmistress's costume of black top hat, red tail-coat opened to show her black and red bra, pants and suspender belt with long, high-heeled boots of black leather.

Unable to help herself Janis put her hand beneath the elasticated waist of her pyjama-style pants and stroked her damp bush, inching down until her forefinger could give her clitoris a good rub. She was soaking wet down there and soon her fingers were sliding back and forth rapidly over the slippery nub, bringing her rapidly to orgasm. She told herself she must get one in before her cue, and the friction became quite frantic as that moment neared. Then, just before she was due to rush on with a bucket of water, she felt the first intense tinglings of her climax begin. She was still throbbing as she made her entrance, slopping water everywhere as she staggered around on weakened knees.

Most of the water ended up over the girls, as intended. Their skimpy costumes now clung to them like wet T-shirts, leaving little to the imagination. The delight of the crowd was obvious, and they began to yell 'Get 'em off!' Playfully Janis went round pulling down pants and unfastening bras while the girls screamed and giggled their ineffectual protests until they were all stark naked. Then they ganged up on Janis and gave her a taste of her own medicine.

The horseplay soon turned to loveplay, much to Tiger Blade's disgust. While the female bodies writhed and groped front of stage, Virgo marched around the cage with her whip, slyly giving him a taste of it every so often by slipping the lash through the bars.

Janis abandoned herself to the action, feeling a second climax rise within her as Pam enthusiastically mouthed her genitals while she did the same to Diane. Her nipples were being expertly manipulated by Lucille, whose own breasts were being sucked by Tina, and all the time the video camera was homing in on the action, relaying every detail to the audience via the screens. She could hear occasional coherent phrases coming from the front rows: 'Suck her off!' 'Make her come!' 'Go for it, Lucille! Tina!' The excitement of the spectators was feeding hers, making her crest the wave of lust and keeping her there in a state of suspended arousal.

Dimly Janis was aware of Blade singing '*I'm still wild, wild about you!*' as he watched Virgo circling his cage. She knew the point was approaching where Virgo would come to the front of the stage and invite someone from the audience to join the girls in their orgy. The music changed to '*Are you man enough for me?*' and the girls began to sing the chorus, swaying provocatively in front of the seething crowd as the men vied with each other to be the chosen one. Virgo took a few steps down in her high-heeled boots, cracking her whip over the heads of the audience, delighting them as she sang, '*I need it hard and I want it hot, so give it everything you've got!*'

While she wriggled away with the other girls, Janis saw Virgo reach down into the clamouring crowd and clasp someone's hand, pulling him up onto the steps at the side of the stage. Security guards kept the rest back as he mounted the steps, followed by envious eyes. When Janis took a good look at him, however, she gasped aloud: it was Adam! He was wearing his usual scuffed jeans and a faded Reading Rock Festival T-shirt that she recognized. Flushed and sweating, his brown hair plastered over his brow, he allowed Virgo to lead him right onto the stage where he stood looking self-conscious while she crooned just for him, '*Give me a hard man to please, and I'll go down on my knees . . .*'

Janis stared at him in a daze. He hadn't seen her yet, perhaps he just hadn't recognized her. His eyes were riveted to Virgo's face and figure, lusting after her red lips, her deep cleavage, the scrap of red and black lace that barely concealed her pussy from view. A sick pain that she recognized as jealousy hit Janis in the pit of the stomach. She knew the routine, knew that Virgo would give him one kiss then deliver him to the rest of the girls who would play with him for a while until the time came for Blade to break out of his cage, creating a diversion.

Then Pam was scheduled to run screaming into the wings with Adam in tow, from where he would be discreetly returned to his place in the audience. But as she looked at him Janis felt the old attraction returning in full force, making her yearn for him with that earlier longing. She remembered what it had been like wanting him but not being able to have him. For six long weeks he'd tried to extricate himself from a dead and bitter relationship with another woman so that he and Janis could be together. Janis had been patient, but had suffered agonies of frustration as they snatched clandestine moments together, never long enough to make love properly.

Once again, he appeared infinitely desirable. His brown eyes were aglow with that sexy light that had been such a come-on, and she was remembering how his lips had felt under hers in those early, wonderful days of infatuation. Now he was kissing Virgo, not her, and the burning pain that spread from her navel to her groin intensified. She wanted him, God how she wanted him!

But the routine that the cast had worked out to include the anonymous member of the audience didn't involve Janis, except in the most superficial way. It was Pam and Diane who would get most of the action, with a bit on the side from Lucille and Tina. Janis was supposed to be diverting Virgo's attention while all that was going on so that Blade could steal her whip and turn the tables on her.

A sullen resentment took over as Adam and Virgo ended their prolonged kiss to tumultuous applause and the four girls dragged him away, tearing off his clothes. Virgo turned her attention to Janis, the mesmeric eyes reminding her that this was their moment, a little bit of a lesbian side-show to the main action. Up to now Janis had always looked forward to this part of the show, since they'd rehearsed it so many times that all the moves went like clockwork. But now she was filled with anger. Adam should be with *her*, not those other girls who meant nothing to him. A dark suspicion hit her that he was doing it to spite her until she told herself she was being irrational. He was behaving passively and the other girls were following their script. It was Janis who was filled with spite.

Yet she couldn't help herself. In her confused, drugged state her thinking and impulses went completely awry and she tore herself away from Virgo's embrace.

'What are you doing?' hissed the other woman as Janis turned on Pam and Diane, who were starting to stroke and lick Adam's naked body into a state of tumescence.

The pair looked equally startled as Janis thrust them away, kneeling beside her ex-lover and kissing his engorged glans. He groaned and a light of recognition came into his eye, which promptly winked at her. Although she could hear the others muttering and exclaiming the crowd was yelling encouragement, and that was music to her ears. She could see Adam grinning in his familiar way and knew that soon it would seem as if they'd never been apart.

'Carry on as if it's all part of the show!' came Virgo's whispered instruction to the others. Aware that she had thrown the timing out, Janis felt a twinge of guilt but it was too late to stop now. She straddled Adam and plunged down on his erection, feeling the welcome fullness in her cunt as she enclosed the full extent of his penis within her fleshy interior walls. The other girls stopped flapping and put on a show of co-operation, stroking Janis's breasts and letting Adam fondle theirs as the pair heaved and thrust their way towards satisfaction. Janis was only dimly aware of the music behind her and of the action that was proceeding without her. The band was stalling, playing several choruses of 'Hard Man to Please' instead of moving on to reprise the 'Wild about You' theme that was supposed to accompany Blade's escape.

For a few minutes, fucking Adam felt like the good old days. The crowd faded into oblivion, and even the other girls were banished to the outer edge of Janis's consciousness as she rode her lover towards a shattering climax. She knew so well how to bring them both to the brink and let them hover there, increasing their pleasure, before she made the final thrust that would tip them over the edge together in one hot, pulsating maelstrom of sensation. A part of her was taking a wicked delight in messing up the show's carefully arranged schedule, in making Blade wait for his dramatic escape bid while she stole all the limelight. It served the rock star right for not letting her make love with him.

Instead she had Adam, dear, sexy Adam. Her fondness for him grew along with her passion as they rode the wild waves of their mutual desire, resurrecting the love they'd once shared and moving inexorably towards the orgasm they both hungered for. Janis began to swivel her hips and grind her mound against his, accelerating the friction until they were both gasping with unfulfilled lust.

At last it broke upon them simultaneously, the way it often had at the peak of their affair. Janis felt swirling hot currents of pure bliss fill her pulsating quim and, at the same time, she was aware of Adam pumping out his seed with a series of groans. The sweat ran from them both in rivulets as they milked every last drop of pleasure from their mutual climax beneath the hot lights and the uproar of the crowd was deafening, although Janis scarcely noticed it. Only afterwards, as she flopped onto Adam's damp, hairy chest, did she remember that they were not alone and then embarrassment set in.

Janis rose unsteadily, eyes blurred, knees enfeebled, and staggered from the stage into the wings. Hardly knowing where she was or what she was doing, she flopped down onto an empty chair and put her head in her hands. For several minutes she just sat there alone, her head reeling, hearing the music change and knowing that the show was going on, as every show must, but not caring about anything. She had been with Adam again, rekindled the fire that had dwindled over the past months, and now she felt totally disorientated. Her private life had suddenly gone very public, and it was extremely disconcerting.

When she peeped through her fingers at the stage again she saw that Blade was out of his cage and the scene was proceeding as planned, with Virgo now inside the cage and the other girls running screaming from the fierce lash of Blade's whip. Adam was nowhere to be seen and her part in the action was over, so she rose wearily from her chair and stumbled down the corridor to the dressing-room feeling terrible.

It didn't take long for Janis to realize that she was suffering from withdrawal symptoms. Whatever aphrodisiac drug Gore had fed them before the show had a hell of a come-down. Her head ached and she felt sick, but worst of all a feeling of utter self-disgust had overtaken her. Janis pulled on her clothes, slipped her feet into her shoes and drank a lot of mineral water but she still felt bad. It was just as well she'd played her part in the show because no way could she have gone on again.

Suddenly there came a tentative knock on the dressing-room door. As she stood to answer it she knocked over her chair and the clatter made her head ache all the more. She seized the handle and flung open the door, then uttered the single word, 'Adam!'

Somehow he was the last person she'd expected to see there. He was looking at her with a quizzical expression, his eyes searching hers. In the background she could hear the show still going on, the audience yelling and whistling, but around the pair of them there seemed to be a bubble of silence and calm.

'I thought you might like a lift home,' he said.

Janis was about to say she'd be going home with Virgo, but

then she realized that to be in Adam's company was definitely more appealing. She nodded and pulled on her jacket. After closing the door behind her they made their way through the maze of corridors and out of the stage door.

'My car's parked over there,' Adam said, noncommittally, leading the way.

It was cold outside and Janis shivered uncontrollably even inside the vehicle. Adam put the heater on as they drove towards the exit but then, as they waited for a break in the traffic along the main road, he put his arm around her and gave her a brief hug. It was just too much for her to bear, and she burst into tears.

'Jan, don't cry!' Adam said, sounding just like he used to when she was upset, which made her weep all the more.

'I'm sorry. It's all been so . . .'

'I know.' Calmly he drove out into the stream of traffic and they headed off down the road. 'Look, I'm taking you back to my place first, OK? We need to talk. You can go back to where you're living later if you must, but there are things I have to tell you.'

Janis was in no mood to argue. The thought of being back in Adam's friendly, warm flat filled her with optimism. But she needed to tell Virgo where she was going. They stopped at a phone box and she called first the Pyramid and then Virgo's flat, where she left a message on the answerphone.

After that, Janis felt more relaxed. But as they pulled up outside the flat she'd once called home the tears flowed again and Adam drew her into his arms. 'Look, I'm sorry for everything, OK?'

She looked at him through tear-blinded eyes. 'What do you mean?'

'I'm sorry I let things go adrift between us. I'm sorry I overreacted to what you said about Blade. I'm sorry I doubted you when you said you'd met Virgo. And if there's anything else I've done wrong, I'm sorry about that too.'

Janis giggled. 'You'll be apologizing for being born next!'

'But one thing you won't hear me say is "I'm sorry I ever met you". Oh Jan, I've missed you so badly these past few weeks!'

'I've missed you too.'

As she said it, Janis realized it was the truth. She had been trying not to admit it to herself, but now it was a great relief to have it out in the open. She clung to him, drinking in the dear familiar smell of sweat, booze and tobacco that oozed from his old jacket and reaching up to touch the springy curls of his brown hair. His lips brushed hers briefly, sending sparks of ecstasy buzzing around her befuddled brain, but then he was unfastening his seatbelt and helping her with hers.

'I know what drug you need now, young lady. Pure caffeine, hot and strong. Come on, we'll get those brain cells of yours functioning again and then we'll talk.'

Meekly, gladly, she followed him up the crumbling steps of the Victorian villa and into the shabby hallway. It had never seemed more welcoming.

CHAPTER FIVE

Once she was back in her favourite armchair with a mug of black coffee Janis began to feel more normal, although her head still hurt a bit. She told Adam about the weird pre-performance ritual that the Shaft band went in for, and about Gore's little present to them all.

'I could tell you were drugged up,' Adam said, matter-of-factly. 'Your pupils were dilated and your breathing was funny. You had a strange look in your eyes, too.'

'Why did you volunteer to come up on stage?'

'I had to find out more about what went on, see what kind of a gut feeling I had.'

Janis laughed. 'I had a pretty good gut feeling, how about you?'

But Adam only gave a brief smile and she could tell he was deadly serious. 'I wasn't there just to get my rocks off. Call it investigative journalism if you like. I've been hearing some strange rumours about Blade and Gore.'

'What kind of rumours?'

'Pretty dark ones. What's your impression of those guys?'

'Blade has been straightforward with me, professional. I have the feeling that he's not particularly interested in me as a woman. Oh, and he seems to be quite antagonistic towards Virgo, which came as a surprise to me. I thought they were lovers off-stage as well as on.'

Adam nodded. 'And Gore?'

'Can't stand him. He gives me the chills. I wouldn't have taken that drug off him except that everyone else did and I didn't want to make a fuss. It was stupid of me really, but no one told me beforehand that I was expected to do the show under the influence.'

'What does that make you think?'

She shrugged. 'I'm not sure. You could say I'm less starry-eyed about it all than I was before.' She gave him a smile, hoping he would return it, but he just frowned.

'I've been dead worried about you, Jan. When you sent me that card giving Virgo's address I knew you were really mixed up with them and that's when I started checking them out. I've always been a bit suspicious of Blade, but what I heard made my blood run cold.'

Janis felt a shiver run down her spine. The uneasy feelings she'd been having for a while were crystallizing into fear. 'Tell me, I want to know everything.'

He perched on the arm of her chair. 'OK. First of all, Blade is not the great hetero lover you imagine him to be. He's gay, and he's Gore's partner. His stage act is just that, an act.'

The news shattered her. It seemed unbelievable, but before she could question Adam he continued, 'There's worse. Not only is he one big sexual sham but he and Gore are also into some weird cult. I don't know a lot about it, except that it involves sex and drugs.'

Janis was sceptical. She'd had her own doubts, of course, but this was all too much to take. 'How do you know?'

'I don't know, not for sure. I told you, it's only rumours.'

She gave a scornful laugh. 'You ought to know better than to listen to showbiz gossip when there's no real proof. What do they say about Virgo, then, is she supposed to be involved too?'

'Again, I don't know. But I think you should get out of that scene, love. It's too risky. I don't want you to get mixed up in all that occult stuff.'

'I'll make up my own mind about that. I've given up my job to join Shaft and I won't jack out easily. Certainly not on the basis of a few rumours.'

'Well, I've given you a warning, so be on your guard.'

Janis looked up at Adam with a rueful grin. 'I suppose I might be kicked out anyway, after tonight. When you came up on stage and those girls started making love to you I couldn't stand it. I was supposed to be doing something with Virgo, but I upset everyone's routine by making love with you instead. They're not going to be very pleased with me.'

Adam took her into his arms and gave her a short but sensual kiss on the lips. She felt warm and loving towards him and her desire was rekindled, but then he drew away. 'You're better off out of it, believe me.'

Janis curled up against him, catlike. She didn't want to talk about it any more. 'Can I stay here tonight? You make me feel safe.'

'OK, but I don't think we should sleep together.'

She felt awash with disappointment, but something in his expression prevented her from arguing. After all, she'd been the one to walk out on him. What had happened at the Pyramid had taken them both by surprise and maybe they should take time to reflect on what they both wanted.

Janis had thought she was too tired to do any more than sleep that night but once she was tucked up in her old bed, with Adam taking the couch in the lounge like a gentleman, she began to remember what it had been like making love with him again. Although the effects of the drug had worn off she still felt randy. Beneath the crumpled sheets her body was hot and roused, the stiff peaks of her nipples brushing against the bedclothes and a warm wetness seeping from between her thighs.

She imagined Adam creeping into her bed in the early hours, no more able than she was to resist the powerful urge that was drawing them together. His hard male body would slide in next to hers, and she would feel the heat emanating from him as he took her into his embrace. Their kiss would kindle her fire even more, making her press her breasts and her hairy mound against him in a bid to satisfy her craving for greater contact. She would sigh with relief as his hands found the solid globes of her breasts, his fingers moving to excite the already turgid nipples into a state of tingling anticipation.

Now Janis could feel her thighs moving against his in restless lust, the thick prong rubbing against her belly and leaving a slippery residue around her navel. She imagined taking his wayward prick in hand, feeling the velvet smoothness of the skin as it moved over his shaft and the sticky bulb of his glans. Then she would grope his balls, loving the way they felt heavy and hot in her palm, rolling them around in their sac until he groaned with tormented delight.

His mouth would fasten on her nipple, arousing her further as he sucked and licked her into a state of tremulous desire. She would feel his hands on her hips, her thighs, moving ever nearer the burning nub of her sex. Her own hands simulated his movements and deep within she felt a first shuddering, a foretaste of things to come. She moved up to part the swollen lips of her pussy, feeling the liquid soak her fingers as she stroked the slick grooves. Her other hand tweaked her nipple, and soon her longing became more urgent, more focused.

Janis plunged her fingers deep inside herself, felt the thick walls of her cunt close over her own hand as she delved and thrust, her thumb pressing hard on the throbbing clitoris. It wouldn't take her long to come now. She heard the slurping noises that her love juices produced as her bunched fingers moved in and out of her quim, simulating Adam's penis.

Then, with a sudden explosion of sensation, she climaxed.

Her lover's name was on her lips as the exquisite feelings flooded through her, but once the orgasm had faded she had to face the fact that she was alone, uncertain whether they would ever make love the way they used to, and she started to sob. What if Adam didn't want to see her after tonight? What if it really was finished between them, despite the fact that she'd fallen in love with him all over again? The thought of losing him now was unbearable. She found she cared even more about that than the prospect of being kicked out of the show.

Maybe she was on the rebound from Blade, she thought, mulling over what Adam had told her. Eight weeks was a long time to lech after someone. If the attraction had been mutual surely he would have made a play for her by now. Yet the thought that he might be gay was disturbing. Didn't they say that about lots of famous sex symbols? Maybe it was just a case of male sour grapes. The confused thoughts whirled in her mind but soon lapsed into dreaming as she drifted off into sleep.

Next morning Adam had to get to the office of *Soundscape* magazine by ten. As they snatched a hasty breakfast together he offered to drop Janis off at the most convenient Tube station. His manner was brisk, and she knew this was not the time to raise personal issues. Nevertheless, she felt bleak as she drank her coffee and ate her toast in the kitchen that was filled with memories, most of them good.

She was still worried about what he had told her, and definitely scared about what Virgo's reaction would be when she returned to her flat. As she travelled towards Docklands she considered her options. To leave the band now and take on some boring office job again would be very depressing, to say the least. She had grown used to the excitement of being in the show, to her glamorous new image, and to the hope that one day she might approach Virgo's level and be a star in her own right.

Then there was Adam. Did she really want to go back to him? How did he feel about her? That he still cared was obvious. He wouldn't have warned her about Blade and Gore otherwise. And the way he'd responded to her on stage still made her melt inside. But last night he hadn't wanted to go to bed with her. Had it just been his male pride stopping him? Janis sighed. Time would tell, so she must be patient.

Virgo was still asleep when she arrived. Janis ran herself a bath and was wallowing in it when the door suddenly opened and the star stood there with her silk kimono draped about her shoulders, exposing most of her naked body. Janis felt a reflex twitch in her groin at the sight of those magnificent breasts with the soft pink splodges of her nipples just asking to be licked and sucked into hard peaks. Yet she felt faintly annoyed that the other woman's body still had the power to arouse her.

'Hi!' Virgo grinned. 'The prodigal returns, eh? You certainly made a pig's ear of your first night with Shaft didn't you?'

'Yes, I don't know what came over me. Was it that pill Gore gave me, do you suppose?'

Virgo sidled into the room, her eyes bright even at that time of the morning. Sitting down beside the bath she took the soap and began to wash Janis's arm. 'That was just to make you randy, sweetheart. We all need a bit of help when it comes to doing a show. Gore is a chemical wizard, he makes his own drugs. The good thing about them is that they're non-addictive and have no known side-effects, but they do the job. You feel OK today, don't you?'

'Yes, fine.'

'Well then, why worry?'

Virgo's soapy hands moved over to her breasts and Janis lay back in the water, lazily enjoying the sensations. The chemicals might be out of her system by now but she still felt horny. And from the way Virgo's nipples were stiffening it looked like she was, too. Despite her misgivings she felt her body responding like clockwork to the gentle, lubricated massage.

'I'm not worried, exactly. The only thing that worries me is how Blade reacted to my performance last night. I imagine he wasn't best pleased.'

Virgo laughed. 'I think he was quite amused, actually. He likes a bit of spontaneity, does our Blade, and he was chuffed to see the other girls dropped in it. So I shouldn't worry, I don't think he intends to kick you out. Of course, there might be a ritual penalty to pay.'

'What do you mean?'

'You'll find out tonight, before the show.'

Slick with lather, Janis felt her tingling nipples send urgent messages to her equally pulsating clitoris and knew that she no longer had any scruples about making love with a woman. All she wanted now was satisfaction. So when Virgo suggested she should step out of the bath she did so eagerly.

They made a fluffy nest of towels on the floor, Virgo slipped out of her kimono and for half an hour they indulged in an orgy of lesbian gratification. This time they used vibrators on each other, revelling in the multiple orgasms as they plunged the dildoes in and out of their cunts and pressed them against their demanding love-buttons. It was nothing but pure sex, pure lust, and Janis gave herself up entirely to the moment. At one point she had her arse filled with a thin dildo, her quim filled with a thick one, and a third was being applied to her clitoris while her nipples were being fiercely sucked and nibbled, all to mind-shattering effect.

Janis had long overcome her inhibitions and made sure that she gave Virgo as good as she got. But afterwards, as they lay entwined on the bathroom floor in a state of utter exhaustion, Janis felt a weary disgust creep over her. Just a little while ago she'd been telling herself how much she loved Adam. How could she make love with another person so soon afterwards?

She decided that it was down to frustration. If only Adam had slept with her last night, if only they could have sealed their reconciliation with a few hours of tender loving care, she would be feeling very differently about Virgo now.

Later, Janis found the courage to ask about Blade. They were sitting drinking coffee in Virgo's sunny kitchen and the time seemed ripe.

'I heard something about Blade yesterday,' she began, tentatively. 'Someone told me he might be gay.'

Virgo gave a knowing smile, as if she'd been waiting for this to come up. 'I told you he wasn't all he seemed, didn't I?'

'It's true, then?'

She nodded. 'Why do you think he has to take drugs? He couldn't make love to any woman stone cold sober, let alone me. I don't turn him on at all. It's a good thing his cock is a fake.'

'What?'

Virgo laughed. 'I thought even you would have sussed that by now – it's a fucking dildo! I mean it's striped black and yellow, for goodness' sake! Honestly, Jan, you are a touch naive, you know.'

She didn't mind if Virgo thought that. Somehow it made her feel safer. But she decided not to mention the other business that Adam had told her about. If she let on about that she might seem less naive and more dangerous, and she still didn't trust anyone around that band a hundred per cent.

They passed the afternoon shopping, then arrived at the Pyramid for the second performance. After this there would be a day's rest before the ten-date tour of Britain began. Blade greeted Janis with an ironic grin as she made her way to the dressing-room.

'Like to do our own thing, do we? Can't have that, Janis. What would happen if there were a free-for-all on stage? Chaos, that's what. You've a lot to learn, girlie, and I shall teach you your first lesson myself.'

His dark eyes glittered at her amusedly, but there was a coldness behind them that disturbed her. As she got into her clown costume the other girls started to carp at her until Virgo put an end to it by saying, 'Look, she screwed up, OK? We all do that from time to time. But tonight she's gonna play by the rules, aren't you, Jan?'

Janis nodded, grateful to be let off the hook.

They gathered on stage at the appointed time, aware of the continuous hubbub of the audience behind the curtain. They all joined hands, but before Gore came round with his magic pills Blade asked Janis to step into the middle of the circle. She did so nervously, remembering what he'd said about punishing her. While the band played and the crowd whooped, Blade's deep voice intoned her misdemeanours.

'Last night you wilfully deviated from the strict routine that we've rehearsed over the past weeks, throwing your fellow performers into confusion. You risked ruining the whole sequence by your selfish desire to seize the limelight. Only the quick-witted response of the other girls saved the show. Do you deny this accusation, Janis?' Shamefaced, she shook her head. 'Very well. Are you now prepared to be disciplined?' She nodded, but a sick dread had turned her stomach to lead.

'Virgo, will you be the first to administer the chastisement?'

Janis looked in her direction. The ringmistress had already raised her right arm and the long black whiplash was snaking to the floor.

Blade's severe tone came again. 'Lower your pants, Janis, and bend over with your bare buttocks turned towards Virgo.'

She did as she was told, knowing full well the nature of the discipline that she must now undergo. Her heart was thudding rapidly as she steeled herself for the sting of the leather thong on her defenceless backside. But when the blow came, with a resounding crack, it was almost a relief. Her left buttock, which had taken most of the impact, was still smarting but the pain soon faded.

She straightened up, thinking she had got off relatively lightly, only to hear Blade say, 'Now it's your turn, Lucille.'

Horrified, she watched Virgo hand the whip to the black girl on her left. A sneer crept into Lucille's expression as she took the leather handle and braced herself, legs apart, to deliver her share of the punishment. It dawned on Janis that she was going to have to submit to everyone in the circle, yet she had to admit that it was only fair. She had wronged every member of the cast so each one should have their turn at exacting revenge.

The next blow hit her square across both cheeks, making her gasp in agony. There was only a brief pause before Pam had her turn, mercifully more lenient. As she turned obediently to present her hind quarters to Diane she caught Blade's eye. His sensual lips were half-smiling, half-pursed, but his eyes glinted frostily at her and she felt deeply afraid. For a moment she was convinced that the man was capable of anything, even murder. What if everything Adam had said about him were true, after all?

Her brief speculation was interrupted by another stinging taste of the whip and she couldn't help crying out in pain. Her defenceless buttocks felt horribly sore and she trembled at the thought that she had several more strokes to endure. Yet Janis vowed she would not break down and cry in front of the whole company. Although she flinched and gasped at each new ordeal, the whip passed around the circle and back to Blade without any ignominious breakdown occurring.

But would Blade's prove the most merciless whip-hand of them all? Although she felt she couldn't take any more Janis submitted her red-striped behind to him, bracing herself for the unkindest cut of all. Then, to her amazement, she heard him say, 'Stand up, Janis. You've taken your correction with due humility, so let that be enough.'

Incredulously she watched him hand the whip back to Virgo. He waved her back into the circle and everyone, including Janis, closed their eyes for the ritual invocation. A deep relief filled her as the pain began to recede at last and she knew there would be no more. As Gore passed around the ring, administering his drug, she heard Tina on her left whisper,

'This will soon take the pain away, you'll see.'

She was right. Less than a minute after Janis had ingested the pill she was floating on Cloud Nine, all her aches and pains dissolved in the erotic glow that was spreading throughout her body. The opening music struck up and they took up their places on stage or in the wings, ready for another show. The make-up girl was on hand with some number-five greasepaint which she carefully applied in a thick layer to Janis's buttocks, to disguise the redness.

This time it all went according to plan. Janis had no urge to muscle in on the act as a good-looking guy was pulled from the audience, his prick coaxed into active life by Pam and Diane. Now she was convinced that it had been Adam, and him alone, who had driven her to intervene the night before. Calmly she went through her part of the act, distracting Virgo while Blade pulled at the bars of his cage and finally bent them enough to slip through. He then picked up the protesting Virgo and threw her in, bending the bars back again to imprison her. Now Blade had the whip hand once more, but fortunately he aimed at Janis's calves instead of her poor bum. She ran off the stage screaming, as her part demanded, then retreated to the dressing-room relieved that she had managed to behave herself this time.

Even so, she found herself longing to quench the persistent itch between her legs. The drug had heightened her desire but without Adam to screw, or anyone else for that matter, she was left high and dry. After pulling on her clothes she wandered down the corridor to the pay phone and dialled his number. To her delight he answered straight away.

'Adam! Look, I'm ringing from the Pyramid so I can't talk long. I just wanted to say I'm sorry I doubted what you said last night.'

'You've found out about Blade and Gore?'

Her voice dropped. 'Had some of it confirmed, anyway. Can we meet somewhere after the show? I'd love to see you.'

'Sorry, Jan, not tonight.' Her spirits fell, and she felt like slamming down the phone. But then he added, 'How about lunch tomorrow? I'll be in Charing Cross Road at lunch time. We could go to that pasta place.'

Janis knew better than to press him, but she was still disappointed. 'Lunch' sounded like they were 'just good friends'. Was he seeing someone else that evening? Had another woman been there at the flat while he answered the phone, smiling up at him from the sofa in a state of undress, lying in his bed stark naked? Was he, even now, stripping off to make love to her? Knowing Adam he was hardly likely to have remained celibate for the past eight weeks. There would almost certainly be at least one girlfriend around by now.

The thought depressed her, making her feel every bit as naive as Virgo had implied. How stupid she'd been to think she could breeze back into Adam's life as if they'd never been apart, as if she'd never maimed his ego by walking out on him! That wild encounter of theirs on stage had been just for show, after all.

By the time Virgo and the others came back into the dressing-room Janis had polished off almost a whole bottle of the hospitality wine and was lying on her stomach on the couch.

'Oh God!' she heard Virgo say. 'Have I got to carry you home, you silly cow?'

'I needed a drink to numb my bum!' was Janis's excuse. Her head ached and she was befuddled. Somehow she managed to get to her feet and, leaning on Virgo and Pam, hobbled out to the waiting taxi.

The confusion in her head soon reached her heart, and she began to sob in the back of the cab. With Blade out of reach and Adam playing hard to get there only remained Virgo. Yet the thought of more lesbian frolics did not appeal. What she wanted was some good, hard cock inside her and no matter how many dildoes Virgo teased her with, the end result was ultimately unsatisfying.

So when they reached home and Virgo started to kiss and fondle her, Janis said she was tired and went into the spare bed to sleep off her bad mood. Some time later she heard her flatmate on the phone, and shortly after that she left and didn't return. Evidently Virgo had found herself another bed to sleep in that night and Janis was surprised to find that all she felt was relief

CHAPTER SIX

When Janis walked into Pasta Pronto! and saw Adam sitting there waiting for her at a corner table her heart leapfrogged. He was wearing his one suit, an Italian job that had cost him a week's wages, and a crisp white shirt, There was even a tie around his neck, navy blue and dotted with green parrots.

'You didn't have to dress up for my sake,' she told him with a grin, as she slid into her seat.

'You wish! Actually I had an interview with the editor of *Style File* at noon, so I thought I'd better look the part.'

'Really?' Janis gave the menu a cursory glance, deciding on the tagliatelle. 'I didn't know you were that interested in men's fashion.'

'They wanted someone to interview rock stars about their wardrobes. I got the gig.'

'Adam, that's great!' She leaned forward and kissed his cheek, which smelt enticingly of Aramis. 'Shall we order champagne, or something?'

They had champagne cocktails, as an aperitif. Soon it felt as if they'd never been apart. There was so much news to catch up on, so many stories to tell, that they were halfway into the afternoon before either of them realized it.

'God, is that the time?' Janis gasped at last, noticing her watch.

'Do you have to be somewhere? I could run you . . .'

'Oh no, I've nothing on at all today. The tour doesn't start till tomorrow.'

'In that case, why don't we spend the rest of the day together? It was lovely weather when I arrived. We could go and walk in a park or something. How about it?'

Janis smilingly agreed, but she couldn't help thinking *And what about tonight?* The alcohol had gone to her head and she was feeling woozily aroused.

They ended up walking on Hampstead Heath, not too far from where Adam lived. There were few people about so Janis felt she could talk freely about the band. She told him how she had been 'punished' before the show and his face darkened.

'I don't like the sound of that at all, love. It sounds pretty ritualistic to me.'

'Don't let's jump to conclusions, OK, it's a bit freaky but then so is the show. A spot of flagellation is usually included in the performance. But you were quite right about Blade and Gore. Virgo admitted to me that they're in a gay relationship and now I can see it all the time. There's something about the way they behave, the looks and smiles they give each other. I noticed it particularly last night.'

'What part, exactly, does Gore play in this outfit?'

'I'm not sure. He makes drugs, maybe he sells them as well. But I've the feeling that Blade is involved with him in some other way, more than just sexual. Gore seems to get away with an awful lot. He sulks and criticizes, has tantrums, and Blade doesn't seem to mind. But when one of us girls puts a foot wrong Blade comes down on us like a ton of bricks.'

Adam put his arm around her shoulder, pulling her close. 'You will take care, won't you, love?' His lips brushed her hair. 'I've only just got you back, and I don't want to lose you again.'

His words made her heart soar. 'Don't worry, I'll be careful. But I would like to find out the truth about what's going on.'

'You keep your eyes and ears open, then, and your head down.' Adam grinned at her, his eyes softening. 'I want you to keep in touch while you're away, Jan. It was horrible before, not hearing from you for weeks on end.'

'I'll phone you every night, if that's what you want.'

They stood still and he drew her face close to his, Their kiss was tender at first but then deepened into passion, their tongues working together sensually until the juices flowed. Janis felt her insides turn into quivering jelly as the delicious beat spread to every part of her, making her desire him more and more. She reached down between them and touched the hard ridge in the front of his trousers, feeling it move slightly beneath her fingers.

'Oh Jan!' she heard him groan. 'I want you so much!'

It was warm and secluded where they were, near a clump of bushes. Heedless of his best suit, Adam drew her into the copse and spread his jacket on the grass. 'It's worth the cost of a dry clean,' he grinned, when she protested.

That was what she'd loved about him at the beginning, Janis recalled, his daredevil streak. There was something wonderfully wicked about preparing to make love in a public place in broad daylight. She pulled off her sandals and knickers, glad that she was wearing a summer skirt and no tights and that she hadn't bothered to put on a bra. Beneath her pink T-shirt her nipples were outstandingly huge.

Smiling, Janis loosened his tie as he kicked off his shoes. She undid a shirt button and her hand crept in to feel his warm chest, with its light dusting of hairs. Her thighs shifted restlessly against his and as their lips met she uttered a low groan, which made him reach up below her skirt and caress her naked bottom. The soreness was gone now and she relished the way he was clutching and pinching at her buttocks, his fingers tantalizingly near her crack.

Adam undid his shirt buttons and unzipped his fly. 'Better

not take all our clothes off, in case we're spotted by some old biddy out walking her dog!'

Janis giggled, putting her hand in through the open zipper and feeling the very satisfactory bulge in his pants. She stroked his tool through the cotton material, loving the way it thickened and strained at her touch. Adam pulled up her top and found the rearing tip of one taut breast. He bent his mouth to her nipple and she sighed, feeling the warmth of the sun caress her naked skin along with his hot, wet lips.

Carefully she extracted his penis from his pants and saw it rear and stretch, like an animal freed from its cage. The dark pink glans was glistening with a bead of love-dew and she spread the stickiness all over the top with her thumb then moved down the shaft, delicately working the loose skin back and forth. His mouth tightened on her nipple, sucking and licking eagerly, and she knew that their foreplay would be brief.

'Jan, it's been so long!' he whispered, feeling her bare pussy with his hand. Janis felt herself opening to him, willing him to explore every crevice of her. His finger slipped straight into her cunt and she moaned as she wriggled against him, feeling the longed-for contact between his hand and her itching clitoris.

Janis had a sudden urge to taste the musky flavour of his cock, and she turned round to straddle him, leaving her pussy within reach of his groping fingers. Eagerly she bent her lips to the slick glans, licking it clean, then she wiped her tongue down the length of his shaft until she reached his balls. Sucking gently she drew them into her mouth, one by one, and felt Adam's hand plunge right into her sopping chasm, filling her completely. His other hand was fondling her bum, one finger probing between the cheeks and sending rich sensations throughout her body, back and front.

A few minutes of this intense stimulation was the most either of them could bear. With sudden accord they swung round so that Adam could penetrate her from the side, keeping a low profile to avoid discovery. Janis lay comfortably, her right thigh over his left one, and sighed with contentment as his rampant organ pushed its way inside her. She squeezed it encouragingly with the walls of her cunny, feeling the hot tingling of her clitoris pushing her towards even greater heights of arousal.

One of Adam's hands passed between their bodies to lodge against her bulging mound while his other hand toyed with her breasts, flicking first one erect nipple and then the other. He increased the pressure on her love-bud and Janis gasped as his thrusting increased, sending her into a dizzying spiral of lust. She began to move her pelvis in response and soon they were one throbbing, thrusting love-machine, every part working in harmony to bring them to their mutual climax. When she felt the orgasmic waves begin Janis uttered a low moan that triggered Adam, and he spurted into her at the height of her first pleasure-peak. They clung to each other in ecstasy, riding the surging tide of bliss together until their heaving bodies gradually subsided into the warm, comforting glow of their embrace.

For a long time they just lay there, letting the sun's rays play upon their exhausted bodies, but eventually Adam murmured, 'That was fantastic, Jan. I'd forgotten how good it could be between us.'

'Me too.' She smiled ruefully at him, disengaging her thigh. 'We let things slide, didn't we? Got too bogged down in routine or something. Stupid of us.'

'I agree. But now you're about to go off on tour.'

He sounded so forlorn. She gave him a hug. 'Don't worry, it's only for a couple of weeks. I'll move back in after that, if that's what you want.'

Adam kissed her and she felt the erotic currents start to move again. But just as they were gearing up for another

session of love-making the shrill voice of a woman called,
'Jessie! Here, girl! Good dog!' and a figure loomed beyond the
trees.

Janis giggled. 'Biddy alert! Better get out of here!'

They dressed quickly and sauntered out of the bushes trying
to look as normal as possible. Adam took her hand and pulled
her across the turf. Running and jumping they made their way
back to the car and tumbled into it, laughing like teenagers.

'Shall we go back to my place?' he asked, and she nodded.
There would be time enough to get back to Virgo's and pick
up her things by ten o'clock tomorrow morning.

Already Janis was feeling at home again in Adam's flat.
Sitting cross-legged on the floor with Darius purring on her
lap, she let her lover feed her titbits while she closed her eyes
and tried to identify them. Teasingly he dangled grapes and
strawberries over her nose and mouth, poked chocolates
between her teeth and let creamy yoghurt dribble over her
tongue deliciously. Before she knew it he had placed his glans
between her lips and she tasted it with the same relish, feeling
a rush of excitement in her belly as she licked all round the
dome and below the ridge, her tongue slipping over the jutting
veins as she proceeded on down.

Adam edged further in, filling her mouth with his firm
flesh and letting her soft lips and wet tongue massage his prick
thoroughly. Janis had always loved doing this, and now she
bent her head back to accommodate him, feeling his glans
stroke her throat and push against the roof of her mouth. She
reached up to fondle his balls in their soft sac and felt them
heave and tighten. After the sickly sweetness of cream and
chocolate she craved the bitter taste of his sperm, and she
began to rub the base of his cock between her thumb and
forefinger to hasten his coming.

It didn't take long for him to lose control, his cock pulsating
hotly and shooting his load right down her throat. Janis

swallowed the acrid juice without a qualm, her mouth working around his penis to the end, milking him of every last drop. She laughed when she realized that the cat had jumped off her lap in alarm at these goings-on and was now watching them guardedly from a safe distance. She flopped back after her labours and took Adam into her arms.

'God, Jan, you give the best head of any woman I've ever known!' he sighed contentedly.

'And you've got the best cock!' she grinned. 'Hey, guess what I've discovered – Blade's enormous tadger is a complete fake!'

'What? You mean he hasn't got one?'

'No!' she giggled. 'I suppose he does have one, but he wears these inflatable dildoes on stage. I don't suppose anyone's ever seen his real one.'

'Anyone except Gore, you mean.'

'Maybe not even him. Hey, suppose he has a really tiny dick. Wouldn't that be a story for the tabloids. I can just see the headlines: "Sex-god has prick of clay!" '

'Or how about "Shaft's Blade can't cut it!" '

'Do you think he's afraid of discovery, and that's why he rules us with a rod of iron?'

'Or plastic, as the case may be!'

'Maybe it's not just the case that's plastic.'

'Giving him a blow job takes on a whole new meaning, doesn't it?'

They fell about laughing as their puns grew more and more outrageous. Soon they were kissing with new urgency and Janis could feel herself growing wet with lust again. This time Adam took her on all fours from behind, his hands reaching under to squeeze her tits and pull at her stiff nipples while he thrust against her buttocks. In his eagerness he came before she did, but after a short rest he was ready to lick her still-pulsating clitoris and bring her off orally while he fingered her insides. She moaned and thrashed out her climax, feeling the whole of her cunt contract over his plunging fingers as she orgasmed again and again.

In the tender aftermath of their love-making their affection for each other was reborn and Janis began to feel safe and nurtured. She realized how pressured she'd been these past weeks, trying to satisfy the sexual demands of Virgo, coping with being in the show, lusting after Blade to no avail, and all the while missing Adam more than she'd cared to admit. This was the first time she'd felt truly relaxed for ages.

'Oh, this feels so *comfortable!*' she exclaimed as, back in what she regarded as her own bed again, she snuggled up to Adam's familiar warm chest. 'If I could duck out of the tour and stay here with you I would, love, honestly.'

He stroked her hair, pulling a strand out of her eyes. 'I don't want you to.'

'Don't you?' she asked, in faint alarm.

'No. I really think you should stay with Shaft for a while, find out more about what's going on. There could be a sensational story in it and we could make loads if we sold it to the Press.'

'But I thought you said to take care. What if it turns out to be dangerous?'

'I trust you to be sensible, Jan. Maybe you could find out something from Virgo. She obviously knows more than she's letting on.'

'Mm,' Janis said doubtfully. 'I don't want to antagonize her. She's kind of a friend.'

'What kind of a friend? A bosom pal, would you say?'

Dismayed, Janis felt herself blush. She hadn't yet revealed the full extent of her relations with Virgo because she wasn't sure how Adam would react. 'You could say that,' she giggled.

'You mean, she's a lesbian?'

'Maybe she swings both ways. I'm not sure.'

'But she does fancy women. Does she fancy you?' Again Janis giggled, unsure what to say. Adam's questioning intensified, his brown eyes sparkling with interest. 'Don't tell me you've been to bed with her!' His grin widened as she nodded. 'Jan, I'd never have thought it of you! How far did you go?'

'All the way!'

He sat up, propped on one elbow. Clearly he was titillated by the idea of two women making love. 'What was it like? What was *she* like? You're not going to disappoint me by saying those gorgeous tits are made of silicon, are you?'

'I don't think so. They felt real enough to me.'

Adam's eyes widened and his hand dropped to her own breast, fondling it casually. 'What happened? I never knew you were bisexual, Jan.'

'Neither did I. It seemed quite natural at the time, though. I suppose I was on a high after the show and feeling randy. Then, after we'd done it once and I moved in with her, it was easier to do it again. Look, you're not jealous are you?'

He gave a scornful laugh. 'Of another woman? Never! I know she can't give you what I can give you, love.'

'We did use vibrators,' Janis said, slyly.

'Tell me more!'

'What, all the details?'

He kissed her soft nipple, his hand travelling down to her moist bush where he toyed with her gently. 'Yes, it's turning me on a treat, the idea of you and her. Did she play the active rôle all the time or did you take it in turns? Did you taste her pussy? I want to know everything!'

Talking about it to Adam made it seem more normal, somehow. As Janis relayed her experiences in answer to his frequent questions, she found she was arousing herself as well as him, She remembered how voluptuous Virgo's body was, how firm her breasts and smooth her shaven pubis. She remembered too the velvety wet feel of her quim and the way those cushioning walls tightened over her invading finger, clutching at her with increasing ferocity as her climax progressed. She remembered the feel of those luscious lips as they closed over her tingling nipples or kissed the equally tumid lips of her pussy.

And all the while Adam's finger continued to dabble in her vulva, making the love juice well up and spill over until she was drenched in it. Her clitoris, swollen and slippery, was pulsating hotly and she knew her orgasm could not be far off. By the time Janis started to describe how she and Virgo had licked and sucked each other to a simultaneous climax Adam was bringing her close to the brink, his fingers sliding around in her cunt and the engorged nub of her clitoris filling her with rich, exquisitely thrilling feelings.

Janis took hold of his now-rampant cock and straddled him, unable to bear any more of the frustrating wait for fulfilment. 'And once I put her tit between my thighs and rubbed my clit on her nipple,' she confessed between gasps as she moved rapidly up and down on his prick. 'It was like sitting naked on one of those bouncing balls. I slithered all over her huge breast with my pussy, and it didn't take me long to come. Afterwards I licked all my juices off her and . . . Oh! Ah! That's lovely!'

The climax came upon her swiftly, and with a ferocity that made her gasp aloud. She increased the pace of her pelvic thrusts to make the sensations more intense and the racking spasms accelerated, fierce and relentless, almost painful. Dazed, she swayed giddily above him as the orgasm went on and on. She felt herself clutching again and again at Adam's hard tool with her pulsating cunny until he also succumbed and the hot spurting soothed her insides, allowing her to wallow in the warm afterglow. They clung to each other, utterly satiated, and although she had more to say to him fatigue soon took over, lulling her into sleep.

Next morning she awoke at nine, and panicked. Adam still

lay asleep beside her, the duvet thrown back over his dark-haired chest. She allowed herself the brief indulgence of kissing his flaccid penis, then shook him awake. 'It's late, Adam. I must get to Virgo's flat by ten!'

In the end they decided it would be quicker if she called a taxi. Before they parted she promised to ring him often, leaving messages on his answerphone if he wasn't there.

'And remember, take care, love!' he cautioned her, as the cab waited outside. 'I don't want to lose you again when I've only just found you.'

She kissed his lips and gave him one last hug. 'I promise. And I'll be back again before you know it. Keep the bed warm for me!'

The taxi was held up by traffic and Virgo was cross with Janis when she arrived. 'Where the hell have you been? I thought you'd chickened out of the tour or something!'

Janis, still high after her night with Adam, gave her an indulgent smile. 'Nothing of the kind. I spent the night with an old friend, that's all. But I asked the cab driver to wait. I thought we could both use it to get to Blade's place.'

Virgo was obviously curious, not to say suspicious, but there was no time for debate. She waited impatiently while Janis threw the clothes and toiletries she needed into a travel bag, then they hurried down to the waiting taxi. As they hurtled through the London traffic Janis felt the first real excitement of the tour hit her. They were playing several major cities at medium-size venues. It was a real adventure.

Blade and Gore were to go in one minibus with the crew, while Virgo and Janis went in another with the rest of the women. Although Janis protested ritually at the blatant sex discrimination she was secretly relieved. Over the past few weeks she had come to enjoy the company of the girls and to be relieved of Gore's sinister presence was a plus. The first stop was Birmingham, where they would be staying in a hotel after the gig.

When they checked in, Janis was surprised to find she was not sharing a room with Virgo as she'd expected. The star had a single room, and Janis had been put in with Lucille. She didn't mind too much, but it did seem rather odd.

'It's nothing personal,' Virgo assured her. 'I always get a single. It's in the rider. Everyone else has to share, including Blade and Gore. Not that they mind, of course.'

At six they were driven to the venue for the show. The Birmingham audience turned out to be even more enthusiastic than the London one, and the number of pairs of sweaty bras and sodden panties that were thrown onto the stage made performing quite a hazard. Fuelled by Gore's love-drug, Janis found herself staring lecherously at the guys in the front row who seemed to be a bunch of hairy bikers. While she went through her paces she started fantasizing about being gang-banged by them and almost missed her exit cue.

Back in the dressing-room she had a while to wait and decided to phone Adam. She was missing him already, and knew that he would want to know how she was getting on.

'Have you found out any more?' he asked, after they'd exchanged greetings.

'Not a lot. I found out that Blade and Gore always share a room when they're on tour . . .'

Someone was coming along the corridor. Hastily Janis said good-bye but just as she replaced the receiver she saw Gore's black slouching figure coming towards her. She gave an involuntary shudder. She didn't often encounter him alone and, whenever she did, the temperature seemed to drop a few degrees.

His eyes narrowed when he saw her and his fat lips broke into a sneer. Looking round to make sure they were alone, he sidled up to her and hissed, 'Janis, isn't it? Janis the canis.

Know what "canis" means, Janis?' Terrified she stared into his cold eyes, shaking her head. 'Pity you've not had the benefit of a public school education like me. Well, "canis" is Latin for dog and that's exactly what you are. You're a dog, Janis. Not a star like Virgo. Not a genius like me. Just a dog. And don't you forget it, because you know what happens to dogs who misbehave, don't you?' Again she shook her head, speechless with fear. 'They get put down!'

He was gone before she had time to breathe. She had seldom experienced such vitriol addressed to her personally and it was both terrifying and bewildering. Why did Gore hate her so much? Probably she would never know. Janis went into the dressing-room and took a long swig of mineral water. She wanted to go back to the hotel but she couldn't even remember its name so she would have to wait for the others.

Once the show had ended the dressing-room filled with all kinds of strange people wanting autographs, interviews or sex. Lucille appeared to be permanently draped around a muscular black guy called Errol, and Janis began to wonder what it would be like sharing a room. Or would Lucille decide not to use her hotel bed that night?

They left in the minibus soon after midnight with Errol in tow, and Janis wondered if she would be able to sneak in with Virgo. She was very tired, shaken too after that weird encounter with Gore, and all she wanted to do was sleep. But Virgo was with some butch American woman called Lee and they were deep in conversation, so it looked like there was no option but to stick to the original room plan.

When they reached the hotel Lucille and Errol made straight for the bar so Janis sneaked upstairs. She got into bed as soon as she could, turned out the light and pulled up the duvet, but it was impossible to sleep. She kept turning over Gore's extraordinary words in her mind. Calling her a 'dog' was a straightforward enough insult, but what exactly did he mean by 'put down'? A verbal put-down was one thing, but in a canine context . . . Janis shuddered. She had never felt such visceral fear of another human being in her life, and the experience was unnerving.

Before long she heard the door being slowly opened, accompanied by Lucille's suppressed giggles. Two pairs of feet made towards the other bed, and then there was a heavy thud as they both collapsed onto it.

'Ssh! We'll wake her!' Lucille cautioned, still spluttering with laughter.

Then came Errol's drawl. 'Can't we put the bedside light on, sugar lips? I want to see that gorgeous body of yours when you strip off for me.'

'It'll be too bright . . .'

'Then drape something over it. Your panties will do.'

'Errol! Hey, watch what you're doing!'

'That's just the trouble, I can't! C'mon, babe, switch that light on. I wanna see your beautiful big ass and those amazing firm tits that I've been creaming myself over all evening.'

'OK, hang on. I'll put my T-shirt over it first.'

Janis was facing their bed and as the light came on she flinched behind her lashes. The temptation to peep was too strong, especially with Errol making so many lewd remarks. She stared through half-closed lids and saw him pull off his shirt to reveal a dark brown chest spattered with black hair. He bent his lips to Lucille's naked breasts and kissed them rapturously. In the amber glow of the bedside lamp they were almost copper-coloured with huge, nearly black nipples.

'Mm, you taste so good!' she heard Errol mumble, his face half buried in the generous mounds. There was the tinkly sound of a belt buckle being undone and soon he was struggling out of his jeans while Lucille pulled off her own. In a few seconds they were both naked except for their pants, kneeling on the bed facing each other. A lascivious smile passed over the black girl's face as she watched Errol's penis growing in its black cotton pouch. She put out a hand and cupped his balls where they swung inside his pants, squeezing them gently, and a look of molten desire passed over his face.

'Shit, girl, you wanna make me come in my pants? I can think of a better way. Lie down and spread your legs, honey cunt. I'm gonna tongue-fuck your sweet pussy to kingdom come!'

Janis found it impossible to listen to such salacious language without becoming aroused herself. Despite her fatigue she groped between her legs and found herself soaking wet down there. Now that the couple were absorbed in their love-play she gave up pretending to sleep and stared at them while she applied the necessary friction to her rampant love-bud, lubricating it from time to time with fresh juice from her open vagina.

As Errol enthusiastically licked between the spread lips of Lucille's pussy Janis could see his great dusky prong swinging beneath him, rearing and probing at thin air. He was groaning too as he swallowed her copious liquids and she was squirming and moaning aloud, grasping her big tits in her hands and squeezing them mercilessly until the nipples stood out like ebony acorns.

Janis wanted to get her own lips around that thick stalk, suck at it until it gave up its milky sap to her. The very thought of it was taking her close to a climax. She closed her eyes for a few seconds and concentrated on the sexy urge that was filling her with exquisite fire, making her press her thighs together and clench her buttocks as she rubbed herself where it pleasured her the most. She pulled at her nipples, feeling an answering twinge in her clitoris that made her desire grow in ever-increasing circles. Now she was staring openly at the rapt lovers while she masturbated, confident that they were far too absorbed in their own passion to pay any attention to her.

Soon the sweet shudderings were convulsing through her, making her oblivious to everything else in the room. Faintly she could hear the low moans of the lovers as they sought the same goal, and she was absurdly gratified that she'd beaten them to it. But as she felt the throbbing fade she could hear Lucille working up a crescendo of lustful sighs and when she opened her eyes she could see that Errol was now inside her, his great prong plunging into her again and again, his hands working feverishly at her nipples on the heaving, erect globes. She could hear the faint slap, slap, of his balls every time he rammed his penis home, and soon Lucille was thrashing around in the throes of a violent climax that Errol was responding to with a deep-throated chuckle.

'Oh, you really are a hungry sexpot, aren't you?' he murmured. 'Your greedy little snatch is clam-tight on me. Talk about rubber suction! You'll suck this condom right off my dick with those tight squeezes . . . ooh, baby!'

As Lucille calmed down Errol suddenly withdrew and peeled off the black condom he was wearing. He shunted up the bed on his knees and put his cock between her panting lips.

'Give me a little kiss, girlie, just a little kiss,' he wheedled. She reached up and took the long, thick tool in her hand, giving the oozing glans an experimental lick. 'Oh, yes, yes! More of that, babe, just a little more of that, sugar!'

He was pulling her tits up around his genitals as she licked away, rubbing the mounds of flesh against his balls and shaft. Janis could see the tautness of his brown buttocks as he knelt astride her, the sinews standing out on his thighs. Suddenly she realized that her own mouth was watering as she imagined what it would be like to fellate that wonderful organ. Lucille was performing the task with increasing enthusiasm, opening her mouth wide to let him thrust in and out, enjoying having her bosom kneaded so thoroughly.

Then, with a long, drawn-out groan, Errol pulled out and

shot his load all down Lucille's deep cleavage, rubbing her jugs together as the slimy residue slipped down them. He collapsed between her thighs, his face coming to rest between her breasts where he could smell and taste his own come. Then Lucille put out her hand and switched off the lamp, plunging the room into darkness. Janis heard Errol sigh, 'You're one hell of a lay, Lucille!' and then there was silence except for the heavy breathing that always follows such exertions.

Janis turned over on her side with a sigh of relief and was soon asleep.

CHAPTER SEVEN

The tour turned out to be far more exhausting, and less exciting, than Janis had imagined. Apart from travelling, most of their time was spent hanging around in hotels and dressing-rooms, and for only three hours of the day did experience match her expectations. When she was on stage, with the turned-on crowd roaring and screaming, helping to bring all those heaving bodies to some degree of satisfaction, Janis felt her life was worthwhile. But afterwards there was a dismal sense of anti-climax and for the rest of the time she was mostly bored out of her skull.

The high point of each day, apart from the show, was when she managed to get through to Adam on the phone. With Virgo now keeping her distance, and making the most of whatever opportunities for casual sex came her way, Janis was missing him more than ever. He was the only person she could talk to about her worries and frustrations, but she had a few interesting bits of information to pass on too.

'I saw Gore reading a book by Aleister Crowley,' she informed him. 'That could mean he's into some kind of sex magic, couldn't it?'

'Sounds highly likely to me.'

'But if he's into any particular cult he's keeping it well hidden. There's just one thing: he has a ring with a weird symbol on it. He wears it all the time.'

'What kind of symbol?'

'I haven't been able to get a really close look at it, but it looks similar to the Shaft logo, except that there's a big ruby between the top two points.'

'Like a drop of blood?'

'Possibly. And Gore always wears black. I've never seen him in anything else.'

'Sounds a pleasant sort of a chap!'

The second half of the tour dragged as Janis found herself wanting to be back with Adam more and more. Although she had plenty of chances to score with any of the fans that constantly flocked around the band, Janis found she had no inclination for one-night stands. It seemed ironic, given her uninhibited performances on stage, but the urge just wasn't there.

At Leicester, the American girl that Janis had noticed at Birmingham appeared once again and this time Virgo introduced her when she came to the dressing-room after the show.

'Janis, I want you to meet Lee. an old friend of mine. I thought we might get together back at the hotel. I'll have champagne sent up to my room.'

The thought of making up a threesome filled Janis with mixed feelings, but on the whole she was excited. Her self-imposed chastity was wearing a bit thin and there were still three more gigs to do before she could get back to Adam's welcoming arms. With her short cropped hair and butch clothes, Lee didn't strike her as particularly attractive but she couldn't help feeling intrigued. Virgo didn't seem like a real lesbian. Did bull-dykes like Lee do things differently? Was it more like being made love to by a man?

By the time Janis entered Virgo's hotel room she was feeling really horny but, to her surprise, the two women were locked in earnest conversation. They hadn't even bothered to open the champagne, which was still sitting in its ice-bucket.

'Janis, come in!' Virgo smiled, beckoning her towards an empty armchair. 'Lee and I were just discussing something, and I'd like you to be in on it too.'

Mystified, Janis sat down. Virgo explained, 'Lee and I used to be in a band together, way back when. She's a fucking good drummer.'

'Really?' Looking at her, Janis wasn't surprised that she enjoyed beating the hell out of a set of skins.

'Yes, really.' Lee turned her amber, cynical eyes in Janis's direction. It was like being looked at by a sleepy big cat who could be dangerous when roused. Janis felt her cunt twitch.

Virgo continued. 'As you might have gathered, I'm not altogether happy with the way things have been between me and Blade lately. At the beginning, when we were on our way up, it was fine. We were more of a partnership then. He respected my input into the show, and I respected his. But since he came under the influence of that fucking toad things have been going from bad to worse.'

'I thought the tour was going well,' Janis said. 'And the album.'

'Oh, the band's a success all right. But I want something else. Call it artistic satisfaction, if you like, creative freedom. But that's exactly what I'll never get as long as Gore is hanging around Blade like a bad smell.'

'I see.'

Janis wasn't altogether surprised. She'd seen the way Blade had appropriated her ideas, presenting them as his own. But was that the whole story? She couldn't help wondering if Gore's involvement with the occult was behind Virgo's unease.

Lee leaned back in her chair and put her boots up on the low coffee table, crossing her ankles. She gave Janis a penetrating look and a reluctant smile. 'You only see part of the picture, honey. The rest is a lot more interesting, believe me.'

Again Janis felt a shiver of desire pass through her as she imagined what those hard lips would feel like, pressed to her own. There was something cool and confident about the lesbian, as if she knew she could give any woman on earth more pleasure than she'd experienced with any man. It was intriguing, but also rather frightening.

'I'll come straight to the point,' Virgo said. 'Lee and I have decided to form a band of our own, an all-girl band. And we'd like you to be a part of it.'

'*Me?* But I've hardly had any experience . . .'

'We'll soon teach you all you need to know,' drawled Lee, and Janis couldn't help thinking, *I bet you will!*

'You have a good stage presence,' Virgo told her. 'And you said you could strum guitar a bit and sing vocals. I think you'd be perfect. At any rate, I'd like you to consider it.'

Janis didn't know what to say. Being in the Shaft company had been beyond her wildest dreams but now, before she had really settled in, she was being offered a second opportunity.

'I'm not sure, Virgo. I kind of expected to get a more interesting part in the next show with Blade. It's been fantastic so far, of course, but I haven't actually had any close contact with him. I thought maybe . . .'

'Dream on!' Lee sneered. 'You're not his type, sweetheart.'

Janis threw Virgo a questioning glance. 'She's right, I'm afraid,' the star said. 'You'll only ever get bit parts in the show as long as Gore calls the shots. For some reason he really dislikes you.'

'I know, but I haven't a clue why. I've never been deliberately unpleasant to him.'

'There's no fathoming that bastard, so don't bother to try. His life follows a different set of rules from most people's.'

Janis remembered what Adam had said about being careful. Perhaps she would be better off keeping her distance from him. The proposition that Virgo had just made her sounded very appealing. An all-girl band! Once she would have jumped at the chance. 'Tell me a bit more about this band you're planning.'

It seemed they had half the rest of the line-up already, and Janis could meet them when they returned to London. Virgo had been writing material for some months now, and so had Lee. They had identified their potential audience as mainly lesbian, and planned to start on the gay pub circuit. But there was every chance that their appeal would widen and they might become a cult mainstream band.

'So, what do you say?' Virgo asked at last. 'You don't have to decide now, but we need to know soon or we'll have to find someone else. We plan to start rehearsing immediately this tour is over.'

Quickly Janis weighed up her options, and her feelings. She wanted, most of all, to talk to Adam about it. With his knowledge of the music biz he would be the best person to advise her.

'I'm not ruling it out,' she replied. 'Can I have till this time tomorrow to decide?'

'Sure.' Virgo grinned, reaching for the champagne. 'Celebration might be a bit premature, but what the hell? At least you haven't said no!'

'I don't know, any excuse to get rat-arsed!' Lee grinned. She didn't smile often, but when she did there was a striking transformation that Janis found very attractive.

Soon the trio were giggling their way through the bottle, with Lee and Virgo reminiscing about the good old days, and Janis began to relax. She kicked off her shoes and undid the top three buttons of her blouse, feeling hot. Lee's eyes went straight to her cleavage, and seemed to sear her naked skin. Between her thighs Janis felt a softening, and a moistening.

It didn't take long for Lee to get close to Virgo, stroking her gold hair and cuddling her affectionately. Janis began to feel out of place. She rose to use the bathroom and when she came out found the pair lying on the king-size bed with Virgo stripped to her panties and Lee still fully clothed, although she had taken her Docs off. They both smiled to see her surprise.

'Don't be embarrassed,' Virgo called, holding out one slender arm to her. 'Come and join us, sweetie. We both want you to.'

Slowly Janis walked towards the bed, intrigued and daunted at the same time. It was one thing to make love with Virgo, she was used to that by now. But Lee was an unknown quantity, a real hard-core lesbian, and she wasn't sure she was ready for that.

Virgo took her hand and pulled her down onto the bed, kissing her mouth softly. 'I've been telling Lee about you,' she whispered. 'She thinks you're just as gorgeous as I do.'

She started to pour more champagne and spilt it onto Janis's blouse, whether accidentally or on purpose she couldn't tell. At once Lee's fingers began to undo the remaining buttons, revealing her padded bra, while Virgo kissed and caressed her neck. Shivering sensations ricocheted down her spine as she saw the naked lust in the dyke's hazel eyes and felt her hot breath sweep over her chest.

Behind her, Virgo was undoing her bra. Lee pulled it up over her rearing nipples, her eyes widening as the full globes of her breasts were revealed. 'Tits to die for!' murmured Lee, her hands clutching them eagerly, squeezing them to make their red tips stand out so that she could catch them in her mouth and suckle to her heart's content.

'Mm, you two look so good together!' Janis heard Virgo say as her back and shoulders were covered in tiny kisses. Hands were pushing down the elasticated waistband of her loose velvet trousers, fingers dipping into the crack between her buttocks and sending her into shuddering heaven, and all the while Lee was sucking fiercely at her breasts, making her nipples enormously wet and tingling.

Her pants were pushed halfway down her thighs now and Virgo's hands were everywhere, teasing her clit through her bush, tantalizing her arse, stroking her thighs. She felt herself become totally abandoned to the two pairs of hands and lips, lying back and kicking off the last vestiges of clothing until she was completely naked and open, back and front, above and below, ready for anything they might want to do to her. It was so long since she'd felt this horny, this alive.

Suddenly those hands and mouths seemed to multiply, every part of her body being caressed at once. With her eyes closed Janis no longer knew nor cared whose fingers and lips were where. Gently she moaned out her pleasure as all the curves and crevices of her body were explored, opening her legs wide to give her eager lovers free access to every part of her.

Now she was being invaded in every orifice, her mouth full of hot, wet tongue, her ears being licked too, her arse and cunt the subject of simultaneously probing fingers. She squirmed and heaved under the onslaught, feeling her imminent climax building to the point where she would explode in a scorching avalanche of hot juices and seismic waves. Recognizing the point just before the release, when her whole body was tense and straining, she suddenly felt a change. Something had happened, a slowing down, a standing off. She opened her eyes.

To her intense disappointment she found that Lee had switched her attention to Virgo's naked and compliant body. Although she continued to stroke Janis's breasts and tweak her nipples, her lips were otherwise engaged. Enviously she watched one of Virgo's large breasts being kissed and licked until the whole of one engorged nipple disappeared between Lee's avid lips. The swirling maelstrom of lust that had caught Janis in its grip just seconds ago now released her and she felt her arousal waning, diminishing, threatening to leave her high and dry.

But that had never been Lee's intention. The hand that was still caressing her moved lower until it tangled in her damp bush and Janis found her libido rising again. She reached out and stroked Virgo's free breast, hearing the sharp intake of breath that her friend made as both nipples were stimulated. Lee gave Janis a brief smile, then moved her fingers down right onto her swollen clitoris and began to rub her there gently, making her moan with the hope of fulfilment once more.

While she continued to mouth Virgo's taut nipple, Lee moved her other hand down until she found her wet crevice. Now she had fingers in both sticky pies. With a low chuckle she began to pet both pussies at once, first with soft, gentle strokes and then more firmly. Janis relaxed as the voluptuous feelings took hold of her again, letting her thighs flop open.

Lee was between them now, thrusting into each hot cunt with a new determination while she divided her attention between the demanding nipples of both women. When it was her turn to be sucked Janis felt the first spiralling towards a climax begin, but before it reached the summit Lee had gone back to Virgo. She was still fingering her ceaselessly down below and varying her approach. Sometimes her fingers made rough invasions as far into her quim as she could reach; sometimes she dabbled in her labia with delicate movements that made her love-juice overflow, and sometimes with expert friction on her clitoris just where it counted the most. But all the time she was holding out on her, taking her two paces forward and one pace back. It occurred to Janis that she was judging how far gone they both were, trying to make them both come at once.

Then, for an instant, the contact stopped. She opened her eyes to see Lee sitting back on her heels, a blissful smile on her face and a finger in her mouth.

'Mm, this is yours, Janis!' she murmured. 'A touch of

Southern-fried flavour, I do declare.' She withdrew her left forefinger and replaced it with her right one. 'Oh yes, pure essence of Virgo, I know it well!' she chuckled. 'Sweet and spicy, with a hint of cinnamon.'

'You sound like an ad for Colonel Sanders!' Janis giggled.

'Sure thing! It's finger-lickin' good!'

Without warning, Lee suddenly bent down and placed her lips to Janis's still-soaking pussy. Janis gave a little cry of surprise that soon turned into one of ecstasy as she felt the long, cool tongue penetrate her. Virgo turned over on her side and began to kiss her breasts until Janis knew that she was on the verge of a cataclysmic orgasm.

'I'm going to come!' she moaned.

But still she had to await her turn. Abruptly the soft lips left her equally soft labia and for a few seconds she felt bereft. Then she saw that Lee had resumed her dual stroking of their two pussies and she lay back again, confident that this time it would not be long before she reached her destination. She could hear the restless moans of Virgo beside her and reached out for those gorgeous breasts once again, to help speed their mutual arousal. Lee was thrusting her fingers deep inside now, moving rapidly in and out and giving her clitoris a good rubbing as she did so.

The electric energy was gathering force in both of them, and just as she heard Virgo give a helpless cry, followed by a fierce shuddering of her whole body, Janis could feel her own climax begin. Wet lips fastened on her throbbing clit as she tipped over into a fierce, pulsating whirlpool of pure sensation and joined Virgo in bliss. On and on the climax went, prolonged by Lee's steadfast tonguing, until she flopped back utterly exhausted onto the pillow beside an already thoroughly sated Virgo.

'Oh God, I'd never have believed it possible!' Janis sighed, as the three of them cuddled up together. It felt weird having

Lee fully clothed between their two naked bodies. She tried to undo a button, wanting to feel the dyke's hard body against her own, but was given a gentle slap. 'I never undress,' she was told, curtly.

Someone turned out the bedside lamp and the trio lapsed into the total blankness of sleep.

Sometime in the night Janis awoke to feel Lee moving around over Virgo's prone body, but she was too tired to join in. Carefully she climbed from the bed, picked up her discarded clothes and crept from Virgo's room into her own. Lucille was fast asleep and snoring after drinking too much, but Janis didn't care. All she wanted now was her own bed and oblivion.

In the morning, Janis awoke with both a literal and a metaphorical bad taste in her mouth. The diversions of the previous evening had left her feeling as if she'd indulged in an overlong wanking session. There was no comparison between that and the kind of love-making she'd known with Adam, and now she wanted him more than ever, wanted the reassurance of his meaty prick inside her and the triumphant outpouring of his seed.

As soon as she could, Janis phoned him. He was having a lazy day and was still in bed at half-nine, his voice appealingly raw and husky. 'Jan! I was just lying here thinking about you.'

'In that case say good morning to Mr Perky for me!'

'I wish you were here to do it yourself.'

'Me too! Look, love, something's cropped up that I'd like to discuss with you. Virgo has asked me to join a new band with her and some other girls. I have to tell her after the show tonight, but I wanted to see what you thought first.'

'An all-girl band? Hardly fashionable right now.'

'But Virgo could be quite a draw, don't you think?'

'Depends which market you're aiming for.'

'She's thinking lesbian band, at least to start out. That's the part I'm not sure about.'

'Hm. To be frank, I think the days of "lesbian chic" are numbered in the pop world, if they're not already over. She'd be better taking the bisexual approach. After all, that's what she's already known for, isn't it?'

'I think she needs to talk to you, actually. I don't think her knowledge of the music scene is that wide. She's been cushioned from it too long by being with Blade. She needs advice from someone with his ear to the ground.'

'OK. Look, I'm free tonight. Why don't I motor up to wherever you are and we can talk after the show?'

Janis felt her heart lighten. She hadn't asked his advice just to lure him up to Nottingham but now he'd suggested it she was overjoyed. Maybe she could change her twin room for a double, just for one night.

In the event, the minibus had a breakdown on the way to Nottingham and by the time they got to the hotel they were in such a hurry that Janis didn't like to make a fuss. It was more important to get Adam put on the guest list, so as soon as they arrived at the venue she sought out Rob the Roadie, who dealt with such things. It was too much to hope that she would be able to pick her lover out from the audience while she was on stage, but nevertheless she tried, scanning the front rows of faces but to no avail.

While she went through her act Janis gave it all she had, imagining that she was performing for Adam's eyes only. She pressed herself against the cage, rubbing her clit against the iron bars and letting Blade caress her breasts through the gaps until she reached a breathtaking climax. These days she usually had to fake it, but not tonight. As the orgasm flushed through her she was afraid she would collapse and clung tightly to the bars of Blade's cage. Afterwards she caught him looking at her with an amused expression and knew he had guessed. At the beginning of the tour she would have flashed her eyes at him, wiggled her hips, tried to make him interested in her. But now, knowing what she knew about him, she didn't bother. Instead she threw him a scornful look. *Only one more show*, she thought, *and then I'm free of you forever!*

Janis realized that she still felt piqued that Blade was unavailable to her, both on stage and off. Even though it would have all been empty show she'd have loved to be at the mercy of that giant dildo, looking up to see his dirtily handsome face staring down at her as he prodded her with the scornful arrogance that was almost his trademark. But it was Gore who held the key to the mystery that was at the heart of Blade, and he guarded it jealously.

Any lingering disappointment on that score vanished instantly in sheer delight when Janis found Adam waiting for her in the dressing-room after her part in the show was over. The room was otherwise deserted and they gave each other a passionate kiss of greeting. As their tongues entwined, Adam's hand reached into the neck of her costume and gave her breast a squeeze, fuelling her already rampant appetite.

'Oh darling, I've missed you so much!' she sighed, pressing her body close to his.

'I've been thinking of you too. And I've bought you a present. It's waiting for you back at the flat.'

'What is it? I hate surprises. Tell me now!'

'No,' he laughed, tickling her. 'You'll just have to be patient.'

'Rotten thing! Give me a clue, then.'

'No, I won't.'

'Beast!'

They began to play-fight and were still at it, chasing each other around the dressing-room, when the others came in. Janis felt incredibly happy. Her days with Shaft were numbered, but by her own choosing, and she was convinced that she would be going on to better things. For, despite her pretence of asking for Adam's advice, Janis had already made up her mind: she would join Virgo's band.

When Adam was introduced to the star, Virgo's eyes lit up. 'So you're the man Jan's so hooked on she can't give you up!' she said, mischievously. 'Well, I hope you're worthy of her.'

'So do I,' he grinned. Janis saw how his eyes skimmed over Virgo's figure in its black and pink kimono, taking in the sexy cleavage. For a moment she felt a pang of jealousy, but then reminded herself that Adam wasn't the type to play around. At least, she frowned, he hadn't been.

Her doubts were swept away as those smiling eyes were turned back in her direction. He pulled her to him, his arm comforting around her waist, and softly kissed her cheek, making Janis feel loved and cherished again.

'Let me remind you two lovebirds that we have just ten minutes to get to the minibus,' Virgo said as she pulled a sweatshirt over her naked breasts and hopped into a minuscule pair of panties. 'We can talk later, in my room.'

When 'later' arrived, Adam and Janis found themselves in Virgo's luxurious room together with the star herself and the inevitable bottle of champagne.

'I presume Jan has told you of my plans?' she said straight away to Adam, lounging on the bed while the pair sat together on the grey velvet sofa.

'Yes, a little. Have you thought of a name?'

'Not yet. I was waiting to see if Janis would join us on guitar and vocals. It's a kind of superstition. I don't want to think about names until I'm sure I've got the right line-up, and that includes Jan. If she's willing, that is.'

Her green eyes looked provocatively in Janis's direction, decisively quashing any last-minute doubts. 'Yes, I'm game.'

'Great!' Virgo bounced off the bed and came to give her a hug and a kiss. For a few seconds Janis was disconcertingly aware of how close the three of them were on the sofa. She felt a warm rush in her belly and wondered what a threesome

might be like. The presence of a red-blooded male like Adam
would make it a totally different experience from that of the
previous night. Janis felt the warm glow inside her build into
a tingling fire, setting her sexual pulse throbbing. But then
Virgo rose to pour the champagne, and the situation was
defused.

'So, Adam, I gather you're a rock journalist. What do you
think are the chances of a new female band making it at this
present time?'

'Depends how big you want to go.'

She frowned as she poured the bubbly. 'All the way to the
fucking top, baby, what do you think? If you want the truth, I
intend to be a big, sharp splinter in Blade's arse.'

'To rival Shaft you'll need a gimmick, something to make
you stand out from the crowd. Got a manager?'

'Not yet. This project is under wraps as long as I'm under
contract to Shaft. I have one more album track to cut with
them and then I'm supposed to renegotiate. That's when I quit.'

'Jan said you were aiming for the lesbian market. Is that
wise?'

'You tell me. I thought we might start out that way, to be
sure of an audience, then move over into the mainstream.'

'Unlikely. You'd better start as you mean to go on: establish
your image – and your audience – from the word go.'

They discussed for some time what that image should be.
Adam suggested that, trading on Virgo's much publicized bi-
sexuality, they should go for an intriguing combination of the
raunchy and refined, with groin-centred music and aesthetically
pleasing appearance. 'Think along the lines of "Model girls
letting rip",' he grinned. They finally settled on 'Eclectic Pussy'
as a provisional band name. With its suggestion of various
musical influences, pun on 'electric' and sexual innuendo Virgo
pronounced herself well pleased.

'Have some more champagne,' she offered, kneeling at his

feet to pour it so that her breasts were thrust almost into his lap. Janis sensed that he was finding it hard to resist the allure of two women at once, and her own excitement grew. The alcohol, and the after-effects of Gore's aphrodisiac, were making her unbearably horny.

'Of course, we have to have sexy-looking girls for the band,' Virgo went on, thoughtfully. 'Looks count for as much as, if not more than, musicianship in this business. That's why I asked you, naturally darling.'

She threw Janis a dazzling smile that sent immediate shivers down her back and then gave Adam a wink. Smiles and glances, full of hidden and not-so-hidden meaning, were flying back and forth between the three of them now like a crazy dance in mid-air.

'You're both lovely,' Adam said, his voice resounding with a throaty tone that Janis recognized as suppressed desire. 'And you're both great on stage. I think you should choreograph your act yourself, Virgo.'

'Of course. And I think we'll be including some audience participation in our show, too.'

'In that case you can count on me being in the front row!'

'Just as you were last time?'

Virgo gave them both a knowing smile and Janis knew she was hinting at Janis's unscheduled dalliance with Adam on stage. The air was heavy with innuendo and sexual heat. She decided it was time to lay her cards on the table. They all knew which way the evening was heading, it just needed someone to break the ice and Janis knew it had to be her.

'I couldn't get a double room for me and Adam,' she told Virgo. 'Could we stay in here?'

A slow smile spread over the star's flushed face. 'Of course. Nothing would please me more. Do you want to use the bathroom? The bath has whirlpool jets and I'm sure it's big enough for two.' She paused, and the erotic tension in the air was almost tangible. 'Or maybe even three.'

Adam giggled nervously in a way that told Janis he was tempted. She whispered in his ear, 'I will if you will, if you will, so will I!' He grinned at her, his eyes questioning, and she nodded, returning his smile. Realizing that it was up to her, as the common denominator, to make the first move, she took their hands and led them into the adjoining bathroom.

CHAPTER EIGHT

When it came to it, Virgo and Adam didn't need much encouragement. While Janis ran the water and added a cocktail of scented oils from the aromatherapy selection on the shelf, Virgo began to undress Adam in slow motion. It was strange seeing another woman seduce him, and stranger still not to feel jealous. Janis sat on the edge of the large bath watching her friend undo her lover's shirt, kissing the bare strip of emerging chest skin as it first lengthened then widened to include his nipples. Adam stood passively at first, evidently relishing the feeling of being made love to by a glamorous and famous rock star. Janis felt good for him, remembering how excited she'd been the first time it had happened to her.

Gradually, her fingers working in concert with her lips, Virgo removed his shirt and set to work on unzipping his jeans. Janis watched her face as she slowly uncovered his erection, which had risen swiftly to its full dimensions for the occasion. The green glow in her eyes intensified as her gaze lighted on the sturdy length of his shaft and the pinkish-mauve dome of his glans, already slick with the first drops of love-dew.

When the bath was full Janis approached them and was instantly included in their embrace. She felt both snug and sensual with their arms around her, the three of them standing there in a tight little circle, radiating energy and desire. Soon two pairs of hands were undressing her, removing her T-shirt and bra, pulling off her jeans and pants, until she was naked.

Virgo was the only one still clothed. Janis began to lift up her navy sweatshirt, relishing the familiar touch of Adam's hands on her own nipples as she revealed Virgo's perfect breasts.

'Aren't they wonderful!' she said to him, taking one rosy, erect tip between her lips as encouragement for him to act likewise.

He took his cue, moaning softly as his mouth became filled with the gob-stopper dimensions of Virgo's nipple. The star fumbled with her own Levis as the pair of them sucked at her, and soon the jeans were dropping to the floor leaving her naked except for her tiny red panties. Adam was becoming more ravenous now, his hands grasping at the mounds of flesh and his tongue working avidly over the huge, reddening nipple. Janis reached down for his prick and felt it leap in her hand, depositing a slimy kiss on her wrist. *Careful*, she warned herself, *or he'll come too soon.*

Breaking free for a moment, Janis moved to the bath and turned the bubble timer to fifteen minutes, then stepped in, expecting the others to follow her. For a while they were too engrossed to move, so she settled down in the seething foam and contented herself with playing the voyeur. She watched Adam lift both of the other woman's heavy breasts and kiss them in turn while Virgo caught the length of his prick between her palms and rolled it like dough, sighing throatily as she did so.

The couple were so hot for each other that, for a while, Janis was afraid that they would fuck right there on the floor, oblivious of her, and she would feel left out. But although Adam had begun stroking the silken pouch of Virgo's pussy, his finger reaching in to feel the moistness of her vulva, it wasn't long before they were moving towards the bath. Janis moved aside to let them in and soon all three of them were lying in the hot foam, squealing with delight as the jets found their tender parts and treated them to a brisk massage.

'Oh, Jan, this was *such* a good idea!' Virgo grinned, her breasts glistening with foam. Adam's hand found Janis's open crotch beneath the water and he gave her clitoris a quick rub. She wriggled and laughed, reaching out to rub white bubbles into Virgo's sleek, warm skin. For a while all three of them played at washing each other, except that certain parts of their anatomy seemed to get far more of a 'washing' than others!

Although the tub could just about accommodate them, it wasn't exactly built for three-way foreplay so when Virgo suggested that they should move back into the bedroom and massage each other with body lotion the other two quickly assented. Wrapped in fluffy warm towels they lay on the huge bed hugging and kissing for a while until they were dry and ready for something more sensual. Virgo produced a bottle of expensively scented body cream in a dispenser which they took turns to shoot at each other, depositing huge globs over breasts and stomachs and thighs.

'I'll do Adam while Adam does you, and you do me!' Virgo said, evidently used to taking charge of such proceedings. Janis had no objections, since the order of play coincided exactly with her own desires.

It was extraordinary how much Janis was enjoying seeing another woman making love to Adam. While he smoothed the rich lotion into her own tingling breasts, and she did the same to Virgo's, the sight of those feminine fingers delicately applying the cream to that fine erection of his made her clitoris throb with hot urgency. The multiple sensual possibilities of their love-triangle were flashing through her mind, and at the thought of each erotic combination her desire increased until she felt a desperate longing in every cell of her body.

It seemed that the situation was having the same effect on the other two because soon they had given up any idea of order and were kissing and sucking and licking and stroking each other indiscriminately. Janis found no difficulty in moving straight from tweaking Virgo's erect nipple to caressing Adam's taut balls. One minute she was sucking at pink pussyfruit, her tongue lapping at the sweet secretions as they flowed around Virgo's enlarged clitoris, the next minute she had Adam's salty glans in her mouth and her lips were moving up and down his stiff shaft.

She was not active all the time, however. Sometimes it was bliss to just lie back and let the others pleasure her, with Virgo concentrating all her attention on her breasts while Adam plunged into her with rapid strokes and brought her swiftly to peak after peak of hot, gushing lust. Another time they made a sandwich layer of themselves with Virgo on all fours over Janis's body giving her cunt a thorough licking, while Adam screwed her from behind.

When they grew fatigued Virgo brought out her collection of sex toys and they experimented with assorted dildoes, vibrators, love-rings for Adam's flagging erections and love-balls for heightening the women's internal sensations. Janis found herself lost in a kind of erotic overload, all her senses working at full pitch and her orgasms growing more frequent and more intense as the night progressed.

She could tell Adam was enjoying it too and, seeing him flushed and excited by having two women at once, she wondered whether this could be the key to making their relationship work. Maybe all they'd needed was to add a little piquancy to their sex life. Well, tonight's adventure was certainly giving them a hefty dose of spice!

And what of Virgo? After a while Janis thought she seemed strangely cool, as if she was just going through the motions. Was this just another performance to her? It was hard to tell.

At last, in the early hours of the morning, all three of them sank wearily to rest on the big bed and Janis flicked off the light. She lay for a while listening to the increasingly regular breathing of her two lovers, wondering how they would all feel about it in the morning, As far as she was concerned there had been a kind of inevitability about it. What she was hoping was that none of them would have any cause to be jealous in future. If Janis and Virgo were to make a go of their band then they would have to put every ounce of energy into the project and they didn't need such complications and distractions.

Janis awoke to find Adam gently snoring beside her and Virgo showering in the bathroom. She cuddled up to him and he opened his eyes, a slow grin spreading over his features.

'Wow, that was some night!'

'Did you enjoy it?'

'Mm.' He nuzzled against her like a hungry puppy. 'I've always dreamed of making love with two women at once.'

'Did it come up to your expectations?'

'I should say so!' But then his face looked suddenly serious. 'But I don't think I would want it all the time. Special occasions only. Most of the time all I want is you, babe!'

Janis felt relieved. She still needed to feel that she was Adam's number one girl after all.

In a few minutes Virgo breezed in to find the pair of them making love with slow sensuality. 'I don't know, at it like rabbits!' she quipped. 'Pardon me if I don't join in. Right now coffee is a priority.'

She moved into the small sitting-room where there were coffee- and tea-making facilities, switched on the TV and completely ignored them. Adam grinned, resuming his long, slow lengthing of Janis's wet and willing pussy until she bucked and moaned her way through a brief but intensely stimulating orgasm. He soon followed suit, jetting his seed into her with an explosive force that she found doubly satisfying, and afterwards they lay kissing and cuddling until Adam decided, reluctantly, that he should get dressed.

'I have someone to interview in Leicester this afternoon,' he told her. 'But it will only be a couple of days before you're back in London, won't it? I can't wait to have you all to myself at home again.'

Janis was looking forward to that too. It would be great to have a stable base for a while. She might have to take a temporary job after she left Shaft and before Eclectic Pussy got under way, but it would be worth it. If both Virgo and Adam had faith in the new band that was good enough for her.

The last two gigs seemed to fly by and at the end of the Oxford one there was a party on stage. When they were all quite pissed, Gore suddenly came up to Janis and put his arm around her. 'How have you enjoyed being in my company?' he asked her, with a leer.

Now that she had something else to look forward to Janis was no longer fazed by having him so near her. She was able to look him straight in the eye and say, 'Actually, it wasn't as much fun as I thought it was going to be.'

'What?' Gore pretended outrage. 'You expected it to be *fun*? Shame on you, child! Rock'n Roll is a serious business, and don't let anyone fool you otherwise! Seriously, though, a little bird tells me that I don't think you'll be staying with us for the next tour. You lack a certain "Je ne sais quoi", my sweet. Not your fault, some girls have it, others don't. But we gave you a fair crack of the whip, wouldn't you say? No complaints, put it down to experience, what?'

Janis hated his patronizing tone, but she told herself she would only have to endure him for a few more minutes. The pervertedly sexy heat of him was nauseating her, making her most uncomfortable, yet she forced a smile and managed to come back with a cool reply.

'It's been nice knowing you Gore – not!'

And she sauntered off, feeling that she'd somehow scored a point. In fact, she was glad that she now knew where she stood with Gore, who had opposed her inclusion in the company from the start for reasons best known to himself. It was clear that her contract would not be renewed, but all she felt was relief that she would not have to go grovelling to Blade.

The rock star's apologies, when the final parting came, were dripping with insincerity. 'It's been nice knowing you, Janis,' he lied. 'And I'm real sorry we can't keep you on. But you were a last-minute replacement, if you remember, and we'd prefer to give a more experienced girl a chance. The routines on our next tour will be even more complicated and . . . well, I seem to recall that you had a little trouble sticking to the script on one or two occasions.'

You bastard! Janis thought, behind her relentlessly sweet smile.

Virgo drove Janis back to London in the small hours and generously offered to drop her at Adam's place first. Janis wondered whether she would expect to be invited in, but Virgo pre-empted her by saying she was going straight to her Docklands apartment and would probably sleep for twenty-four hours non-stop. She promised to phone and zoomed off, leaving an exhausted Janis on the pavement with her two heavy bags.

Despite being woken in the middle of the night, Adam was delighted to see her. He made hot chocolate and they sat chatting until neither of them could keep their eyes open, then they tumbled into bed together. Fortunately the next day was Sunday, so they could have a lie-in.

When Janis awoke, the first thing she saw at the end of the bed was a Fender Telecaster, with sunburst finish and humbucker pick-up. Round its neck was a pink satin bow with a card that read, 'I belong to Janis'.

'Wow!'

Excited as a child at Christmas, she leapt to the end of the bed and embraced the gorgeous guitar, hugging its broad back to her chest as she kissed its knobbly neck.

'Well, you need a decent instrument if you're going to cut it in Rock 'n Roll,' Adam grinned, watching her with delight. 'Look after that one. It's a 1976 model. I picked it up for a song, so to speak.'

'Oh, thank you, thank you!' Reverently Janis put it on her knee and strummed a few chords. 'I'll practise like mad now, honest I will.'

He came up behind her, putting his hands on her breasts. 'How about thanking me properly?' he suggested, huskily.

Their love-making was joyful, ecstatic, with Janis in such an optimistic mood. He entered her almost immediately and they moved swiftly from position to position, relishing the new sensations each provided. Janis came three times before he did: once when she was on top, once while she was lying on her side, and again when he took her on all fours from behind. Each time seemed more powerful, more abandoned, so that when they finally climaxed together she was swept up in the pulsating torrent of fire that burst from him, filling her to capacity and sending aftershocks of shuddering ecstasy throughout her body.

I'm so happy, she thought, and part of her happiness was being released from the sneering presence of Gore and the cold indifference of Blade. She hadn't realized what a blight those two arrogant gays had cast over her life until now, when she was free of them.

But the best part of her happiness was being with Adam again, just as in the old days, with all their petty bickering behind them. Ironically it had been Blade who had driven them apart, but Virgo who had brought them together again, and now both of them could only go from strength to strength as they pursued their exciting new careers.

*   *   *

Three weeks later, however, Janis was in a very different mood
as she sat in the London flat by herself with Darius on her lap.
The cat had become her confidant lately. As she stroked his
downy fur she spilt out her troubles to him.

'I'm starting to wonder if this band will ever get off the
ground,' she sighed. 'Virgo's got the band together, except she's
not sure about the bass player, but we've not even had any
rehearsals yet. She's supposed to be putting together some
more material.'

But that wasn't her only worry as she sat in the deserted
room, listening to the tick of the old clock that Adam had
inherited from his grandmother. The longed-for domestic bliss
that she had hoped for now she was back in her old domain had
failed to materialize. Instead, she was bored out of her skull.
After the excitement of the tour and the kinky sex, everyday
life seemed dull as dull and she craved the thrills she'd
experienced in Virgo's company.

But Virgo was busy in the studio most of the time, fulfilling
her last obligations to Shaft, and Adam was dashing around
interviewing fashion and rock icons like there was no
tomorrow, leaving Janis to her part-time job in a record store
and Darius. 'Not that you aren't delightful company, old
moggy,' she informed him, brushing her lips against his furry
face. 'But you aren't exactly the world's best conversationalist
and as for sex . . . well, I've heard what a hard time you give
those feline females out in the back yard so . . . thanks, but no
thanks!'

Their tête-à-tête was interrupted by a ring at the doorbell.
Janis got up, deposited the cat on the floor, and went to answer
it. A girl with cropped black hair and small, darting eyes stood
there, carrying a guitar case.

'Er . . . are you the person advertising for a bass player?'

Janis frowned, puzzled. 'I might be. Did you see an ad
somewhere?'

'Yes, there was a phone number, someone called Virgo. She said to call here and see you, because she was busy.'

'She might have told me!' Janis muttered, inviting the girl in. Wondering just what she was supposed to do now she tried to smooth over the awkward hiatus by offering her tea.

'Thanks. My name's Dagmar. I'm German, but I've been in London a long time. Used to be in a band called Jezebel's Gels. Have you heard of them?'

'Sorry, no. Milk and sugar?'

Janis decided she could do no more than chat to Dagmar for a while. She didn't feel competent to give the German girl a proper audition, despite the fact that she'd brought her guitar along. Resentment was still festering in her. She was angry that Virgo had landed her in it without warning. However, the girl seemed pleasant enough and was touchingly self-effacing when it came to talking about her musical prowess.

'I've got a tape, if you'd like to hear it,' she offered at last. 'It's me doing some solo stuff'

'Solo bass?' Janis asked, surprised. She slotted it into the machine and pressed the button. A surprisingly rich and mellow sound emerged. 'Is that you?'

Dagmar nodded with shy pride. 'Yeah, I was just messing around.'

'It's very impressive. Tell me about your experience with the other band. Why did you leave?'

'We broke up, went our separate ways. We weren't getting anywhere together and, besides Kelly, our lead singer, got mixed up with this guy . . .'

She stopped, evidently not wishing to express her feelings on that subject. Janis asked her outright if she was gay.

'Yes, but I don't mind working with straights. Only two of us in Jez were lesbian.'

'I suppose you know that Virgo is bisexual?'

'How about you?'

Dagmar's grey eyes were level with hers, making it impossible to pussyfoot around the subject. It was the first time Janis had been directly challenged since she'd made love with a woman and she hesitated for a moment, then smiled. 'I suppose I have to say that I'm "bi" too, although I'm in a steady relationship with a man.'

'You and Virgo?' Again the directness of her question demanded candour. Janis nodded. 'Lucky you! She's my icon, if you must know. But I don't want you to think I'm trying to get into the band just because of that. I really like her music and I feel I can do it justice. I was disappointed when she said she had no time to audition me, but she said to come and have a chat with you anyway.'

They did some musical fooling around, playing guitar together and singing some of Virgo's songs. It felt good, and by the end of the afternoon Janis's spirits were high again. She decided to recommend her to Virgo for the band, and told her as much as she was leaving.

'Thanks!' Dagmar said, eyes glowing.

'I can't promise anything, mind. Final decision rests with her, and all that.'

'I understand.' Dagmar stared at her for a few seconds and the atmosphere turned suddenly electric. Janis found herself looking at the girl's soft, curving mouth with its appealing sheen and a shudder of lust caught her unawares. Just as it registered, she felt Dagmar's mouth move swiftly towards hers and there was a brief kiss, enough to whet her appetite without satisfying it. Then, before Janis had made a full recovery, she was gone.

'Wow, what a woman!' she said to Darius, who turned up his nose at her and stalked into the kitchen as a cue for her to open a tin.

After she'd told Adam about her visitor he asked, 'Do you fancy her, then?'

'As a matter of fact I do. Trouble is, there's no room for you there. She's only into girls.'

'I don't mind, you know,' he said, softly nipping the back of her neck in a way she found very arousing. 'If you have sex with other women, I mean. It's just other men I draw the line at. Of course, I'd rather be in a threesome with you if possible.'

Janis thought wistfully of Virgo. She had been missing her friend. Not just for sex – Adam more than made up for that – but because they were mates, and she had precious few of those. The girls she used to know had become strangers since she'd joined the Shaft road show, some out of disgust and others out of envy or shyness, and she knew she could never recover her former easy friendships with them.

The recording sessions came to an eventual end and, one Thursday night, Virgo phoned out of the blue to say she'd arranged a rehearsal for the full band, including Dagmar, on Saturday morning. Janis was delighted. She'd started to have doubts, but now it really looked as if Eclectic Pussy was about to get off the ground after all.

Things seemed to move very swiftly after that. Virgo had taken the plunge and booked a month of pub gigs, three a week in the London area, to give them maximum exposure. But they had to work very hard to get all the new material down. It seemed that Virgo had been jotting down ideas in the recording studio between takes, and working them up into complete songs when she got home at night. Her output was impressive: twelve new numbers, ten of them usable and two to be worked on. They couldn't use any of her previous material because it was all tied up in copyright under the Shaft name.

'That prick Blade had me conned out of half my royalties,' she moaned. 'But you know what they say, "Don't get mad, get even!" And I fucking intend to, darlings, I can promise you that. We're going to be bigger than Blade ever dreamed of being. Just stick with me, kids!'

Janis felt disinclined to believe Virgo's hype, but as their first gig approached she started to have more faith in the band. They'd got things really tight and the material was very good, despite being composed in a hurry. Janis surprised herself, too, by her prowess on guitar. Most of her old skill had come back easily, and she had built on it through hours of daily practice until she felt much more confident. Her singing had improved too, thanks to a few lessons from a singing coach. Now there were only details like costume and make-up to consider before their début performance at the Tragedy Queen in Soho.

They all went to the fetish-wear shop to get kitted out and ended up with catsuits in black and red vinyl with holes cut to show just their nipples. They were incredibly sexy garments. As Janis pirouetted before the mirror admiring her tight buttocks, thrusting nipples and the provocative bulge of her Venus mound, she began to feel powerfully aroused. The other girls looked fantastic too, transformed with wigs and glittery make-up into prancing super-dykes.

Adam's eyes nearly popped out of his head when, visiting Janis in the crowded dressing-room upstairs at the pub, he saw her in her stage gear for the first time.

'Christ, Jan, I fancy you something rotten!' he leered, tweaking her protruding nipples. Lowering his voice he added, 'Will you wear it at home for me sometime?'

'Maybe!'

He was stroking her plasticized buttocks, making her feel really horny inside the tight-fitting suit. She didn't need any love-drugs to get her high for this performance, she concluded. Although there was to be no actual sexual contact during the act, she suspected it would be even more of a turn-on to be flirting with the punters, titillating the audience with their teasing unavailability.

When the five of them walked onto the small stage there was uproar. Word had got around the gay scene and there were men there as well as women, all eager to see what new persona the fabulous Virgo had dreamed up for herself. The place was packed and they were having to turn people away. Even though Adam was on the guest list Janis saw him arguing at the door before they finally let him slip in at the back.

The minute she played the first crashing chord of 'Woman to Woman' Janis felt perfectly at home in the band. It was such a relief to be playing a useful rôle for a change, instead of mere window-dressing to make Blade look good. On reflection she'd realized that even Virgo had played second fiddle to him, despite her apparently equal status. They were both well out of it.

Once the pounding rhythm of the first number got under way the audience was totally won over, clapping and cheering and stamping so that the music was almost drowned out at times. Janis felt the adrenalin coursing through her veins as their enthusiasm lifted her higher and higher.

The excitement mounted throughout Virgo's carefully orchestrated set, climaxing in the superfast 'Devil's Daughter'. Janis could feel the sweat coursing down her, making her body feel liquid inside the hot suit, but still she wriggled and thrust her pelvis, pushed out her tits with their nipples bursting through the peepholes, waggled her tongue at the salivating girls in the front row and generally acted in a totally uninhibited fashion, loving every minute of it. Her crotch was on fire, the tightly packed vulva seeping at the edges and her clitoris responding to every move as the clinging material moulded itself to her grooves. She was hot and throbbing down there and the need to do something about it was growing by the second.

At last, unable to help herself Janis hooked one leg over her low-slung guitar and rode its solid body mercilessly. She just about managed to keep up the thrashing rhythm as she masturbated, egged on by the screaming crowd. They knew the exact moment she came, in a series of violent spasms that nearly had her rocketing off the stage, and a huge cheer went up. Everyone in the room loved it.

When they retreated to the dressing-room, Janis felt totally exhausted and drank a pint of mineral water without stopping. Virgo came up with a wry smile. 'Trying to fucking upstage me, were you? Well, you succeeded!'

Janis hoped she was only pretending to be miffed, but she knew that Virgo was right. For the whole of the last number she had been the star of the show. Maybe she'd better take a back seat in the second set and let someone else have a chance.

But the audience wouldn't let her. 'Ja-*nis*! Ja-*nis*!' they chanted insistently, and she was obliged to acknowledge them with a smile and a few sexy thrusts that had them chanting all the more. Soon, however, Virgo was pulling out all the stops and the spotlight was on her. Janis couldn't help admiring her professionalism, the way she worked the crowd up and kept them focused on her unique blend of soft porn and sweet music. There were several slower numbers in this set, sultry songs that aroused listeners in a totally different way from the harder, rockier numbers. Expertly Virgo wove her sensual spell over them, quietening them down into a mood of languid eroticism that was nevertheless extremely sexy.

For the last two numbers they increased the pace until the whole place was in uproar. Janis and Virgo did a number face to face, flirting outrageously with each other, and the crowd yelled for more. When all four of them were lined up front of stage, with Lee bashing away behind, Janis felt a great sense of solidarity, of acting in harmony to produce one great sound. It was something she'd never felt before and it made all their hard work worthwhile.

Afterwards they were besieged by fans wanting autographs.

In the Shaft band they had all been well protected from this kind of intrusion but here, in this London pub, they had to cope with it themselves. Janis found she was touched by the genuine sentiments expressed and the feeling that they were doing something really worthwhile for people whose lives were often fraught with the stress of living outside the accepted norms of society.

'Wasn't that great!' she smiled, glowing with satisfaction as Adam's cheerful face appeared.

'Fantastic! You're a star, Jan. You're all stars!'

'You bet your sweet life we are. But help me off with this outfit, will you? I know exactly what shrink-wrapped bacon feels like now!'

Virgo came up, flushed with excitement. 'Someone's offered to pay for us to make a CD! They say we should put it about ASAP. What d'you reckon, Adam?'

'If you make it a good one I'll review it for you. More important, I'll get you some air time. Maximum exposure, that's what you should be aiming for. You're worth it.'

Virgo hugged him, then Janis, then all three hugged together. For a moment Janis felt they were in their own secret, erotic world again but then the clamour of the fans and the bustle of the dressing-room intervened and it was just her and Adam again. They stole away together, eager to get home where they could sate their appetites on each other with another night of non-stop, fabulous sex.

CHAPTER NINE

Much to Janis's delight, Adam's offer to manage the band was accepted by all the girls. Only Dagmar had any reservations about being managed by a man, and Adam's network of contacts in the music world finally won her over.

To Janis it seemed only right that he should be more intimately involved with Eclectic Pussy. After all, he'd already been extremely intimately involved with two of its members! But Virgo put her finger on it when she said, 'Some women get so strident when they're driving a hard bargain, but men have a natural advantage. They can talk quietly, and other men will listen.'

Adam was relieved that they'd accepted him too. He told Janis he was getting fed up with talk about lapels and turn-ups. The fashion world was taking up too much of his time and attention and he needed to get back to his rock roots again.

'I can get you a good recording deal if the CD is up to scratch,' he told them. 'But you have to put your hearts and souls into it, girls. Make it the best thing you ever did.'

To make sure, he put them in touch with a producer friend who worked with one of the best recording engineers in the business. They agreed to give the band several hours of their time at a reduced fee. Only after they had sweated it out for three days in the studio did Rolf and Pete drop by to give their expert opinion. With their help the raw recording was licked into shape by Friday the thirteenth, and the result astounded everyone.

'It's bloody marvellous!' Virgo said as they listened to the final version of 'Spider Woman' for the third time. 'Let's hope Friday the thirteenth turns out to be lucky for us.'

'It should do,' smiled Sal, who was into lunar astrology. 'The thirteenth sign is Arachne, the spider goddess.'

Adam managed to get them air time on Virgin Radio and also on the new, prestigious 'DJ Harvey' show, whose ebullient host enthused about the track, playing it four times in one week. They began to talk about making a video, but finances were tight.

'I should be getting some Shaft royalties soon,' Virgo said. 'I'll put fifty per cent aside in a fund for Pussy.'

One Sunday afternoon the band, and Adam, were gathered together in Virgo's flat. It was Lee's birthday, and they were celebrating with cake and champagne. That evening they had another gig at the Tragedy Queen and everyone was in high spirits, knowing that there would be a fantastic reception from the audience. It was the last time they would be playing such a small venue, since they could now command an audience of several hundred.

Suddenly there was an imperious rapping at the door and Virgo got up with a frown.

'Hope that's not the boys in blue!' she quipped as she went to answer it. Once the door was opened, Blade and Gore strode in and the girls instinctively shrank from their menacing faces.

Virgo was scowling. 'Hey, what d'you think you guys are doing, fucking bursting in here uninvited? This is a private party, and you're not welcome.'

'Shut it, bitch!' Gore snapped. 'We're here on business. Serious business. Is this the motley crew you call a band?'

'I'm not standing for this . . .'

Calmly, Adam got to his feet. 'Can I help, gentlemen? The

name's Adam Richardson, and I manage this band. If it's business . . .'

Blade said, 'It's between us and Virgo. I think it would be better if we saw her alone.'

'The hell you will!' Virgo walked dramatically to the door and pointed out into the corridor. 'Fuck off, the pair of you!'

Gore gave one of his nastiest smiles. 'I don't think you'll be so ready to insult us, sweetheart, when you hear what we've got to say.'

'Anything you want to say can be said in front of these people. I've no secrets from them.'

'OK, if that's the way you want it.' Gore delved inside his black velvet jacket and pulled out a folded document. 'Recognize this, Virgo? It's the contract you signed when you joined Shaft. And you know what they say about contracts, don't you? Always read the small print.'

'If you have a point to make, please make it,' she said, wearily. 'We were having a pleasant afternoon till you turned up.'

'Sorry to interrupt your little party, but breach of contract is not something we can ignore and we're off on tour again tomorrow. Take a look at clause twenty-three, would you?'

Janis noticed that Virgo's fingers were trembling slightly as she took the papers and opened them out. When she read the relevant passage her face dropped. Gore gave a gloating bark of a laugh. 'Now do you see? That bit about your stage name being copyright, owned by the band. You can't be "Virgo" in any other band, but it's come to our notice that you have blatantly flouted this rule. You're trading on the name to promote your new outfit, and that's illegal. We could take you to court and sue for every penny you've got!'

Everyone in the room was dumbfounded, none more so than Virgo herself. She looked pale and drawn, seeing her hopes and dreams disappear before her in the Cheshire-cat grins of Gore and Blade.

'Is that what you intend to do?' she asked at last, her voice little more than a whisper.

'Well, that depends on you,' Blade said, slowly. 'We could settle out of court, of course. And you'd have to promise that you would never call yourself Virgo again.'

'But it's her name now!' Janis interjected, unable to stand by and say nothing. 'We all know her as that. She can't change it.'

'Rubbish, people change their name all the time,' was Gore's brisk response. 'We've all done it. She can go back to being Miss Angela Sykes any time she likes, and she knows it.'

Janis looked at the star, whose glittering image already seemed somewhat tarnished by the banality of her real name. Virgo gave her a rueful smile that clearly said, 'Can you blame me for changing it?'

The two men turned towards the door. Having delivered their bombshell they were obviously disinclined to stick around. 'You'll be hearing from our legal chaps in a few days' time,' Gore sneered over his shoulder as they made their exit.

The room fell into stunned silence as they all tried to calculate the effect of the news on their band. Without Virgo's name, would they be such a draw? And if she had to pay a hefty sum to avoid a court case, how would they finance a video, let alone an album? Everyone knew she'd been counting on putting money from Shaft into Eclectic Pussy.

'I'm sorry, everyone,' Virgo said at last. 'But it looks like I've dumped us all in the shit.'

'Let's not be hasty,' Adam said. 'OK, it looks bad right now, but we don't know what kind of a sum they're going to come up with. It may just be possible to raise a bank loan, although my credit's not so good these days.'

'But what about Virgo's name?' Sal moaned. 'That's worth its weight in gold to us. Without it we're just another dyke band.'

'We've already had some good plugs, though,' Janis reminded them, trying hard to be optimistic. 'A lot of people already know that it's Virgo's band. Did Prince sell any fewer records when he started to use that weird symbol instead of his name?'

'Are you suggesting she calls herself "the artist formerly known as Virgo"?' Lee sneered.

'No, of course not.'

'What's in a name?' Virgo sighed. 'Several thousand pounds, apparently. Oh God, if we only knew what kind of sum they were thinking of.'

'Don't worry about the money, that's my job,' Adam said. 'If we can get a record company interested in you we might be able to swing it.'

'But you know how it is in this business, Adam. You have to have backers, money up front. Then if you're lucky, and *only* if you're lucky, you get to recoup later.'

'Look, we already have an excellent single. The initial response has been good.'

'Yes, but Virgo's name is on that,' Dagmar reminded them. 'We'll have to have all those promo leaflets re-printed, all the CD sleeves, gig posters. It's going to cost us a bomb!'

'Look, that's my worry as your manager, OK?'

Janis felt proud of Adam. He was certainly doing his best to limit the damage to their morale. But Blade and Gore had been the real party poopers, and nothing could restore the festive spirit now.

'What about tonight's gig?' Lee reminded them, gloomily. 'It's advertised with Virgo's name on the poster. Will we have to cancel it, or what?'

'I'm not in the mood anyway,' Dagmar muttered.

'Neither am I,' sighed Sal. 'What a rotten end to your birthday, Lee.'

'Hey, I've had a brilliant idea!' said Virgo, suddenly. She'd been sitting quietly thinking while the rest of them were debating and now her eyes were bright again.

Rushing to a drawer she drew out one of the Eclectic Pussy posters they'd had printed, with blank spaces for the venue and date. Above the band name was printed the legend, SENSATIONAL NEW BAND STARRING THE FABULOUS VIRGO! She picked up a black marker pen, inserted an 'A' in her name between the 'R' and the 'G' then faced them with a triumphant smile. 'See? That can be my new name. Isn't it brilliant?'

'Virago!' Janis read aloud. 'Like the feminist publishers!'

'What do you think?' Virgo asked the rest of them. 'Will it do?'

'Virago!' Lee repeated. 'That means some kind of harpy, doesn't it?'

They searched for it in a dictionary and discovered that, despite its hellcat connotations, its original meaning was 'a woman of masculine strength and courage'.

'Like Brünnhilde! That's marvellous!' Dagmar grinned.

They all looked towards Adam for the casting vote. He was still contemplating but eventually he gave a smile of approval. 'I think it will do. It satisfies the legal requirements but it should still remind people of her former incarnation. Best of all, it's one in the eye for those two bastards. I think it'll work.'

Janis thought it was a brilliant coup. To give such an obviously sexy woman the name of a virgin had always seemed rather affected to her. Now the image would be of a female warrior, a woman with guts and strength and pride.

Virgo flexed her arms to display her muscles. 'OK, everyone, from now on I'm Virago. If you call me Virgo I shan't answer, so you'd better remember.'

The feeling of having got one over on Blade and Gore was exhilarating, and that night they played the best gig they'd done so far. The crowd was ecstatic and almost mobbed the stage, so they were glad that Adam had laid on a few extra bouncers for the occasion. One thing was obvious: Eclectic Pussy were on a roll, and nothing must be allowed to prevent their meteoric rise to fame!

Afterwards, in the restful quiet of their flat, Janis and Adam discussed the future. Tired as they were, they didn't feel like going to bed yet. Entwined on the sofa with a couple of brandies, they debated how they might raise the much-needed cash to promote the band as it deserved.

'I've no capital and no credit,' Janis moaned. 'If Virgo – oops, Virago! – can't come up with anything, what are our chances of getting either a backer or a loan?'

'Slim, but I'll do my best.' Adam pulled her close and kissed her brandied lips, making them tingle with anticipation.

'Who can you approach?'

'Maybe Ivan Craig. He's a rogue and a villain, but he's one of the biggest names in the business. First we have to put together a really good presentation, though. Some publicity photos to go with the CD, and as pornographic as possible. He's a bit of a dirty old man.'

'Shall we start now?' Janis grinned, pulling down her top to show one ripe, bulging nipple.

He promptly took it between his lips murmuring, 'OK, if you insist!'

'I meant the photos! Ooh, that feels nice!'

They were soon tearing the clothes off each other, all their earlier lust returning now they had rested. Janis knelt on the floor and began licking Adam's shaft until it stood straight and tall in his lap. She leant forward and took it beneath her breasts, rubbing them together with the fat cock sandwiched between. Adam groaned and threw his head back. Janis felt her cleavage become wet and sticky and she grew excited herself, aware of the seepage from her pussy as she massaged his straining erection.

In a few seconds Adam was coming all over her, spraying her tits and belly with globs of liquid white that trickled down over her skin when they met her hot flesh. Janis sighed with bliss as his hands rubbed the copious juices over her nipples, making them tingle with new urgency. Down below her clit was tingling too, eager for its turn. She scrambled up onto his thigh and began to rock back and forth, rubbing his hardness against her. The wet labia squelched apart, exposing her inner lips to the delicious friction and hastening her climax. Oblivious of everything except her own quest for satisfaction, Janis rose and thrust her mound into Adam's face. Obediently he began to lick her, cooling her overheated flesh with his saliva and giving her the more direct stimulation needed by her pulsating love-button.

Helplessly Janis surrendered herself to the oncoming tide of her orgasm, letting Adam's eager tongue probe right into her cunt as the thrills escalated within. She moaned and thrashed her way through a long, fierce climax that left her weak and exhausted. Dimly she was aware of Adam lifting her up and carrying her into the bathroom, where he lovingly washed their mingled juices off her satiated body, then put her to bed.

Although they didn't have a gig booked for another four days, Virago rang Janis three days later and said she was calling a meeting at her flat. For some reason she didn't want Adam to be there. He happened to be out doing some business, but Janis was worried. Was he about to get the sack as their manager in his absence?

Janis was the last to arrive. The other girls were sitting there in sober silence and she knew at once that something was wrong. 'What's happened, Virago?' she asked, careful to get the name right.

'I've had a letter from their solicitors. They wasted no time.' Virago handed her the letter but didn't give her time to read through all the legal jargon. 'They want six thousand,' she went on, bitterly. 'That's practically all I have coming from the last of the Shaft royalties. I shall be left with hardly anything, bar what I've put by for my own future and I can't afford to risk that.'

'Of course not, none of us would want you to,' Sal reassured her. 'You worked damn hard for those bastards. You're entitled to keep your share of the profits.'

Virago sighed. 'So the question remains, how are we going to finance this band? How can we raise enough money in a short time to capitalize on the good start we've made?'

It was an open question, but one which no one had a ready answer for. Several frivolous suggestions were made, such as putting money on the lottery or robbing a bank. Then Sal said, tentatively, 'I used to make a lot of money when I was a student . . .'

'How?' they chorused. She seemed reluctant to say.

'OK, let's be straight. Are we talking prostitution here?' Virago said, impatiently.

'I suppose so, but it was money for old rope. I worked for a woman who ran a dominatrix service for wealthy businessmen. They had to be wealthy, the prices we charged! There was nothing to it, though. Sex was forbidden, although if they were very good and paid a lot you could sometimes wank them off. But what they really got off on was being bossed around and, sometimes, spanked. It could be great fun, actually, and you got to wear a lot of fabulous costumes. A bit like being on stage, in fact.'

Dagmar said, 'Well, I'd be up for it. I wouldn't have to pretend to be nasty to the men, either. I really do hate those poncy business types. I was married to one once – for ten minutes!'

The others laughed, but Virago looked thoughtful. Then she said, 'Do you know, I think it might just work. We could offer our services in pairs, just to be on the safe side, and I wouldn't

mind using this flat. It's a posh address, which means we could
charge over the odds, and I intend to move out soon anyway.
Can't afford the rent any more.'

When she realized that Sal's proposition was being taken
seriously, Janis felt a twinge of excitement, bordering on fear.
What would Adam say if she decided to do it? Would she dare
tell him?

They all began working out the details, deciding which
magazines to advertise in, how much to charge, what to wear
and how to act. Sal was a great help, and as the afternoon wore
on the venture began to seem more and more feasible. At six
o'clock they decided to put it to the vote. It would have to be
an 'all or nothing' issue, they decided, because it would
obviously be unfair if some band members worked to raise
money in that way while the others didn't.

'I'm not sure what Adam is going to say about this,' Janis
said, before the vote was cast.

'He's our manager,' Dagmar snapped. 'We're employing
him, not vice versa.'

'I know, but you're asking me to take a vote which could
affect my personal life with him,' Janis explained. 'The rest of
you don't have regular partners, so it doesn't apply. But surely
I can have time to think about it and, if necessary, talk it over
with him.'

'Ring him now,' Lee suggested. 'We don't want to wait.'

Aware that she was holding up the proceedings, Janis went
to the phone in the bedroom and dialled the flat. Adam had just
got in. She cut short his report of his unsuccessful meeting at
the office of a Sony subsidiary, telling him where she was and
what had been proposed as a moneymaking scheme. There was
a short silence, then he broke into laughter.

'By God, if you can pull it off that would be a great
publicity stunt!'

'We'd only be doing it for the money, Adam.'

'Yes, I know, but if you can make capital out of it publicity-wise so much the better. Hey, this might mean a whole new angle for the band. Really exciting!'

'So you've no objections to me going along with it, then?'

'None at all. There's no sex involved, is there?'

'Not as far as I can see.'

'Well, then. How much did you say those poor geezers would pay per session? Over a hundred? What, per girl? My God, you'll be quids in after a few weeks!'

When Janis returned to the others the smile on her face said it all. They voted unanimously to put their plan into action and Virago said she would target the men's glossies for next month. Sal knew of some hotels where staff would, for a small consideration, pass their phone number on to potential clients, so they decided to start there on Monday.

'Training session here, tomorrow, three p.m. sharp!' Virago announced, her green eyes brighter than Janis had seen them in a long time.

The 'training session' turned out to be hilarious. They took it in turns to play the client while two of the other girls played out their rôles. Sal naturally was the expert, and she proved to be an exacting teacher. Her criticism flowed freely all afternoon.

'No, Dagmar, look at your face! You must frown and pout as if you're really angry with him! Lee, do try to put more conviction into that slap. You look like you're swatting flies. Don't be afraid to hurt him. They like it rough, honestly!'

Janis was surprised to find she really enjoyed playing the harridan. Dressed in a provocative outfit of black leather bikini, thigh-length boots and elbow-length gloves, she began to practise a harsh, rasping tone of voice and a commanding stance. It made her feel extraordinarily strong and powerful, especially when she managed to make Lee cringe as she knelt on all fours. Previously she had been a little intimidated by the drummer's lesbian aggression, but now she was acting as meek and obedient as the rest and Janis was making the most of it.

'Lick my boots, worm!' she commanded, and Lee did as she was told. 'Now crawl over and bring me that magazine in your mouth, like the dog you are!'

The others sat on the sidelines, giving encouragement and making suggestions. Soon it was Dagmar's turn to dominate Janis. Seeing the other woman towering above her as she knelt there naked was a frightening experience, and she found it humiliating to obey her commands without question.

'God, how can anyone get off on being ordered around like that?' she wondered aloud, after she'd been made to lick crumbs off the carpet, and had her bum used as a practice pad for Dagmar's drumming technique.

'Those businessmen get tired of being in control all the time,' Sal explained. 'They want someone else to take total responsibility for a while. Being a slave for an evening revitalizes them, helps them do their job better.'

They began to organize a rota. Each of them would be working with each of the others on a 'one night on, one night off' basis. Janis was relieved to find that her first job would be with Virago. Their experience of love-making in a threesome with Adam would no doubt stand them in good stead.

When it came to it, however, it felt very different from that. Virago offered to take the first client, whenever he appeared, and two nights after Sal had briefed her contact in the hotel a call came. The man, known to them only as 'Cecil', would be arriving at eight o'clock on Wednesday evening. He wanted a three-hour session, which didn't sound too gruelling. Janis went over to the flat an hour earlier to get herself ready.

Cecil had obviously done this kind of thing before. He came with a mask, which he wanted to wear, also a pair of handcuffs and a padlock and chain to go round his crotch. Janis felt a bit out of her depth but fortunately Virago was completely at ease with the situation and her confidence was infectious. Gleefully the two women discussed in front of Cecil what they would do with him.

'Since his hands and prick are completely useless, we'd better make full use of that mouth of his,' Virago said.

Janis saw the man's erection twitch and guessed that he was finding their words arousing, so she played along. 'Yes, I think my feet could do with a catlick. I'll make him clean my boots first, though.'

While Cecil's tongue worked overtime on her boots, Virago kept up a constant haranguing, slapping and pinching him whenever she accused him of slacking. The man grovelled, promising to do better, and Janis kept having to quash her feelings of pity, reminding herself that he'd paid for exactly this sort of treatment and the worse they bullied him the more he would be satisfied.

To feel his wet tongue on her naked feet was a sensual experience and Janis sat back, revelling in it, as he worked between her toes. Virago now had him by what remained of his hair, jerking his head back painfully every time she accused him of not doing the job thoroughly.

'Are you satisfied, mistress?' she would ask Janis at every turn. And she would answer 'yes' or 'no' as the mood took her, ashamed to find that she was thoroughly enjoying her new power.

Virago could see that Janis was enjoying herself and when Cecil finished both her feet she asked, pointedly, 'Is there anywhere else you would like him to lick you, mistress?'

Janis pulled off the leather pants and exposed her pussy. She was already hot and wet down there, and looking forward to a long and satisfying session of cunnilingus. The man set to work eagerly, despite the tongue fatigue he must be feeling. While he made a thorough job of it Virago whipped him for being a 'naughty boy' and it was obvious that he was in seventh heaven.

The tireless efforts of the man to lick and suck her to orgasm succeeded three times in succession but by then his time was nearly up. As one last humiliation, Virago tore off his mask and made Janis walk all over him in her high-heeled boots.

When Cecil had changed back into his clothes he suddenly became the businessman once more. Janis was astonished at the change in him. He held his head high, looked them in the eye, gave each of them a firm handshake as he thanked them for giving him 'twice the pleasure'. It was the first time he'd had two women working on him at once, but he assured them it wouldn't be the last.

'Success!' Virago grinned, brandishing the wad of notes as soon as she'd closed the door. 'With luck, he'll tell all his friends!'

'Maybe we should have cards printed,' Janis suggested.

'Excellent idea! We're onto a winner here, girl, and no mistake! Best thing is, it's so easy and I really enjoyed it!'

'So did I,' Janis confessed.

And so did Adam, by proxy, when she described the whole episode to him later that night. 'Maybe I should join you,' he suggested. 'We should offer the service to women, too.'

'Hey, that mightn't be a bad idea!'

She put it to the others when they met later that day at rehearsal. Adam had insisted that they should continue to rehearse regularly and not get side-tracked by their new career as dominatrices. They still had a few pub gigs to do, but with the debt to Blade hanging over them their more ambitious plans had had to be curtailed for the time being.

The other girls were in favour of Janis working with Adam. It meant that they could split up easily into two pairs. But Dagmar said, 'If you and Adam are going to offer this service to women, why can't we?'

Everyone thought it a good idea, wondering why they hadn't considered it in the first place. However, when they asked Janis whether she and Adam would take on men as well she laughingly shook her head. 'I'm sure Adam wouldn't stand for that. Still, I'll ask him.'

How things have changed, Janis thought as she went back to their flat. Once she would not have given Adam a second thought, but now she was scared of doing anything without consulting him. Was she afraid of losing him?

Yes, she decided. He was that important to her. Whatever happened with the band she felt emotionally committed to him and nothing would be allowed to interfere with their relationship, not even Eclectic Pussy. At least they now had a joint and equal commitment to the band.

CHAPTER TEN

When Janis told Adam about the suggestion that they should take men as well as women clients, he reacted with caution. 'Let's see how it goes with women-only first, love. I don't think I'm ready to see you bossing another man around. Not if I have to play my part too.'

Adam and Janis decided to rent accommodation for their new venture. They didn't want people coming to their home, which would mean they could never get away from their work. They found a cheap flat which they kitted out with a thick-pile carpet, red velvet curtains and assorted stools, chairs, small tables and a sofa, which they thought would be useful props. On Sal's advice they advertised with cards at lesbian clubs and the more upmarket haunts of career women. It wasn't long before their phone started ringing.

The first time was scary for both of them, despite the fact that they'd already swapped ideas and agreed on the ground rules. The client, who called herself 'Chantal', enquired on the phone whether any lesbian sexual activity could be incorporated. After checking with Adam, Janis agreed. But she was still horribly nervous. She'd never made love to another woman in cold blood, so to speak, and now she was being called on to remain in control of the situation, to pretend she knew exactly what she was doing. It would be quite an ordeal.

The minute she saw the woman, however, Janis realized it was not going to be so bad after all. Chantal was simply gorgeous. Her blonde curls cascaded about her shoulders and her sexy blue eyes glinted mischievously as she entered with a sway of her slim hips. She wore a thin white sweater through which her dark and prominent nipples showed at the tips of two generously proportioned breasts. When Janis looked at Adam he gave her a wink and she knew he fancied Chantal something rotten too.

Once the money was handed over Janis fell into her rôle, demanding that she should strip so they could both get a good look at her. Pretending to be offended, Chantal refused.

'In that case, we shall have to do it for you!' Janis snapped. 'Master, take control of her.'

While Adam held Chantal's arms firmly behind her back, Janis undid her velvet trousers and slid them down over her thighs, exposing the tight white triangle of her lacy panties. She left the trousers hanging about her knees and roughly lifted up her sweater to expose her bosom in the white lace bra.

'We'll teach you to defy us!' Janis muttered, as Adam let go of her arms just long enough to get the jumper over her head. 'Adam, unhook this cheeky hussy's bra!'

He obliged, and the heavy breasts swung free from their confines and hung there provocatively, nipples rearing. Janis longed to touch them. She gave the right tit a sharp slap and watched the taut flesh shudder. It was so satisfying that she repeated it with the other one.

'Now perhaps you will be more obedient,' she said, staring into the girl's insolent blue eyes.

Adam came round to face her, his expression stern. 'Take off your trousers!' he commanded. Slowly Chantal removed her sandals then pulled the trousers off until she stood there naked except for her small panties. 'Those too!' Janis ordered.

Chantal hesitated, but Adam had no hesitation in reaching out and pinching one of her nipples really hard. 'Ouch!' she exclaimed, with real tears smarting in her eyes.

'Do exactly as you're told and you won't get hurt,' he snarled. 'Off with those knickers!'

Pretending to sob, Chantal pulled the scrap of lace down her thighs to reveal a tightly-curled dark blonde muff. When she stepped out of the pants Janis saw the pink pouch of her vulva and the dark slit of her sex and felt a warm rush of excitement. She wanted to take command, to make this sexy, gorgeous female do whatever she wanted, yet the presence of Adam was slightly inhibiting.

It was he who made the next move. He made the girl kneel over a stool and began to smack her beautifully rounded bottom with his bare hand. 'This is to show you that we mean every word we say!' he announced. 'But just to prove that we are not entirely heartless, if you take your punishment well the Mistress will reward you by soothing your aching buttocks with some nice cold cream, won't you, dearest?'

'Oh, yes!'

Janis went over to the dresser where they kept their equipment and took out a jar of cream. She waited for Adam to finish slapping Chantal's behind and then made her lie face down on the sofa with her reddened cheeks uppermost. Adam gave Janis a wink as she settled beside the prone girl and dipped her finger in the pot. Already her own clitoris was throbbing wildly beneath her black lycra catsuit and she suspected that Chantal was equally excited despite her passive pose.

Slowly Janis smoothed the cream into the girl's plump buttocks, making sure she went well into the crack between them. Chantal started to wriggle and moan slightly. Growing bolder, Janis let her finger slip between the parted thighs and found the sodden chasm of her sex already open to her. Slyly

she poked into the warm, slippery entrance to her cunt and felt
the cushioned walls contract eagerly around her finger. But
she knew better than to continue, and withdrew at once.
Titillation was the name of this game and she must play by the
rules.

'That's enough!' Adam's voice barked, breaking the
expectant silence. 'We don't want to spoil her, do we? She's
here to work for us. Up you get now, slave! I have one or two
jobs for you to do.'

They set her to 'work' with a feather duster. As she went
around the room Adam followed, running his finger over the
surfaces she was supposed to have cleaned. He devised a neat
system of reward and punishment. If he found no dust she
would be titillated with a feathery tickle of her nipples or
clitoris, administered by Janis, but if there was the least speck
of dust on his finger she would be thrashed on her naked
bottom with the plastic handle of the duster, carried out by
himself.

The game continued until Janis suspected that Chantal was
bored by it and then she brought in an idea of her own. 'I want
you to pay lip service to my pussy,' she announced. 'Help me
undress.'

The sapphire eyes of the woman gleamed with new interest
as she came forward, her luscious breasts bobbing enticingly.
Janis couldn't resist playing with them as Chantal's fingers
found the hidden fastenings of her catsuit. Although there
was no change to her expression, Chantal's nipples tautened
as they were stimulated and her already large breasts
seemed to swell even more. Janis gave a sigh of relief as
the clinging garment was pulled off her body, leaving her
naked.

'Kneel before me!' she told her, and Chantal obeyed.

Janis spread her legs wide and parted her labia with her
fingers, exposing the red bud of her clitoris. Chantal stared

straight at it, her face slightly flushed. Adam came to stand behind her, naked too now and with his erection at full strength. Janis remembered the threesome with Virago and her lustful feelings intensified.

'Lick me right there!' she said, and the soft, pouting lips approached her tenderest parts.

Slowly Chantal applied her wet tongue to the tip of her clitoris. Janis winced. 'Not there, clumsy creature! You hurt me!'

Adam reached over the woman's shoulders and pinched each of her nipples, hard. She squealed. 'That'll teach you to be rough with the Mistress!' he said. 'Treat her gently, the way she deserves.'

'I'm sorry, Mistress,' Chantal said, hanging her head.

'Maybe she should use her fingers,' Adam suggested. 'She can save her mouth for your breasts.'

'What a good idea,' Janis smiled, seeing an answering glint in Chantal's eye as she raised her head again.

The woman was soon working hard for Janis's pleasure, her fingers deftly working around her clitoris in the way she liked, making her juices stream, and her mouth softly enjoying her breasts in turn, kissing them and licking around the tawny areolas before she took the whole of one pert nipple between her lips and began to suck more strongly. Janis felt the warm bliss coursing through her veins and rocked unsteadily, but soon she felt strong arms supporting her from behind, Adam's arms, as he kissed the back of her neck where she liked it most.

The fierce contractions soon came, bringing voluptuous sweetness in their wake as Janis rode out her orgasmic peaks, one after the other. Through bleary eyes she looked down at Chantal, who had a smug smile of satisfaction on her face.

Afterwards Janis felt self-conscious and silly, quite unable to carry on acting as dominatrix, but Adam stepped into the breach and found Chantal some trivial task to do while Janis recovered on the sofa. The time was nearly up and she watched the other woman's waggling buttocks and swinging breasts as she pretended to polish a small table vigorously. She would have liked to watch Adam take her from behind, but she knew that their client wasn't into men except as slave-masters. Maybe next time he would be lucky.

Chantal left apparently well pleased with her prolonged session but as soon as she had gone Adam leapt on Janis with all his pent-up lust and thrust into her without preliminaries. Once again she felt the build-up to a climax begin, deep inside her still-warm and wet cunt, and the feeling of having him banging into her with unrestrained passion was extremely sexy. His lips greedily sought hers, their tongues duelling for supremacy as he shafted her over and over with increasing speed, the musky scent of him strong in her nostrils.

Janis almost screamed as the first tremors of her orgasm ripped through her body, wild and free, taking her up into an orgiastic sunburst of pure self-indulgent pleasure. She could feel Adam coming too, spraying her inside, voiding himself of every lingering drop of liquid fire as he kept on thrusting, thrusting, thrusting until he was totally spent.

They lay exhausted on the sofa for a while then looked into each other's eyes and began to giggle. Janis said, 'Well, I don't know what this evening has done for Chantal's love-life, but it's certainly given a hell of a boost to ours!'

Over the next few weeks the sexual subjugation business threatened to take over from the music as both Janis and the rest of the band reported an unending stream of clients. They were making money hand over fist, even after allowing for expenses. The trouble was they had no more gigs booked, and the rehearsals that Adam insisted they kept holding were turning into lacklustre affairs.

'Look, just when are we going to get another gig?' Dagmar demanded at last.

Janis shrugged. 'Adam's trying as hard as he can. But none of the places that we played before will have us back.'

'I don't understand that,' Virago frowned. 'We packed those pubs, the enthusiasm was fantastic. What's going on?'

'Maybe we were just a bit too successful,' Lee suggested. 'You know how Adam had to hire extra bouncers. Maybe the management got cold feet, afraid of a riot or something.'

'Then he should be looking to bigger venues,' Sal said. 'He's not much of a manager if he can't get us any gigs, is he?'

Janis duly reported the general feeling to Adam, who looked fed up. 'It's not as if I'm not trying. You've seen me, love, on the phone for hours on end several times a day. The extra money we're earning at this domination lark is going to end up subsidizing our phone bill.'

'What are they saying then, that we're no good?'

'No one's saying that. I have the feeling I'm getting the run-around, to be honest. It's a case of "We're fully booked at present" or "We'll give you a ring if we get a vacancy," all that kind of stuff. It's weird.'

Janis stared at him, saw him get the same idea at the same time as her. Together they groaned, 'Blade!'

Was that possible? Could he, or someone acting on his behalf, really be blocking them?

'It's perfectly possible,' Adam said, grimly. 'In fact, it's highly likely. Now we have two options. We can fight it, or we can scrub round to find venues outside his sphere of influence.'

'New venues might be best. After all, we have revamped our image, what with the sub-dom theme and Virago's new persona. I'd go for a different circuit. We said we always wanted to go more mainstream and not rely on the gay scene entirely.'

'Good! My own thinking exactly. I'll have a rethink and then we should get some new handouts and demos done.'

By the time they got home that night Janis was confident that they had started to overcome the dirty tricks that Blade and his gang had probably been up to. She rang Virago about it next day and the star exploded on the other end of the line. 'The fucking bastard! I knew he wouldn't be satisfied with his pound of flesh, he'd have to go the whole hog!'

Janis did her best to reassure her that Blade wouldn't win, that they'd overcome all opposition in the end. And their new tactics seemed to pay off. Soon Adam reported that a trendy venue in North London, The Cage, had agreed to a date in a month's time.

'It's not much, but it's a start,' he smiled. 'And don't forget I'm still working on the big boys. I had a drink with Gerry, Ivan Craig's assistant, the other day and I think I'm worming my way in there. But it's softly, softly with him. I don't want to wreck our chances by being too pushy.'

But then something even more disturbing started to happen.

Janis turned up to rehearsal one day and found the other girls acting jittery. When she asked what was the matter Virago told her she'd been receiving threatening phone calls.

'And that's not all. We've been getting some pretty peculiar clients, too. They sound OK on the phone, but when they arrive they seem like thugs. They come on all stroppy when we try to tell them what to do and one or two have actually become violent.'

'You don't think it could be Blade behind it again, do you?'

Virago glowered. 'I wouldn't put anything past that man. Not with Gore egging him on.'

Janis frowned. 'Tell you what, why don't I join you next time? With three of us they won't be so inclined to cut up rough.'

Virago was doubtful but Lee and Dagmar thought it was a good idea. It was their turn that night and they accepted with enthusiasm Janis's offer to join them. She rang Adam, not wanting to go home again in between times, and he was encouraging.

'If you can defeat those buggers it might persuade them to stop pestering the girls. But do take care, won't you, love? Above all, if he has any kind of weapon . . .'

'Don't worry, we'll have the others waiting in the next room. With five women against one man he wouldn't stand a chance. And we'll make sure we get him shackled or manacled, or both, at the first opportunity.'

Janis found she was looking forward to it. Although the sessions with Adam had been exciting in themselves, and had led to some even more exciting love-making afterwards, she missed the all-woman camaraderie of the band now they only met at rehearsals twice a week.

The man who had booked for that night was called 'Derek'. Virago was sure he was another of Blade's henchmen, if that was what they were, because of his gruff voice and uncertain tone. 'I can tell them from the genuine clients by the way they keep asking questions,' she explained. 'Most of the regulars already know the score.'

By eight o'clock Janis was waiting with Lee and Dagmar. They had planned a few strategies, but in case they didn't work the others were listening in next door, ready to burst in if it sounded as if the situation was getting out of hand. The doorbell went and Dagmar answered it, showing a balding middle-aged man into the flat.

'We hope you don't mind having three of us tonight,' she said. Derek's brown eyes darted suspiciously from one face to the other, but he grunted his assent. 'It's just that Janis is new to the work and could do with some practice,' Dagmar continued, conversationally.

Money changed hands and when Dagmar had flicked through it she nodded. Right on cue Lee came forward, brandishing a pair of handcuffs. But Derek scowled. 'I'm not having those on. No bondage, OK? I said that on the phone.'

'All right,' Dagmar agreed, smoothly. 'But you'd better behave yourself.'

'That's what I'm here for, innit?'

Something about the man's uneasy manner confirmed that he was unused to this scene. Lee gave Janis a wink and said, 'Take off your shoes, then.'

'No, I'm not taking nothing off. I said on the phone no bondage, no nudity. Course, I've got no objection if one of you lovely ladies wants to take yer clothes off!'

'Insolent swine!' Dagmar shouted, cuffing him. He grimaced and looked like he was going to hit back, but then thought better of it.

'Get down on all fours, like a dog!' Lee commanded him, and he obeyed. 'Now crawl over to that vase of flowers and drink the water from it. Every last drop!'

Janis felt sick at the thought. She hated the smell of rotting foliage. Derek hesitated, but was obviously unwilling to blow his cover so early in the game. She guessed he would be well paid for this assignment. He shuffled towards the low table where the vase of carnations stood and put the glass vessel to his lips while Lee stood over him. He belched and gurgled his way through it, a look of disgust on his face.

'That's better!' Lee declared. 'Now we know you are prepared to do as we ask of you. Goodness, it's getting hot in

here. Remove my clothes, will you? And mind you don't
pull my hair or pinch me or anything. I shall tell my friends if
you do and they will be very angry indeed, do you
understand?'

'Yes,' he said, meekly.

'Yes, *Mistress*! You will address each one of us as Mistress
while you are in our domain. Is that clear?'

'Yes, Mistress.'

'Right, then. Start with my boots and work your way up.'

Janis and Dagmar watched as he carefully pulled off the
tall, brown leather boots and then unfastened the black
stockings from their suspenders. Janis wanted to laugh and
didn't dare look at Dagmar in case she lost control of herself.
But just as she was in danger of issuing a spluttering giggle the
man made a mistake.

'How dare you!' Lee crowed. 'Incompetent fool! You've
snagged one of my best stockings. Punish him, darlings, both
of you!'

Given something to do at last, Janis gave him several hearty
whacks on the bare backside as he lay across Dagmar's lap
with his trousers down. He was more careful after that,
undoing all the zips and buttons with exaggerated caution until
Lee was stark naked.

'Good. Now I want you to breathe on my breasts, good and
hard!'

'*Breathe* on you, Mistress?'

'How dare you question my orders!' Lee snapped, and
slapped him across the cheek. Janis saw him flinch and knew
that he was growing vengeful. But still the charade must
continue.

They watched Derek exhaling vigorously over Lee's small
tits, fanning the pale pink nipples, and again the urge to laugh
came over Janis and Dagmar. Sensing that her two companions
were finding it hard to keep a straight face, Lee told him,

'Enough of that. There are two more mistresses to be served. Come here, Dagmar darling, and let this worm have the honour of divesting you of your garments. I feel like cuddling your gorgeous naked body.'

Dagmar was wearing a multi-buckled, all-in-one black leather catsuit, and it was amusing to watch the man trying to figure out how the thing was fastened. He fumbled with a seemingly endless array of buckles and zippers until strips of her pale skin were exposed all over her body. The sight was quite erotic, and Janis found herself becoming intrigued by what Lee and Dagmar got up to in their spare time. The pair had become passionately involved with each other since they'd been in the band.

At last both of the lesbians were stark naked, and to Janis's surprise Lee told Derek to lie face down on the floor. She then lay on top of him, back to back, and looked up with a grin.

'He makes quite a nice, comfy bed,' she said. 'Come and join me, Dagmar darling. Kiss my pussy, there's a dear, but be careful you don't end up kissing that ratbag's arse!'

The girls dissolved into peals of laughter, but Janis couldn't help feeling like a gooseberry as she saw the two of them clambering onto Derek's prone body. He groaned as the air was pumped out of his lungs by the double load, but did not attempt to push them off. Janis went to kneel at his feet and experimentally tickled them. He groaned louder and kicked a little, so she slapped the soles of his feet quite hard and he stopped.

From her vantage point she could clearly see the wide open chasm of Lee's cunny and the tight pink rose of Dagmar's arse. She was very tempted to join in their erotic play but was afraid of intruding, so she decided to bide her time and await her cue. While Dagmar sucked noisily at her lover's juicy quim, Janis had to content herself with tickling the soles of Derek's feet intermittently but now he steeled himself to remain immobile.

Then came the words she'd been longing for. 'Come and join us, mistress! There's room for one more on top!'

Smiling, Janis accepted Lee's invitation and added her body to the weight. She felt Derek sink further into the floor with a groan as she sat astride him right behind Lee, with her arms around her, and found the hard points of her breasts with her fingers. 'Mm, that's good!' Lee murmured. 'Pull those nipples for me, that'll get me off quick!'

Janis looked down at where Dagmar was still nose-deep in Lee's pussy, looking as if she had a hairy black moustache. Her own clitoris was throbbing clamorously so she began to slide back and forth along Derek's back, grasping more and more fiercely at Lee's small breasts. She heard the other woman's climax arrive, in a series of moans and groans accompanied by much wild thrashing around, until she tumbled right off Derek's back.

Dagmar, dazed and with her lips glistening with love-juice, looked up and caught Janis's eye. She smiled and wriggled up over Derek's fat bottom until her mouth was at crotch level, then continued her cunnilingus almost without a break. Gratified, Janis leaned back and let the expert tongue work its way around all her grooves until her clitoris was throbbing wildly and she knew she was on the point of coming. Another pair of hot, relentless lips fastened on her left breast: Lee had returned, to join in the fun. The extra stimulation tipped her over into a gushing orgasm that propelled her off Derek's back and onto the carpet in her extremity of excitement, rolling over and over as the delicious spasms racked her through and through.

The three women had all but forgotten about Derek, who was still lying there like a corpse. Lee went over and gave him a hefty kick with her bare foot. 'Turn over, worm!'

But the worm had, indeed, turned. The look on Derek's face was terrifying as he glared up at them, 'Dirty bitches, all of you!' he snarled, leaping to his feet with surprising energy. Since they were all thoroughly knackered by their exertions it didn't take much to overpower them. They fell to the ground like ninepins and Derek proceeded to dole out the same treatment he'd received, kicking out at them viciously. The crucial difference was, he was wearing industrial-weight Doc Martens.

Janis was completely winded by the first kick which took her completely by surprise. Too weak to stand she tried to roll away from him, but he caught her again on the left buttock. Their screams attracted the others who burst in from the adjacent room, taking Derek by surprise, and in a matter of seconds he was overpowered, much to Janis's relief.

Once again Derek was biting the dust, with his hands tied behind his back and two women pinning him down. 'Get the canister!' Virago hissed. Evidently they'd been cooking something up in the other room. Sal returned with a can of blue vehicle paint and proceeded to spray his backside with relish.

'Here, let me have a go!' Virago grinned, seizing the spray-can from her.

When all five of them had vented their spleen on Derek's buttocks they 'breathed' on him to dry him off then untied his hands. He rose with a sullen snarl, only vaguely aware of what had been going on as the girls hooted with laughter. Virago brought a small mirror out of the bedroom and showed him her handiwork.

'There! Take your arse back to whoever told you to come here tonight and tell them not to fuck with us again!'

'No one sent me!' he bleated feebly, but when Lee brandished the paint at him he hastily pulled up his trousers and staggered towards the door. The laughter echoed down the corridor as he disappeared into the night rubbing his sticky bottom.

'Oh God, I nearly died laughing!' Sal declared, flopping onto the sofa alongside Dagmar.

'Me too!' Janis grinned. 'But do you think it really was Blade who sent him?'

Virago's face turned suddenly cold. 'If it was, this is outright fucking WAR!'

CHAPTER ELEVEN

The money was piling up very nicely in the band's bank account. The only trouble was, it wasn't coming from gigs. Although Adam had managed to get them a couple of bookings in December they were not very well paid and it was hardly the meteoric rise to fame and fortune they'd all been expecting.

To make matters worse, a snide article had appeared in a major music magazine claiming that Virgo was finished on the rock scene now that she'd split from Blade. There were scathing references to her 'cobbling together a motley crew of assorted dykes calling themselves Electric Pussy' (*sic*). A review of one of their early gigs said they'd 'tried to make up in sex appeal for what they lack in musicianship, but they failed miserably in both areas.'

Adam was sure that Blade had influenced the journalist, whom he described as 'anybody's for the price of a pint'. It was sickening, but there was nothing they could do about it. A glowing review in *Lesbian and Gay News* was small consolation. The girls felt angry and frustrated, and Janis was afraid they'd eventually take it out on Adam. She knew he was doing his best against the odds, but would they believe it? Although they had all enjoyed playing the domination game at the beginning the novelty was wearing off, and they were starting to mutter that this was not what they had expected to be doing when they joined Eclectic Pussy

But then Adam came up with something that silenced all complaints. He'd managed to get Ivan Craig interested. His patient courting of the great man's assistant had finally paid off, and Craig was considering them for the prestigious Bollox label. Adam had managed to arrange a meeting with him for the following Monday.

'Don't count your chickens,' he warned the girls, when the euphoria had died down. 'He likes to make out he calls the shots at Salamander but he still has to get the approval of the board. Even so he has considerable clout, so don't try and be clever with him, OK?'

Adam was addressing his words to Virago, since she would be the spokesperson for the band. She nodded, impatiently. 'Give me credit for knowing how to deal with these jerks, Adam. I have been in the business a while, you know.'

'Sure. Anyway, I'll be on hand to smooth over any ripples. Just make sure you're all looking your sparkling best at nine-thirty on Monday, OK?'

There was a groan from the girls, most of whom seldom got up before ten. Adam said, 'One more thing. Ivan Craig has a bit of reputation for . . . well, for demanding payment in kind, if you know what I mean.'

'Casting couch stuff, is that it?' Virago grinned. She looked round at the others. 'I think we can handle that after all we've been through these past few months, eh, girls?'

Dagmar shrugged. 'Whatever it takes, boss!'

'Does that go for the rest of you?' They all nodded. 'I'm glad you agree. Don't worry, Adam, we'll make the old fart feel like a million dollars – as long as we get a million back.'

They all laughed, but Janis felt uneasy. Maybe she was just picking up on Adam's nerves. Or did he know something about this character that he wasn't letting on?

Later, when they were alone, he confided in her. 'We're

unlikely to get such a good break as this again, love. I just hope we don't blow it, that's all.'

'What can go wrong? We can only do our best.'

'It's not the music I'm worried about, or the band's image. It's more of a personality thing. Ivan likes people who do as they're told. I'm afraid Virago will come over as too stroppy. She already has a reputation as being difficult. If Ivan dislikes her he won't take the band on.'

'Would you like me to have a word with her?'

'No, that might make things worse. We'll just have to hope she has the good sense to tone down her remarks when it comes to it. I'll do my best . . .'

'I will, too. Oh Adam, wouldn't it be absolutely fantastic if he signs us up?'

Adam grinned. 'Best thing is, it would make Blade sick as a parrot!'

The offices of Salamander Records were on the fourth floor of a new building in Docklands, not far from Virago's flat. Every suite was devoted to one of the labels and Bollox was the largest, with a fine view of the Thames. A receptionist with cropped blonde hair, oozing street cred from every pore, asked them all to wait in a room whose walls were covered with gold and silver discs, press cuttings and photographs. Janis tried to envisage Eclectic Pussy amongst them.

After waiting for nearly twenty minutes, they were finally shown into Ivan Craig's office. In the middle of a sea of pink carpet was a sleek black desk, with a stainless steel and leather chair behind it. A semicircle of similar chairs had been set out in front – precisely the right number, Janis noted. Craig was evidently a man who liked things just so.

'Good morning ladies, Adam,' he smiled, from behind the smoke-screen given off by a slim cigar.

Janis surveyed the man who held their fate in the balance. Thinning ginger hair, thick sandy beard and vivid blue eyes gave him a 'Van Gogh' look, and she noticed that every one of his fat fingers was loaded with rings. He wore a black T-shirt and jeans with expensive trainers, and his voice was deceptively mild and pleasant. Deceptive, Janis decided, because of the steely look in those eyes and the obstinate set to those broad shoulders.

'I've listened to your track, and I like it,' he went on, flicking ash onto the carpet with a nonchalant air. 'I've also seen the video Adam made of your act which, I must say, leaves a lot to be desired.'

Janis felt her spirits sink. She looked at Virago, whose lips were clenched tight as if she were willing herself to remain silent. Ivan Craig rose from his chair with a deliberate air and walked round to the front of his desk, observing them all more closely.

'However, I think you show promise. Your style could be revamped, your image moulded. You have talent, you have looks. But, girls . . .' he threw up one disparaging hand. 'Eclectic Pussy! Let's put the name on hold for a while, shall we? Right now I need to see you perform.'

The girls looked nervous. No one had expected to be put on the spot like that. Adam said, 'It's all right, girls. I've had your instruments brought and set up in the room next door. Shall we go through?'

A huge door slid to one side revealing a kind of studio, with their guitars awaiting them on stands before microphones and the drum kit set up on a dais at the back. Even Janis was flabbergasted. She knew why Adam had kept this to himself: he hadn't wanted them to get too anxious, or to over-rehearse. The instruments had been left in the hired van after Saturday's gig, and no one had questioned it when he'd offered to keep them secure until their rehearsal on Tuesday.

For once Adam had shown himself to be quite devious. *Maybe he does have the guts to be a good manager after all,*

Janis thought with a smile as she strapped on her Tele.

'Now I realize this has been sprung on you,' Ivan smiled, his eyes winking coldly at them. 'But I needed to feel the raw energy of your performance and I don't have the time, or the inclination, to stand around in grotty pubs like the rest of the fellas.'

Janis saw that Virago was inwardly seething, but fortunately she was still containing her emotions. Adam stepped into the breach, taking control of the proceedings with surprising ease. 'I suggest you play that medley you did on Saturday night, "Spiderwoman" followed by "Sweet Skin" and "Invitation". When you're ready, girls.'

They sounded really wobbly at first, until they got used to the idea of playing for real at eleven in the morning. Virago warmed up a treat after the first minute or so, and Ivan never once took his beady blue eyes off her. The music started to sound great in that room, which had, obviously, been designed for good acoustics.

When the last clanging chord had died away there was silence. Ivan took the cigar stub from his mouth and tossed it into an aluminium waste bin, then turned abruptly and marched back into his office. The girls looked at each other in dismay. Had they really been that bad?

'Come on,' Adam urged them. 'Ivan wants to talk to you.'

Once again they were ranged on the chairs opposite his desk and Ivan looked at each of them in turn, his face giving nothing away. Then he nodded, slowly and deliberately.

'I think you might just be worth the gamble,' he said. 'But I need to be sure that each one of you is one hundred per cent committed to the band, to Salamander, and to me. That is why I intend to interview you individually, starting with Miss Virago, as I think she now likes to be called. The rest of you can wait outside, where coffee will be served.'

Uncertain whether to be pleased or worried, everyone

except Virago rose and left the room. In the waiting room
Adam did his best to be optimistic. He looked at his watch.
'We've already taken up half an hour of Mr Craig's valuable
time,' he pointed out. 'And he seems prepared to give us even
more of it. We've got to be in with a chance.'

But everyone was wondering just what was going on behind
those closed doors. Ten minutes went by, then fifteen, then
twenty, and still Virago had not appeared. Then, when almost
half an hour had elapsed, she emerged looking flushed and
amused.

'Next!' she winked. 'I think it had better be you, Jan.'

Nervously, Janis rose and went in through the open door.
She was surprised to see that Ivan had changed into a black
towelling robe and beads of sweat stood out on his brow.
Remembering what Adam had said about the man wanting
payment in kind, she felt a faint tremor of anticipation in the
depths of her body.

'Ah, Janis, isn't it? Shall we go through into the next room,
dear?'

His unctuous tones nauseated her. Nevertheless she followed
him through the door as he slid it open, and immediately
uttered a gasp. There was now no sign of the instruments they
had played. The room had been transformed by invisible hands
into a kind of boudoir with a huge black leather sofa bed
spread with cushions, a shower unit that Janis realized had
been screened off before, and a magnum of champagne. Ivan
poured her a glass straight away.

'Now I'm going to lie here and watch while you strip for
me, darling,' he told her.

Janis flinched. She'd never come across such a blatant abuse
of power before. Yet she understood perfectly well that every
member of the band would have to go through this test. If only
one of them demurred Eclectic Pussy wouldn't stand a chance
in hell with Ivan Craig.

It's only the same as we've already been doing for money, Janis told herself, taking up a seductive pose. But somehow it didn't feel like that. It felt dirtier, more corrupt. She pushed aside the feelings of revulsion and imagined she was dancing to one of Virago's tunes, smiling archly at Ivan as he lounged on the bed, wiggling her tits and bottom at him as she slowly revolved.

'Cut the ballet, sweetheart, I want to see that gorgeous body of yours.'

Janis was wearing a skin-tight silver lurex cropped top and black vinyl hot pants with spangly tights and high-heeled pumps. Slowly, she rolled up her top to reveal her black bra. Ivan's beady eyes gleamed even more salaciously at her as she unfastened it behind her back. Her tits were now hanging loose, and as she lifted her arms to take the top right off she felt them slip down beneath the bra-cups so that her nipples were barely covered.

With a deft gesture she removed the garment entirely, feeling her nipples start to firm up on exposure to the air. She had to force herself to look at Ivan, whose hefty erection was now obvious beneath the black robe. He was staring greedily at her, as if he were running through a mental menu of things he might do to her, or get her to do for him. She found it unnerving.

Slowly Janis undid the zipper of her hot pants and pulled them down over her hips. She stepped out of them and began to roll down her tights from the waist, showing her black lacy briefs. She stepped out of her shoes, removed the tights, then turned her back on the lecherous figure on the bed so that he could glimpse her buttocks through the see-through lace of her panties. At any moment she expected him to come and grab her tits or her arse, but he did no such thing. The ball was definitely in her court – for the time being.

Gradually, and with much wiggling of her hips, Janis pulled

the knickers down her legs and showed him her bare backside. When she was completely naked she raised her arms above her head, with her black pants still in her hands, swaying to inaudible music. On impulse she tossed the garment over her shoulder, high into the air before, very slowly, turning round.

Ivan had caught the scrap of lace and was holding it to his face, eyes closed, sniffing the faint odour of her sex which lingered in the material. He opened his eyes and saw her posing: breasts full and taut, tipped with their ruddy, aroused nipples; dark brown hairy delta, still matted from the close-fitting panties; thighs crossed to guard her secret, the hidden cleft where, despite herself, Janis could feel the juices silently flooding grooves and folds.

'Delicious!' she heard him murmur, before throwing the panties aside. With his eyes fixed on her body, Ivan untied his robe and revealed the full extent of his arousal. Like some exotic fungus his prick stood thick and white and tall, capped by a violet-coloured glans. Janis shuddered. What would he want her to do now?

'Come here,' he cooed, half inviting and half commanding her. She obeyed without demur, feeling her breasts jiggle in front of her as she crossed the carpeted space between them. Soon Ivan was gazing up at her, a rapt smile on his face and his hand at the root of his thick stalk.

'Do you like giving head?' he asked.

Janis nodded, slipping into her rôle as prostitute without hesitation. 'Yes, I do. Especially when the man has a lovely big one that fills my mouth right up.'

'Good girl!' he smiled, his eyes gleaming with anticipation. 'Kneel down, then, and see what you can do with mine.'

She fell to her knees on the bed, with her breasts resting on Ivan's chubby thighs. They felt slightly clammy. He lay back with his hands behind his head while she bent her mouth to the task, licking the tip of his sticky glans with her tongue and letting her fingers creep along his thigh towards his balls. Ivan uttered a low moan and a sigh. Janis knew she had to give the performance of a lifetime, not just for her own sake but for the sake of all of them in the band. The main thing was not to hurry the proceedings. Slowly she licked down the bulbous head and on down the shaft, lightly still, taking her time. Her tongue reached his scrotum, probing the loose skin of his sac to feel the loose balls within. He groaned loudly and rubbed his thighs restlessly against her pendant breasts.

Delicately Janis caressed his bollocks while she licked up and down his shaft, feeling the veined ridges as she tongued him. It didn't take her long to realize that his cock was too big to fit into her mouth. She managed to slide her lips over his glans, but that was all. Slowly she circled her tongue around the salt-tasting tip while she encircled the straining shaft with her hand and rubbed gently. The penis thrust against the roof of her mouth, making her gag, but she continued to stroke him with her hand while she licked along the tiny groove in the top.

Realizing that he needed more thrills, Janis moved up until her breasts hung over his erection and she squeezed them together with his prick in between, lowering her head so that she could maintain mouth contact with his glans. From the accelerated moans that issued from Ivan's mouth she gathered that he regarded this as an improvement. Making sure her boobs had his meaty shaft in a tight embrace, she used them to massage him while she flicked her tongue back and forth over the tip, tasting more and more of the milky juices that were oozing out.

Janis was getting aroused herself and her fingers caught hold of her enlarged nipples while she used her palms to press her breasts into a cleavage. The sight and feel of that enormous dick was turning her on, although she wondered how she could possibly accommodate such a huge penis. Involuntary moans and sighs were issuing from her lips now as she gave Ivan's erection the maximum friction. She was sure he was going to come very soon, spurting all over her tits and making her all wet and sticky. The thought of that excited her even more.

By now she was rubbing her Venus mount against his legs, trying to gain some stimulation herself to ease the throbbing ache in her pussy. It didn't take Ivan long to catch on. He made her turn around so that he could reach her nether end and, as she continued to suck his cock and rub it between her breasts, he thrust his fingers into her with both hands, back and front. Janis gasped with the shock of having both orifices filled at once, but she soon relaxed her sphincter as she got used to the idea. While she squeezed her own nipples and tasted the musky flavour of his juices he was making her cunt flow copiously, thrusting in and out of her with his bunched fingers and giving her love-button the longed-for attention it craved.

Within a minute she was coming, clenching tightly with both her vagina and anus as the spasming pleasure went on and on, filling her with complete satisfaction. Evidently Ivan found the experience of fingering her tight little arse and well-lubricated quim most arousing too, because just as her intense climax began to dwindle his began, shooting hot spunk into her mouth and down her chin from where it oozed onto her firm breasts.

Immediately afterwards Janis collapsed onto the bed, oblivious of where she was and who she was with. Her whole body was vibrating with pleasure, and she was only dimly aware of the hand that was stroking her breasts to prolong the warm bliss. After a while, though, she remembered what this was all about and opened her eyes to see Ivan staring down at her with a faintly sardonic smile on his face.

'There, that wasn't so bad now, was it?' he purred. 'Uncle Ivan likes to make sure his handmaidens are happy, too. Why don't you toddle over to that shower and freshen up while I call in the next willing victim?'

Janis did as she was told, glad to feel the warm water flush over her sticky body. Through the shower curtain she could see another member of the band entering, and soon realized that it was Dagmar. She couldn't help smiling at the thought of that lesbian being forced to service the insatiable Ivan. Just what would he get her to do for him? Lingering in the cubicle, Janis eavesdropped on their conversation.

'So, you prefer women do you?' she heard Ivan say, his tone disapproving. 'Well, that's all right, because I do too.'

Janis heard him give a deep, raucous laugh and she could only guess at how Dagmar must be feeling. His next words astonished her. 'I can tell you like to be in charge, don't you? Would you like to take charge of me? If I'm a naughty boy I'll let you spank me. How does that sound – is it fair?'

'Perfectly fair,' Dagmar answered.

'Good. Take a look in that cupboard, then. You might find some of the things useful.'

Janis couldn't resist peeping out between the shower curtains. She let the water continue to rain down, keeping up the pretence that she was still washing herself, but she was far more interested in the proceedings in the room. Dagmar had removed a supple cane from the cupboard and was swishing it forcefully in the air while Ivan watched her cunningly, his robe wrapped around him. It was a familiar scenario.

Dagmar drew herself up and said, in an imperious voice, 'Come on then, naughty boy, let me see you touch your toes.'

'Shan't!' Ivan grinned.

'What? Are you defying me?' Dagmar took a menacing step forward. 'I said, bend over and touch your toes.'

'Don't want to!'

'Then I'll make you want to.' She held out the pointed end of the thin cane and lifted up a flap of Ivan's robe to reveal his erection. It had grown strong again, no doubt excited by the prospect of more stimulation. 'What a dirty boy you are! I've met your sort before, always playing with yourself. You are sorely in need of correction. Now on your feet and bend over!'

Ivan shook his head, staring at her wilfully. Janis wondered what she would do next. She watched as Dagmar brought the cane down sharply on the soles of his feet, making him wince. He started to blubber like a schoolboy.

'That was just a taste of things to come!' she told him. 'Now if you'll do as I ask you will get six of the best on your bare bottom followed by a nice soothing rub down. But if you continue to be obstinate I shall have to thrash you harder and longer, and there will be no nice massage afterwards. The choice is yours.'

Sullenly Ivan rose from the couch and stood on the carpet in front of her. He lifted up his gown to waist height and bent over, exposing his large, pale buttocks. Dagmar raised her arm and the cane came swishing down. Ivan's bottom wobbled on impact. He groaned and she repeated the action, making his bum cheeks flush bright pink. She lifted the switch a third time, getting up a rhythm.

Dagmar was smiling and Janis guessed that she was thoroughly enjoying herself She had entered the room not knowing what to expect, fearing some sexual humiliation at the hands of this powerful man. Instead, to her obvious relief, she was being allowed to do something she relished: administering punishment to a man. She continued with gusto until the pale cheeks were criss-crossed with red marks. Then she stood aside, panting with exertion.

'Now lie face down on the bed!' she commanded him.

He did as he was told. Dagmar took some massage oil that she'd found in the drawer and approached the bed. Soon she was smoothing it into his smarting behind and, from her vantage point behind the curtain, Janis could see that she was working the exotically scented oil well into his arse-crack, making him moan and wriggle on the bed. She was anointing his balls too, which soon appeared sleek and shiny as they peeped though his outspread thighs.

With Dagmar fully occupied and Ivan lying prone, Janis decided it was time to make a quick exit. She turned off the shower and towelled herself down, then grabbed her clothes and tiptoed towards the door. The others were awaiting her on the other side, agog with curiosity, and Janis began to describe what had gone on in there.

As the morning went on each girl had her 'private audience' with Ivan Craig, and by lunchtime he pronounced himself well pleased with the band. He'd already got the go-ahead from the board, who had said they would trust his judgement on this one. With five major hits in the current Rock charts they could afford to take a few risks.

Ivan told them he would advance them the money to make an album and a video, but the cash would have to be recouped before they earned any royalties. The faces of the girls fell. After all their hard work they had expected something more promising, but Adam said it was a generous offer. Many producers these days required their bands to finance their own recordings by taking out bank loans, if necessary.

'And you can be sure that when I take a band on it goes into profit pretty soon,' Ivan added, smugly. 'You'll earn back your advance, girls, don't you worry. But . . .' He paused, his expression growing stern. 'You must all agree to do *exactly* as I say.'

Virago opened her mouth but a look from Adam silenced her. 'Of course they will, Mr Craig, you have my personal guarantee on that. No one knows how to make a sure-fire hit like you. We are privileged to have the benefit of your wide experience in the rock industry.'

'Yes, you are!' Ivan beamed, his ego suitably massaged.

Once they were safely away from the offices of Salamander Records, however, the girls burst into helpless laughter.

'What a *jerk*!' Sal exclaimed. 'Do you know what he made me do? I had to wank in front of him while he pulled his disgusting prick. At least he didn't stick it in me, thank goodness!'

'Well, I did warn you,' Adam said. 'And fortunately all your noble efforts proved not to be in vain!' He waved a thick sheaf of papers at them. 'One contract, ladies! To be gone through with a fine-tooth comb then signed by all parties. I'll get a lawyer I know to look over the fine print. And we'll need a producer. I recommend Karl Yates. He's one of the best in the business – as long as you keep him well supplied with his favourite drug.'

'What you have to go through to succeed!' Virago sighed. 'Then there's the little question of what we're going to call ourselves. Do we decide that, or does Karl?'

'It'll probably be down to Ivan in the end,' Adam admitted. 'But there's no harm us making some suggestions. Now, how about nipping into this pub for a bite and a celebratory tipple?'

The pub turned out to be a rather good one. They had a merry afternoon with a couple of bottles of champagne and some delectable seafood, then made their way to their respective homes. But after all the excitement, and with the effect of the bubbly wearing off, Janis found herself in a more sober mood as they drew up outside the flat. Adam put his arm around her and gave her a kiss.

'Cheer up, darling. Anyone would think you're about to sign your death warrant instead of a contract with one of the top names in the business!'

She smiled ruefully at him. 'I'm sorry. I know how hard you've worked for this, Adam. But I have the weirdest feeling that it's all going to go wrong.'

'What could possibly go wrong? Don't be such a wet blanket, Janis.'

Yet the mood persisted through the days that followed.

Maybe it was just superstition, or a feeling that they somehow didn't deserve their good fortune. Perhaps it was the sordid way they had acquired the contract. Whatever it was that was bugging her Janis kept it to herself, not wanting to upset Adam and the other girls.

The band performed twice more on the London pub circuit as Eclectic Pussy, then they began discussing their new image with Karl, the producer. He wanted a more heavy-metal feel to the music, and more subtlety to the lyrics. They were all encouraged to write material, and he said he would use any that fitted the new image. Janis and Adam collaborated on one song, called 'Storm in your Eyes', and were delighted when it met with Karl's approval. That meant they would eventually get songwriters' royalties as well which, as Adam explained, could be worth a lot more long term.

Everything seemed to be going well. After an intensive two weeks in a rehearsal studio, flogging their guts out every day, both Karl and Ivan pronounced them up to scratch and able to travel down to Dorset for two weeks of recording in the state-of-the-art studios owned by one of Salamander's top bands.

So why, Janis wondered on the eve of travelling down to the sticks, did she still feel so weird about it? There had been a sick feeling in the pit of her stomach for weeks, but there was no rational explanation for it. Maybe Adam had been right with his diagnosis, and it was just nerves. There was a heck of a lot riding on this album and, with the exception of Virago, they were not exactly the most experienced of bands. Whatever faith Karl and Ivan had in them must still be justified by some excellent tracks, the kind that would catapult them up into the 'Rock Newcomers' slot on Dave Garrett's famous radio programme, or earn them some brownie points in the music press. Adam had promised to do his best there but he wasn't the only music hack in the business and once his involvement with the band became public knowledge he could hardly write glowing reports of them, not even under a pen-name.

No, Janis told herself, in the last resort everything rested on the efforts of the band. She was just praying that she herself would be good enough, and would not let the others down.

CHAPTER TWELVE

Since the recording and video were being funded by Salamander, Adam suggested that they should spend some of their hard-earned dosh on a new van in which to travel down to Dorset. Janis was excited at the prospect of working in a top-notch recording studio, but she was still feeling nervous. As they all piled their instruments into the back of the van she felt a sense of foreboding that would not go away.

'Cheer up, love,' Adam whispered, as she climbed into the seat beside him. 'This is going to be great!'

The girls began the journey in high spirits, singing some of the new songs as they bowled down the M3. They stopped at a motorway services and gorged themselves on coffee and sticky buns. Janis looked round at the circle of happy, excited faces and wished she didn't feel such a killjoy. Why couldn't she just be optimistic like the rest of them?

North of Winchester it began to rain and the road became dark and slick. Janis stared through the windscreen, half mesmerized by the hypnotic swish-swish of the wipers as they sped along. Suddenly there was a thud on the driver's side of the car. There was a jolt and then they swerved to the left. Adam cursed, but before Janis realized what was happening they were careering right out of the middle lane and into the path of the traffic in the slow lane. There was a blaring of horns and a squealing of brakes. Something just nudged the back bumper and they were swerving again, this time onto the grass verge. It all happened so rapidly that there was no sound from the girls until the van was bumping wildly over uneven ground and slowing to a halt.

'Shit! Stupid fucker!' Adam exclaimed, pulling hard on the hand brake. The van jerked unsteadily to a halt. 'He might have got us all killed!'

'What happened?' Janis asked, her voice barely audible. There were squeals from the back and someone was sobbing.

'Someone fucking pranged us, that's what. There was no need for it. He was in the fast lane, must have come too close or something. I really don't know why it happened. There was no excuse for it, none at all. Must have been some kind of maniac.'

'Maybe he fell asleep at the wheel,' Sal suggested.

Adam unbuckled his belt and went out to inspect the damage, returning after a few seconds grim-faced. 'Well, we've got a dent in the side and one of the tyres has blown. Could have been worse, I suppose. But we have to change the front wheel.'

While he and Lee got the wheel off the others sat in moody silence in the van, contemplating their near-death experience. Janis's thoughts were even darker. What if that 'maniac' had been acting deliberately, trying to scare them or put them off the road? She knew she was mad to think that way, but the idea persisted. It seemed too much of a coincidence that they were on their way to the studio to cut their first album.

No, I'm being ridiculous, she told herself firmly. The superstitious foreboding she'd been feeling must not be allowed to cloud her judgement. Better by far to put it down to bad road conditions and Adam not being a hundred per cent used to the new vehicle. When he finally returned to the driver's seat she gave him a hug and a kiss. 'Sure you're OK to drive?' she asked him.

Adam nodded. 'Yes, fine. It's just a bit of a nuisance. We're going to be half an hour late.'

It didn't seem to matter when they finally arrived at The Gables, an old stone-built manor house in darkest Dorset that had been converted into a set of studios, offices and living quarters. They set about exploring the place with gasps of enthusiasm. Besides the two superb recording studios there was a spacious mixing room, with a vast 48-track desk, computers and video-editing facilities. The rooms were all interlinked by closed-circuit TV. Jake and Baz, the two sound engineers, were rakish types who eyed the girls with undisguised lust, making Janis feel instantly randy. Not that she would be taking up their unspoken invitation, she firmly told herself, not with Adam around. She had so much to thank him for, both professionally and personally, that she would not dream of putting it all in jeopardy for a cheap thrill.

The atmosphere in the huge, wood-panelled dining-room where they all assembled for a delicious lunch cooked by one of the resident staff was lively and flirtatious. Janis could see Virago responding to the macho vibes of the men, and she wasn't the only one. Sal was giving Jake decidedly randy looks too. Janis felt envious, wishing she were fancy-free again, until she reminded herself that they were there to do a job and the fewer distractions the better.

In the afternoon they set to work recording the first track which happened to be the song that Adam and Janis had composed together.

'That's a really nice number,' Jake said after the first run-through. 'I reckon you ought to release that as a single. Only my personal opinion, of course.'

Even so, Janis felt flattered. Someone in the business had admired their song, so it couldn't be that bad.

Although they'd got all the material pretty tight in rehearsal, once they got before a microphone and were conscious of how much every minute was costing, the girls made lots of nervous errors. It was a frustrating afternoon, each of them trying not to get riled with the others when they had to go over the same ground again and again. By six o'clock they were all feeling ratty and fed up.

'It's always like this on the first day,' Baz assured them. 'Nerves, tensions. Unfamiliar surroundings. Once you get used to the place and start to relax things will go better.'

'I bloody hope so!' Lee muttered beneath her breath. 'Karl's coming down tomorrow.'

Another splendid meal had been prepared for them. 'I could get used to this,' Adam grinned, as they tucked into steak and chips washed down with a decent red wine. Round the huge table they began to feel like one big, happy family. The alcohol helped. Soon everyone was in helpless fits of laughter as Jake and Baz told stories of some of the big rock stars who had stayed at The Gables in the past.

'You know Beano, from the Catalysts?' Jake asked. Everyone nodded, instantly seeing a vision of the shock-haired, bearded weirdo with his flat cap. 'Well, he suddenly came up to us around three a.m. and woke us up demanding "Girls, girls, girls!" I told him we were in the middle of nowhere, in the middle of the night and not even the call girls worked round the clock in our neck of the woods. So then he said, "Well, if you can't get me no fuckin' women get out there and round up some sheep!" I told him if he was that desperate he could do it himself. He said he'd been doing it himself all night and he wanted someone to do it for him. God, what a pervert!'

'But do you remember when Stu was here?' Baz broke in.

'Oh yeah – Stu Mayfield. He brought his entertainment with him. Two of the fattest black women I've ever seen, twins they were. What they got up to defies the imagination!'

'Go on, tell us!' Virago coaxed, her eyes gleaming.

'Well, how that guy didn't suffocate, I'll never know. We watched them on the TV – they'd forgotten to turn the camera off in their room. Apparently he got turned on by lying between them, like a human sandwich. He had these great long straps that went all round the three of them. When they were all strapped together, one on top of the other, they'd go rolling around the room. It was so bizarre! I wanted to keep the video but he made us give it to him when he found out.' Jake grinned at Baz. 'We could have sold it to the *Sunday Sport* for a bloody fortune!'

As the anecdotes continued Janis found herself wondering whether stories would be told about them in future. She could see that some of them were becoming aroused by all this sex talk, and when they moved through into the sitting-room they seemed to fall naturally into pairs. Lee and Dagmar were together, as were Adam and Janis, but Virago made a point of sitting next to Jake on the sofa while Sal seemed more than happy to be near Baz.

The gossip continued, becoming more salty as the evening wore on and the wine flowed more freely. Virago began to tell a few tales about Blade and Gore who, as it turned out, had both attended a minor public school notorious for its homosexual culture.

'When Shaft first started out there were always pretty boys hanging around the dressing-rooms,' Virago said. 'I was a bit naive in those days and it took me a long time to twig what was going on. But then the guy who was managing us said it was bad for our image. For a long time after that nobody knew Blade was gay. He and Gore didn't frequent the gay scene, they kept themselves to themselves. If there were any others involved it was kept discreet. In fact, we deliberately played up the hetero image on stage.'

'It's ironic, isn't it?' Janis said. 'There was I fantasizing about Blade, along with hundreds of other women, while all the time he was gay.'

'It's no different from those Hollywood stars, like Rock Hudson,' Sal commented.

They had reached that quiet, intimate time of night when confidences seemed possible. Jake asked straight out which of the members of the band were lesbian and which, if any, were straight. He seemed relieved when Virago said she was bisexual, and moved a bit closer to her on the sofa. By now Janis was convinced that the pair would be spending whatever remained of the night together. She was feeling tired herself, however, and whispered to Adam that she'd like to go to bed.

They said their goodnights and retreated to the room they'd been allotted. The décor was restful – floral curtains and duvet, cream walls and carpet – but Janis felt very restless. She had a bath while Adam lay in bed flicking through half a dozen music mags that he'd taken from the collection in the sitting-room. When she joined him in bed they cuddled up, but neither of them seemed to want to make love. 'I don't feel ready to sleep,' Janis said.

Adam sighed. 'Neither do I. It's excitement, I expect. Shall we see what's on the telly?'

The television was on top of a chest at the bottom of the bed. Adam turned it on with the remote then began to flick through the channels. Suddenly they were looking at a scene that was very familiar. It only took them a few seconds to realize that they'd hooked into the closed-circuit television in the house.

'Ooh, how naughty!' Janis giggled. 'We can spy on them!'

They had a clear view of the whole sitting-room. Virago was lying on the sofa with her head in Jake's lap, Lee was sitting on the floor with her head against Dagmar's knees, and Sal was snuggling up to Baz, who was passing a joint around. There was an air of erotic expectancy about the scene which made it compelling viewing.

'Are you thinking what I'm thinking?' Adam said, his voice low and husky.

'What, that they seem to be pairing off? I thought that earlier.'

Adam, evidently aroused by the idea, began stroking her breasts. She moved over and placed her bottom between his open legs, letting him caress her as she lay back on his chest. Adam's genitals were squashed against her bum and, as his erection developed, he readjusted his penis so that it lay more comfortably along the divide between her buttocks.

As they watched, the pace on the screen hotted up. Virago whispered something in Jake's ear, leaning forward to show off her cleavage, and he passed it on to Baz, who sniggered and began to caress Sal's hand then got up to put some new music on. Janis could hear the slow, sultry strains of some jazz singer in the background as Virago and Jake began kissing in earnest. Dagmar and Lee noticed, smiling at each other, then Dagmar slipped down to the floor and began to embrace the other woman, covering her neck with little teasing touches of the lips until Lee pulled her close and they kissed with passionate fervour.

By now it was obvious that they were all feeling randy and Janis was no exception. With her eyes still fixed to the screen she shifted to one side and began to stroke Adam's rampant penis while he pulled gently at her engorged nipples. 'I think they're going to have an orgy downstairs,' Janis murmured. 'Are you envious? Should we go back and join them?'

'No,' came Adam's throaty voice in her ear. 'I'd rather stay as we are. It's more fun to watch, don't you think?'

She turned and grinned at him. 'It's certainly less complicated.'

In just a few minutes the others were stripping off and soon they were completely nude. The scene downstairs was developing into a free-for-all, with four female and two male bodies writhing and groping on the thickly carpeted floor. The two engineers had huge erections and were clutching at anything that came within their reach: breasts, buttocks, thighs, pussies. Lee and Dagmar tried to keep out of their way but even they got groped a few times by the two men, who seemed to be completely out of their heads. Soon the two lesbians retreated to the corner where they set about enthusiastically drinking each other's juices and triggering off a series of wild orgasms. It was obvious that they were well practised in pleasuring each other by now.

For the others, though, it was their first encounter and they all seemed determined to make the most of it. Janis watched Virago take Baz's cock into her mouth while Sal hoisted herself onto Jake's prick and began to ride him vigorously. Baz was stroking and kissing Sal's breasts as she worked herself back and forth, while Jake did the same to Virago at his side. Just as Baz was about to spurt, Virago took her mouth away and let him shoot it over her tits while Jake smeared the sticky mess all over her hugely erect nipples.

Seeing all this going on was very arousing, both for Janis and, apparently, for Sal who started to climax, throwing her head back and moaning as she heaved up and down with increasing speed over Jake's stiff organ. He was on the edge too, and the pair of them were soon caught up in paroxysms of pleasure.

'Oh God, I can't stand any more of this!' Janis heard Adam say, pushing her roughly onto her knees. She fell forward on the bed and his hands clamped onto her buttocks as he probed into her from behind making her cry aloud, half with surprise and half with pleasure as his fat cock wormed into her sopping quim.

'Oh, yes!' Janis moaned, still staring at the screen where now both men were sucking at the women's musk-laden pussies while they waited for their own potency to be restored.

Janis bucked her hips in practised synchronicity with Adam's thrusts as they worked themselves up towards a climax. She was moving her pelvis round and round while she squeezed him inside, and he gasped with increasing urgency and clasped her dangling breasts, giving the nipples some rough treatment in his eagerness to hasten their joint fulfilment. It didn't take long for them both to come. Through bleary eyes Janis watched Virago thrashing and moaning on screen and it propelled her into a mighty orgasm of her own, the bursts of sex energy spasming through her like an electric shock. Her contracting vagina sparked off Adam, who bit into her shoulder as he climaxed, making her squeal.

They collapsed in a heap, dimly aware that above their heads the lewd pictures were still showing like some porn movie they'd hired to turn themselves on. Except it was for real, and all happening downstairs. Janis stared at the images of Sal and Virago being thoroughly shagged in the missionary position and gave a faint smile.

'I guess a good time was had by all tonight!' she murmured, as Adam flicked first the remote then the light switch to plunge both themselves and the others into darkness.

Next morning, feeling very much the worse for wear, Janis and Adam came downstairs to the kitchen where breakfast was to be served. In an hour's time Karl was due to arrive from London and the real work of recording could begin. Except that the faces of Jake, Baz and Virago which met them around the kitchen looked rather more than hung over. 'Doom laden' seemed better to describe the atmosphere. Worried, Janis asked, 'Is everything OK?'

Jake threw Virago a despairing look. She said, grimly, 'I'm afraid not. There was a burglary in the night. The computer's been stolen.'

'What?' Adam was instantly on his feet despite the earliness of the hour and the fragility of his nerves. 'What do you mean, stolen? Don't you have adequate security in this place?'

'Of course!' Jake sounded sullen. 'We have no idea how anyone could have got into the studio. Unless someone stole a set of keys and had a duplicate made.'

'What time did you go to bed?' Adam asked. Janis remembered what they had been up to until the early hours and, despite the seriousness of the news, had to stifle a giggle.

'About three, I think. But the theft could have happened any time, if they were quiet enough. The alarm had been disabled. Whoever they were did a good job.'

Adam said, 'We've got Karl coming down, and it's important not to waste his time. Do we need the computer for today?' Jake shook his head. 'OK. So you've got a couple of days to sort out another one. I trust you're insured.'

'It's not as simple as that. We had programs stolen, too. We can't redo them all in a couple of days.'

'Well, do your best, we can't ask more than that. Have you checked to see if anything else has gone?'

'Yes. As far as we can tell it's just the computer and a few floppies.'

Even so, it was a setback they could have done without. The effect on morale was bad, especially on Jake and Baz who went through the day like a couple of ill-natured teenagers set to do household chores. Adam tried very hard to smooth things over with Karl. He knew the producer of old, and by the end of the day they were developing a relaxed working relationship which made the girls feel more at ease.

'It's going well ladies, despite this morning's setback,' Karl told them as they assembled in the kitchen at the end of the afternoon. His grey eyes surveyed them all shrewdly and his mouth was smiling beneath the black moustache. 'But I need to hear more conviction in the singing. Virago and Janis, you need to practise those harmonies on "Storm in your Eyes". Just get more passion into it, more fire. We'll run through it again first thing tomorrow.'

Janis felt subdued. She knew she wasn't giving of her best, and she was ashamed of letting Virago down, but somehow her nervousness was spoiling everything. The old superstitious dread had returned. First that near-accident on the motorway, now the theft. There was bound to be a third catastrophe, there always was. And who knew how serious that would be?

Over the next few days Janis did her best to quash her misgivings. When some equipment broke down, setting them back a whole day, she tried to shrug it off. Then, when Jake broke his arm falling off his bike when he cycled down to the village for some milk, she accepted that the accident had just been bad luck too. But the tally of 'bad luck' dogging them seemed to mount every day, slowing down the recording process and affecting everyone's morale.

Adam gathered them together in the sitting-room one evening, in front of a roaring fire, and gave them all a pep talk. 'Look, I know we've had some setbacks but what we already have down is very good. I like it, Karl likes it. I sent a copy to Ivan and, believe it or not, the word came back that he likes it too. So we're not going to let a few minor misfortunes spoil a great album, now are we?'

Janis felt proud of Adam. He'd worked very hard over the past ten days, sorting out any problems – technical, business or personal – making sure that everyone was in the right place at the right time and in a fit state to work, and generally making life easier for everybody. As a manager he was proving to be worth his weight in gold. Their sex life had been great, too. They hadn't bothered to spy on the others again because they hadn't needed that kind of stimulation. After a hard day in the studio their libidos had been rampant and they had revelled in the chance to make love without any of the day-to-day distractions of living at home.

One evening, Janis was feeling particularly randy and persuaded Adam to retreat to their room soon after ten instead of joining the others in a game of Risk. She ran a bath and they both got into it, wallowing in the spicy scent of some expensive foaming oil. Their hands smoothed the cleansing froth all over each other, paying particular attention to their erogenous zones, and then they patted each other dry with white fluffy towels and went through to the bedroom. A delicious sense of luxury pervaded her being, the luxury of not having anything else to do just then and of having all the time in the world. It was as good as going on holiday.

Janis decided to pamper Adam by giving him a massage. She started at his head and tenderly ministered to his face and neck, then spread her palms down over his broad shoulders and deeply-sculpted chest. For a brief moment she remembered how their relationship had grown lacklustre, how indifferent she had become to his body, and she felt ashamed of herself. She should never have allowed things to slide like that. Thank God she had come to her senses and realized what a treasure she had in Adam. They were suited in every way, but particularly physically. By now they had harmonized their desires and habits, their preferences and appetites so that they each sensed exactly what the other was feeling, what they wanted at any given moment. It was instinct that had led her to soothe away the cares of the day like this, for example. Smiling to herself, she went on down to the smooth plane of Adam's stomach, which she stroked with gentle circular motions.

His prick was already beginning to rear up, craving her touch, but Janis let it wait knowing that the feeling would be all the sweeter when she did get around to it. Instead she concentrated on his legs, smoothing down his thighs with firm strokes and then on to his knees and shins. She spent a long time on his feet, enjoying the spectacle of his erection as it strained and swelled with desire, the bulging glans seeming to grow purple with rage at being frustrated. His balls were tight and expectant, also longing to be held, and as Janis began her long, slow ascent up his legs towards them they started to heave.

At last she had them in her hand, scrunching them softly while she bent to lick the salty juice from the slit in his glans. Adam moaned at the meagre contact, desperate for more, and Janis widened her mouth to take in the whole glans. When she began to lick all round the slippery surface his moans became more sensual, less protesting. She scratched at his scrotum lightly, the way he liked it, and moved on down the shaft until she had almost the whole of his penis in her mouth. He thrust impatiently but she wouldn't let him choke her. Instead she began to lick all over the smooth skin of his sheath.

'God, Janis, you do a fabulous blow job!' he sighed.

Janis was relishing the faint spiciness of his taste as she gave him a thorough licking. Already she could feel herself moistening below, the soft profiles opening up and the nub of her clitoris hardening. She contemplated how she would like to make love. With her on top, perhaps, controlling the pace. Or maybe, when he was good and ready, she would let him take her from behind as she knelt on all fours. It was just a question of how to begin. She knew that they would pass through many different positions before they both reached their first climax.

Sliding up his legs with her own apart, Janis felt the friction of his hard flesh opening her up, loosening her labia and making all the sensitive surfaces of her sex come alive. She wanted to continue this sense of being in control and knelt above him with his hard prick poised just below her pussy. Gripping the warm, taut shaft she gave her clitoris an experimental rub with his glans and shuddered as the rich sensations passed through her.

'Let me come in!' Adam pleaded.

'In a minute.' She smiled down at him, lying there in her benevolent power. Her love-lips were kissing the top of his organ, she was making them do it with her internal muscles. He groaned as she enclosed him briefly with her labia then let him go again, over and over, making little sucking noises. For an instant she let him sneak inside her but then she drew back and he sighed out his disappointment.

'Rotten prick tease!' he chided her, affectionately.

'Don't worry, you'll get there in the end!'

After a while, to their mutual content, she let him rest just inside her. Skilfully she caressed him with her cunt, but if he began to thrust she withdrew. For a minute or so she kept this up, then let him in further, very gradually, until the whole of him was inside her and she gave him a long, welcoming squeeze. He moaned and writhed under the sweet torture. Janis felt her clitoris buzzing away and gave it a little manual help, uttering a sharp breathy noise as her approach to orgasm began.

Eager to be satisfied, Janis started to ride Adam hard and soon the combination of her pelvic movements and his deep thrusting brought her off. She threw her head back and gave a series of mewing cries while her body caught fire, hot pulsing waves filling her from head to foot as the climaxes went on and on, each stronger than the last, and finally began to wane. She flopped down onto Adam's chest, exhausted, and wondered if he had come too.

'My turn now,' she heard him say, as if reading her mind.

Gently he rolled her off him onto her back and penetrated her immediately. For a while Janis felt numb below, but once the sensation returned to her vulva she began to kick into a second slow ascent towards orgasm. The determined thrusting was exciting her beautifully, and she clung to Adam's broad back, responding to his energy with renewed enthusiasm.

But just as she was moving into a state of bliss, something alien invaded her consciousness. At first she tried to ignore it, but soon she identified it as a smell, an acrid and unpleasant one at that. She sniffed and stiffened, her whole body alert to danger. Adam paused in his fucking and looked disconcerted. 'What's the matter?'

'That strange smell. Can't you smell it too?'

He frowned, but his annoyance at having his coitus interrupted soon visibly changed to fear. 'God, it's smoke!' he gasped.

Coincidentally there was a sudden shrill noise as the alarm system kicked into action. Adam pulled out of Janis's cunt and dashed to where their dressing-gowns were hanging behind the door. He threw hers onto the bed and thrust his arms into his own.

'Come on, we must get out of here at once!' he called, cautiously opening the door.

To Janis's relief no orange flames leapt into the room. Adam told her to wet some towels so she rushed to the bathroom and soaked two hand towels. She pulled on her robe and joined him outside the room where the smell of smoke was stronger.

'Get down on your hands and knees,' Adam told her. 'If there is smoke around it will rise from the floor. If we have to go through any flames we can put these towels over our faces.'

Fortunately they managed to get out of a back door without encountering any fire directly. But once they were outside in the courtyard they could see thick black smoke pouring from the studio on the other side of the building. People were screaming and rushing about on the lawn. Adam took Janis's hand and they began to run to where the others were.

'Oh, thank God you're safe!' Virago exclaimed, when they appeared.

'What about the others?' Janis asked, anxiously.

'Everyone's out and Jake's gone to the phone at the end of the lane to get the Fire Brigade.'

They all ended up standing on the lawn in a miserable huddle waiting for the firemen to arrive. Baz and some of the other staff were doing their best to throw water on the blaze in the main studio but clearly the fire had taken quite a hold. By the time the two fire engines arrived naked flames were sweeping to the night sky, illuminating the scene with an eerie Guy Fawkes glow. Janis buried her face in Adam's shoulder and burst into tears.

'It's all right, love,' he tried to reassure her. 'No one's been hurt and the studio's insured.'

That's not the point, Janis thought. The feeling that they were somehow doomed was now inescapable and she was convinced that someone, whether human or superhuman, really had it in for the band. But if that was the case, what could they do? For a moment Gore's malevolent face swam before her eyes.

'Are you cold, love?' she heard Adam ask, pulling her closer to him.

But, cold as the night air was, that was not the cause of her unstoppable shuddering. Her teeth chattered, her body trembled and her knees felt incapable of supporting her. Janis knew that she was in the grip of some atavistic fear that had nothing to do with the temperature. She had never been so scared in her life.

CHAPTER THIRTEEN

The fire at The Gables should have been the last straw but, somehow, it wasn't. A new studio was found, not too far away, and the work was continued. When Ivan heard about the series of catastrophes that had beset Eclectic Pussy he gave a great guffaw, according to Karl, and suggested a new name for the band: Jinxed!

Amazingly, the name stuck. Both Karl and Adam thought it had just the right whimsical, slightly sinister feel to it, and Virago agreed.

Janis was less convinced. 'Don't you think it's tempting fate to call a band by that name?' she said to Adam.

He laughed. 'But don't you see, that's just the point!'

At any rate Jinxed! they were – and jinxed they continued to be. A few days after moving into the Black Cat studio near Dorchester the whole band came down with some bug. For three days they were confined to their rooms while vomiting and diarrhoea took hold.

'I blame the catering,' Adam said when the worst of the symptoms began to wane.

But now Janis felt she really had to speak her mind. Alone in her room, feeling weak and depressed, she had been brooding over the catalogue of disasters they'd been through ever since they had begun work on the album. Her suspicions could not be kept to herself any more. When she and Adam were feeling almost well again she broached the subject as they took a walk in the grounds. 'Do you honestly believe it's all been just coincidence, or bad luck?'

He shrugged. 'Of course. What else could it be?'

Janis paused, then whispered, 'Black Magic?'

'What, you mean some local witch or something? I know Dorset is a bit rural and remote in places, but . . .'

'No, Adam, I mean Blade and Gore! Think about it. You said they were into some cult or other. Isn't it just possible that they could be working magic against us, trying to ruin the album and the band?'

'Don't be ridiculous, Jan. Most of what has happened to us has had a perfectly rational explanation. We've just had a run of bad luck, that's all.'

'OK, even if you don't want to believe in magic you must admit that some events could have been deliberate. Remember how we were pranged on the motorway coming down? Then there was the computer breakdown, the theft, the fire. And now food poisoning. All perfectly possible for Blade and Gore to bring about, even if they had to pay other people to do it.'

'I think you're being a bit paranoid there, Jan. Truly I do.'

She fell silent. It was the response she'd half expected, yet she'd hoped that Adam would take her more seriously. Still, she had no proof. Unless, or until, something really blatant happened she would only have her own suspicions and gut intuition to go on.

The recording went well and, in another ten days, they had all they wanted. There would have to be a final mix, and Ivan Craig would have to give his approval, but everyone was optimistic. When they gathered once more in Ivan's office at Salamander there was an air of excited confidence amongst the band members that was very infectious.

When Ivan greeted them with champagne they knew that their high hopes had not been unfounded. 'It's excellent!' he grinned, his blue eyes twinkling under the ginger brows. 'With the right video to plug the single it should go straight into the charts.'

No one yet knew which track would be chosen as the single but it seemed Ivan had decided. He gave Karl the nod and the first notes of 'Carnival Queen' came blaring out. Virago gave a whoop of joy. She had written the song and stood to make a bomb out of the royalties, but it was also her favourite on the album. Jan's disappointment that he hadn't chosen 'Storm in your Eyes' was only momentary. She knew it was not an appropriate track for a single, being a slow number with little dance potential, and her hopes had not been high.

'So now there remains only the question of the video,' Ivan continued, when the hubbub had died down. 'There's only one time and place to shoot a film with that name. Mardi Gras, carnival time – in Rio!

'Rio!'

The band chanted the magic name in unison. Again excitement filled the air as the word conjured up an image of sexy women in fantastic costumes, showing off their semi-nude bodies on colourful floats to a non-stop driving beat, while all around them people were dancing in wild street parties.

Everyone agreed that it would be perfect. Only Adam expressed reservations. 'Isn't that going to be incredibly expensive?'

Ivan's eyes lost none of their sparkle as he said, 'Yes. But we're prepared to fund it.'

Adam said, 'Of course, it will eventually come off our royalties . . .'

'Who cares?' Virago sighed. 'It's the chance of a lifetime. I doubt whether we would get to be in the Rio carnival otherwise.'

'Salamander is prepared to use its Brazilian contacts to arrange a float for you,' Ivan went on. 'You'll be performing all the time so it will be good publicity. By the end of the festival we'll be selling plenty of singles in Rio, if nowhere else!'

The next few weeks went by in a whirl of planning and publicity. Adam worked hard to get the news into as many publications as he could. He arranged for interviews at several radio stations, even got Virago onto a chat show on peak-time terrestrial TV. The costumes were being made for the band and travel was being finalized. The script for the video was written and rehearsals were held, as far as they could be, with a wooden platform in a draughty hall substituting for the moving float. Everything looked set for a successful trip, a brilliant video and an even more successful hit at the end of it all.

Yet still Janis could not think about the trip to South America without that old sick dread. She couldn't tell anyone about it, least of all Adam, and she felt ashamed that she was not a hundred per cent enthusiastic about the prospect like the rest of the band. She felt both hypocritical and churlish, unable to enthuse sincerely about the trip along with the others and annoyed that the sombre doubt in her heart would not go away.

When they finally flew in to the Brazilian city and saw the famous sugar loaf mountain and the gigantic welcoming statue of Christ silhouetted against the sky, Janis finally lost most of her misgivings. The hotel was packed with tourists who had come for the carnival and the atmosphere was already festive. They were there for just three nights, and the girls were determined to make the most of it.

On the first day they explored the city, which was already buzzing with carnival energy, and on the second day they prepared for the long night ahead. Dressing up in their costumes soon put them in the mood when evening came. Janis put on her exaggerated stage make-up and the skimpy pink spangly triangle that only just covered her pubis. Fishnet tights and high heels accentuated the length of her legs and her bosom was almost completely bare, with just two stick-on pink stars concealing her nipples. She looked like a fabulous showgirl at some Parisian night-spot.

On the way in the van, they crawled through traffic while revellers danced all around. Everywhere Janis could hear the complex, insistent rhythms of the various samba schools, and after a while the beat became as familiar as her own pulse. People were wearing fantastic costumes and some wore masks, dancing in the streets and shouting affectionate abuse at those who were still in vehicles. The noise was immense, and Janis was wondering how their own song could possibly be heard above the hubbub.

They reached the place where the camera crew were awaiting them, on a trailer attached to the main float. Filming amidst all that mayhem was going to be a tricky operation but the mainly Brazilian crew seemed undaunted, eyeing the girls with blatant lust. Janis felt her sexual fuse ignite as she climbed up onto the carpeted platform with the other girls. Her desire was on a slow burn, and the night ahead was long. Who knew when the tension that had already started building in her would reach its flash point?

While the others were taking up position on the float, Janis turned to Adam who would be travelling with the film crew. 'Wish me luck!' she smiled.

'You don't need it, darling. You look fabulous and irresistible. But if anyone tries it on, remember I'll be right behind you!'

For a moment she gazed into his eyes, two lovers isolated in their own private world from all the noise and bustle around them. Then Adam jumped down and the generator kicked into life, powering the dazzling lights and deafening music that qualified them to take part in the Mardi Gras parade.

'Carnival Queen, you're my Carnival Queen!' came the familiar words, blaring through a tinny loudspeaker. The float

gave a couple of jerks then started to move, slowly and
steadily, down the side street that led to the main procession.

The theme of their tableau was 'The Carnival Queen is
Prepared by her Handmaidens'. Virago was lying, almost nude,
on a huge bed covered in red velvet. All around her the other
girls fussed over her adornment. Sal brushed her long, blonde
hair with rhythmic strokes while Lee pretended to shave her
bikini line – a totally unnecessary process since Virago always
had a depilated pussy. Even so, it was obvious that Virago was
enjoying the experience of having shaving foam sprayed over
her groin and massaged into her smooth skin.

Janis and Dagmar were assigned her two naked breasts.
Wielding large swansdown puffs, they stood on either side of
her supine form, powdering her nipples with talc. A feature of
their display was a canopy lined with mirror tiles that showed
every detail of the adornment going on below. Two large,
Egyptian-style feathered fans were criss-crossed over the head
of the bed to give an exotic touch and a gaudy bejewelled
crown was displayed at the foot, on a red velvet cushion
trimmed with gold braid.

The 'handmaids' had rehearsed a dance which they broke
into from time to time when the music changed. Wiggling
their hips and jiggling their breasts they titillated the
bystanders with their erotic movements. Cheers and shouts of
encouragement followed them everywhere, and Janis was soon
on a permanent high. The slow procession wound its way
through the crowded streets, and every so often she would
catch a glimpse of another float displaying Inca or Aztec gods
in colourful and gilded splendour, a flock of 'Birds of
Paradise' or a human rainbow. Sometimes the whole bright
snake would come into view for a few seconds, a moving
column of colour and light, movement and noise, that dazzled
all the senses and turned all the participants into one dancing
tribe of humanity.

Hours went by, but they could have been days for all Janis knew or cared. So it was with something of a shock that she realized the float had been diverted from the main parade and was now approaching what looked like a huge warehouse. They ground to a halt, the music stopped and the generator stuttered into silence.

'Is that it?' Janis asked, mystified. 'End of the performance?'

Adam jumped up onto the float to explain to everyone. 'We've got a problem with fuel. There must be a leaky tank somewhere. Anyway, we daren't go on using this float. Juan says there's a party going on here and if we join in the film crew can complete the video inside.'

'Let's party then!' Virago exclaimed, evidently relieved to be able to get to her feet after all that lounging around.

Inside the corrugated iron walls the house party to end all house parties was in full swing. The revellers were gyrating to the synchronized samba beat of two different bands while all kinds of opportunists circulated amongst them selling food, drink and drugs. Many of the party-goers wore masks, some quite fantastic creations covered in sequins and lace, others fashioned into grotesque animal or ghoul shapes. Janis shuddered as two men in black turned round to reveal fluorescent skeletons painted onto their chests and grinning skull masks.

'Okay, everyone, if we get separated here's the drill,' Adam said, struggling to make himself heard above the din. 'I'll be back at the float all the time. If you want to rest, or tell me something, you know where we're parked. The hotel we're at is the San Antonio, remember. If you get completely lost just make your way back there. We'll rendezvous sometime tomorrow evening. You'll all be comatose during the day.'

Janis felt a chill strike her at his words. She was tempted to say she would go back to the float and wait with him, but the others were pulling her on, insisting that she should join in the dancing and be filmed for the video. 'This is stupid, pull yourself together!' she told herself. But without Adam to watch over her she felt ridiculously vulnerable.

Virago was pulling her into the seething throng of bodies where the temperature was hot and the smell was of sweat and perfumed passion. Men and women were fondling each other indiscriminately and most of them were very scantily dressed, exposing plenty of flesh to be caressed. Soon someone was stroking Janis's bare buttocks and her breasts were being intermittently fondled too. It was dark in that part of the room, only the musicians' corner being floodlit, and the revellers were taking advantage of the anonymity to have a secret orgy.

A bottle was passed around and Janis, now desperate with thirst, took a long swig. She realized that the other members of the band had disappeared, melted into the crowd, and another bout of fear assailed her. She put her hands around Virago's slim waist to make sure they kept in touch and felt her hips working continually to the beat, just as hers were. Locked into the samba rhythm their bodies were on autodrive and their minds were fuzzy at the edges.

The crew finished filming her and Virago and went off in search of the others. Soon after they'd gone Janis grew aware that someone was making weird bird calls in her ear. She turned around and saw a mouth grinning at her beneath a black mask covered in trailing feathers.

'Cucuricu! Trrr! Trrr!' he went, Then, as someone blew loudly on a whistle, he imitated the sound with a long trill.

His hands grasped hold of her breasts from behind, tearing off the remains of the stars so that he could reach her bare nipples. Janis closed her eyes, moaned and leaned back against him, feeling the hard bulge of his member, clad in soft cloth, brushing against her naked buttocks. With her clitoris pulsating in time to the music and her cunt dripping wet she was helpless to resist the lure of sexual promise. Wiggling her buttocks she felt them roll across his erection from side to side. It was extraordinarily arousing.

'Coo, coo, coo!' the bird man was calling, seductive as a randy dove. Janis reached round and grasped his swaying hips, pulling him closer. She could feel his lips on her neck now, cool and wet, her nipples throbbing urgently beneath his tickling fingertips.

For an instant Janis opened her eyes and saw that Virago was also being seduced by a masked man standing behind her. A latex mask representing some prehistoric beast covered his whole head, and Janis couldn't help thinking he must be hot inside there. She glimpsed where his hands were and concluded that he must have his finger right inside Virago's cunt as his hand was beneath her naked buttocks and she was squirming ecstatically. Enviously Janis seized the right hand of her own lover and placed it on the inadequate scrap of material that was supposed to be preserving her modesty.

His fingers burrowed beneath the sweaty triangle and found her slippery nub. Janis gasped with relief as the heightened sensations thrilled through her. All her inhibitions were gone now and no one around her seemed to care what anyone else was doing. They had become one dark, vibrating mass of energy synchronized to the eternal rhythm of the samba.

With knowing confidence the stranger's fingers played on her clitoris, taking her right to the edge and then slackening off, prolonging her desire with a mollifying 'Prrr!' Janis continued to rub against his thick penis, hoping that she was repaying him in kind for what he was doing to her. But the dance-beat was quickening and the crowd was moving, milling around.

Still drugged by the delicious feelings that were making her head swim, Janis let herself be taken back, back through the slippery crowd in the stranger's arms. Dimly she perceived that Virago was still near, still in front of her. She had to be moving backwards too. It must be a new pattern of the dance, she concluded, the dance that had them all in thrall, making them do whatever it wished now they were in a trance-like state.

Teeth grazed her neck and fingers tweaked cruelly at her nipples, but Janis remained in a daze. They were on the edge of the crowd now, near the thronged entrance to the warehouse. Somewhere outside Adam was waiting on the float, but she never gave him more than a passing thought. All that mattered was the immediacy of this stranger's hands and lips upon her overheated flesh, and the subtly changing beat of the music, that was becoming indistinguishable from the rhythm of love.

She had her face up against the rippling tin wall now, still in darkness where no one could see. Not that anyone would have cared. Her breasts pressed against the cold metal as the stranger fumbled with his loincloth and then she felt him hard against her, the erection huge as it probed her arse-crack. Thinking to guide him into her quim, Janis tried to seize his prick but he caught her wrists and continued to thrust between her buttocks. The realization dawned on her too late. She screamed as sudden pain shot through her and she tried in vain to wriggle free of him. He chortled in her ear, 'Cucuricu! Cucuricu!' then gabbled something in Portuguese.

Janis was frightened, her fear tinged with anger. She hadn't come all this way just to be buggered by a total stranger! Recovering her presence of mind she stamped as hard as she could on his toe with the sharp heel of her sandal. He gave a yelp and let go of her hands. Following up with a jab in the ribs from her elbow, Janis found she could slip out of his grasp and she began to push her way through the crowd.

But her assailant was hard on her heels. He caught up with her and took her in a fierce embrace, lifting her off the ground. She kicked and screamed, but no one took much notice. Desperately she looked round for Virago and saw that she was being hustled along behind her. Brontosaurus-face had one arm twisted around her back and he was marching her forward with his other hand over her mouth. Virago's blue eyes, staring back at Janis for a moment, looked absolutely terrified.

'Oh God, they're going to take us away and rape us. Maybe even kill us!' Janis thought.

They were being pushed in the opposite direction from their float, down a narrow alleyway which appeared deserted. Janis felt herself tremble and weaken. Anything could happen in a place like this, while everyone else was enjoying the carnival. Her mouth felt dry and tasted foul. Her heart was battering in her ears. Behind she could hear a heavy tread accompanied by the irregular clack of high heels, and she knew that Virago was suffering too.

Then Janis caught sight of a white van parked at the end of the alley. Was that where they were being taken? The imaginary scenario grew more horrific. First abduction, then rape, then murder. And who would know, or care? After all it was carnival time, when anything goes. A chill went right through her as the back doors of the van were flung open and she was pushed inside, scraping her shin against the metal in the process.

The man held her down with her face on the filthy floor, waiting for the second man to arrive. Virago was screaming, 'Let me go!' and then there came a loud slap and she shut up. Soon she was also being hurled into the open van. Janis realized they only had a split second to do something before they became total prisoners.

The men had to stand back to close the doors. She kicked out as hard as she could in the direction of her captor's groin and felt a surge of triumph when she hit the target. He gasped, 'Fucking bitch!' and a pair of cold eyes glittered at her from behind the mocking feathers of his mask. Then she knew, beyond doubt, just who was behind all this. She sprang down and punched the other man straight in the face, causing him to reel back.

'Quick, let's get away!' she told Virago.

While the men were still in shock the two girls ran as hard as they could to the end of the alley where people were watching the procession. Janis realized their way was barred by bodies. 'Please, let us through!' she pleaded.

Some curious bystanders stared at them and Janis pressed home her plea. 'Some men want to kill us! Please, we are in danger! *Danger de mort!* Let us pass!'

Fortunately someone spoke enough English to understand the urgency of their case. He spoke to his neighbour and they shepherded the girls through the crowd. From behind came shouts and exclamations as their pursuers attempted to push through in their wake.

As they got near to where the float was the cries from behind grew fainter and Janis began to feel safe. Adam was watching them at a distance and Janis waved to him, immensely relieved. When she finally tumbled into his arms the strain she had been under finally caused her to snap and she began sobbing desperately.

'God, Janis, whatever's the matter?' Adam asked, his face pale beneath the bright lights.

'Get as out of here, quick as you can!' she told him, aftershocks quivering through her body. 'Two men tried to kidnap us. They're still out there, after us!'

Fortunately Adam did not try to argue, or even talk to them, but led the way into a sidestreet away from the crowds that was a short cut back to the hotel. Janis kept looking nervously over her shoulder to see if they were being followed, but there was no sign of their captors. Both she and Virago were panting as they hurried over the cobbled streets and up the hill to where the San Antonio stood in the midst of semi-tropical gardens.

Dishevelled and exhausted as they were, no eyes were raised as they went up into the lift to the suite of rooms they had hired for the band. Evidently the hotel staff were used to people returning in such a state from the carnival. Once they were in comfortingly familiar surroundings, however, Janis broke down. She wept hysterically in Adam's arms trying to explain, through her tears, what had happened to them.

'It was Blade and Gore, I *know* it was!' she insisted, fiercely, anticipating Adam's disbelief. 'Gore had me, and Blade had her. Tell him, Virago, tell him it was true!'

Wearily, she nodded. 'I'd know him anywhere. God knows how they got here, or what they thought they were doing. Trying to scare us, I expect.'

'Are you quite sure?' Adam frowned at them, unable to believe yet unwilling to disbelieve.

'Maybe it was some kind of blackmail attempt,' Virago speculated. 'I wouldn't put anything like that past them. If they held us to ransom they could ask whatever they wanted, make us give up the band, anything.'

'Hm.' Adam's face was grim. He strode over to the phone, took out his diary and asked the operator for an outside line. While he waited for his connection he nodded towards the bathroom. 'Why don't you both clean yourselves up? You'll feel much better then.'

Janis ran a hot bath and they both slipped into it, sighing as the delicious heat soothed their battered bodies. They were still lying there, eyes closed and surrounded by foam, when Adam appeared in the doorway.

'Well, I've checked one or two things out,' he began. 'And it's certainly possible for those two villains to be here. They finished their British tour ten days ago. Rumour has it that audiences have halved since you left the show, Virago.'

She thrust her fist up into the air. 'Yes! Now all we have to do is make sure that the audiences for our band are twice as big!'

'Blade must be furious to come all the way out here, just for revenge,' Janis said. But it gave her theory that he'd been behind their misfortunes more credence.

'It's not absolutely certain,' Adam said. 'You girls were pretty out of it, and could easily have been mistaken. Did they say anything to you?'

'The guy who was with me was weird. Kept making bird noises,' Janis said. Then she remembered. 'Oh, and he said something in Portuguese at one point.'

'That means nothing,' Virago said. 'Gore speaks the language. He spent some time in São Paulo years ago. He could have been doing it to put you off the scent.'

Adam leaned his head against the doorjamb, looking wrecked. Janis was relieved that he was coming round to the idea that she was not paranoid and they really were out to get her.

He straightened up, a determined set to his mouth. 'OK, supposing that you are in danger from those bastards, there's only one thing for it. We'll have to hire some bodyguards.'

'You mean here, in Rio? But we're going back tomorrow.'

'I know, and if we're very vigilant we should be able to get you to the airport without any problem. No, I was thinking more of the British tour. If Blade and Gore are up to mischief it will be a lot easier to do it there.'

Janis said, mischievously, 'Like they tried to when we were in Dorset, you mean?'

She hadn't mentioned it to Virago before, and now her blue eyes widened with horror when Janis ran through her earlier suspicions. She ended by asking her what she thought.

'Like I said, I wouldn't put anything past those fuckers!' Virago took hold of the cake of soap and began to wash herself vigorously. 'If you knew what I knew . . .'

'Why don't you tell us, then?' Adam intervened, sitting down on the bathroom stool just inside the door. 'If they are the enemy we have to know them as well as we can. It might help us to predict their moves.'

Virago smoothed a hand down the length of her arm and sighed. 'I'm kind of sworn to secrecy. But I don't suppose it matters now. They've got it in for me no matter what. The thing is, they're into this weird cult . . .'

'I heard,' Adam said.

'How?'

'Press grapevine. It doesn't matter. What can you tell us about it?'

'Basically it's a sex cult. The ritual they perform before each show is like a trigger, increasing the sexual charge that builds up on stage between the band and the audience. They store it in their bodies and use it to channel power from some demon character. I don't know quite how it works. It's complicated, and I only got to know about it when I came upon some literature. Gore got involved with the cult here, in Brazil, and took it back to England with him. He initiated Blade when they became lovers.'

'I knew Gore was evil, the first time I met him,' Janis said. 'Those eyes – so chilling! And for some reason he's hated me from the start, too.'

'Don't take it personally, love. He hates all the women in the show. Apparently they're necessary to provide some kind of polarization of sex energy, something that he and Blade can't achieve on their own. They need us, so they hate us. Same boring old battle of the sexes story. Only this one has a twisted ending.'

Janis felt a shiver run down her spine, despite the warmth of the bath. 'What's that?'

'You don't want to know. Look, I've probably said too much already.' Virago sank down into the water and closed her eyes. 'Just take it from me those bastards are dangerous. Take precautions, OK?'

'We certainly shall,' Adam said, grimly. 'But I think it would be best if we didn't mention anything to the others. They don't have to know what happened tonight.'

'Fine,' Janis smiled. 'The sooner we forget about it the better, as far as I'm concerned.'

Adam came up and knelt by the bath. He started to soap her breasts with slow, gentle fingers. 'I'll ring the airport in a minute and see if we can get an earlier flight tomorrow. Just in case a reception party has been arranged for us at the airport.'

'Mm, good idea!' Janis moved languidly in the water, enjoying his soothing touch. She felt very tired, but it was the kind of tiredness that would allow her to wallow in sensuality while Adam did whatever he liked to her compliant body. Somehow she hoped that might exorcise the memory of Gore's brutal assault on her.

CHAPTER FOURTEEN

'And now for this week's chart buster. Blasting into the stratosphere out of nowhere at number nine, the fabulous Virago has got Blade well and truly *shafted* with the first single from her new band, Jinxed! Here it is, our hot tip for number one, "Carnival Queen!" '

An adrenalin high hit Janis's system like cocaine as the band burst into action on the cramped stage in the TV studio, surrounded by the usual bobbing zombies. They yelled and cheered to order as Virago flirted with the mike, shook her tits and ass, put all of her energy into the song. This was the moment they'd been not so much waiting for as working towards, their success in the charts being a foregone conclusion once Salamander had decided to make it their single of the month and push it for all they were worth.

Number One in the satellite charts was their first objective, which was why they were there on the Star Singles show, making the most of their peak-time exposure. Janis thrashed her guitar like a rock legend and her ear-splitting grin wasn't forced, she was patently loving every second of it. Behind the band was a screen showing the video they'd made in Rio. Their costumes for the TV appearance were a bit more discreet, but still sexy. Janis's breasts were banded with paper-thin black latex so that her nipples stood out in stark relief, and she was encased from toe to groin in the same material with just a

couple of pink plastic hands groping her, back and front. The
guitar clung stickily to her bare, sweaty midriff making slurpy
noises as she moved around.

Virago ground her pussy against the mike stand as she sang,

> *'Carnival Queen, she's the best on the scene,*
> *If you know what I mean!'*

The audience roared and cheered, most of them members of
the newly formed fan club, drafted in by Adam. During the
month since their single had been released he had worked so
hard to get them maximum publicity, and most of it had paid
off. Hardly a day went by when a photo of the Jinxed Minxes,
as they'd already been dubbed, didn't appear somewhere in the
press. The raunchy Rio video had helped too. It was climbing
steadily up the music vid charts and would no doubt hit the
number one spot around the same time as the CD single.

The song wound its way to a nerve-shattering climax and
Janis felt her own crotch on heat, her clitoris throbbing to the
beat, her vulva as wet as a drowning pussy. She rubbed her
mound against the guitar, hoping for some relief but only
succeeded in frustrating herself further. The sweat was running
down her forehead into her eyes and she hoped her make-up
was as waterproof as it claimed to be. Glancing to her left she
caught a wink from Sal, who was posturing wildly, her tits
bouncing almost out of their inadequate dayglo slings. Behind
them Lee administered savage correction to her Premier drum
kit and Hellride cymbals.

By the time they got off the stage Janis was pulsating all
over, her body in sexual overdrive. She sank into Adam's arms
in the dressing-room, glad to feel his warm body against her
own but wishing they could go off and fuck their hearts out
right away. No such luck! There were interviews and
photographs to be endured, fans to meet, autographs to sign.

Adam had made it plain that they couldn't afford to miss out on a single opportunity to plug the record and the band.

Most of the attention was on Virago, of course. Her split from Blade had been headline news in the music press and the fact that Shaft were not doing so well without her was all good publicity. She revelled in the limelight, tossing her blonde mane in thinly disguised contempt whenever Blade's name was mentioned, preening and smiling at the flattery which usually followed, since most of the journos were men. On Ivan's advice they had played down the lesbian image, emphasizing instead that they were dedicated to freeing the libido from its strait-jacket and allowing people to find themselves sexually, however weird or wonderful the expression of their liberation might be.

While she listened to Virago spouting these and other platitudes, Janis sat in the background sponging herself down. She longed for a shower, but the dressing-room was swarming with people and some of them actually wanted her autograph so she couldn't disappear just yet. Then a voice suddenly purred in her ear, deep and wickedly seductive.

'Janis, the wonderful Janis! Please may I have your pussy print?'

Startled, she turned to find herself staring into the most riveting pair of blue eyes she had ever seen. They came set like sapphires in golden-brown skin, and below them a perfect snub nose and full, sensual lips completed the picture. A flash of lust careered down Janis's spine.

'I beg your pardon?' she said, her voice faltering.

'Pussy print. It's my speciality. I already have a whole raft of female rock stars'. My ultimate ambition is to get Princess Diana's.'

'I'm sorry, I don't understand.'

She smiled, showing perfectly shaped white teeth. There was something oddly synthetic about this girl's appearance, but who cared? She was absolutely exquisite.

'The colours I use are vegetable dyes and perfectly harmless. There's a whole rainbow to choose from. All it entails is for me to paint your pussy, and then you sit down on a piece of paper. What could be simpler?'

'I . . . I don't know.' Janis looked around for Adam. She was out of her depth here. Would this count as good publicity material? 'What about Virago and the others, are you going to do them too?'

'All in good time,' she smiled.

Adam came up, drawn by the woman's incredibly erotic aura, and introduced himself.

'Hullo, I'm Leantha,' she smiled. 'And I was just trying to persuade Janis here to give me her pussy.'

'*What?*'

Leantha chortled sweetly. 'Only for a few seconds, for artistic purposes.'

'She wants to take a print of my private parts,' Janis explained.

'It's for an exhibition of pussy power that I'm putting on at the Tate next month,' Leantha smiled. 'I'm their Director of Alternative Arts.'

'Really?' Adam's eyes lit up at the prestigious words 'Tate' and 'Arts'. Janis could read his mind. In the pop terminology of a certain pundit, if they could attract the interest of the 'trendies', as well as the 'wendies' (the eternally youthful) and the 'bendies' (the sexually adventurous), their reputation would be made.

'We could go to your hotel,' Leantha suggested. 'I'm sure you'd feel more comfortable there.'

An hour later the three of them were sitting in the hotel bedroom drinking wine and chatting about the fusion of art and music that was the contemporary pop video.

'Some people argue that the visual imposes restrictions on the listener's aural imagination,' Leantha declared. 'It's been called audio-visual fascism. Others rejoice in the emergence of a new art form. Where do you stand on this, Adam?'

'If videos help to sell more songs, I'm all for 'em!' he said, deliberately crass.

Leantha frowned. She didn't realize that she was being sent up. 'I don't think that's in doubt, is it? But it's aesthetic values we're debating here, not commercial ones. Why make a filmic interpretation of a subjective musical experience? What price artistic integrity, when one's creations are being manipulated by someone else's imagery?'

'Quite!' Adam poured himself more of the wine. He was looking lecherously at Leantha's thighs. They peeped out from the slit in the front of her long black skirt. Janis couldn't blame him. She'd been mesmerized by those large and perfectly round breasts, revealed in braless splendour beneath a transparent pink blouse when Leantha removed her jacket.

'Shouldn't we get on with the job?' Janis giggled, rising from her chair as she sensed that Adam had no more time for intellectual debate. 'I'll take my knickers off.'

'Fine.' Leantha opened her bag and took out a collection of small pots which she placed on the coffee table. 'You can choose your colour, or colours. Please feel free to express yourself in any way you wish.'

Janis took off her jeans and then her panties so that all she had on was her skimpy T-shirt. There was something excitingly kinky about the prospect of covering her love-lips with the sticky, tinted cream. She decided on buttercup yellow.

Leantha clapped her hands together. 'Oh, lovely! Only one other woman has picked that one before. Now who was it? Let me see.' She searched through a small notebook. 'Here it is. Yes, of course, it was . . . But yours won't come out the same shade as hers, of course.'

'Why not?'

'Well, that's the marvellous part about it. Every woman's

secretions are different as well as her configurations. The chemical reaction is individual, rather like firing pots with different glaze. The other girl's came out more of an acid yellow. I expect yours will be softer, more orangey, but I don't know for sure. It's unpredictable. That's what makes it so exciting!'

Leantha cleared away all but the yellow pot then she untied her bundle of paper and took out one sheet. 'This is finest hand-made rag paper.' She held it up to the light and a crown appeared. 'See the watermark? I always use the very finest materials. I feel I owe it to my subjects. Now, are you ready? Just lie down on the bed and I'll smear the paint on, then we'll take a test impression on inferior paper.'

While Adam watched, amused and curious, Janis spread her legs for Leantha to stroke the gooey paint into the sensitive tissues of her vulva. Her touch was delicate, sensual, and Janis soon found her erotic tension heightening. She gazed at the honey-coloured breasts that were hovering above her, the darker brown nipples just visible in a state of soft relaxation. A gut-wrenching desire to tease them into prominence took hold of her and she felt a sudden increase of secretions down below.

'Mm, nice and wet,' Leantha murmured. 'That will make for a better print. Up you get now, but try not to close your legs too tightly as you walk over to the table.'

Janis did her best to walk with an open-legged gait and then got into position, straddling the low table where a sheet of paper had been placed. Leantha directed Adam to hold one of her hands while she took the other, to steady her.

'This is just a first impression, to soak up any excess dye,' Leantha explained. 'Now, lower your pussy onto the paper nice and slowly. Don't wriggle or squirm, just a normal sitting position will do. Ready, steady, go!'

Janis bent her knees and gripped tightly onto their hands as she sat down on the cool paper. She remained there for a few seconds then stood up again, looking down at the imprint. It was an interesting shade of mustard, a vaguely bivalvular smudge with a white snake-shaped hole in the centre.

'Not immediately recognizable as the female pudendum, I shouldn't have thought,' Adam commented, dryly.

'The second print will be better,' Leantha assured them.

Janis braced herself to repeat the process, This time the print had a more conch-like appearance. Leantha pronounced herself well satisfied with the work of art.

'I think we should drink a toast all round. To pussy power!' she grinned.

'Pussy power!' the other two echoed, swilling down the rest of the wine between them.

Janis wanted the woman to go now so that she and Adam could get down to some serious fucking. But after Leantha had packed away her paints she produced a large tub of cream and said she would clean Janis up.

'Soap and water won't do it,' she said, seeing her hesitation. 'It's a vegetable dye, remember? You have to use this special cleanser.'

Lying on the bed again with those titillating fingers massaging her labia, Janis felt her lustful desires returning. She wanted Adam, of course, but she was growing increasingly more excited by the presence of a third party. Leantha was smiling down at her, thrusting her huge breasts out and now Janis could see that the dark nipples were hardening beneath the see-through blouse.

'I'm very grateful to you, Janis, for letting me take a print of your pussy,' she said, her fingers delving lightly into the wet recess of her vagina. 'And I'd like to do something in return.' She turned round and threw Adam a dazzling smile. 'For both of you.'

'Really?'

Adam was evidently thinking along the lines of more publicity for the band. But Leantha reached up with her free hand and pulled him down onto the bed beside Janis. Once he was there she put her hand on his thigh, smiling seductively. 'I'm rather a special woman, though I say it myself. Nature has given me a rare and wonderful gift which I really enjoy sharing with others.'

It was obvious that she had something other than business in mind. Janis saw Adam's fly bulging and her own libido increased. It seemed a threesome might be on the cards after all.

'What do you say to we three getting together more . . . intimately?' Leantha suggested.

Adam threw Janis a questioning glance. She smiled and nodded. He said, 'How could we refuse?'

'I'm so glad you said that. Perhaps you'd like to undo my buttons, Adam.'

She turned around to let him get at the buttons down her back. All the time her right hand was stroking the warm cream into Janis's vulva, making her long for more action. She watched achingly as Adam removed the flimsy blouse and Leantha's fine pair of tits was exposed. They stood out firm and proud from her chest, the dark brown nipples long and stiff, crying out to be touched with lips or fingers. Slowly she began to unzip Adam's fly and free his already rampant erection.

Janis sat up and pulled off her last remaining garment, wanting to be in on the fun. She reached out and stroked Adam's head while Leantha pulled his cock out of his pants and admired it, fondling the shaft. She was still wearing a pair of baggy black velvet trousers. Adam reached for her breasts and began to suckle eagerly. Janis moved in closer and Leantha resumed her slow pleasuring of her pussy.

'Mm, so good!' Janis sighed as she squirmed away against

the other woman's fingers. One slipped right inside her, gave her a thorough internal massage then slipped out to give more friction to the hard nub of her clitoris. And all the while Adam was fondling and sucking at Leantha's magnificent boobs, making the long brown nipples look like luscious, sticky dates.

Seeing Adam's stiff penis made Janis hungry for more and she began to stroke his buttocks, reaching right down to where his balls dangled and giving them a fondle too. Adam groaned, evidently finding the two women rather hot to handle. Then Leantha withdrew her hands to undo her own fly and Janis lay back, pulling his head down towards her quim so that he could give her a good licking.

He had only just begun, his long tongue probing into her, when Janis looked over his head and saw something that made her gasp aloud. Leantha had taken off her trousers and was wearing a close-fitting pair of pants with a very masculine-looking bulge in the front.

'My God, are you what I think you are?' she said, faintly, looking from tits to crotch and back again.

A slow smile spread over Leantha's lovely face. 'I told you that Nature has been specially kind to me.' She pulled the waistband of her pants right down and up sprung an unmistakably erect male organ of a very respectable size.

'Good God, you're a hermaphrodite!' Janis exclaimed. 'Were you really born like that? I'm sorry, I don't mean to be rude, but . . .'

'No offence taken,' Leantha smiled, as she pulled her pants right off. Grasping her penis firmly by the shaft she gave it a few strong tugs. 'Actually I have had a little help from a famous gender reconstruction surgeon, but only to enhance the cosmetic effect. And I had implants in my boobs but, what the hell, so do lots of women!'

'But how much of you is male, and how much female?' Janis wanted to know.

Leantha explained in a matter-of-fact tone that showed she was well used to dealing with such enquiries. 'Genetically I'm female. I have a vagina but no testicles.' She stroked her penis fondly. 'Technically this thing is just an overgrown clitoris. But it's capable of full penetration and although I can't ejaculate I get wonderful orgasms.'

While Janis was staring incredulously at the freaky spectacle of a woman with a prick – or a man with boobs, whichever way it was – Adam had abandoned his cunnilingus and was doing likewise. She could see the thoughts passing through his mind, his expression was so transparent, and she giggled because the same thoughts were occurring to her. What fantastic possibilities the prospect of three-way sex with Leantha was opening up!

Over the next couple of hours they explored just about all of them. Janis thought it was fantastic when the 'she-male' was fucking her and they were fondling each others' breasts, while Adam came into Leantha's tight little cunt from behind. But then it was all-change: while Adam screwed her from the front, Janis gave suck to the other woman's cock. The only thing that Adam didn't feel too happy about was sucking Leantha off, but Janis was more than happy to oblige so it wasn't a real problem.

Both Janis and Adam were getting off on the novelty of having a lover like Leantha and their passion knew no bounds. After her third orgasm, Janis stopped counting. The enormous sexual urge she'd felt while performing on the TV show was being well and truly satisfied. The weirdest moment was when she and Adam were fucking, and performing fellatio and cunnilingus on Leantha at the same time!

After their night-long orgy, Janis and Adam overslept. They woke to find themselves alone and immediately panicked. They were supposed to be meeting the rest of the band in the hotel lobby at nine-thirty for a press conference before their first tour rehearsal, and it was already quarter to ten. Hastily they showered and dressed then, trying to look as if they hadn't a clue what the time was, they sauntered downstairs.

A reporter thrust a copy of *New Musical Express* at them the minute they appeared.

'Could we have your reaction to this article by Blade please, Adam? Virago refuses to comment.'

'What?' Adam took hold of the paper and read the headline with a frown. Peering over his shoulder Janis saw that it said, 'Slagging off the "Slags!" '

'What's this about, Mack?' Adam asked, sternly.

The reporter grinned in a way that made Janis want to punch him on the nose. 'Allow me to summarize,' he said. 'According to Blade, Jinxed is, and I quote, "Just another dyke band pretending to go straight to sell records." Is that true, would you say?'

'Certainly not!' Janis said, indignantly. She ignored Virago's warning look and continued, 'We're not all lesbian, for one thing. I'm certainly not, anyway. And even if we were, we make no particular issue of our sexuality. To borrow a phrase from the Swinging Sixties, as far as we're concerned it's "whatever turns you on". And if our music turns people on, so much the better.'

'Well said,' Adam murmured. He smiled at the reporter, handing back the paper. 'I think you have your answer. But I'd just like to add that Shaft doesn't seem to be doing too well since Virago left to form her own band. Isn't it more likely that Blade's outburst is a classic case of sour grapes?'

'That's for our readers to decide,' the reporter said. 'But thanks Adam, Janis. You'll get some sympathetic coverage, don't worry.'

'See you in the Pig and Whistle later, Mack?' Adam said as the man turned to go. 'I'll buy you a drink.'

He nodded with a grin, and was gone. Adam winked at

Janis, then turned to the other two reporters who were still scribbling. 'That's all, folks! Thanks for coming but we have a show to rehearse. The Jinxed tour starts on April the first!'

The other girls groaned. 'Oh, must we?' Virago sighed. 'We're all shagged after last night. Can't we put off the rehearsal until tomorrow?'

'Definitely not! You're professionals, remember? Any slacking and you immediately give ammunition to the opposition.'

Yes, Janis mused, it really did seem as if Blade and his pals were the enemy, now.

Everywhere they went these days two bodyguards went with them. They stood on guard outside the rehearsal space in West London that Adam had rented. They accompanied them to restaurants and pubs when they took breaks to refresh themselves. They even hung around outside Adam's and Janis's flat all night, watching for suspicious vehicles or personnel. And it seemed to be working. Although Blade periodically slagged them off in the Press he made no attempt to get near to either Janis or Virago physically.

On the eve of the tour to promote their first album, Jinxed were invited to a party held by Salamander Records at a five-star hotel in Kensington. It was to be a very grand affair, with several famous faces from the pop world and a sprinkling of film stars present, and Janis enjoyed dressing up in a shocking pink, figure-hugging gown. Elegance, rather than blatant sexiness, was the keynote for all the girls that evening. Ivan had explained that he wanted the band to appear 'classy, just like their music.'

The enthusiastic reception that the album had been given throughout the media was very encouraging and some had even tipped it for the 'Best Album of the Year' award. It had recently been released in America, to equally good reviews, and Janis had been on a high for days. She felt even more elated than when she was first chosen to join the Shaft company. This time she had more of a rôle to play in the band and 'Storm in your Eyes', the song that she and Adam had composed, had been singled out for quite a bit of praise in its own right.

So it was in buoyant mood that she and Adam went by taxi to the hotel where they would meet the rest of the band. The press photographers were there, snapping away as they emerged from the cab, and in the lobby the others were waiting in their splendid gowns. Even Lee, who had never been seen offstage in anything but scruffy jeans and T-shirt, looked surprisingly feminine in an emerald green taffeta gown with a bouffant skirt and high heels.

'Don't we all look wonderful!' Virago smiled as she greeted them with a kiss. 'And guess who are coming later – David Bowie and Elton John!'

'Fantastic!' Adam beamed. 'Good old Ivan. He's certainly pulled out all the stops tonight!'

The large hotel conference room was done out in carnival style in homage to the album, with balloons and streamers everywhere. Janis couldn't believe her eyes as she glanced around and recognized faces that she'd only seen on television. 'Have all these famous people really come just to see us?' she whispered to Adam.

He laughed, hugging her briefly. 'Don't forget, darling, you're famous too now!'

The rest of the band were in high spirits, revelling in all the attention. They were scheduled to perform one number live, at midnight, but the album was playing constantly and the video was being shown over and over on a large screen in the corner. Janis was slowly getting used to the sycophantic phrases that kept coming her way like a scent on the breeze: 'Loved the album . . . adore the band . . . thought the video was terrific . . . bound to be a wonderful tour.'

Around eleven, Elton and Bowie made their brief appearance and Janis had a few seconds of conversation with each of them, helped by Adam through her tongue-tied lapses. As she accepted yet another glass of champagne or bit into a delicious cocktail snack, Janis wanted to pinch herself. She kept having to remind herself that she was not here as a guest at someone else's function. This was all for *her* – and the others, of course. Handsome men were flirting with her. Some pretty women were, too. And she had the extraordinary feeling that if she wanted to she could have anybody in that room – with the possible exception of Elton and Bowie!

The 'performance' was simply a matter of the five of them singing along with their own single. They had no instruments to play so it was just a token gesture, but it was received with rapturous applause all the same. Everyone seemed delighted, Ivan was grinning from ear to ear along with the other Salamander bosses, and Janis found herself being enthusiastically hugged by a very drunk Virago.

'Will you come with me to the Ladies?' she asked, in an exaggerated stage whisper. 'I don't think I can get there by myself!'

'Of course!'

Janis took her by the hand and led her through the crowd, some of whom were already heading for the exit. The cloakrooms were on the next floor. They staggered upstairs and into the luxuriously appointed Ladies. Janis had a pee, then waited for Virago to emerge. She did so a few minutes later, giggling. She caught sight of herself in the mirror.

'Oh shit, my make-up's a mess. What am I going to do?'

'Here, sit down. I'll help you.'

Absorbed in the task of reapplying smudged lipstick and eye shadow, Janis didn't realize that the door was being stealthily opened. Eventually a moving shadow in the mirror caught her eye and she looked up. With a cry of horror she recognized the two figures that were standing right behind them. They were both wearing carnival masks, just as they had in Rio. Before she could do or say anything, a pad soaked in some foul-smelling spirit had been clamped over her nose and mouth and that was the last thing she remembered before falling into a dreamless sleep.

CHAPTER FIFTEEN

The place that Janis found herself in when she came to was cold, dark and dank. She shivered, trying to adjust her eyes to the black void. There was a sick emptiness in her stomach and her head ached horribly. She whispered, 'Virago, are you there?' but received no reply and she sensed that she was alone. Her hands were free but she soon discovered that her ankles were chained and padlocked.

Janis reached out and touched a rough stone wall. There was a faint light seeping in round a wooden door and another smell beside the dankness, a manurelike, animal smell. Maybe the place used to be a cowshed. From the quietness outside she guessed the barn was somewhere in the country.

Her body felt sore all over, but she began to explore her prison as best she could on all fours, dragging the clanking chain behind her. Her handbag had been thrown into a corner and there was a jug of water and an enamel mug. She drank two cupfuls straight off. The liquid slurped around in her empty stomach making her long for food. Her mind was numb with incomprehension. She recalled seeing Blade and Gore in the Ladies at the hotel, then the stifling pad over her face. Had they really abducted her and Virago, brought them to some out-of-the-way place and held them prisoner? She would dearly love to come to some other conclusion but it seemed clear enough. Those bastards were out to ruin Jinxed as a band

and they would stop at nothing to do so, not even kidnapping. They'd tried it once before in Rio, and this time they had succeeded.

Janis didn't want to speculate any further. Reaching the door she strained to peep out through the crack, but it was all grey outside. She had no idea of the time. How much longer would she have to wait before anyone came? Maybe it was best to let them know that she was awake, at least. Whatever they had in store for her would happen sooner or later and nothing could be worse than this horrible lonely suspense.

'Hallo! is anyone there?' she called, faintly at first but then with gathering strength. At least they hadn't gagged her. She changed her cry to 'Help!' and it wasn't long before she heard someone coming. A bolt was drawn back and the rotting wooden door was flung open.

Janis looked up at the two men. They'd removed their masks and Gore was sneering at her, gloatingly. Behind him, Blade looked more circumspect. They both needed a shave.

'So you're awake, bitch!' Gore snarled. 'You'd better stop that racket or we'll tape your mouth. And get away from the door!'

He kicked out at her, making her shrink rapidly back into the gloom. In the dim light that now filled the hut she could see that the floor was of bare earth and there was straw in one corner. She was being kept like an animal. 'Where's Virago?' she asked Blade. 'What have you done with her?'

'Don't worry, she's still alive – for the time being!' Gore snapped. 'But you won't see her.'

'Why are you doing this?'

Gore stroked his rough chin, pretending to think. He turned to Blade with a sardonic smile. 'Well now, let's see . . . just why *are* we doing this, Blade? Any ideas?'

Blade grinned back. 'Because we feel like it?'

'Yes, that'll do. It makes us feel good, see. In fact . . .' He thought of something, his grin widening evilly. 'Talking of making us feel good, there's something you can do for me right now. I just happen to have my early morning hard-on and it's a real stonker.'

Gore started to unzip his jeans and Janis felt her heart sink like cold porridge. The fact that he was gay was no consolation whatever. She remembered how he'd pawed her at the carnival, and felt sick. Terrified, she shrank back into the hut, longing for the darkness of oblivion again, but it was light enough for her to see the huge dimensions of his prick as he pulled it out of his pants. He waved it at her, mockingly.

'Get back against the wall! By the way, this used to be a pigsty, so I thought it would be appropriate for you. Back, I say! Sooo-ey! Sooo-ey!'

He lunged forward and caught her by the hair, pulling her towards the stone wall. Janis screamed, shuffling backwards on her bottom to avoid more pain. She felt the thud of the stones against her sore back, then he thrust his stinking cock in her face with the crude command, 'Suck me off!'

Blade was still at the door, standing astride with a blank look on his face. Janis threw him a glance of mute appeal but, after catching her eye, he turned and wandered off. Her spirits sank further. Somehow she had felt safer with Blade there as a witness.

The excruciating pain flashed through her again as Gore jerked her head back. 'Open your mouth, bitch!'

The huge glans was now between her lips and tasted sour. With her head against the wall Janis had no control over the procedure and he thrust into her mouth mercilessly, making her gag. She seized the base of the shaft hoping to restrain him, but he snatched her hand away, squeezing it so hard she feared he would break her fingers.

'No hands!' he snarled. 'And don't even think about using your teeth. If you give me any trouble you'll get it in the arse!'

With a great effort Janis resisted the urge to vomit, relaxed her throat and allowed him to push into her. She tried imagining it was Adam, but the organ was too big and dirty and she felt too humiliated. Again she felt her gorge rise and coughed to prevent herself from spewing. She glanced up and saw him staring down at her coldly, implacably, and with real hatred. She closed her eyes.

The relentless probing went on and on, with punishing force, and Janis loathed the bitter taste that was filling her mouth. Behind it all was the fear of further punishment, of pain and even of death. She felt her soul retreat from her plight, detaching her from reality and keeping her in some dark limbo of horror and misery. The bludgeoning cock began to move faster as the climax approached, battering against the numbed roof of her mouth. Gore was grunting and gasping above her and she knew, with a desperate satisfaction, that the end was near.

At last she felt the hot acid sear its way down her throat and she gulped, feeling a strong urge to bring it back up. The last few spurts came and then her teeth scraped lightly against the retreating penis. She shuddered, fearing she had hurt him and terrified of the consequences, but Gore said nothing. He pushed the slackening organ back into his pants, zipped himself up, then strode out, slamming and bolting the door behind him.

Janis lay down on the bare ground in relief, tears stinging her eyes. For a while she dozed, then woke and drank more water, glad to swill the filthy taste of stale spunk out of her mouth. Her stomach growled, reminding her of how dependent she was on those two bastards for everything now.

And where on earth was Virago? The place must be some kind of farm, probably abandoned. Although they were being kept apart Janis was sure that Virago would be in another building nearby. If only she could free herself, get out of her prison. She tugged experimentally at the ankle chain which bound her two legs together. It had been placed around her feet in a figure of eight, just allowing her to hobble.

Heavy footsteps warned her that her captors were returning. She lay down again, feigning sleep. More light came this time when the door was opened and she guessed that it must be around midday. Someone came towards her and she flinched, but then a dish was put beside her. She half opened her eyes and looked up through her lashes. It was Blade. She opened her eyes completely and sat up. 'Blade!'

He looked at her indifferently, placing a plate of bread and cheese beside the jug. 'Food!'

Janis ate some of it while he watched. The bread was stale and the cheese had spots of mould on it but she didn't care. Then he turned to go. She reached out and touched his leg. 'Please, Blade, for God's sake tell me if Virago is all right.'

He glanced at her briefly, as if afraid of the mute appeal in her eyes. 'She's OK.'

Janis grasped the leg of his jeans more firmly. 'Why have you brought us here, Blade? What are you going to do?'

He shrugged. 'Gore wants your tour to be cancelled and the band to split up. He's going to make that demand by phone today, as a condition of your release.'

'But that's crazy! We're only just starting out, we can't stop now.'

'If your people don't agree to it then the band is doomed anyway. You'd be nothing without Virgo.'

'Virago,' Janis corrected him without thinking, then sighed at the absurdity of it. What did it matter now what the woman was called?

'But what if they refuse? What will happen to us?' Blade averted his face, and Janis suspected the worst. She was still clinging in desperation to his leg. 'He wouldn't kill us, would he?'

'You don't know Gore. He'd stop at nothing to get what he wants.'

For an instant their eyes met and Janis realized, with a shock, that Blade was just as afraid of Gore as she was. She could almost smell his terror. What kind of a hold did that bastard have over him? Was it drugs? Was Gore some kind of psycho, possessed by demons? Virago had known more than she'd let on. If only she'd been persuaded to reveal more maybe they'd have known just what they were up against.

Janis's mind started racing again as she realized that these few precious minutes might be her only chance to save herself, and Virago. 'Blade, you've got to help me!' she begged. 'It's Virago he wants, you said so yourself. Why drag me into it?'

'You were just in the wrong place at the wrong time. I'm sorry.'

He made for the door but she crawled after him. 'Please wait! Won't you help me a little?'

'What?'

Blade was still looking anxiously through the door, keeping watch for Gore. She thought quickly. 'You could loosen my chains, just a little. Then I could try to escape when I was alone, and you were with Gore. That way he'd never suspect you had anything to do with it.'

'But I'd have to undo the padlock.'

'Where's the key?'

'Gore has it. I . . .'

There was a shout outside and Blade hurried through the door, waving her back. He shut and bolted the door after him and Janis felt despair seize her again. She could hear the two men talking outside.

'What the fuck are you doing, Blade? Leave that bitch alone!'

'I was only giving her some food.'

'OK, but don't talk to her. She's a cunning little vixen, that

one. If you're not careful she'll be saying things to weaken
you. Remember who it is we serve, Blade. Remember our goal
and be steadfast.'

Janis felt her last hope ebbing away. She and Virago were
in his power. What if he waited until the tour was cancelled,
and the reputation of Jinxed ruined, then had them killed them
anyway? She gave a grim smile. They'd certainly chosen an apt
title for the band.

Hours went by and the crack of light through the door faded
into night again. Janis dozed intermittently in the pile of straw,
but she was freezing cold and aching all over so there wasn't
much chance of sleeping properly. She wondered what was
going through the minds of the others. Had the police been
informed? Or had Gore got a message to them already,
warning them against saying anything?

Then, when Janis had consumed the remains of the food
and water and was longing for more, the bolt slid across very
quietly and the door was opened. For a second a dark figure
was framed in the doorway and she feared it was Gore. But it
wasn't. Never before had she been so glad to hear the
reassuring sound of Blade's voice.

'Gore's gone to the phone box. I've only got five minutes,'
he said, tersely.

Bending down he unlocked the padlock that bound her
chains. For a second Janis contemplated leaping up and
making a dash for it, but then she thought better of it. For one
thing her legs were stiff and she would almost certainly be
caught by Blade as she stumbled around. Or, even if she did
manage to give him the slip, she would be getting him into real
trouble with Gore and her life wouldn't be worth living for fear
that he would track her down. No, she must play this one by
the book and do exactly as she'd promised.

'Thanks a million,' she told him, rubbing her chafed ankles.

'I've got to lock it again,' he reminded her. 'But I'll give you a bit more leeway. I'll make it look as if this chain's wound round twice but in fact it's only fastened in one loop. That means if Gore comes here before you've got away you have to be careful not to move too much or he'll notice and then I'll get it in the neck.'

'I really appreciate this,' Janis said. 'But where is he keeping Virago?'

Blade's eyes narrowed in the half-light. 'You're not going to do anything stupid, are you?'

'No, I shan't try to free her by myself.'

'OK. At the moment she's in the cellar of the farmhouse. But if Gore suspects anything he'll move her.'

'Where are we?'

'Wales.'

'*Wales!*'

'I've got to go now. Good luck.'

Janis sat in stunned silence after she heard him bolt the door again and trudge off, presumably back to the farmhouse. She wished he'd brought her some more water, but knew she had to be grateful for small mercies. There was the noise of a car engine and she guessed that Gore was returning. She debated the best moment to make her getaway. If only she knew the time, or how far they were from the nearest town.

More heavy footsteps came and this time it was Gore. He stood in the doorway with a torch. Janis could see a fine mist of rain illuminated in the beam. She shrank away from him, terrified that he would discover her secret and get both her and Blade into dreadful trouble. Even in the dark his eyes looked unnaturally bright, as if he were high on something.

'More water.' He put the jug down. 'We don't want you fading away just yet, do we? Not when Salamander Records have agreed to pay a ransom for you.'

'A ransom? But I didn't think you wanted money.'

'I want all I can get. I reckon I'm owed some compensation

for the way that bitch ruined *my* band. No one shits on Gore and gets away with it. Just remember that.'

'If they pay up, will you let us go?'

He gave an evil chuckle. 'You'll just have to wait and see, won't you? I've a whole shopping list to get through before I give you up. You're probably more valuable right now than you would ever have been with that poxy band of yours. Think about it!'

Janis just wanted him to leave. But he squatted down and put his foul face close to hers, staring malevolently into her eyes. 'Why do you hate me so?' she whispered.

He gave a croaking laugh. 'You knew, didn't you? From the moment we met. It's because you had it all so fucking easy, that's why. You walked into that dressing-room and Blade handed you your chance, just like that. It's always been like that for you, hasn't it? Well, now you're going to find out just how hard life can be for the rest of the poor buggers.'

He got up and aimed a vicious kick at her leg. Janis pulled it back and realized, too late, that she'd let the chain slacken. She hugged her injured shin to her chest, hoping he hadn't noticed. Cowering in the dark she felt sick with fear, but he just laughed at her and strode to the door.

'You feel sorry for yourself now, don't you?' he mocked. 'But you ain't seen nothing yet. Oh no! If you knew. If only you knew . . .'

He was rambling on, no doubt under the influence of one of his home-made drugs. Janis sat still and silent, longing for him to go. When his footsteps had faded into silence again she took stock of the situation. If she waited too long she might not be able to get far enough away by daybreak, when Gore might check on her again. On the other hand, if she went too soon he might still be awake. If only she knew the time.

Then fate dealt her an unexpectedly good hand. Suddenly, blaring out into the night, came the sound of Shaft's latest

single. Janis guessed they were playing it to taunt her and
Virago. The words seemed appropriate:

> *'What's keeping me here? I just don't know.*
> *What's keeping me here, when I'd rather go . . .'*

They'd obviously turned up the sound full blast. It took Janis
only a few seconds to realize how fortunate she was. She
reached down and pulled the chain first over one ankle and
then the other, rubbing her legs vigorously to restore the
circulation. Struggling to her feet she put on her discarded
shoes, went over to the door and gave it a hefty shove with her
shoulder. It didn't matter how much noise she made right now
– the din outside would drown it! The door was old and rotten
and it didn't take much effort to splinter the wood. Soon she
had a hole large enough to put her hand through, and then it
was easy to draw the bolt across. She picked up her bag and
stepped out of her prison.

The damp night air hit her full in the face with refreshing
force. Only one window in the stone farmhouse was lit up,
throwing a yellow stream of light across a muddy yard. Dark
shapes of hills rose all around, but there was the outline of a
truck at the side of the house. The road must be near there.
Stealthily she began to hobble over the uneven ground. The
cold and wet began to seep miserably into her skin after that
first, exhilarating, exposure to the elements.

As she neared the building Janis was terrified that Gore
would come out to see how she was enjoying the 'entertainment'
put on for her benefit. It would be just like him to gloat. She
contemplated getting into the van but she knew he would have
the keys so there was no point. She was better off on foot.
Under cover of darkness she could surely find a place to hide
if he did come looking for her.

After a few minutes Janis found herself in a muddy lane

with stone walls on either side. She hurried along, her once-glamorous gown soaked through now and clinging soddenly to her body. Her legs felt weak at first but strengthened the more she walked. It was only temporary, she reminded herself, the result of getting used to moving them again. In an hour or so she would be exhausted and freezing cold.

The lane went on and on without sign of habitation and she grew worried. There must be a phone box somewhere. She couldn't phone the police as long as Virago was still a prisoner, but at least she could let Adam know where she was.

Twenty minutes later she came out onto a main road. There was little traffic, however, and she was nervous about getting a lift from a stranger in her condition. What if someone took advantage of her? That would be unbearable. No, her best bet was to find a phone and get Adam to come for her. She would find a place to hide nearby and wait for him.

At last she came to a phone box in a small village. To her utmost relief it took coins, not just phone cards. She found twenty pence and slotted it in with trembling fingers. 'Please Adam, be at home!' she prayed as he dialled the number.

It was wonderful to hear his voice. He seemed equally delighted to hear hers. 'Where are you, love? Are you all right? Is Virago with you?'

'Wait a minute, and I'll tell you!' she laughed, relief flooding through her. 'I'm in some part of Wales with an unpronounceable name. I just saw a road sign.'

She spelled it out for him and then he went off to find a map, but before he returned her money ran out. 'Damn!' she exclaimed, scrabbling around in her purse for another coin and finding only coppers. Still, if he had any sense Adam would guess she'd be waiting for him in the phone box. It was risky, she knew. Gore was no fool, and if that was the same phone he'd used he would come there looking for her. Still, if she went on there was a real risk of hypothermia. Uncomfortable

as the cramped cubicle was at least she had some shelter from
the wind and rain.

She dozed, awoke shivering, and dozed again until dawn.
Still no sign of Adam, but Gore had not come looking for her
either. Janis peered out at the misty morning. Should she
knock on a cottage door, ask for help? Just a blanket would be
a luxury. But they might inform the police. She tried to
estimate how long it might take Adam to drive to Wales from
London, but since she had no idea how long ago she'd phoned
it seemed a futile exercise.

Gloomily Janis stared through the small square panes of the
old-fashioned phone booth. There was a dull tension in her
stomach that was worse than the hunger, a perpetual fear that
gnawed at her remorselessly. Were Adam and Gore already
engaged in a race against time, both of them speeding towards
her? Which would reach her first? With a shudder she
speculated that the outcome might well prove to be a matter
of life and death.

Slumped on the concrete floor, knees under her chin, Janis
didn't hear the approaching car until it braked in the road
outside. It was bright daylight and, as she looked up she saw at
once that it was Adam's blue Renault. Pushing herself to her
feet she banged on the glass.

'Hey, Adam! I'm in here!'

He leapt out and came straight to the phone box, arriving
as she heaved the door open. They clung to each other
rapturously for several seconds, but then Janis's anxiety
returned. 'Let's get away from here as quickly as possible,' she
muttered. 'They could be on my tail.'

On the journey back to London they swapped news
endlessly. After Janis had related what had happened to her,
Adam told how they'd scoured the hotel looking for her and
Virago. Ivan had wanted to go straight to the police but Adam,
sensing that Blade and Gore were behind it, had restrained

him. Even so, he'd gone through hell in the past twenty-four hours and when the call came from Gore he'd been hard pressed to restrain himself

They decided to say nothing to Ivan about Janis's escape. She would stay in a hotel and Adam would look after her. It seemed the safest course. Adam was meeting the others later.

It was bliss to be in a hotel room again, with hot water on tap. As Janis luxuriated in a warm bath she felt her old strength and optimism returning. Horrific as her ordeal had been she had survived, and she was sure that Virago would too. While she waited for Adam to return from his meeting with the rest of the band, she began to feel sexy again for the first time since her kidnap.

He returned with a broad smile on his face. 'Guess what, we've got some allies!' he said, sweeping her into his arms and giving her a great big kiss. 'You'll never believe this, but you know the album's doing really well in the States?' She nodded. 'Well, a bunch of lesbian bikers have come over for the tour. Of course they're mad as hell that it's been cancelled, and madder still now they know why. I wouldn't like to be in Gore's shoes when they find him.'

'What? You mean they're going after him?'

'That's the general idea. Of course we can't just let them go storming the place. That might put Virago in worse danger. But if we can manage to surprise those bastards we can certainly outnumber them. The plan is to go down there tomorrow.'

'Then I'm coming too.'

Adam's face darkened. 'Don't be ridiculous, Janis. You've been through enough already.'

'But I'm the best person to find the place again. OK, I didn't see it in daylight, but I have a rough idea of where it is, and the general layout of the land. I'd be invaluable to you.'

He still looked doubtful. 'I just don't want to put you in jeopardy again, love.'

'Don't worry, I'll keep out of danger. But I'd be so fed up staying here while you were all down there. It would be hell for me, knowing how much I could help.'

'I suppose you're right. But only if you get a good night's sleep and you're feeling up to it.'

'You'll never guess what I'm feeling up to right now!' Janis put her arms around him. 'Come to bed with me, Adam. After what that bastard did to me I need reassuring.'

He smiled tenderly at her and they kissed with slow passion. Janis knew she had to exorcise Gore's ghost from her body. She needed to cleanse herself of the humiliation, the pain. Slowly she undressed her lover, smiling to see that his erection was already full grown. His prick stood clean and tall, a prize, not a weapon. She bent her lips to the smooth pink glans and tasted his sweet flesh, banishing forever the memory of that other foul organ. Adam stroked her hair as she sucked and licked at him, moaning softly when she moved down his shaft and enclosed the full length of him in her softly willing mouth.

'Oh, you're so gorgeous!' he murmured. His hands moved to her breasts, fondling gently. Her nipples tingled at his touch and grew bold, hardening and yearning against his fingers until she felt an answering itch in her groin. He twisted round so that he could taste the luscious juices she was secreting from her quim. Janis moaned at the first touch of his lips against hers, wriggled to let his tongue reach the eager bud of her sex that was already pulsating with desire. She squeezed his balls softly, feeling his prick strain against the roof of her mouth as she licked all round the shaft.

Her pussy was awash now, aching for him, and she lifted his head away then guided his prick towards her entrance. The contact was exquisitely lush, his glans pushing straight in without delay and filling her up entirely.

'I didn't dare think about this while I was . . . there,' she told him, her heart expanding with joy. 'It was too much to hope that we'd ever be like this again.'

'Where there's love, there's hope,' Adam smiled down at her, his head haloed with light. She smiled, feeling his radiance reflected in her own face. His hands continued to stroke her breasts as he began the series of long, slow plunges that would take her up to heaven.

They seemed to make love for hours, neither of them being in the mood to hurry. Adam took her up to a blissful plateau and there she stayed, meltingly oblivious of all that had happened to her, revelling in the prolongation of their love-making. Her cunt seemed to expand to infinity, accommodating his gentle thrustings. Sometimes she gripped him with her inner walls, feeling the length of him slide in and out. At other times she went limp and open, letting him plumb her secret depths without hindrance. She was simmering on a slow heat, coming very gradually to the boil, and when she first climaxed the onset was so gradual that she gasped with surprise as it gathered momentum, taking her into a series of delicious tremors that filled her body with voluptuous pleasure.

Wonderful as their love-making had already been, Janis felt hungry for more and she realized that her lover was still hard. In a few seconds she was on top of him, letting him reach up to her jutting breasts as she rose and fell in a smooth rhythm. This time they took it faster so that their mutual climax, when it came, was fierce and strong. His outpouring seemed to go on forever, douching her with warm bliss as her cunt filled with his seed.

They collapsed with sighs of contentment and Janis snuggled into his embrace, feeling she had wiped the slate of her memory clean of all its dark stains. With her cheek against Adam's gently heaving chest she murmured, 'Oh, that's done me so much good! I feel ready for anything now.'

'Are you ready to meet a bunch of bike-dykes from hell?' he grinned down at her.

'As long as they're on our side,' she whispered, sleepily.

'You'd better believe it!'

CHAPTER SIXTEEN

Early next morning Adam and Janis drove to Lee's flat in the van. The drummer had offered floor space to four of the Americans and the other four were staying with Dagmar, but they were all due to meet at Lee's at nine. Adam had phoned to let them know that Janis was safe and would be coming with them to Wales. The news had been greeted with great jubilation by the biker girls, but Janis felt nervous at the prospect of meeting them.

The scene that met their eyes as Lee let them in was one of total devastation. The four butch-looking women were sitting round smoking and drinking Special Brew, while all around them the floor was littered with empty bottles, cans and cigarette packs. At first Janis felt repelled by their clothes: the filthy T-shirts with grinning skull motifs, torn and oily jeans, battle-scarred leathers and heavy Docs with metal toecaps. They all had pierced ears, eyelids, lips or noses and probably other parts of their anatomy too.

Janis didn't know what to make of their hairstyles, either. The one called Bex had her head completely shaven and tattooed all over. Another had cropped hair with a five-pointed star cut into it. A half-caste woman called Dolores had long, greasy dreadlocks interwoven with beads of a dark-brown sticky substance that must have been either opium or hash, and the fourth wore her hair in punkish spikes of various lurid hues. They made a formidable bunch. But when they saw her, the faces of all four women broke into welcoming grins and Janis warmed to them. Their eyes sparkled at her with genuine friendliness as they rose to their feet and, one by one, shook her by the hand.

'Great to meet you, Jan! And congratulations on escaping from that shit-head!'

'Yeah, I'll second that! Jest wait till we get our fuckin' hands on him!'

'We'll get Virago back, you bet your boobs! We came over here to hear the band and that's what we're fuckin' gonna do.'

'When we get going, babe, there ain't no power on earth can stop us. We'll chase those bastards off the face of the planet, no sweat!'

The sheer raw power emanating from the women was exhilarating. They were buzzing with sexual energy and lust for action. Just being with them was like playing on stage at a gig. When the other four arrived with Dagmar the small flat was filled with noise, swearing and laughter. Just having them around made Janis feel more secure. It would be a brave man, or woman, who dared mess with the likes of them!

They had a natural leader, a girl called Harley like the bike she rode. The rest of the girls respected her and always listened to what she had to say. Janis found herself admiring her too. With her flowing mane of dark red hair and huge hazel eyes she was the most strikingly attractive of the bunch.

'We'll travel down in convoy to that village where Adam picked you up,' Harley said. 'Then we'll stay there until you've located the farm. We don't want to give 'em no advance warning, now do we?'

Janis wondered how two men and a girl could possibly escape from such a heavy bunch but she knew they must take no chances. Her impression had been that the farm was in wild, mountainous country. It could be an area that Blade or Gore knew well, but none of the bikers were familiar with the territory and neither were Janis and Adam. The surprise factor was their best weapon.

At last they set out on the road to Wales, the van containing Adam and Janis, Lee, Dagmar and Sal flanked by the convoy of bikers as if they were a police escort. The other road users gave them due respect and they reached the Welsh border without incident. After stopping for a bite at a motorway services they proceeded, with Adam leading the way, to the small village where he'd picked up Janis.

The nearer they got to it the more nervous she became, wondering whether Gore would choose to use the phone box again and spot them. But the place seemed just as quiet as before, with only a few local youths staring in open-mouthed amazement at the sight of eight leather-clad dykes, with fearsome images on their backs, sitting arrogantly astride gleaming red, black and silver machines. They drew up at the only pub.

'We'll go into this bar,' Harley announced, swinging her leg over. 'Find out what we can about the lie of the land and get some of your great English beer down us at the same time.'

'More likely to be Welsh beer,' Adam grinned. 'You're in a foreign country now, you know.'

The publican and his wife were clearly overwhelmed by the sudden influx of outlandish females but they did their best to appear unfazed. When they were all served Adam engaged them in casual conversation. 'We're looking for a place to camp,' he told them. 'Somewhere near here would be good. You don't know of any farms that could take half a dozen tents, do you? Or maybe there's somewhere deserted, where we wouldn't be troubling anyone.'

The publican scratched his bald patch. 'Well now, there's quite a few empty farms round by yer. One up the lane, old Pritchard's place, been empty this twelve-month. Dreadful shame! Ewan Pritchard, he's the only son, should have taken it over by rights but he's in prison and the old man died, see. Left to go to rack and ruin, it was. I remember when old man Pritchard was the richest farmer around here . . .'

Realizing he was set to go on all afternoon, Adam broke in. 'Is it far, this Pritchard farm?'

'No, not so far. Like I said, just up the lane a few yards on from the phone box. You go up about a mile or so and look for a gate with a holly tree, then turn off to the left. You can't miss it.' His face clouded with suspicion. 'You're not squatters, are you? Not plannin' to settle round yer?'

'Oh no!' Adam laughed. 'Our friends are from Los Angeles, only here for a holiday.'

'That's all right then. Only the Welsh Nats don't like immigrants, see.'

During the conversation Janis sat nervously watching the door. What if Blade and Gore came in for a pint? Even though they heavily outnumbered them Janis didn't trust those two. Her mind raced on. What if they'd moved Virago to a safer place? It would be difficult to track them down in those hills.

Adam finished his pint then took her hand. 'Come on, Jan, we'd better get going while the light's still good.'

'What if we find them?' she asked. 'What then?'

With a grin Adam produced a mobile phone from his deep pocket. 'Harley has one too, so we can keep in touch.'

The biker grinned. 'Jes' say the word, boss, and we'll make Stormin' Norman look like Sergeant Bilko!'

They decided to go on foot to the farm, so there would be no engine noise. Janis held tightly onto Adam's hand as they made their way along the lane. She remembered how she'd felt the last time she was there – cold, wet and terrified – and the thought of her ordeal was chilling. Were they simply walking back into danger? The mobile phone was small consolation.

What if Gore took them both prisoner before they had time to warn the others?

Yet she knew that they had to act as scouts before an effective campaign could be launched. The whole thing had to be planned like a military operation if they were to take those villains by surprise and ensure Virago's safety.

They reached the gate and saw the dilapidated farm buildings in the distance, with the bare hills behind. Deciding to cross the fields rather than use the cart-track they began to walk over the uneven ground, keeping close to the stone wall for cover. The light was already fading into a grey gloom that made Janis feel both anxious and depressed. On and on they went in silence, eyes and ears wide open, until they were close to the outbuildings. Janis thought she recognized the low stone shed where she had been kept a prisoner. She could see where a hole had been punched through the door.

'Let's go round the other side of the house, see if their van's still there,' Adam whispered.

But when they looked at where the van had been it was gone. Cautiously they approached the farmhouse but it had a dead, silent air about it and Janis became convinced that Gore and the others were no longer there. After peering through the windows they went inside. There were many signs of recent habitation: a torn page of *Melody Maker* on the floor, dated just a few days ago; several empty cigarette packs and milk cartons; a length of rubber tubing and a discarded syringe; a folded piece of newspaper that looked as if it might have fallen out of a wallet.

Adam opened it out. There was a photo of a stone circle in the middle of some woods and the headline was, 'Black Magic Rituals Desecrate Stones'. The brief article described how a goat's skull had been found at the ancient site and blood daubed over the stones. Janis felt her own blood chill. She had a strong intuition that Blade and Gore had taken Virago there, but where was this stone circle? The report didn't say, but she guessed it was local.

They went down into the cellar and found an empty water jug and mug, similar to the ones that Janis had used. She told Adam of her suspicions, and he nodded.

'I was thinking along the same lines.' He dialled up the pub and spoke to Harley. 'Look, we think we know where they are. Please ask the landlord if he knows of a small stone circle in the middle of a wood near here.'

They hung on awaiting the reply. Harley's voice came back with the information that there was one such site just two miles away, off the Llanberis road. Time now seemed of the essence. The bikers were to pick up Janis and Adam and take them there at once.

When Janis first saw the convoy bearing down on them she felt a flutter of excitement in her loins, bordering on fear. 'Thank God they're on our side!' she whispered to Adam as the pack pulled up all round.

'Jump up behind me!' Harley told Janis, brusquely.

She did as she was told, quashing the urge to ask if there was a spare helmet. Adam got up behind Bex, the half-caste, and they started off down the lane with a great roar. Once on the open road they set off at a steady pace and soon saw the wood about two hundred yards from the road, as described by the landlord. The bikes stopped at a gap in the hedge. 'I say we rush the place,' Harley said.

'Yeah, let's Desert Storm the fuckers!' Bex grinned.

'OK,' Adam said. 'But if they're working black magic in there we'll do some of our own. We'll split up into two's and come at them from all points of the compass. If we time it right, they won't know what hit them!'

To maintain the surprise factor they walked their bikes across the fields until they reached the perimeter of the wood. A weak sun had come out from behind a cloud. It was low in the sky and glowing a dull, coppery red that gave Janis the willies. Suddenly all the dykes took off their leather jackets and T-shirts until they were stripped naked to the waist. Janis gasped. Every one of them had dark blue spirals tattooed on their breasts. Harley looked particularly magnificent with her enormous tits thrusting arrogantly forward. There were small gold rings through each of her nipples, linked by a silver chain. She took a stick of blue-black paint from her jeans pocket and turned her large, stiff nipples blue as well.

'Boadicea's warriors!' Harley grinned. 'It's our insignia. We paint our faces with woad, too!'

She proceeded to make curling patterns on the face of each girl. When it came to her turn Janis felt the greasy stuff being daubed on her forehead and cheeks. Defiantly she pulled off her jacket and top, letting Harley decorate her breasts and nipples with blue. Now she was an honorary member of their tribe.

'OK, away you go, we can't waste another moment!' Adam said when they were fully prepared, directing the others to go off in pairs and await the signal. Janis could feel her heart pounding as she clung to the solid flesh of Harley's waist.

Adam waited edgily, seated on the pillion of the bike behind Bex. Around his neck was the whistle he was going to blow when the time came to charge. They were gambling that if Blade and Gore were performing any rituals they would climax at sunset, which was only about ten minutes away. As they waited, Janis prayed that they were not already too late.

'When we get going hold onto my tits!' Harley grinned over her shoulder as she manoeuvred the bike into position. 'If you get me excited I'll scream harder!'

After five minutes Adam said he'd give the signal. Harley gave her machine a kick start and it throbbed into life. She revved loudly as he blew the whistle and there were answering roars from all around the wood. Janis pressed her naked breasts against the other woman's warm back and her excitement mounted. She felt safe behind such a seasoned warrior.

'Ready, steady, go!' yelled Adam, blowing hard on his whistle a second time.

Soon the small wood was reverberating to the sound of eight powerful engines on full throttle. Janis clung to Harley's ample breasts as they crashed through the undergrowth, heedless of track or path, and the amazon gave out a blood-curdling scream. Soon Janis was yelling too, finding a primal voice from deep within her soul that came out of her like a banshee's yell. It was tremendously exhilarating, but terrifying too.

Janis could see a clearing up ahead but the bike was still going at top speed, crashing over fallen branches and tree stumps, shaking her up and down until she was clinging onto Harley's boobs for dear life. Through the thinning trees she could just make out some greyish-white shapes and knew that they were approaching their destination. But what if Blade and Gore had already fled with their quarry? What if they were just too late and this incredible rescue mission was no more than a hollow charade?

Right through the last of the trees they hurtled until the circle of ancient stones was in full view. Janis gasped as she saw the grim scene taking place in the centre. Only dimly aware that the other bikers had arrived from the other directions, Janis was mesmerized by the sight of Virago lying naked and bound on an improvised stone altar while Blade stood behind her holding a smoking firebrand in one upraised hand and with a weird dragon mask over his head. The most horrific aspect, however, was the way Gore was standing there clad in scarlet and black robes covered with grotesque symbols and holding a long-bladed dagger aloft. He looked round at them, his black eyes darting everywhere as his wits sized up the situation.

The bikers drew to a halt outside the circle, uncertain what to do next. Adam dismounted and began to walk towards the nearest stone. Janis felt both terrified and proud of him as he called out, 'We have you surrounded, Gore. Don't try anything stupid now. You're well outnumbered.'

Gore gave a chilling laugh. 'If one of you steps into the circle I shall immediately make our sacrifice to the Lord of Blood. It is too late for negotiation. You had your chance and you blew it. This bitch must die. Our Lord decrees it!'

Janis looked on in horror. She could tell, from the stunned silence of the others, that they were horrified too. Beneath her hand, still clutching at the ample breast, she could feel Harley's heart going like a two-stroke engine. Were they about to witness a particularly disgusting murder?

Adam spoke again, his voice deliberately measured, and Janis knew he was struggling to keep control of himself. 'If we let you go, will you promise not to harm Virago?'

The sun was sinking fast and Janis realized that Adam was playing for time. If his hunch was right, and the sacrifice was supposed to happen exactly at sunset, it would very soon be too late.

'What do you mean, let us go?' came Gore's scornful, impatient voice. 'We shall continue our ritual. The evil virgin bitch-queen must die. It is ordained. And after the deed is done you shall be punished for your interference. Get on your knees and pray now, profane ones, for you have incurred the wrath of our Lord!'

Janis thought quickly, spurred by panic. It seemed essential to create some kind of diversion, to give the others a chance to act. With scarcely any thought for her own safety she dismounted and called out to Gore, 'Let me take Virago's place, then!'

Behind her she heard Adam groan 'No!' but she ignored him. Cautiously she approached one of the weathered stones.

There was a deathly silence from the circle of bikers all around.

Gore was staring at her with a triumphant hatred in his eyes. 'Bitch!' he snarled. 'Let me make a double sacrifice to my Lord! Come, I shall bind you to this vixen, then you two hellcats shall go straight to hell!'

He gave a bloodcurdling laugh, insanely shrill, and Janis's first instinct was to run. Instead she steeled herself to walk forward, across the muddy grass to where the centre of depravity was. As she approached Gore lowered the knife and gave her a sardonic smile. She glanced down at the half-sunken stone where Virago lay, bound and gagged. A pair of dark blue eyes stared up at her in mute appeal, strengthening her resolve.

When she was right before him Janis summoned up all her strength, drew herself up and looked him straight in the eye. 'How do you imagine I escaped, Gore?' she said, quietly. 'I had help, you know. Blade helped me. He has betrayed you.'

'You're lying! Blade is my blood brother. He would never betray me.'

Janis continued calmly, 'Then explain how I managed to unlock my chains. I could never have done it without his help. He loosened them for me so I was able to slip out of them and break down the door.'

She saw the slight faltering in his expression, the glint of doubt in his eye and pressed home her advantage. 'He hates you, Gore, hates you and fears you. That's the only reason he obeys you.'

'No, he worships with me! We both adore and follow the same master, with music and ritual. How could he hate me?'

Nevertheless Gore's face turned towards that of Blade, which was half hidden by the grotesque mask. Spiky black fronds covered his hair and in place of his ears were two phallic-looking horns. Only his red mouth and frightened eyes were revealed beneath the green, warty latex.

Gore said, in a chilling tone, 'You're saying nothing to defend yourself, Blade. Why not?'

Blade's voice came out from behind the rubberized hood sounding uncharacteristically feeble. 'Would you believe me if I said I had nothing to do with it?'

The two men were facing each other now and Janis suspected that the confrontation would last several seconds at least. This might be their one and only chance. She beckoned behind her back, hoping the others would take the hint and start to close in on the unsuspecting pair.

'*Should* I believe you?' Gore snapped. 'Why should this cow lie? She's supposed to be one of your *fans*, isn't she?'

Blade retorted angrily, 'She was until the bitch-queen poisoned her mind with lies about me! Don't get side-tracked, Gore. It's all Virgo's doing. She must be killed and ritually dismembered, the way we agreed. It is she who has betrayed you, and me. Don't let this silly cow divert you from the main . . . Ah!'

While he was speaking, two of the bikers had crept up on all fours behind him and now had him in a firm arm-lock. Adam and Harley grabbed Gore at the same time and Janis lent a hand, wrenching the knife from his grasp as he was taken by surprise. The rest of the women piled in to help and soon had the two men completely helpless on the ground.

Janis hurried to untie Virago. As soon as she released the gag both women began to sob with relief They hugged and kissed each other like long-lost sisters reunited while the others applauded, looking on with a mixture of feelings written on their features.

While Virago was wrapped in a lightweight thermal blanket produced by one of the bikers, the two villains were stripped naked and led over to the sacrificial stone that, seconds ago, Virago's flesh had been warming. They were then tied there, side by side, in her place. With the mask ripped from his face it was apparent that Blade was terrified, but Gore maintained his usual superior cool.

Harley stepped forward, brandishing the flaming torch. She looked magnificent, with the light gleaming on her gold nipple-rings and lending a burnish to her auburn hair. She was obviously enjoying every minute of the unfolding drama.

'I reckon you reckoned without the bike-dykes from hell, didn't ya, fellas?' she grinned.

'Who the fuck are you?' Gore muttered.

She stepped forward and flipped him across the face with the back of her hand. He winced and she laughed. 'Show some respect, worm! Back in LA no male of the species would dare answer back to me or my sisters. We eat sperm like you for breakfast, poured all over our cereal. Adds a little more crunch to our Crunchy Nut Flakes, if you catch ma drift!'

Bex sauntered up, grinning. 'What we gonna do with 'em, Harl?'

'Well, I ain't sure yet, but I think we might just have a bit of fun while we're decidin', don't you?' She pushed her great jugs together so the chain clinked and flashed. 'What do you reckon to ma deadly weapons, boys?'

Janis watched in fascination as she sank to her haunches beside the stone and thrust her enormous mammaries into Gore's face. She held them there, grinning wickedly, as he wriggled his head ineffectually. Blade lay there wide-eyed with fear as the seconds ticked by and muffled groans came from beneath the mounds of flesh.

'Hey, don't suffocate him completely, Harl,' Dolores said, when his whole body appeared to have gone into convulsions. 'That won't be no fun for the rest of us!'

Harley feigned disappointment. 'OK. Let's give him the countdown.'

The women began to chorus: 'Ten – nine – eight – seven . . .' When Gore was at last released from his torment his face was bright red and he gasped down great lungfuls of air.

Virago giggled. 'That was the perfect punishment for that creep. He has a real thing about women's tits – he can't stand them!'

Dolores was shaking her dreadlocks at Blade, who cowered as she loomed over him. 'What'll we do with this one?' She pointed to his shrivelled white dick. 'Hey, he won't miss that a helluva lot, will he? Shall we "bobbit" him, girls?'

Lee came up, brandishing the knife that Gore had been holding. She put the point to each of Blade's nipples in turn, making them invert. Then she placed it at the base of his penis. He was visibly trembling, and not just with cold. 'P . . please . . .' he stammered. 'N . . . no . . .'

'Why not?' Lee answered, moving the blade down to his balls. 'You were getting ready to carve up poor Virago. Why shouldn't we do the same for you?'

'It was all an act,' Blade said, growing more articulate in his desperation. 'Like on stage.'

'Where was the music, then?' Dagmar grinned. 'Where were the lights, the audience? Not much of an act without those.'

'We . . . we just wanted to frighten her. To make her stop competing with us.'

Virago came and stood over him. With the silver thermal cape around her shoulders she looked magnificent, imperial. 'You couldn't stand it, could you, Blade?' Her tone was full of pitying contempt. 'Me being successful without you, I mean. You thought I was riding on your back, while all the time it was you riding on mine. That's what really hurts, doesn't it? It was me the crowds came to see, me they called for, me they adored. Not you.'

He fell silent, finally acknowledging the truth of her words. Janis knew it was true, too. Blade had been a sham from the start, a gay poser under the influence of an evil manipulator, his offstage self a mere shadow of his onstage persona. Whereas Virago had always been the Sex Queen that she appeared to be, voracious in her appetite for men and women alike and emphatically her own mistress.

Their exchange seemed to take the wind out of Harley's sails. She turned away with a shrug and a curt command, 'Give the pair of 'em a good beatin', girls, then let's get the hell outa here!'

Janis watched as the seven bikers took off their belts and, walking around the recumbent pair, delivered an almost ritualistic thrashing. One after the other they laid into the helpless bodies of the two men until their skin was striped red and they were moaning with pain. Yet there was a token quality to their chastisement and it was evident that they would survive the beating. When every girl had administered three stripes Harley called them to heel.

'C'mon, let's get goin'! We'll leave these bastards to the wolves!'

'We don't have wolves in England,' Adam pointed out. 'But after a night in the open maybe these two losers will reflect on the futility of their lives.'

'You're not going to leave us here?' Gore groaned.

'Oh yes we are. Chained to the rock, like Prometheus!' Virago smiled, sweetly. 'You didn't have any qualms about making Janis and I prisoners and leaving us alone in the dark, now did you? Like I always say, what's sauce for the goose . . .'

The two men moaned and lay back against the rock, resigned to their fate, as the women returned to the bikes. It wasn't long before they were zooming through the wood again in high spirits, the Americans breaking into a chorus of 'Ghost Riders in the Sky' and the English girls joining in with enthusiasm.

It was ten o'clock by the time they arrived back in London, both elated and exhausted by the day's events. When they gathered at Lee's flat once again there was a sense of anticlimax. Virago expressed everyone's secret thoughts when she flopped down in the nearest armchair and asked, 'Now what?'

'First thing is to ring Ivan and tell him you're both safe,' Adam said. 'I imagine he'll want to go ahead with the tour straight away. Some of the dates could probably be salvaged and others rearranged.' He gave Harley a rueful smile. 'Don't know whether it'll be fixed in time for you guys to see a gig, though. When are you going back to the States?'

'We can stay to the end of the month,' Harley said. 'But hey, why wait for a gig? If you five gorgeous creatures are willing we can stage a gig of our own. Better yet, let's party!' She asked Dolores, 'Where did you say that squat was? The one where they have all those fetish rooms?'

'West London.'

'OK, we'll go over there tonight and check it out.' She put on a fake English accent. 'You'll be hearing from us tomorrow, chaps. Tally-ho for now, and toodle-pip!'

They rose to leave en masse. Adam and Janis got up too. It had been a long, hard day and they wanted to get back to their flat. The prospect of an all-night fetish party with the bike dykes, appealing though it was, made them suddenly need their beauty sleep.

But when they were, finally, tucked up in bed together their cuddling led predictably to sex. Janis needed the warm reassurance of Adam's body, needed to know she was still loved and cherished after the brutal treatment that she had undergone. His fingers moved over her curving breasts, gently brushing her nipples into firm nubs, making her stomach flutter with anticipation as they moved on over the flat plane of her midriff and down to toy with the crisp hair of her muff. All the while he was kissing her with soft persuasion, letting her know how deeply he cared, soothing away the terrors of the past twenty-four hours.

But as his lips played gently with hers she couldn't help wondering how Virago was feeling that night. She had opted to stay in Lee's flat and so probably she was now tucked up in the king-size bed along with Lee and Dagmar.

Then she thought of Gore and Blade, strapped to the rock like a living sacrifice to their black demon, and couldn't help smiling. Adam felt her lips curl against his and drew back, his expression quizzical. 'What's the matter, love?'

'It's OK, I just had a thought. About those two bastards.'

'What?'

Janis giggled. 'Well, my Mum used to say that sitting on cold, wet stone seats gave you piles!'

CHAPTER SEVENTEEN

Janis was wondering what to wear to the celebration party when there was a knock at the door of the flat and a large parcel was delivered. She opened the box and her gasps of surprise soon turned to squeals of pleasure as she unfolded a pink latex mini-dress, with clear plastic bubbles for her nipples and crotch to show through. She glanced at the accompanying card then held it up for Adam's approval. 'It's from Harley – isn't it gorgeous? Oh, there's something else.'

From a second parcel she brought forth a pair of shiny black leather boots and some long black vinyl gloves. Just to complete the outfit there was also a black leather dog collar, with silver studs.

Adam gave a wry smile. 'That's you kitted out, then. But what am I going to wear?'

'Something outrageous, obviously. I'll leave it to your imagination. Right now I can't wait to try this lot on.'

The sight that met her eyes in the mirror a few minutes later was extraordinary. The tight rubber material caressed her breasts and thighs intimately, like a second skin, and the see-through sections made her nipples look pale and delicate by contrast with the stronger pink all around. Janis had found a small can of silicone spray hidden in the wrapping and the gloss on her leather gloves was brilliant. The slim boots clung seductively to her thighs and although she tottered on the extra-high heels she knew that they made her legs look terrific.

Janis was not satisfied with the way her pubic hair was revealed, however. It just didn't look right. Stripping off her finery she made for the bathroom and picked up her electric lady shaver. Then she started hunting around for some cream to soften her skin.

Adam entered, still in the nude. 'What are you doing, Jan?'

'I've decided to shave myself down below. I don't look good in that dress with my hair showing.'

'Let me do it for you, then.'

She lay passively on the bed and opened her legs. Adam rubbed in some rose-scented cream to give the shaver a smooth ride, then switched it on. At first it tickled her but she soon got used to the feeling of gentle pressure and vibration over her tender parts and started to enjoy the process. Carefully Adam went over all her nooks and crannies while Janis lay perfectly still, trusting him not to hurt her. At last he pronounced himself satisfied. He put a blob of cream on a tissue and gently wiped the stray hairs from her naked mound and vulva.

'How does it look?' she asked him.

'See for yourself!'

He took her by the hand to the wardrobe mirror. Janis gasped to see her sex so blatantly displayed. She could only dimly remember being like that naturally. Cautiously she reached down and stroked the smooth, soft surfaces. 'It feels nice,' she smiled. 'Strange, but nice.'

'It's very nice indeed,' he said throatily, replacing her fingers with his own. 'So nice that I can hardly keep my hands off it.'

He led her back to the bed. Janis was extremely excited at the thought of him playing with her bald pussy. It was like having a brand new toy. She spread her legs and sighed with gratification as Adam bent his head to lick her newly sensitized skin. It was good to feel so clean and exposed. She purred with pleasure as he licked all the cream off her and then sucked in her natural juices, his tongue moving into every smooth crevice without hindrance.

It didn't take Janis long to come, pressing her denuded mound against his lips as she milked every last ounce of sensation from his probing tongue. Just as she felt the last tremors melting away Adam got to his knees and placed his oily glans between her labia. He rolled it all around her pubis and she revelled in the feel of his slick flesh against hers, producing exquisite after-tremors in her quim. Then, unable to resist any longer, he pushed into her open and sodden cunt and thrust his cock in to its fullest extent.

The experience was new for both of them, and within a few minutes Janis was ready for more stimulation of her clitoris. She reached down and parted the velvet-smooth labia, letting the thick base of Adam's penis ride up and down against her bulbous love-button, taking her once more on the way up to a climax. This time her frenzied moans set him off and they came together. Afterwards he wiped his spunk into her bald pussy just as he had with the cream and she spasmed over and over, with little whimpering cries, until all the wild energy in her sexual store was exhausted.

After a while the pair of them went into the bathroom and showered. Adam was still fascinated by the feel of Janis's depilated flesh and his intensive lathering of her pussy almost distracted them once more, but Janis reminded him there was no time. He'd not yet decided what to wear to the party and she didn't want to be late. Their love-making had been a titillating hors d'oeuvre to what she was sure would prove a most satisfying main course.

Suddenly Janis had an idea. 'Why don't you wear some of my clothes?'

He stared at her in alarm. 'What, go as a transvestite?'

'Why not? I know you won't be a hundred per cent

convincing, but we could have a go. It would be a giggle! I'm
sure the girls would play along.'

'I'm sure they would, too.' He gave her a rueful smile, but
in the depths of his brown eyes she could see a spark of real
interest. Had she hit on some secret fantasy of his? The more
she thought about it the more exciting the prospect seemed.

Soon Janis was rifling through her wardrobe and underwear
drawer, wondering what would best suit her lover. Onto the bed
she tossed padded uplift bras, corsets, suspender belts and
various styles of panties: French knickers, tangas, open-
crotched bloomers. Then she added a leather miniskirt with
lacing, clinging velvet pants with an elasticated waist, a shiny
red nylon dress with a mandarin collar, and various tops. She
surveyed the collection thoughtfully, aware that Adam was
growing increasingly turned-on at the thought of wearing such
feminine garments.

'We don't have time to shave your chest,' she remarked.
'That means we have to go for the padded bra and high neck.
Try this one on.'

She handed him a black bra into which she had stuffed two
large shoulder pads to fill out the top half of the already
padded cups. With the aid of a handy 'bra extender' she was
able to fasten it behind his broad back. Then she made him get
into the matching black lace tanga. His prick and balls were
just about contained but she pulled a firm-hold pantie girdle
over his hips to cover the tell-tale bulge. Adam was tightly
constrained and had difficulty in breathing but he insisted that
he could survive the evening.

'OK, now let's see about stockings.'

Janis found some spangly silver and black ones that she
eased over his muscular calves and attached to the girdle's
suspenders. She selected the red nylon dress and, when she'd
managed to do up the zipper at the side she sprayed it all over
with the silicone to give it a high gloss.

'Gorgeous!' she exclaimed. 'Now for the trickiest part – gloves and shoes!'

A pair of black, elbow-length net gloves proved to be the best since they stretched to fit his fingers. None of the shoes seemed possible, though, and Janis was foxed until she remembered a pair of black canvas sandals with cork wedge heels. The canvas stretched to accommodate Adam's broader feet and the heels were not too spiky for him to walk on – perfect! Now all that remained was to make up his face.

Janis thoroughly enjoyed the process of transforming Adam's features with her extensive range of cosmetics. Although there was no time for experimentation she was pleased with the results of her labours. A subtle smoky grey gave depth to his eyes, enhanced with black, long-lash mascara, and she made his cheek-bones seem more pronounced with skilful shading of foundation and blusher. His lips were outlined in plum, filled in with a lighter cerise then painted with a long-lasting and glossy sealant. From her wig-drawer Janis selected a blonde bubble-curl number that perfectly completed the image. When Adam saw himself in the mirror he gasped with delight. 'You've made me look fantastic! No one will recognize me like this.'

'That's the general idea,' she smiled. 'Now find yourself a cloak and let me get on with my hair. Oh, and ring for a taxi. I don't imagine either of us will feel like driving!'

The pair that arrived at the large, derelict building in Notting Hill looked dressed to kill. Janis glanced up at the peeling, cockeyed letters hanging over the once-impressive portal: Hotel Hollander. From the seedy wreck came distant sounds of music and laughter. She followed Adam's unsteady gait up the steps and waited while he rang the bell. Surprisingly it sounded. In a few seconds a half-familiar face appeared. 'Janis!' the black lips screeched.

It was Bex, her face painted with sombre colours to match her tattooed scalp. Her small breasts were on view, with their nipples chain-linked and clamped, and only her sex was obscured beneath a black latex tanga. She wore leather studded cuffs, dog-collar and anklets.

Taking Janis by the hand, Bex led her into the main hall of the hotel where the party looked as if it were at least in half swing. Although not yet crowded there were enough people to make it look busy. A long table festooned with toilet paper in various pastel hues was laden with decorative food and there were big black balloons everywhere. It only took Janis a few seconds to realize that they were condoms. Loud music blared from a smaller room off the main one where more people seemed to be dancing.

'Janis, Adam – you both look wonderful!'

Harley had sneaked up on them, put her arms around them both and was delivering wet kisses. She looked exotic in a skin-tight yellow vinyl catsuit with her ringed and tattooed breasts and labia exposed through cutouts. On each visible cheek of her behind was a skull and crossbones.

'This is amazing!' Janis declared, looking about her. 'What is this place?'

Harley attempted a cockney accent. 'Fucking bloody marvellous innit, doll?' She began to lead them over to a statuesque woman clad in black with deathly white face, black eyes and hair and blood-red lips. 'Come and meet Esmerelda. She lives here.'

The vampirish female grinned at them, showing small, filed teeth. Despite herself, Janis recoiled slightly. Esmerelda said, 'What do you think of our squat, friends?'

'A squat, really?' Janis giggled. 'It's the grandest hovel I've ever seen.'

'It's what you might call semi-licensed. The council don't know what to do with the place. It's condemned, but they can't

afford to pull it down and no one else can afford to do it up. So
they leave us to our own devices.'

'And "devices" are what you guys are great at, yeah?'
Harley grinned. 'Have some champagne, darlings.'

Janis turned around to see a 'maid' standing obediently
with a tray hung around her neck. She was dressed in a black
latex mini-dress with white apron, puff sleeves and extremely
low neckline. Her delightful breasts, with their gold nipple
rings, pointed proudly naked over the glasses of champagne.
Harley reached out and tugged gently at one of the rings, then
took two fizzing glasses off the tray and handed them to Adam
and Janis.

'Are you hungry? We have some very special food over
here.'

They followed Harley's taut yellow rear with its firmly
jutting hemispheres over to the long table. Janis gasped when
she saw the dishes laid out before her. Every one had been
fashioned in a suggestive style to represent male or female
erotic parts. There were the obvious pairs of pink jellies topped
with cherries, and cucumbers stuffed with cream cheese. But
other culinary creations included a complete mermaid with
fishy tail and conch-like vulva fringed with seaweedy pubic
hair and breasts like jellyfish; a cake fashioned like the back
half of a kneeling female, tanned buttocks uppermost and
clearly displaying the two orifices between her legs; sausage
rolls fashioned from delicate, skin-coloured pastry out of
which peeped a purplish 'glans'. Adam picked one up and,
with a wink, placed the end in his mouth then bit into it.

'Delicious!' he smiled. 'And furthermore, it's the nearest
I've come to fellatio in my life!'

When Janis declined to taste the food, preferring to wait
until later, Harley suggested, 'Why don't you come with me?'

They left Adam to his titillating gastronomy and moved to
where the music was coming from. There were about twenty

women in the dimly lit room, all slowly gyrating to the beat.
Janis saw that many of them were half-naked, flashing breasts
and bottoms provocatively. Then she noticed something else,
something strange. Between the legs of each of them was a
metal pole. She stared through the gloom and heard Harley
give a low chuckle.

'Yes, take a closer look sweetheart!'

As her eyes became more accustomed to the half-light Janis
realized what she was seeing. On top of each pole was fixed a
dildo, and the women were dancing up and down on them with
rapturous ease, wriggling and squeezing to increase their
sexual pleasure. It gave a whole new meaning to the phrase
'dancing on the spot'.

'Maybe you'd like to try later,' Harley whispered. 'Right
now I don't think there's a spare parking space. Let's go
upstairs. There's plenty more to see!'

Janis began to realize that the whole building was given
over to erotic entertainment. This was going to be a very
special kind of party! She wondered where the others from the
band were, whether they'd arrived yet. Where had all these
people come from?

'Esmerelda is famous for her fetish parties,' Harley
explained, sensing her questions.

'She certainly does it well.'

'Oh, you ain't seen nothin' yet! Come on, let's wander down
the corridor and see what's behind a few of these closed doors.'

The long corridor was red-carpeted and every door bore a
label. The first one they encountered was called 'The
Nursery'. There was a shutter in the door over an observation
window. With a wink, Harley opened the shutter and let Janis
peep in. She saw three large cots, each occupied by an adult
dressed in baby clothes. A 'nurse', in a starched white overall
with her generous breasts half exposed, was attending to a girl
in a pink vinyl Babygro with matching bonnet and bootees.

The poppers of her crotch were open and the nurse was rubbing baby lotion into her shaven pussy. Next to them a male 'baby' in nappy and rubber pants was sucking on a bottle. In the third cot a girl in white vinyl baby-doll pyjamas was cuddling a doll. Mobiles hung over the cots and there was the tinkling sound of a music box. Harley put her fingers to her lips with a 'Ssh!' and quietly closed the shutter.

'Amazing!' Janis smiled. 'Do people really get off on that?'

'Whatever turns you on, babe! Come on, let's see what's happening next door.'

The notice on the door stated 'Schoolroom'. Before Harley could slide back the shutter there came the sound of a sharp *thwack!* leaving no doubt as to what was going on inside. Janis felt her heart thumping with excitement at the realization that there was something weird and wonderful happening in every room of the hotel, that any secret dreams the guests might have could be catered for, within reason.

When Harley uncovered the window the 'teacher' was just administering the last stroke of the cane on a boy's bottom. His trousers were concertinaed around his ankles and his Y-fronts were pulled down, exposing the reddening cheeks. Six other pupils sat at their desks wearing school uniform. Janis noticed that the girls wore no bras beneath their white blouses and their skirts were very short, exposing navy blue knickers beneath. The boys wore short trousers that were far too tight and could barely contain their very obvious erections.

The schoolmarm noticed them peeping and called out, shrilly, 'What do you want? Do you have a message?'

She drew herself up to her full height, the black mortar-board perched ridiculously on her blonde hair drawn back severely into a bun. Beneath the black academic gown she wore only a black bra and pants, black suspender belt and black stockings with high-heeled lace-up shoes. Janis shook her head while Harley stifled her laughter.

The teacher snapped, 'If you are going to join the class, come in and sit down. Otherwise shut the window and allow me to proceed with the lesson.'

Reluctantly Janis closed the shutter. She would have liked to stay and watch the fun but it was clear that observers were not allowed and there were many other rooms she wanted to peep into. Her appetite was whetted now. She thought of Adam, who had opted to satisfy a different appetite, and thought she was probably enjoying herself more right then.

She was surprised by the notice on the next door: 'The Clinic'. When she peered in, her first impression was of dazzling white tiled walls and bright lights. There were several people inside and a few weird-looking machines with tubes and dials. One woman was lying on a gynaecological examination couch with her feet in stirrups. She was wearing a gas mask and skin-coloured vinyl gown raised to her waist. A 'doctor' in white coat and stethoscope was performing an internal examination, his hands clad in surgical gloves. Nearby stood a 'nurse' in a shiny white uniform putting nipple clamps onto a naked female 'patient' who already had tubes leading from rubber bulbs in her vagina and anus to a machine that was pumping away to keep the bulbs inflated. A second nurse was giving a naked man with a rampant erection a 'blanket bath'.

'Weird!' Janis murmured as the shutter closed on the scene. Yet the spectacle of so many people indulging so freely in their favourite fantasy scenarios was starting to turn her on quite strongly. Would there be one for her? she wondered. Although she'd had many different sexual thrills during this past crazily wonderful year, perhaps there was something she had yet to experience, something new and strange that was just what her secret erotic self was yearning to try. She smiled wryly at the thought that if she didn't find it amongst the entertainment on offer tonight it was unlikely she ever would.

They moved on to the door marked 'The Oratory'. The

room was decorated like a small chapel, with two very phallic candles on the 'altar' and a rail where four 'nuns' were kneeling. Organ music drifted faintly from behind a red curtained alcove. Behind the altar rail a man in a dog collar and black vinyl cassock was standing, legs apart, his large cock being 'worshipped' by the lips and hands of one of the nuns. All the women had their habits hitched up to the waist, exposing their round pink bottoms as they knelt. Another nun walked up and down the row with a black leather whip, the handle shaped like a thick dildo. Every so often she slashed at the bottom of one of the nuns who sighed her penitent gratitude. As Janis watched, she thrust the dildo end in between the bum cheeks of the nun who was sucking off the priest and she gave a loud moan of pleasure.

'Such devotion!' Harley commented, her eyes twinkling. 'I'm almost converted to phallic worship!'

They walked on to the end room on that side. It was called 'The Bathroom'.

'You might find this a bit disgusting,' Harley warned her. 'It ain't to everyone's taste.'

Cautiously, Janis peered in. Four naked people were wallowing in a large bath of what looked suspiciously like shit.

'Ugh!' she exclaimed, making a face at Harley. 'Is that what I think it is?'

'It's stinking mud, but those guys are into toilet games. Want to move on? I think you'll find what's happening on the other side more interesting.'

There was only one door on the other side of the corridor and it was labelled 'The Paddock'. Janis walked up to it curiously and raised the wooden flap that concealed the peephole. She gasped with surprise to see that the long, rectangular room had been turned into some kind of arena with sawdust on the floor. Going through their paces were two 'pony girls' harnessed together and guided by their trainer.

One of these 'ponies' was a palomino, her blonde hair plaited with ribbons and stuck down her back like a mane with another swathe of yellow hair issuing from between her taut buttocks like a tail. The other had dark brown skin and black hair, fashioned in the same manner, and both of them were trotting round awkwardly on all fours wearing shiny black shoes with heels so high that they were forced to walk on points and with black leather boxing gloves on their hands. Their naked rear ends were sticking high into the air and an elaborate system of harnesses twisted around their torsos.

They rounded the bend and revealed their faces. Janis gasped, 'It's Virago! And Dolores!'

'That's right. Don't they look splendid together? That woman behind is Caterina. She's about the finest pony trainer in London. See how she has them trotting in perfect time already.'

As they came down the straight they certainly were an impressive sight. Their rounded breasts were tightly bound with leather from which horse brasses swayed and the nipples were hard and pointed. Every visible inch of their flesh was covered with a light film of sweat but their faces were impassive, their eyes blinkered so that they could only see the way ahead. The reins held by Caterina kept their heads up high and proud.

Janis turned her attention to the extraordinary woman who wielded those reins. She also stared ahead, her eyes bright and unwavering, holding aloft a long black whip. She wore a black rubber corset fastened with an elaborate system of buckles and lacing that thrust her breasts up into a deep cleavage, a black leather cowboy hat, thigh-high close-fitting black boots and gauntlets. Every so often she would let the tip of the whip snake between the buttocks of whichever girl was lagging slightly behind.

Janis stared, utterly fascinated, until Harley reminded her that there was more to see. Reluctantly she drew herself away.

'Guess you might like to get some of that training yourself?'
Harley grinned.

'Mm. Maybe.'

Janis threw her a flirty grin. She was certainly aroused now,
her appetite whetted for more of the naughty sights. Harley
pulled her close and gave her a brief but very sexy kiss that
made her even hotter. 'Is there much more?' she asked.

'Sure is. A whole lot more. Let's go upstairs now.'

The long corridor upstairs had the same layout but the doors
were unlabelled. Janis went up eagerly to the first door and
drew back the shutter. Inside she could see two women sitting
on high chairs dressed in glamorous corsets and stockings,
with their long legs outstretched. Two men in lackey's uniforms
sat on footstools and were caressing, kissing and licking their
feet and ankles. A vast assortment of high-heeled shoes in all
colours and styles were littered about the room and every so
often one of the men would ease a shoe onto a foot with great
reverence.

'Foot fetishists!' Janis murmured. She was taken by the
strange atmosphere in the room, detectable even through the
window. The faces of all the participants in the strange ritual
were rapturous, each locked in their silent world of fantasy and
fulfilment.

The next room was stranger still, lit only by one small-
wattage lamp and even more eerily silent. A person sat in
solitary confinement, covered from top to toe in a constricting
rubber wetsuit over which a strait-jacket had been tied with a
series of tapes and chains. No part of the anonymous person
was visible, since their face was covered by a mask through
which they breathed oxygen from a tank nearby. Janis shivered
and closed the shutter. It was hard for her to imagine what
satisfaction anyone could gain from such sensory deprivation.
Just what was going on beneath that latex cocoon in all that
darkness and silence?

Swiftly they passed on to view the other rooms on that floor. Janis had a series of surreal glimpses: of men in dog collars being subjugated by elegant and demanding dommes; of couples squirting each other with aerosol cream and licking it off their bodies; of girls playing with a collection of weird and wonderful dildoes; of a woman in a 'Nell Gwynne' style costume being ravished by a dashing blade whilst strapped down on a four-poster bed. There seemed to be no end to the invention behind Esmerelda's entertainment.

On the other side of the corridor was another large room, filled with rail upon rail of exotic and erotic costumes for the party-goers to play out their own favourite fantasies. Janis's imagination was already teeming with ideas. Harley put her arm around her waist and led her towards the stairs at the end. Through the silky-smooth latex she could feel fingers pressing against her flesh, stimulating her with subtle pressure. Her tits were tingling and hot. Her pussy likewise. She didn't know how much longer she could remain a mere *voyeuse*.

They returned to the ground floor, where the party had hotted up. Janis looked around for Adam and eventually found him dancing with a small Chinese girl wearing a red rubber dress with a mandarin collar and a slit in the skirt, just like his. They looked like sisters. Smiling, Janis decided to leave them to it and went to nibble on some of the delicacies at the long table. While she was there some of the other biker girls came up, kissing and embracing her. She felt loved and wanted, filled with a blissful sensuality that was slowly coming to the boil. But how would she decide to satisfy this longing for new experience? She was still unsure.

When she had drunk some more champagne and eaten her fill of the buffet, Harley returned. 'Ready for another round, Janis?' she enquired.

'You mean there's more?'

'Oh yes!' Harley gave a mysterious grin and her tattooed

breasts heaved provocatively. 'Shall we go down to the dungeon, princess?'

Janis felt a dark shudder pass through her. There was something ominous in the other woman's tone and in the knowing glint of her eye. She took her firmly by the hand and led her through the increasingly intoxicated crowd. The sweat was running all over her now, making rivulets between her naked breasts and labia. She loved the feel of her newly shaven pussy as the tight outer skin of her dress filled her crevice. Every time she moved she gave herself a fierce little thrill.

They walked down the stairs into a subterranean world of cellars and dim lighting, where pillars and screens concealed a series of strange horrors. Men and women were playing out their grotesque power games clad in bizarre costumes of leather and metal, and employing a range of medieval-looking equipment. Janis felt as if she were moving through a nightmare, yet there was something fascinating about it. She could feel her pulse racing and her body tensing as she wondered what strange desires, compulsions and satisfactions those people were experiencing.

They paused at a dank alcove where a domina in Viking costume was standing with her spiked heel in the cleavage of a blindfolded and half-naked woman who was kneeling with her hands bound behind her back. Janis watched the Viking grind her heel between the plump, harnessed breasts then move her booted leg down to slide between the submissive's open labia. A film of sweat covered the body of the kneeling woman who was trembling slightly, no doubt in anticipation of the next taste of the long whip that was tucked into the Viking's belt.

Harley gave Janis a grin. 'Which would you rather do, darling: give or receive?'

'I'm not sure, really.'

'Then maybe it's about time you found out.'

She put her arm around Janis's shoulder and moved her to the end of the cellar where a harness hung from a hook in the ceiling and a rack containing various whips and canes was fixed to the wall. Silently she reached out and pulled the clear plastic discs from the pink latex dress Janis was wearing. She gasped: she hadn't realized they were detachable. The last flap was peeled from her behind and she stood exposed. Smiling mysteriously Harley softly touched each of Janis's nipples, her shaven mound and then her naked buttocks. She kissed her lips briefly then led her over to the harness where they paused for a few seconds. 'OK?' she whispered.

Deep inside her vagina Janis felt an ambiguous spasm, a sensual twitch that could have been the start of an orgasm or the onset of labour pains. Her throat felt dry and her heartbeat was accelerating. Her head was filled with dizzy confusion. She swallowed, then nodded.

Harley gave a knowing little smile. She pulled open the harness and helped Janis to get inside. The straps went tightly over her breasts, making the nipples bulge out of their peepholes, and across her hips and thighs, allowing her buttocks and pussy to remain exposed. Her wrists were manacled behind her back and a hood was pulled down over her eyes, leaving her nose and mouth free.

Standing there in the darkness, with her body tightly constricted, Janis felt her excitement and terror increase in equal proportions. She heard the ring of Harley's boot-heels on the stone flagged floor and then a grinding noise as she worked the handle on the wall. Slowly Janis was being drawn up by the shoulders until her legs dangled in the air. Harley then passed something over her right foot and pulled it taut. As the noose was tightened she realised that she was being tethered. When the same thing happened with the other foot her thighs were pulled apart and the air was playing freely around her naked pussy. With a shudder Janis realized that she had been immobilized in a very vulnerable position, with her naked pussy and arse completely open and accessible beneath the short skirt.

There was a short silence. She imagined Harley standing there, observing her plight, planning what she might do to her, and her cunt spasmed again, more strongly. She could feel herself becoming wet, so wet that she expected to feel drips of juice trickling down her thighs. Her breasts were straining against the harness with the nipples forcibly thrust out, big and hard. They were throbbing hotly, tingling with a tantalizing mixture of frustration and anticipation, just like her enlarged clitoris. She clenched her buttocks and worked her internal muscles in a vain attempt at self-stimulation but her cunt sucked emptily at the air.

Then Harley's voice broke the interminable silence. 'I'll be back!'

Janis listened to her retreating footsteps and sighed. How long would she be left in suspense? The ache inside her was acute now and her arms and legs were starting to hurt. She could hear faint moans and sudden squeals coming from the other parts of the 'dungeon' which did nothing to reassure her. Just what had she let herself in for? Would Harley be her tormentress, or was she going to bring someone else? Had she gone to fetch Adam?

Janis began to imagine what might be done to her in that very defenceless state. She had no idea how high off the ground she was. Could someone stand right under her and give her a good licking? Could they reach her tits? They could certainly give her thighs and buttocks a whipping. What about using a dildo? Maybe she didn't even have to remain at the same height, but could be lowered to the ground at whim. She had a sudden vision of the paraphernalia on the wall-rack and a shiver passed through her.

As the minutes ticked by Janis's imagination became her

own worst enemy. She began to almost feel the sting of leather on her buttocks, the cruel prickles on her thighs, the tormenting clamping of her nipples. She longed for some kind of physical contact, preferably sensual and sweetly gratifying, but almost any kind would do. Her flesh was aching for it, her nerves were crying out for it with every wafting current of air that gently brushed against her ultra-sensitized skin and sent erotic impulses winging impatiently through her fevered body.

Still no one came. But then, faintly at first, Janis heard familiar music penetrating down to the cellar from the floor above. Someone was gradually turning up the volume. She recognized the sound of Virago's voice singing 'Storm in Your Eyes' and found new meaning in the lyrics that she and Adam had written. A different kind of excitement gripped her and her lips curved into a smile. Maybe she'd just found a new direction for the band to go in.

CHAPTER EIGHTEEN

Last night, at the Candy Bowl, a new rock genre was born: Fetish Rock. Jinxed, the all-girl band from England that has taken America by storm, strutted their incredible stuff in a prick-teasing display of raunchy singing and dirty dancing that will go down in the anals (*sic*) as hard-core groundbreaking.

From the moment the lights went up on a futuristic set – part medieval dungeon, part sci-fi superlab – the audience knew they were in for a helluva show. We were not disappointed. While lasers scanned the roof and images flashed on the video screen at an almost subliminal rate, five mean-assed bitches began the process of mass seduction through a mind-boggling mix of groin-scorching music and pervy sex. Cleverly they appeared to be totally oblivious of the yelling crowd, making no concessions to our presence and turning us all into salivating voyeurs.

Hearing Jinxed was a liberating experience. Watching them was sheer orgiastic bliss. Their show began with a foray into the marginal field of Rubber-Dom that soon got the juices flowing. Center-stage the luscious Virago ('Virgo' in another life) wielded her power with a proud display of tits and ass that had every one of us leching to be her willing slave. Forget the posturing narcissism of the likes of Madonna and Prince: this was the real McCoy. Virago pulled no punches in whipping her fellow musicians into a frenzy of guitar-flagellation and drum skin battering as they hammered their way through 'No Holds Barred', one of the band's three hit singles in the US charts.

Having delivered an adrenalin-fix to our libido, the band slowed the pace to a smoochily insinuating beat that cocooned the senses in warm chocolate. In a silken drawl, Virago extolled the delights of 'Wet Play' while Lee and Janis stripped off her rubber gear and massaged her delectable body with cream. The scene led on naturally to 'Baby, Baby', a nod in the obscure direction of adult-baby territory, with the girls googling and frolicking in babydoll, complete with bonnets and bootees, bottles and diapers. The redoubtable Dagmar played nursemaid while the soothing music coaxed us all back into a cosy world of lullabies and cuddles. Emotive stuff!

The sense that we were being invited to explore a parallel universe deepened with 'Thrashold', a pagan hymn to the god of pain. Wet dream or nightmare? This managed brilliantly to be both. In paying homage to this erotic subculture the girls put us through an emotional masochism every bit as harrowing as the physical kind.

The macho-mechanical world of screwing and clamping, of drilling and hammering, was transformed by the quirky lyrics and offbeat harmonies into a provocative study of flesh as matter, a material like wood or plastic, to be subdued and molded at will.

Even if S & M is not your trip I guarantee you would have been titillated by their next number, the viscerally directed 'Vision of Heaven and Hell' (currently number eleven in the charts and rising). Here Virago became Female Pope in her rôle as psychopomp, leading us through the erotic underworld of our collective libido. The patriarchal and fetishistic roots of religion were turned inside out as pedal worship took place, with the girls as nuns trying on boots in an orgy of foot-fondling that had everyone in the audience itching to kick off their shoes. With its driving rhythm and hymn-like harmonies the music gave a weirdly effective commentary on the swooning pseudo-mysticism of the nuns' devotions, the whole adding up to an audio-visual sermon on the sins of the flesh. The conclusion I came to: if hell has angels like these, who needs heaven?

Leading us further into uncharted waters, the band made mock of our phallocentric egos when they rode on giant, inflated dildoes during 'This is the Big One' then, at the supercharged climax of the song, burst them with a pinprick. An orgy of anal sex followed, with the band's hilarious cover-version of Spinal Tap's 'Big Bottom'

including an arse-rending solo by no-mean-guitarist Sal.
By now the audience were on heat, high on adrenaline
and testosterone, and the band catered to our mood with
an all-out lesbian number which I shall now proceed to
describe in detail for the sheer horny pleasure of it.

The downright dirty mood was re-established with a
bluesy, lascivious bass riff and some sensual, suggestive
drumming from Lee. While Sal downloaded her lust-laden
guitar sound directly to the crotch, Virago launched
straight into 'This Dyke Likes' accompanied by some
mutual foreplay with Janis, who soon abandoned her
playing in favor of girly sexploration.

We were then treated to the sight of Janis grinding her
scantily clad mound against her instrument while Virago
stroked her shapely breasts and tweaked her nipples into
bullet-hard prominence. The couple moved to front of
stage where panties were torn off and both women
exposed their naked pussies for our inspection – and I
mean naked! There was not a hair in sight on those
peachy pubic mounds. The audience reaction rose to a
frenzy when the pair began playing hunt-the-button with
each other, opening up their glistening folds to give the
video camera a wicked close-up of their steamy open
crotches.

When the girls began tonguing one another you could
feel the temperature rise and everyone around me started
to fidget and wriggle. I grew aware of a strange buzzing

noise: was it the whirr of a thousand vibrators, secretly doing the business for us sex-starved spectators? This was audience participation with a vengeance! The rest of the band were getting turned on by the super-slick performance of their fellow musicians. Lee was jerking off with a drumstick, Dagmar was astride her bass, thrashing its strings with more than usual ferocity, while Sal had given up all pretense at musicianship and was indulging in some rhythmic frottage with the mike stand.

Now the groove was downright filthy, the only coherent sounds being Lee's one-stick drum improvisation and Dagmar playing Lady Five Fingers on bass. The whole band seemed to come at the same time – and so, judging from the moans and gasps around me, did half the audience. It was the climax of the show, in more ways than you could possibly imagine.

Jinxed have moved from margin to mainstream in a couple of months, a true rock phenomenon. Their subversive version of sex-rock with its mélange of wry lyrical humor, memorable melodies and erotically charged vaudeville-style performance art trawls the alt.sex. scene to challenge the boundaries of what is acceptable and flirts outrageously with our subconscious and primal urges. Their ultra-libidinous cavortings produce an orgasmatronic entertainment which, if it took place in your bedroom instead of on-stage, would have you up against the Law for running a bordello. But will society tolerate such wantonly anarchic behavior? One thing is for sure: if Jinxed don't live up to their name, and 'Fetish Rock' does have a future, it's MEGA!

Guy Whitfield
Ramblin' Rock magazine

Janis put down the magazine with a smile and leant back on her sun-lounger, letting the warm rays caress every naked inch of her flesh. It was the third review she'd read that morning, all of them excellent. Since that article was written, 'Vision of Heaven and Hell' had risen to number seven in the American singles chart, and 'No Holds Barred' and 'Thrashold' were hot on its heels.

Her smile of satisfaction increased as she lazily surveyed the scene before her. She was lying beside the generous-sized pool at the villa they'd rented in Beverly Hills. Within hailing distance a gorgeously tanned and naked hunk was kneeling on all fours with a tray of iced cans and bottles strapped to his back. His large prick hung flaccid between his legs but she knew that she could have it good and hard in a moment, ready to service her if she so desired. On the opposite side of the pool lounged Lee and Dagmar, oiled and tanned and holding hands across the narrow divide between their sunbeds. In the turquoise water, which was dappled like a Hockney painting, Virago frolicked with Sal and a couple of Babewatch lookalikes they'd picked up on Sunset Boulevard last night.

Janis was enjoying the attractive picture the four water-nymphs made as they played an impromptu game of water polo, their golden breasts bouncing as pneumatically as the beach ball. From the house came intermittent laughter and, from the road beyond, the occasional roar of a motor bike. Harley and her friends were in residence, plotting their next

sortie into enemy territory, maybe a dawn raid on the head-
quarters of a rival gang. As long as they were in the vicinity Janis,
and the other band members, felt protected. Knowing this, Harley
made sure that there were always several of their number around.

Yet, fond as Janis was of the bike dykes, their petty rivalries
held no appeal. Now that they were back on home ground their
conversation was almost unintelligible to her as they swapped
gossip about other gangs and their exploits, discussed drug
deals in the local slang and indulged in various in-jokes.
Security apart, the best thing about having them around was
their habit of turning up with celebrity guests from the rock or
movie world, people they thought the girls would like to meet.
Already Janis had made the acquaintance of her favourite
horror writer and Heavy Metal heart-throb. The hardest thing
of all to get used to, though, was the fact that she herself was a
celebrity and people were actually thrilled at meeting *her*!

The sun was making her randy, as it always did. How much
longer would Adam be? These days she always looked forward
to his return from the offices of the record company, publicity
agent or wherever, because the news was always good. And
good news meant they got to retire for a while with a bottle of
champers and a rampant libido. Already she could feel her
body gearing up for sex, the sweat trickling and tickling down
between her breasts and over her smoothly naked mound to
join those other musky juices in her vulva. She stretched and
sighed, then decided that the sun was just a little too scorching
on her skin.

'Boy!' she called, in her best upper-class 'Lady Muck'
accent. All the Americans loved it.

The kneeling Adonis looked up instantly, his eyes
smouldering at her. He was a lusty Hispanic with filmstar
features, strong chest, legs and arms from working out on
Muscle Beach, and a butt to die for! He began to crawl towards
her, like one of those magnificent silver-backed gorillas, his

buttocks clenched tight with the effort of keep the tray steady on his back. 'Yes, mistress? What is your pleasure?'

Janis thought of several delightful possibilities but settled for a drink and a massage with suntan oil. If Adam didn't show by the time he'd finished, well, she might just give him some new orders!

She took a few swallows of the ice-cold beer then lay face down on the thick towel with a contented grunt and waited. There was a faint hiss as her masseur squirted a fat blob of the rich, scented cream into his palm. Janis's toes squirmed in anticipation as he straddled the sunbed and his hands fell lightly upon her shoulders. She relaxed as he smoothed his palms down her back to her waist, covering her skin with a light film of oil which he then proceeded to rub into her with firm strokes. His strong fingertips snaked up and down her spine, worked at the knotty sinews around her shoulder-blades then came to rest at her hips.

Was that his prick she could feel against her buttocks? As he leaned over to massage her shoulders again Janis was sure his glans was brushing against her arse, and her lust surged. Was he becoming aroused by her? Moving her head slightly, she peered out from beneath her half-closed lids and caught a glimpse of one lean, bronzed thigh against hers. Craning her neck round further she finally glimpsed his erection and settled back with a sigh of satisfaction. It made her feel good to know she was turning him on.

The capable hands were kneading her bum cheeks now, pinching and knuckling until they felt loose and soft. Janis let her thighs fall apart so that his busy hands pulled against the skin of her labia from time to time, giving her a buzz. She was in no hurry to increase the stimulation. There would be time enough for that when she turned over. His hands passed on down her thighs, making the sensitive inner surfaces tingle, then her calves and finally her feet.

Janis adored having her feet massaged. She smiled, remembering how often she had climaxed on stage during the 'Heaven and Hell' number. It would be easy to let this guy's expertise lead her into orgasm but she preferred to wait. It was always better if you waited. Besides, with luck this massage would be just foreplay, getting her in the mood for when Adam returned. As long as she didn't have to wait too long, of course.

Lazily she turned over and surveyed the young man with a smile, thrusting out her breasts so that the brown nipples stuck up proudly. He smiled back, self-conscious about his erection that was now cavorting between them like a naughty child seeking attention. Janis knew the taste and feel of that organ. Although she'd not had full intercourse with him, saving that privilege for Adam alone, she had sometimes played with his magnificent dick and sampled its exotic flavour.

Now, though, she was happy to lie passively and let those capable hands stroke her body into willing compliance. Her mind drifted back through the extraordinary weeks since they had picked up the threads of the band's career and enjoyed a steady rise to the top. When the tour finally got under way it had been a triumphant success, the more so because those two villains were in police custody, charged with kidnapping and intent to murder. Putting her ordeal at the hands of Blade and Gore firmly behind her, Virago had inspired them all during their tour of the UK but she had also given due credit to Janis, whose 'Fetish Rock' idea had been unanimously accepted by Ivan and the band.

Janis sighed contentedly as her masseur leaned forward and moved up her legs, his fingers pressing either side of the shin-bone then smoothing their way up her thighs, carefully avoiding too close a contact with what lay between them. The slight degree of frustration she felt was nothing compared with what she had experienced in Esmerelda's London dungeon, suspended in mid-air. The memory of it made her shiver, even now.

Eventually Harley had returned with an anonymous other, and the subtle torture of their victim had proceeded. Thinking about it now, Janis decided that the suspense had been both the worst and the best part. Harley and her accomplice had dreamed up a tantalizing mixture of erotic stimulation for their willing victim, now stinging her exposed buttocks with a single taste of the whip, now brushing her naked pubis with a velvet glove. They had lowered her to the ground and made free with their mouths on her tender parts. They had penetrated her orifices with assorted dildoes and given her feet a dunking in some kind of warm cream. They had strung her up again and played a hose on her private parts from below, making her squirm. Yet always the main thrill had been the 'what will they do next?' factor. And that, in a lesser way, was what she was getting off on right now.

Janis felt her skin tingle all over as her obedient servant reached her stomach and, with featherlight caresses, traced a path around her navel. She could sense where the nerve-rich contours of her vulva began, just below the Venus mount, and his oiled wrists brushed against it to exquisite effect as he made circular motions around her abdomen. Her breasts heaved and yearned for his favours but he was taking his time, the way she liked it. In the few weeks that she had been resident at the villa this guy had certainly come to learn her preferences. She had Mr Mariani to thank for that. Apparently the two 'houseboys' came with the territory.

It was Harley who had suggested that Adam should contact Joe Mariani, who had arranged their US tour. He had proved invaluable in getting them maximum publicity and had also provided them with the luxurious Villa Palmetta where they'd been staying in between tour dates. From there Adam and Joe had masterminded their American career, which had gone from strength to strength.

Slowly the tormenting hands reached the lower slopes of

her boobs and massaged their taut fullness with tickling strokes. Janis gave out a loud sigh and saw her masseur smile, his prick jerking in sympathy at her frustration. He moved his hands round and round her tits, outlining their rotundity then gently squeezing them. Still he ignored her aching nipples. For consolation she pressed her thighs close together and felt her clitoris throbbing away, hard and insistent.

Now practically all her skin was covered with suntan oil, except her arms and face. Janis groaned as he abandoned her bosom and moved to those areas, dealing firmly with her hands and arms, more delicately with her face. The rest of her body was on hold, awaiting the imminent return of his attention. He gently smoothed his way down her neck, then his hands fanned out above her breasts, tantalizing her. The motion was repeated until she was almost gasping for him to sweep further down, to touch the yearning tips of her nipples and make them slick.

At last his searching fingertips reached the top halves of her breasts and stroked them all over with a circular motion before fixing on their russet tips. Janis sighed out her relief as he moulded them between finger and thumb, rolling and squeezing and gently pulling until she felt an answering twinge in her cunt and her longing became acute. She stared boldly at his erection, imagining how its length and girth might feel inside her, could almost feel him plunge into her, again and again, good and strong.

The guy was excited now, she knew it. He wanted her, his prick hot and tingling and ready, but he knew he couldn't make the first move and that was his burden, just as her desire to be at least technically faithful to Adam was hers. Her lover had given her so much, given up so much for her, and it was all thanks to him that she and the rest of the band had got to where they were today. She owed him her fidelity, at the very least.

Still, it was fun to dream. Janis closed her eyes as the

pressure of those fingers moved down across her abdomen to
the bulge of her mound, just above her pink, pouting nether
lips. The oil was enabling his fingertips to slip easily over her
pubic bone and down between her labia to the wet cleft of her
sex. She shuddered as his soft touch found her clitoris and
began to tease it, then moved on down to the depths where her
cunt was oozing, filling her pussy with musky liquid. Eager to
please, he gave her whole vulva a thorough going-over and she
sighed languorously, feeling her clitoris swell and her quim
contract, readying her for the incipient climax which she knew
would be hers very soon.

'Enjoying yourself, darling?'

Janis started at the familiar voice and her eyes snapped
open. Adam's shadow fell across her face but he was smiling
down at her, perfectly at ease. She smiled back.

'Hi! I was hoping you'd show up soon.'

Her masseur had drawn back from the sunbed, a look of
faint disappointment on his handsome face. She gave him a
sweet smile. 'Thanks awfully. That'll do for now.'

He bowed and went back to being a dumb waiter. Adam sat
down on the foot of the bed and began to caress her toes. The
interrupted orgasm took new heart and her clitoris throbbed
once more, but she momentarily ignored it in her eagerness to
hear the news. 'What have you been up to?'

'I'll tell you later, with the others. Meanwhile, I think you
have some unfinished business of your own to attend to. Why
don't I help you sort it out?'

Janis could see the bulge beneath his shorts and knew
exactly what he meant. Her cunt convulsed at the prospect of
his cock being inside her. She gave him her hand and he helped
her up, putting the towelling robe around her shoulders. Then
they walked the short distance into the villa. It was cool inside,
the elegant décor lifting her spirits, as it always did. In their
room the bed was freshly made and the air-conditioning

hummed benignly, wafting a faint scent of jasmine through its ventilator slats.

'God, I've been thinking of your body all morning!' Adam groaned as he ripped off his shorts and T-shirt. 'Seeing you with that beachboy made me horribly jealous.'

'He was about to frig me, but this is far better. Your timing was perfect!'

Joyously she flung the robe onto a chair and opened her arms for him. They collapsed together onto the bed and kissed with hungry mouths. Then she sat astride him and her hands made sure his erection was at its most robust before she slithered down on it, her well-lubricated cunny receiving him with an enthusiastic caress. She wasted no time in working them both towards a climax, squeezing his glans with the tight muscles around her entrance as she rose up high, then clenching his shaft with the walls of her quim as she thrust down again. Pumping away she heard him gasp and felt him spasm just as her own clitoris brought her to the brink and the pair of them were soon in tune with each other, their orgasms synchronized into one throbbing, harmonious wave of pure sensual pleasure.

'OK,' Janis grinned, swigging beer from a bottle as they lay in bed, recovering. 'Now tell me the news.'

'Only when you and the others are all together.'

Janis pouted, but she knew he was right. This was band business, and they all deserved to share it. She rose from the bed and went into the bathroom to take a quick shower, then put on her silk mini-kimono and sprayed herself with perfume while Adam showered. 'Come on, then,' she urged him, fluffing out her hair. 'They're all around the pool. Let's go!'

After ordering champagne to be brought out to the terrace, Adam sauntered over to the poolside and called to the girls. The beachboys and girls were sent indoors, then the band members assembled at the tables. Harley and two of her mates appeared from the house, scenting good news, and Adam cleared his throat.

'Well, ladies, I've been with Joe and Chuck Newnes all morning at the office of Lou Steinberg.' He paused for his words to take effect. Everyone knew that Steinberg was the head of Optimax, the dynamic film company that specialized in high-quality, low-budget movies and had won three Oscars in succession. Janis realized she was holding her breath and let it out with an audible sigh.

'The upshot is, Lou is very interested in making a "rockumentary" about the band.' There was a whoop of joy from everyone. Adam held up his hand for silence. 'He wants to show everything, including the kidnap of Virago and Janis. Of course that would make excellent cinema, but we'd have to wait until after the trial of Blade and Gore. Joe and I wanted something more immediate, so he has proposed an alternative: a film about the LA "dyke bikers" with Jinxed providing the music for the soundtrack and playing at a bikers' music-fest. What we must decide is whether we can afford to wait for a film to be made exclusively about the band, or whether we're happy to take what's on offer right now.'

There was a pregnant pause. The prospect of Optimax making a film about the band was enormously exciting, but could they afford to wait? It was a tricky decision. Janis frowned, the memory of Blade's scared face suddenly presenting itself to her with vivid force. Any film that emphasized his part in the kidnapping would put paid to his career even after he came out of jail, yet it was Gore who was the real villain. She decided to speak out before waiting to hear what the others thought.

'Personally, I think we should go for the second option. We've no idea how long our success is going to last, so I reckon we should go for the "bird in the hand". Besides, I don't know about Virago but I don't particularly relish the idea of reliving our ordeal in any form.'

'I agree,' Virago smiled, much to Janis's relief. 'Let's strike while the big boy's hot to trot!'

There was some mild opposition from Sal and Dagmar but their arguments were soon overridden and, with the enthusiastic backing of Harley and her gang, the decision was made.

Later that afternoon, as they drove in the minibus back to the offices of Optimax, Janis mused on her hidden motive for backing the biker film rather than the other one. She couldn't forget the way Blade had helped her during her imprisonment, despite the risk to himself. If she hadn't escaped, what hope would there have been of saving Virago from Gore's evil clutches?

Besides, she owed Blade another debt. He had defied Gore to invite her into the band, which had given her the invaluable grounding in rock that enabled her to pull her weight in Jinxed. Despite everything, she was grateful to him for those two chances. Now she'd been offered a chance to repay him, and she was glad that she'd had the courage to take it.

Perhaps Virago, too, understood. As Janis sat between her and Adam on the back seat of the bus, Virago gave her a spontaneous hug and a kiss. 'I think we made the right decision,' she smiled. 'I consulted the yarrow sticks last night and the oracle told me, "No blame. She who forgets the pain of the past is herself forgiven." I think our present success is triumph enough, don't you?'

And Janis, flanked by the two people she loved most in the world, couldn't help but agree.

EVELYN D'ARCY

MIDNIGHT BLUE

When attractive young journalist Susanna James goes down to Cornwall to see what her boyfriend Jon Mitchell is really up to with Gothic writer Alicia Descourt, she discovers more than she's bargained for. Strange, disturbing erotic dreams are just the beginning of Susanna's journey of discovery into bizarre new realms of sensual experience. Soon dreams become reality – an exotic reality of dark hungers that will sweep Susanna into a whirlpool of forbidden passions and taboo pleasures of the flesh . . .

Midnight Blue is a brilliantly compelling erotic odyssey to the danger zone of desire.

HODDER AND STOUGHTON PAPERBACKS

EVA LINCZY

VAMPIRE DESIRE

Intercourse with the vampire!

Diabolus has lived in Hell, where he is the Master, for three thousand years. He is demon, archfiend – and vampire. He is Evil Incarnate. He forces his revolting sexual needs on the she-devils who are compelled, under duress, to pander to his every depraved erotic desire.

Bored with the sexual pleasures of the Pit, Diabolus returns to Earth. To Africa, where he conceals himself in a rare uncut red diamond – for red is the colour of blood. From this supernatural hiding place, Diabolus can assume any human form – male or female – that he wishes. His sexual excesses on Earth start with Kindhu, an African tribal woman. Her torment is just the beginning . . .

In Amsterdam the diamond is cut and in London the individual stones are set in pieces of jewellery before being sent all over the world. In every one, Diabolus lurks. Which is bad news indeed for Marijka in Holland, Peggy in England, Janet in Singapore, Tania in Russia – and a myriad more . . .

Vampire Desire is a hypnotically compelling story of the outer limits of lust where the erotic and the occult meet in an explosion of terror and twisted passions.

HODDER AND STOUGHTON PAPERBACKS

RAY GORDON

SUBMISSION!

Would they take it lying down?

The time: early in the next century. There's been a massive backlash against the domination of society by women. Special 'correction centres' have been set up by the brutal new male dictatorship to bring militant female liberationists into line.

Most feared of the custody officers are Fowler and his sadistic lesbian sidekick Swain. Their lustful treatment of attractive female prisoners is legendary among the members of the resistance movement. When Fowler is captured by resistance leader Hanna Kelley, the jackboot is on the other foot – for a while. But Fowler escapes and takes Hanna captive in turn. Now she's at his mercy. Not that he's inclined to show her any . . .

Submission! is another outstandingly inventive novel of the wilder shores of lust by one of the most powerful talents on today's erotic fiction scene.

HODDER AND STOUGHTON PAPERBACKS